A JANUARY QUAIL M...

Death Visits
January

A JANUARY QUAIL MURDER MYSTERY

Death Visits January

Fiona Sherlock

POOLBEG
CRIMSON

Published 2022 by Crimson
an imprint of Poolbeg Press Ltd.
123 Grange Hill, Baldoyle,
Dublin 13, Ireland
Email: poolbeg@poolbeg.com

A catalogue record for this book is available from the British Library.

ISBN 978178199-713-0

www.poolbeg.com

About the Author

Fiona Sherlock is a crime writer from Bective, in Ireland. Her murder mystery games are played across the world. She also writes poetry and prose but cannot stay away from a good murder. After spending a decade in Dublin working in public relations and journalism, she moved to the country for midday fires and elderflower champagne.

FionaSherlock.com/BespokeMurderMystery.com
Twitter/Instagram: @fionasherlock

Acknowledgements

A sincere thank you to Paula, Gaye and the team at Poolbeg for letting January Quail loose on the world. She has been fighting to get out there for the past few years. This book has a very special place in my heart and was created in the midst of chaos when my daughter was napping as a baby. Thank you to my agent, Lina Langlee, for championing me, and to Julie Fergusson and the team at the North Literary Agency.

For believing in me, and listening to all of my random questions, thank you to my friends and family. Especially Macken dearest. For making it worth doing, thank you, Sephie and Archie. Thank you to my parents Deirdre and John, for encouraging me in every way, and to Monica Sherlock for exposing me to poetry so early.

Thank you to my secondary school English teacher, Ms Walsh, for teaching me the importance of discipline. To Suzannah Dunn and my CBC Creative colleagues, thank you for helping me think of myself as a writer.

Thank you to Nigel Heneghan for all those marked-up press releases.

Thank you to Meath County Library and The Arts Council for supporting my work, and to Alan English and Jody Corcoran in the Sunday Independent for allowing me to comment on the issues of the day. Meeting my lecturers and colleagues in Cambridge, especially Midge Gillies, has been transformative to my writerly life. I am so privileged to have met you all.

For helping with this book, supporting my writing and reading early drafts, thank you to Joan Revington, Michelle McNicholas, Eamonn P. Kelly, Evelyn Sherlock, Linda Farrell, Philippa Grant, Hillary O'Brien, Les Hanlon, Alan Conlon, Creative Ireland, Meath County Council Arts Office and all my lecturers in Trinity and DCU. Thank you to Lisa Carolan, Aisling O'Brien, Linda Daly, Jane Halvey, Antonia Daly, Helen Malone, Eoghan Harris and Patrick Lawlor. I'm sorry, I've forgotten someone special, thank you too!

Dedication

To Sephie x

Chapter 1

Bog water holds secrets, suspended in time, perfectly preserved. Ireland hadn't seen rain in six weeks. The viridescent shamrock grass of the hedgerows around Girley bog had faded to a tawny brown; the pre-emptive elderflower buds dried out to a feathery fist.

Rivulets of sweat ran down the bare backs of the Flanagan men. Six feet deep in the land, they worked in perfect tandem. The older man cut sods into clean rectangular chunks, as his nephew lifted them to the surface. Like blocks of chocolate cake spread in the hot sun.

"Is this global warming at work? I tell you, I'd be half inclined to give up recycling for more weather like this. I never saw a second cut of the bog before – such a mad thing to do on account of the heat." The young man paused to slug from his water bottle.

"Well now, Jack," his uncle spoke without disturbing the rhythm of his work, "I don't know. I'm wondering about diversifying the farm in the long-term. Sure the lakes up at home are bone dry. They've brought out an emergency frog-rehoming grant, to let the little beasts spawn in puddles."

"Puddles? What size of puddles?"

"I'm not sure there's a set size of puddles. Any body of water on my land is long dry."

"You'd only be overrun by frogs. Maybe that's the next thing, a plague of frogs after this drought."

"Arrah, go away with that. Will you be let down for a few pints this evening?"

There was an unspoken agreement not to mention the pub until their day's work was almost done. Talk of the pint gave Jack a push of energy and he took over the cutting.

Work on the bog drew a big thirst. Since the hot weather began in March, most evenings the Gallops pub heaved with the weight of the farm-tanned mullockers of men downing beers.

"Oh, aye," Jack nodded as the slean sliced through the earth.

The usually sharp sound of the blade was dulled. The two men stopped and cast a curious eye at each other.

"There's something caught there," warned the uncle. "Go again."

The tip of the metal implement ran through the bog, but rested on something.

Jack was wrangling the earth away with his hand.

"What is it?"

The shape looked familiar, yet strange to them.

Jack pushed aside the dry soil with his fingers. "It's a – *Jaysus*. It can't be."

Drawing it close to his face, he spread the clots of black soil from the toenails of a slender, severed foot.

Chapter 2

January Quail swirled her bright green liqueur, washing the last vestiges of the mint drink through the crushed ice. Anyone could pop in for a drink or two on her own, accompanied by the paper or a good book. A third crème de menthe solo was a line she did not cross. However, getting all but sacked seemed like a reasonable excuse.

Two raised fingers summoned a double. Her role as Features Editor could be terminated at the end of the month, if she didn't up her act. Alf had announced a number of drastic editorial changes as part of the newspaper's bid to remain profitable. She could re-interview for another, more junior, reporter job in a few weeks, if she could demonstrate her ability to drive traffic to the website in the interim. The whole thing seemed barely legal. She blinked in rapid succession to push back the tears attempting to break through. *Don't think about it*, she chastised herself.

The darkness of McDaids suited January's pallor;

she refused to sully her skin with a suntan, real or chemically manufactured. The pub had once been used as a morgue, and tall windows rose to the cathedral-like ceiling, casting shadows of blue and green across her rubescent bob. But still the air inside was sweltering. She loosened the knot of her yellow tie. Under the linen suit, the chambray shirt clung to her body.

The Bostonian drawl of two American tourists broke the museum-quiet. They eyed her drink as the barman set it down. She averted her gaze to avoid conversation.

January was beautiful in a troubled way, with damson lips and precariously delicate bones. Although only in her late thirties and fresh-faced, she favoured the style of an older woman from a bygone age.

There was no sign of the highly touted graffiti artist, Lady Anon. January should be interviewing her, not mainlining liqueurs. It had been scheduled for weeks. But this glorified spray-painter was already an hour late. January wasn't stupid – she heard the constant talk of metrics and audience. This interview had been her attempt at getting a story to go viral. To give it life beyond the newspaper page and trending on Twitter. Now she really needed it to happen. The artist had never before given an interview to a member of the mainstream media. Engaging only with her fans through social media and a podcast, she had approached January to offer the interview. Now where was she?

January stared at the door. Her eyes searched the pub for the umpteenth time that hour. Commemorative mirrors featuring famous Irish writers, whiskies and characters of ill-repute hung in shadow over the dado rail.

The barmat fell apart in her fingers. With the newspaper under new ownership, numerous online editors advised that her stories weren't converting to online traffic. Nor should they, she had argued – those who care for antiques are themselves antiquities. This interview had been her chance to reach a wider online audience.

January was professionally and personally offended. She could not quantify the feeling as hurt, although that's what it was. Two decades of her life were spent at that newspaper. Twenty years. Through numerous paycuts and departmental reorganisations she had remained a loyal member of staff. She loved the institution and what it had stood for, clocking eighty-hour weeks during busy times. The few friends she had maintained in university never saw her and moved on. She had stalled all the other aspects of her life, for a newspaper, and this was how they rewarded her?

From the front pocket of her blazer, she pushed aside the ink pot and stamps to fish out her smartphone. Nothing from the hipster influencer. She checked her social-media inboxes to ensure no communication had arrived there. In her feed, amidst the pictures of makeshift swimming pools and chilled drinks, one post drew her attention. It had a few hundred retweets and some of the online news sites were covering it.

With squinting eyes, she observed what appeared to be a sunburnt man holding, what was it, an old boot? Was it? It was dark, tanned. She zoomed in.

"Is it a foot?" she asked aloud, catching a few sideways glances from the Americans sitting at the next table. She didn't mind. She liked people to think she was mad. It was a good disguise.

She clicked through to the *Irish Sunday Chronicle*'s article. It was written by Laura, an unpaid intern.

BOG BODY DISCOVERED
Laura O'Brien

Farmer Jack Flanagan put his foot in it quite literally this afternoon, when he discovered a human foot whilst cutting the bog outside Ardee, in County Louth. Flanagan took to social media to enthusiastically report the find, sharing a selfie holding the wizened trotter, which appears leathery and dark in colour.

"*Found this foot in the bog – chap who left it behind was legless.* 😄 😄 😄

Social-media users are speculating that Flanagan may have unearthed another bog body, the ancient remains which can be up to 3,000 years old and preserved in the marshy bog conditions. An Garda Síochána is investigating the matter.

January swallowed the final menthol drop as she read the responses and posts, her fingers rapping on the empty glass. She would have to write about it on Sunday. She jotted the following words down on a pad.

"A millennium is a relevant unit of measurement in the bog. The peat accumulates dead things in the waterlogged muck. Once dried out, the sods are burned in Irish country síbíns and by grandmothers drying their drawers by a hot range."

If this was a legitimate bog body, it would be a significant find. Bog bodies were relatively rare in Ireland. Two had been found in 2003. The first, the preserved body of a male in his early twenties, was nicknamed the Clonycavan Man. Found in County Meath, it was dated as 2,300 years old. His head and torso were safeguarded by the bogland. The second, Old Croghan Man, was found in the Midlands. Reputedly of noble birth, his headless midriff revealed manicured fingernails, never having used his hands to labour. Several hundred others had been found around Europe, some so perfectly preserved by the conditions in the bog they could be mistaken for being asleep, like Denmark's Tollund Man. When schoolchildren happened upon the Lindow Man in Cheshire in 1984, the tabloids nicknamed him "Pete Marsh". The skin of these corpses turned a dark brown colour, like leather. Usually the bones would be dissolved by the bog components, but lots of tissue would endure. January had reported on both these finds, and filed copy to various newspapers, which eventually led to her securing a full-time job with the *Irish Sunday Chronicle*. Two more were discovered in Ireland, but January was well-established in her Features role by then and she hadn't thought readers would be interested. But this was already getting considerable traction on social media, so intrigued her.

This social-media post braced her. With no word from the artist, she plonked her empty glass on the counter and pushed out into the glaring sunlight of the April heatwave. Her mind was a half-drunk hothouse of jumbled thoughts. This was still unverified. Best not to get ahead of herself. She needed to sober up and get onto the story. Giddy, she laughed, skipping through the well-proportioned brown ponds of St Stephen's Green. Talk about good timing, she thought. She needed something to secure her job.

January's house on Leeson Street in the heart of Dublin's Georgian Quarter was built for a wine merchant in 1720. The Quail family bought the house 150 years later, to accommodate the family when they visited the capital. It wound its way through the generations to January, who heavily remortgaged it to bridge the gap between her expensive tastes and mediocre salary. She needed that wage. It was impossible to risk losing the last vestige of her family line.

Now converted into flats, January resided on the bottom two floors. Although it looked grand reflected in the Grand Canal, the shower and other mod cons had been shoved into awkward corners, leaving only one decent room per floor.

She had forgotten bird food. Dumping her post on the well-worn sideboard, she basked in the coolness of the fridge and sipped a cannikin of chilled peppermint tea. Leopoldina was a mute parrot. She rubbed her feathery forehead against the brass bars, before stretching her head back to open her beak.

"I am sorry, old girl," January said, tapping the bird's head. "I will be sure to pick some up later. Those weasels at work want to give me the heave-ho! Can you believe it?"

She stared at the outline of herself in the dark pupil of the bird and sighed. Who else could she confide in?

Try as she did not to think of the humiliating meeting with the current acting editor, Alf Timmoney., it stole into her thoughts. The *Irish Sunday Chronicle* was in a state of flux, with the senior section writers rotating as Acting Editor, before the Board would elect a permanent chief. January was considered the least qualified. She had minimal political reporting experience. Her cheeks flushed with embarrassment to recall that she had put herself forward for a promotion. All the while, her head had been on the chopping block. She swallowed her pride. It would be wise to run the bog-body story by Alf.

At home she preferred to operate a heavy black Bakelite rotary-dial telephone. It required her to put a finger into the circle dedicated to each number and drag it to the exchange, which gave her time to think before a call. The phone was heavy and awkward but it helped to designate time spent on a call as an official communication between her and the outside world. Each call carried more gravity as the handset weighed heavily on her shoulder, decades of conversation gathered in the little ventilation holes of the earpiece.

The line connected.

"Alf, I think I have something better than Lady Anon."

"Hello to you too, Janie," he answered. "Are you okay?"

Alf had winced his way through their earlier meeting. From the muzak playing, she guessed her editor was now in a trendy rooftop bar, tinkling highballs of champagne mojitos. January would never imbibe there, amongst the glass walls and white cubed plastic furniture. But that was his means of obtaining the latest information from the elite and exclusive of Dublin.

"Jolly well fine. But listen –"

"You know it wasn't my decision, right? I argued for you –"

"Yes, yes, all down to the Board. Anyway I'm not calling to discuss it."

"Okay, well, you can talk to me anytime –"

"Her Ladyship never showed. But I have something better."

"Lady Anon is enchanting – I've just seen her down an entire Bloody Mary in ten seconds flat. A deconstructed one at that."

11

"Wait, how did you know it was her?"

"Let's just say I have an inside track."

"For Christ sakes, I was meant to interview her in McDaids and she never showed up! Will you remind her she agreed to talk to me first?"

"Of course I bloody will – that's a serious story, we want to nail it, Jan. It's your story."

"Have you heard about this body in the bog?" she enquired, pouring some crème de menthe into a thimble-like sherry glass. Even at home, she tried to maintain some standards when it came to glassware. The freshness of the mint counteracted the warm, slowing draw of the alcohol, and not even a bloodhound would detect the intoxicant on her breath.

"Yes – apparently they've found the rest of her left leg, head and the torso with both arms." The former crime editor was accustomed to body parts being found separately to their owners. January was not.

"Her?" she queried. "That's interesting. The other two I reported on were male. You know, that's more flesh than was found with the last two bodies."

"Good news, Jan – they will be scanning her tonight. I knew you would want to cover this. I've already spoken to the State Pathologist and she agreed you can attend. But don't spend too much time on this, January, okay? If you want to secure your job you'll have to get the results in."

Chapter 3

The gold hands on Clerys clock read nine o'clock. January had a thin sheet of sweat under her hairline as she walked down O'Connell Street, Dublin's best-appointed thoroughfare. She had changed into a fresh white shirt, but it was already damp.

She hoped the artist had just got drunk and forgotten about their arrangement. Securing her in the first place had been a serious coup. In normal circumstances, she would trust Alf to convince the interviewee to commit to it again. But in the current landscape, she couldn't trust that he wouldn't usurp her.

Although it was dark, it was still nearly 30° Celsius. The warm weather had made it a centre for happy tourists and hopeless drunks, so it bustled despite the late hour. She popped her lips to spread her mulberry lipstick, hurrying along to Dublin University Hospital.

This was the third year in the last decade with record-breaking temperatures. Her thoughts drifted back to when the last two bodies were dug up. It too had been a hot summer. She wondered what link there was between hot weather and such discoveries. She spent weeks shadowing the museum's team, reporting each new discovery. Setanta Molloy was a junior curator and had been as excited as January about the significant discoveries. He was generous in explaining the techniques they used to analyse the bodies.

One evening, after basking in the park beside the lab, soaked in cider, he confessed his fondness for her. She awkwardly avoided him until the story ran its course, and hadn't spoken to him in the nearly two decades since, although she spotted him at cultural events around Dublin.

This particular area of the radiology department was rarely used. At such a late hour, there were no patients in the waiting area. A few curious hospital staff stood around in their blue scrubs, peering into the glass trolley. Inside, the peat-packed mummy waited to be scanned.

The State Pathologist floated down the corridor in a pink floral dress of gold roses, kitten-heeled sandals clipping ominously. January considered the overall look too hoydenish for a woman who dealt in corpses for a living.

Recognising her from the news, January stuck out her hand. "Professor Traynor, a pleasure to meet you. I'm January Quail from the *Irish Sunday Chronicle*."

They shook hands, and January caught the orange

smell of a slow-developing tan moisturiser from her skin. She was a handsome woman in her fifties with a strong jaw and rosy cheeks.

"Interesting case here, isn't it?" January continued. She had to get the woman onside. It was always useful to be able to pick up the phone to a source to check something. Sometimes they often would get the inside track on a breaking story.

"It's usually your colleague Alf who is bombarding me with questions," Professor Traynor said with a smile. "I'm surprised he's not here tonight."

The comment threw January somewhat. Alf hadn't been covering crime in months. She tugged a lock of bright red hair behind her ear and changed tack.

"When the 2003 bodies were found I covered the investigations comprehensively. I'm still fascinated by the secrets they hold."

They moved over to the glass trolley.

"Here is our girl," said Professor Traynor, pulling her plastic gloves on and bending to take in the face of the victim.

January felt like she was looking at an antique statue, hewn from wood. The body was lying on its side in the foetal position. It looked as if the woman had succumbed to slumber, she was so still and calm. The skin was dark brown, almost a shiny black, from the chemicals in the bog. But the details of her face were clear. She was unlike any other withered bog body January had seen pictures of. Of course, Old Crogan Man didn't have a head and the face of Clonycavan man had not been well preserved. These remains were that of a beautiful woman, with a high brow and full lips with an accentuated cupid's bow. Reborn from the turf, she was almost perfect, and her missing arm was barely noticeable. She must have been tall, her long and slender legs now drawn up to her chest, with one arm casually lying across her knee. She had a fine figure, with delicate collarbones and an obscenely generous sweep from her waist to her hip. Her foot, after being severed by Jack Flanagan's shovel was now returned to its leg. One unusual thing, January noticed, was that her hair had been shorn. The calcium in bone would disintegrate but skin, hair, nails and leather clothing would be preserved by the acidic conditions of the bog.

Professor Traynor and a radiologist wheeled the trolley into the darkened chamber. From behind a glass panel in the control room, January watched as they placed the trolley in front of the CT machine which looked like a giant Polo Mint with a horizontal raised platform coming through the hole in the centre. They delicately lifted the body onto the platform and returned to the control room.

Traynor waved two men into the chamber.

One was Setanta Molloy. January's breath was taken away as the door slammed behind her. She managed to conceal it with a quick downward cough. The heat in the room was intense. January reached for a chair to steady herself, but instead the wheels slipped forward and Setanta caught her around her waist as she almost crashed to the floor. The intimacy of the moment did not help January exit the swoon.

Somewhere behind his grey eyes she thought she saw a flicker of recognition. He either didn't remember her or didn't want to acknowledge their previous familiarity with each other. He was a tall thin man, with red skin no doubt darkened by the scorching sun. The last time she'd seen him, he'd been wearing a faded Pearl Jam T-shirt and had shoulder-length blonde locks. Now, he was a man with presence. Now, he wore a cream linen suit, and a bright crimson pocket handkerchief was folded into his left breast pocket.

Professor Traynor spun around the chair and beckoned January to sit.

"Don't worry, I had you pegged for a fainter," she chuckled, unscrewing the lid of a water bottle. "Happens all the time." She handed the bottle to January.

"I–I was just a bit hot –"

"Drink some water and take deep breaths, you'll be fine," Traynor assured her, returning to her station.

"Boys and girls, can we all introduce ourselves?" Setanta Molloy's booming voice was a glad distraction from the sweating January. "I am Professor Setanta Molloy, Chief Curator at the National Museum of

Ireland." His accent had oriented itself much closer to London over the last two decades. "Professor Traynor, I'm sure you're known to the room as the State Pathologist of Ireland, the final authority line on forensic pathology in the country under the remit of the Department of Justice –"

"January Quail, from the *Irish Sunday Chronicle*." She boldly offered her hand to him across his briefcase. She was determined not to look weak.

"Ah yes, now I remember," said Molloy. "Your colleague, Alf Timmoney, requested that I allow you attend – with the caveat that any details we request will be withheld from your story."

Still clogged with light-headedness, she didn't have time to counter the bargain before the police officer spoke.

"Detective Inspector Colm Cooney."

Her eyes settled on the second man's stunning bright-blue eyes. A cultured tan across his broad brow, the police detective was extremely good-looking with straight white teeth and an immodest smile. He was the sort of man women know will be trouble, but excitedly jump into conversation with regardless.

"I've been heading up the investigation on the ground so far." His attractiveness was somewhat spoiled by his flat midlands drawl. "Delighted to come along this evening, to hand her over as such."

Setanta Molloy interrupted impatiently. "We believe

this body to be at *least* a thousand years old. It is a finding of great significance to the State, the Irish people and the broader Celtic community, so the National Museum of Ireland will lead the investigation. A member of Professor Traynor's team made the initial examination. Dublin University Hospital has kindly agreed to allow us use its CT and X-ray machines."

January interjected, "Has she a name yet?"

"Not as yet, but it will no doubt adhere to the convention in naming all bog bodies. Depending on her age at death, she will be the Girley Woman or the Girl from Girley. That should suit your sub-editor, Ms Quail."

Professor Traynor diffused the atmosphere as she pointed into the machine. "This is the most cutting-edge CT machine available in Ireland – it essentially uses X-rays to form transverse images through the flesh. We anticipate it should reveal more detail about our bog lady."

They silently watched the screens as the machine slowly scanned the sinewy muscle. The Girl from Girley moved through the gap in the centre of the giant cylinder, like ham through a slicer. The slow journey of the body through the scanner was mesmerising, the repetitive motion of the scanner doing nothing to dispel January's nausea.

She glanced at Setanta Molloy, but the two men were watching intently. She felt silly for letting some old flame get to her at such a moment. She was all over the place this evening, she needed to focus.

"There's something wrong," the radiologist said quietly as the scan finished, moving the dial and flicking some switches on the dashboard.

Her brow was furrowed as she looked at the black-and-white images on the screen in front of her.

"It looks like it's some sort of metal," she said, now getting agitated. "There's one, two, three, four ... aneurysm clips."

"*Aneurysm* clips? Are you sure?" Professor Traynor's eyes widened as she focused on the screen.

"I am certain – this person had those put in to stop a bleed on the brain."

Traynor's nose was now millimetres from the screen. "This body isn't a thousand years old. She died much more recently."

Chapter 4

Professor Traynor massaged her temples. Her eyes were fixed to the screen, her hair frizzing from a stressful sweat as she realised her mistake. The small control room was stifling as they looked over her shoulder at the humming screen.

"Professor," said Cooney, his phone already in his hand, "you're saying those clips are modern?"

"Yes – 1930s at the earliest, I would say. They're used to stop a bleed in the brain. She must have had one at some stage –"

"I need to make a call," said Cooney. "We will need to ascertain for certain the age of the remains, but it could well stand as a criminal investigation."

Professor Traynor said, "Professor Molloy, I'm afraid I can't allow you to stay. The Office of the State Pathologist will assume responsibility for confirming the age, but I need to complete a full post-mortem examination." All colour had drained from her face.

Setanta Molloy did not hold back as he bellowed,

"You examined her, and failed to notice that she wasn't a few thousand years old! I can't possibly allow you to damage an artefact that may be of national historic interest!"

"This body is absolutely *not* of historic interest. I am the State Pathologist – it's my say that counts. And you needn't worry – she will not be damanged in any way." She nodded at Cooney who was chewing his fingernails, uneasy with the unfolding developments.

"This is an exceptional case," said Setanta Molloy, his slim cheeks turning puce. "I am going to take this to the Minister for Heritage and the Taoiseach, even UNESCO if needs be – otherwise we risk an almost intact bog body being irreparably damaged." He gesticulated towards the scanner, his teeth bared towards Professor Traynor.

January almost couldn't conceal her bemusement at Molloy's threat of involving UNESCO. She pictured Lara Croft-type rangers with a portable vacuum chamber. She had to capture this ridiculous conversation. She reached into her satchel to start the voice-recording app. Her hands were still sweaty and she almost dropped it.

"Just so you know I'm recording this exchange for my notes," she said, still looking into the satchel.

Setanta Molloy exhaled loudly, shaking his head. "Good, good to have an official record."

"I can't speak for the entire position of the Irish media unfortunately but I understand both of your positions." January dreaded being dragged into this discussion, and wanted to fade back into the role of impartial advisor instead of committee member.

"I will perform further investigations thoughtfully, and will agree to allow the National Museum to consult." Professor Traynor sighed. "But, for now, we don't know how compatible the metal is with the MRI. If it is a recent corpse the metal would be okay but if it is any older the metal clips will blur the images, and potentially damage the machine and the surrounding tissue. I will agree to other scans when we know more, but only An Garda Síochána may attend."

The air of the control room was hot with the tempers of those gathered, Setanta Molloy and Professor Traynor now seeking the detective as adjudicator. January watched carefully, conscious that she could also be ejected. She dug her nails into the soft flesh of her hand in an attempt to focus.

"Detective Cooney," said Setanta Molloy, anger simmering through his tightened lips, "I am not satisfied that there will be sufficient cooperation from Professor Traynor's Office. We must use a complex archaeological process to ensure the remains are kept intact. Even if this is a fairly recent body, its condition can give us valuable insight into –"

"You're not listening to me here – there is *no* chance this is an ancient body," said Professor Traynor. "You need to accept that. I will allow you to advise me on the processes if required." Nodding towards Cooney, she said, "Detective, I trust that I can rely on An Garda Síochána to support this decision?"

"I will need to speak to the Commissioner on this but, as an interim measure, it seems to make sense. Professor Molloy, you heard her, this is not an archaeological find, so I don't see how you'd have any say in the matter." He was furiously texting on his iPhone.

Molloy wasn't giving up. "Mistakes have been made many times before both here and abroad. Until we have more evidence, I must state the museum's interest. May I remind you that the gardaí announced yesterday that there was no investigation? I will be apprising the Department of Heritage of the situation."

"Fine," Professor Traynor said.

Cooney was agitated. "January, the situation has clearly changed – can we be assured that nothing will be published until all the agencies involved have a better understanding of what's going on here?"

"I'll need something for tomorrow's online edition," she said. "I'll keep it vague." As it was, there was an unfolding war between three State agencies and possibly two government departments and now even the Taoiseach's office. "And nothing goes to any other media," she said firmly, making sure to catch Molloy's eye. Why was he so irate in the face of clear, scientific evidence?

"I will agree to let you both attend my office tomorrow at two o'clock," said Professor Traynor to

Setanta Molloy and January as the assembled group filed out.

As they walked out of the long hospital corridor onto Eccles Street, Molloy disappeared in the direction of the carpark.

Cooney stayed close to January as they walked towards Dorset Street, although completely engrossed in the screen on his phone.

"Checking what's being said on social media." He looked up to maintain eye contact with January. "What a shit storm. Setanta Molloy is good friends with the Minister."

"And what's she going to do about it exactly? Traynor and Setanta Molloy have to be careful about how things are handled," said January.

"Can you believe Traynor didn't realise that it wasn't a real bog body?" His eyes were still flickering between January and his phone. "Do you fancy getting a drink?"

The occurrences in the radiology department had temporarily distracted her from a growing hangover, throbbing at the base of her skull.

"I'd better get back to the office," she lied. "I have a few other stories to work on."

"At this hour? Anything interesting? You won't forget our agreement?"

"Not as long as you honour ours."

"What other stories are you working on?" he asked again, with surprising insistence.

Most people didn't know her writing and if they did they were not usually interested in her feature articles or "puff pieces".

"Buy the paper on Sunday and see," she said, sticking her tongue out cheekily at him.

"Funny, but I'm interested. The weather has slowed the news down." He stopped walking as he read the screen on his phone. "See you later."

As she hailed a taxi, January was left smiling as Cooney marched off in the other direction. What was all of that about? Had he been flirting with her, or was he an avid reader of the paper? Time would tell, she thought.

Chapter 5

Dublin was not a city used to heat. Its residents were ill-equipped to manage on that searing April morning. Inner-city young mothers pushed buggies, with legs too dark to be natural in short denim cut-offs, their cargo stripped down to their nappies, suckling on fast-melting ice creams. Travelling in packs of three or four units, with buckets and spades and soft sun hats, they were heading for Dollymount Strand. Some of the children's fathers laboured topless, constructing Dublin's new office block on the South Docks. In existing offices, boardrooms sweltered through floor-to-ceiling glass, the air-conditioning no match for the hot baked air.

January pinched her black silk dress forward, allowing the breeze to dry the sheen of perspiration resting on the bosom of her thin chest. It was only nine o'clock but already she was thinking of the cooling condensation on a glass of green crème de menthe, sitting outside Bruxelles. She carried on up the tight staircase to the confines of the newspaper office.

As she opened the second-floor door to the open-plan office, a thick, briny fog of human scent hit her heavily. Each of the three sash windows were open wide, allowing the sounds of the early buskers and street artists in, but little in the way of fresh air. There were reporters sitting in the bay, each workspace not much wider than the desktop screen.

"January," Alf said sharply as he stuck his head out of his office. "Can I see you?" It was a demand, not a request. "Why haven't you been answering your phone? Where have you been?" He was in a blue short-sleeved shirt, with a cerise tie and navy trousers. His thick black glasses slid down his clammy nose as he closed the door behind her.

"Calm down, Alf, it's only nine in the morning. I've got an exclusive – it's a pretty tasty –"

"*Exclusive!*" he erupted. "I gave you a bloody exclusive and you haven't started it, have you? You've been running around investigating ancient mummies. I told you not to spend too much time on that."

He was a nasty little shit, she thought. Gone was yesterday's sense of remorse. Didn't he know how important this story would be to her? He had even arranged for her to attend the scan, so why was he now reprimanding her?

"May I remind you that you are acting editor in a caretaking capacity only – you don't have the right to speak to me like that." She looked across his desk, and amongst the piles of papers and old editions and discarded coffee cups, she saw the pictures of the politicians with the prostitutes. He had left them on her desk yesterday. In a few of the pictures he had made circles in red marker.

"I'll speak to you any fucking way I want, January – you're only staff for a short while – you said it yourself that Laura is up to this – I'm going to work on it directly with her. And since when do you not turn up to editorial meetings? You're a joke. If you're going to have any chance of getting another job here –"

She felt the perspiration was settling in her T-zone, through her ice-white foundation. She imagined her forehead was frozen, her mouth cold, so she could interrupt him calmly.

"It's not an ancient mummy. She died recently. They didn't realise it until a CT scan showed up metal clips in her brain." She plonked her phone down on the table in front of him with the voice-recording app open. "This is the exchange between the State Pathologist and the Chief Curator of the National Museum of Ireland."

Through the echoey phone-speaker Setanta Molloy's voice said: *"You examined her, and failed to notice that she wasn't a few thousand years old! I can't possibly allow you to damage an artefact that may be of national historic interest!"*

"This body is absolutely not of historic interest. I am the State Pathologist – it's my say that counts."

"This is an exceptional case, I am going to take this to the

Minister for Heritage and the Taoiseach, even UNESCO if needs be, otherwise we risk an almost intact bog body, being irreparably damaged."

Alf blew from his bottom lip up, dislodging some of the dark blonde hair from his eyes. "Shit," he said, sitting down into the saggy black leather of his chair, which squeaked as he exhaled and sat forward again. "The Minister is going to have bigger things on his mind than Setanta Molloy's whingeing," he said, nodding toward the pictures.

Slowly it dawned on January. "He's not – I mean, he *is* in one of these?" she said, picking up the matt photo print.

"Did you even look at the pictures properly?" he asked.

She shook her head in denial. In truth she had seen them on her desk, glanced at them and instantly decided she would pawn them off on another reporter. After she had been told about the re-interview, she had stormed straight over to McDaids without looking at her desk again. Of course it could be a sensational story, but she didn't do that now. It wasn't her style, tearing apart someone's life to sell papers, not anymore. She had come to realise that there was a price for such prurience. Everyone was entitled to a private life, even politicians, in her books.

"Dear Alf," she pleaded, "now listen, let me run with this, even for the next day or so and see what we get."

He flung his pen across the desk. "Okay, January, I guess." He bounced over and back in his chair. "How old do they think the body is?"

"The State Pathologist is doing more tests now as we speak – but she said they weren't clipping together brain tissue any earlier than the 1930s," she said.

"Okay, let's see if it's more recent. I will keep on digging around about Minister Fitzpatrick and his hoors."

"His hoors? Where did they come from?" she asked, relieved he had the sense to let her story play out.

"He's in New York. I want to get together more information before I go to him."

There was a knock on the door. "*Come in!*" he barked and Laura entered.

She has a fair old bosom, thought January.

"Those pictures – we had an anonymous package dropped off at reception," Alf said to January. "I want you to cover it."

"Hi, January," said Laura. "I meant to say my friend came through with the number for that guy who found the bog body." She nibbled on her fingernails, glancing at Alf.

"Great, please write it down," January said, getting up.

"Er, I'll text it to you," Laura said, "if that's okay?"

"Fine," said January. There was every chance Laura's generation had lost their pincer-grip to hold a pen, she thought, never mind the strength to handwrite thirty pages of notes.

"Will do," said Laura, making for her seat. She set a typed A4 page in front of Alf.

Scanning the text, he cautioned January, without looking up. "Let me know where you're at with it before you go home today."

"Fine," January nodded, one leg either side of the door across the rickety threshold.

With almost twenty years' service to the paper, although her desk was in the open-plan part of the office, it was a prime spot. It had a landline telephone and sockets at eye level but, most importantly, she wasn't overlooked. She perched on her swivel chair, a gift for her tenth anniversary of working at the paper. It was an antique bankers with soft green leather studded into mahogany-stained rosewood. In ten years she had fallen from lauded and loved staff member to one rung lower than a stipended graduate.

Over a hundred emails. Nothing from Lady Anon. She found the most recent email in their lengthy conversation and replied, requesting to reschedule their chat.

Scanning through the deluge of press releases, she found the most recent police statement on the bog body.

A spokesperson for An Garda Síochána has confirmed the discovery of a body in a bog located

outside Ardee, Co Louth. The force is engaging with a number of state agencies but the death is not being treated as suspicious.

It was unlike them not to send new information, but Cooney had agreed to January taking the story exclusively. She figured there must be some other reason they were staying tight-lipped about the revelations. She cleared through her emails for the next hour or so.

How had the Pathologist not realised it was a more recent body? She would need to explain, at some further date.

What had Alf circled in the picture? She was uneasy that the package of pictures had arrived to the paper anonymously, especially now that anything could be doctored.

Grateful she had the good sense to take a picture of the images on her phone, she pinched the screen to zoom into the background. This image showed Fitzpatrick and another man driving through the gates of an apartment complex. She zoomed in to see that the name of the complex was Laurel Hill.

The next picture showed the two men getting out of the car, Fitzpatrick glancing back over his shoulder to the road behind as two scantily dressed women awaited them at the door of the apartment..

The third picture showed Fitzpatrick sitting on a black leather couch. She had to squint to see, as only a sliver of his face was visible behind the profile of a woman in her underwear pulling the curtains closed.

Alf had circled the second man, the Minister's advisor, Pat Dennehy. January had crossed his path at the raucous drinking session that happened every year after the Dublin Horse Show. She shuddered at the memory of his thin, elderly lips.

Another red circle had been drawn around the number of the duplex apartment, 42, and the last ring highlighted a barely visible red light beside the Minister's car. A cigarette-butt maybe? It could be anything. January made a mental note to ask Alf what else he knew.

Her phone buzzed as Laura sent through a new contact, which she saved down to her phone.

BOGBODY Jack Flanagan

She would call him on the walk over to the mortuary. She had better leave if she wanted to have a quick *sipín* in the Bailey before.

She packed up her satchel and Laura smiled a thin sneer at her as she passed by.

"He's a bit mad, the man Jack," Laura warned. "He wanted money to talk to the radio station apparently, so good luck with him."

January had resisted remote working for as long as she possibly could. Through the unrelenting rise of the internet, she had considered becoming an antiques dealer or a cook, but ultimately journalism was a vocation. Not totally dissimilar to indentured servitude, she thought. She checked the paper's website, and read Laura's update, now halfway down the page. It was old information but it was more recent than what everyone else had.

In the Bailey, she grabbed the last stool at the end of the bar and ordered a bowl of soup. She took a look at this farmer's Twitter page. He was apparently "mad for it", whatever he meant by "it". He declared himself a fan of Volkswagen cars and farming, followed by emojis of a car, tractor, pig and a pint. His tweet of the foot had been retweeted over 10,000 times. He had favourited tweets with tags from the great and good of journalism. The youth of Ireland were avid social-media users, January regretted, even this hapless chap.

She checked Google Maps again, and saw that his farm and the bogland were between the towns of Ardee and Drogheda but actually in Meath, not Louth. She had grown up not too far away, although she rarely visited now. There was no reason to.

The call connected.

"Mr Flanagan?" The hum of a crowd chatting and laughing was audible on the line.

"This is Jack the lad – who's this?"

"This is January Quail from the *Irish Sunday Chronicle* – I was hoping to speak to you about your discovery," she said, catching the attention of the barman, who looked away.

"Well, how's ith going? I'm afraid ith'll cost ya."

Jack had a thick country accent.

"Okay, how much?"

"Eh, how much have you goth?"

"Meet me for a chat, please? I've come from the examination of the body so I'm sure you're curious about what they have discovered so far."

"Aye, aye, thath seems like a fair exchange. Can you come up here to Arday?"

"Sure, I can be there this evening – say six o'clock?"

"Grand job – you'll find me here in the Gallops pub. And answer me this –"

"Go on." She'd better leave it at the one.

"Is there a whole lottha Janie?" he said, finding his own Delphic remark humorous.

"No, there's not so much. Don't get leathered – I want to get some sense out of you later," she said, hanging up the phone as her lunch arrived.

Chapter 6

It was January's first time in an active mortuary. As she approached the city morgue, her mind was full of images of graverobbers in billowing shirts hauling still-fresh wretches for examination on the slab. Grave-robbing had been rife in Dublin. Many 19th century medical students had viewed the intimate details of a human liver or brain whose provenance was questionable. Porters and university professors turned a blind eye to how the bodies had been procured. January had written about this many times.

Colm Cooney held the door open for her.

"Good afternoon, Detective." She ambled in under his arm.

He had his short sleeves rolled over his elbow. He did not place much value of the positioning of a cuff, but was otherwise well-presented.

Inside, January was surprised at the building's modernisation. The ceilings were now high, the floors a modern marble instead of the old green crushed granite.

"How are you this fine day?" she asked.

"Not great, to be honest, didn't manage much sleep. And that eejit Setanta Molloy is insisting on being here. I am making an exemption to keep him onside while we are saying it's a bog body. It would look strange if that was the case and he wasn't here."

He led her down a white corridor, through automatic doors into a viewing room.

The room was windowless. An industrial white light emanated through a large pane, where she could see the body laid out a raised dais.

"Welcome, Ms Quail," said Professor Traynor from inside, through the microphone. She was wearing fluorescent pink scrubs, her face shielded by what looked like a welder's mask. Her cute kitten heels had been replaced by white wellies.

Setanta Molloy was already there. The space was dark and carpeted, with all the stillness of a crypt. January recognised a foreboding portrait of the Morrigan, the Irish goddess associated with battle and the foretelling of death.

The room was usually used by the families of murder victims who would come to identify their loved ones. An almost-expired diffuser hinted a sniff of rose and geranium into the space.

Professor Traynor turned the dimmer switch on the other side of the glass. January squinted as the bright light flooded around the body.

"Let us begin," said Traynor.

An automatic red light appeared on a camera situated at the head of the body.

"Wednesday April 28th, 2018. The time is 2 pm. Our testing has revealed that this body is no older than twenty years." She coughed to clear her throat. "That is, she was buried in the bog in the last twenty years. The clips used in her brain point to previous subarachnoid haemorrhages. These particular clips were first used in the early 90s. From the insect life present, we believe the body was buried within twenty-four hours of the time of death. Attempts have been made to remove the bones – the right humerus is missing. It seems they tried to remove all the bones – there are marks that would indicate it here on the other leg. Perhaps the person was not strong enough to continue the butchery. That, or they were concerned at how it might damage the aesthetics."

Setanta Molloy furrowed his brow in confusion, before leaning to whisper in January's ear, a little too intimately. "The bones are usually dissolved in the bog."

January nodded as he snaked back out of her personal space, a warning stare from Professor Traynor piercing through the glass.

Traynor continued: "The skin was dyed a dark brown, giving the appearance of a much older corpse – leading the anthropologist to mistake it as such on initial visual identification."

She was blaming the anthropologist now, thought January. Neither of them must have thought to check.

"The body is that of a woman, aged approximately between eighteen and twenty-two. She was tall, at six foot, and had given birth. She died as a result of a blunt-force trauma to the head, with indentations on the skull that are ridged. The body also has a number of," she paused and focused on her audience, "unusual post-mortem injuries. There are marks on her knees as if she was pinned down. Large nails were hammered through each joint. There are also incisions to the nipples." She gestured at the victim's chest area.

January was unnerved by the body lying in front of her. This was the recent corpse of someone who had inhabited the earth at the same time as she had. Could she even know her? They were similar ages.

Setanta Molloy broke the silence. "The nipples of Old Croghan Man had also been cut. Sucking the nipples of kings was a sign of submission in Ancient Ireland and –"

"That's it, Professor Setanta Molloy," said Professor Traynor, "or I am turning off the microphone and stopping the post-mortem. *Now*. There was also a noose made from hazel discovered in the bog beside her. However, there are no visible ligature marks on the neck. Examining the tissue microscopically there are no burst blood vessels so it most likely was a prop used by the murderer."

It was the first time murder had been mentioned, and although the bog bodies were nearly all murdered, the passage of time insulated the nastiness of it, the visceral reality of taking life from a breathing creature.

"The person who killed this woman went to great lengths to make it look like an authentic bog body. However, none of these incisions were committed when the victim was alive. We can't rule out that the crime was unplanned and the killer used the various elements to cover his tracks." Traynor pushed her plastic goggles up the bridge of her nose. Her gloves were dirty with soil and tissue so she used her littlest finger.

"Professor," said Cooney loudly, "given the sensitive nature of this crime, I would request that the rest of the examination is conducted in private." He gestured to Setanta Molloy and January. "It's highly unusual for external persons to be privy to what is now a murder investigation."

Setanta's colour rose. "I'm not going anywhere. You'll need someone with an academic knowledge of the bog bodies to interpret the crime. And, in case you don't know, there was a case in Egypt recently where a mummy was discovered near an existing archaeological site. When put through the MRI machine, she was found to have had gold fillings. So it was bumped to a murder investigation. DNA revealed it was an ancient mummy after all – who happened to have her cavities filled. An immensely valuable object destroyed."

"This isn't Egypt," said Traynor, "this person isn't ancient remains and I am not discussing the matter further."

"And what about Tin Tin here?" Setanta jabbed a finger towards January's shoulder.

Cooney turned to face her, taking in the statement. With a deep sigh he looked at January and exhaled. "I'm sorry but you'll have to leave. We'll get a press statement out as soon as possible."

January was unwilling to leave without a fight. She was resentful of what Cooney was asking of them, although it seemed inevitable.

"Yes, we may need your expertise, Professor Setanta Molloy, but that will be at our discretion," said Cooney.

Before January could argue her case, the light in the gallery went out, leaving them standing in the dark apart from low orange nightlights in the plug sockets.

Traynor said: "My colleagues in An Garda Síochána agree with me. I must insist you both leave." Still speaking from the blacked-out room, her disembodied voice said, "Goodbye."

"Is she serious?" January asked Cooney. "This is a joke. I am going ahead and reporting what has been discovered here."

"January, this is an open murder investigation – please do not do that. It's unethical and in direct contravention of our agreement." His blue eyes searched hers for some sort of reasonableness.

At the start of her career she had received a number of complaints and had been reprimanded by the Press Council of Ireland for pushing things too far when covering entertainment stories, following celebrity chefs to do cocaine in the toilet of posh nightclubs and such. Although she had long since abandoned those practices, any allegation of unethical reporting resonated with her.

"Fine – but you'd better have a statement or something for me."

She followed Setanta Molloy out of the viewing room.

"What a total fuck-up!" said Setanta. "This will look bad for the police and that daft woman." He meant Professor Traynor.

They walked down the corridor.

"You were there when the last two bodies were found," he said, finally acknowledging their previous encounter.

They were now standing outside the heavy metal door of the old police station, the hot, humid air hitting them with a thump.

Setanta took out an e-cigarette, shaking the replacement fluid vigorously into the clear chamber. January noticed it was caramel flavour, which would be more fitting for a teenage girl than a middle-aged museum curator.

"What do you think it means?" she asked.

"What does what mean?"

"The hazel noose, the removal of the nipples?" She watched him inhale.

Blowing a plume of fruity-saccharine vapour into the air, he said, "Well, whoever did this is trying hard to make it resemble a bog body. Those are finishing touches though – the real work must have come with aging the skin like that, making it such a resemblance to the real thing. It's a work of art."

They were now crossing Griffith Avenue, headed towards the city. January was pretty wary of Setanta, but she still valued his take on things – if she could manage to strip away his own agenda.

Her thirst prevailed. "Do you have time for a drink?" They were approaching the Cat and Cage, an old favourite amongst locals and country girls alike.

He did not hesitate. "Why not?"

He pushed back the brass handle of the pub door as January slipped by him. It was quiet – there was no one else there apart from the barman. Any of these old boozers without a beer garden had been abandoned during the warm spell.

With her usual liqueur not available, January joined Setanta in drinking a pint of Guinness. They sat on the bouncy felt lounge seat, watching the brown beer separate into the black stout and its creamy white head. Setanta held his e-cigarette up to the bartender who nodded in response, giving his permission for the professor to inflict his ridiculous confectionary fog on

January. He had not asked her permission.

"They will come crawling back for advice." He sipped his pint with relish, licking the creamy moustache of foam from his top lip. "Mark my words. My own ego apart, the case in Egypt is a cautionary tale."

"They weren't clipping aneurysms two thousand years ago?"

"Maybe they were. It's no more unexplainable than how stones weighing ten tonnes were transported over twenty kilometres in the construction of Newgrange, when we aren't even sure the wheel was invented."

"You think the killer was an archaeologist? For him to go to such great lengths?"

"That's what he wanted us to think, but anyone could Google bog bodies and see those features amongst some of the bodies discovered." He looked intently at January. "Are we on the record here?"

"We are talking, Setanta, talking. Now that the gardaí are involved again I'm not sure what I can report."

"Right, well, I think whoever did this ..." He took a deep mouthful of his beer.

"Wanted the body to be found," January said. She was sipping hers cautiously, conscious that she would need to be sober for the hour-long drive to Ardee.

"Exactly, no one would go to such lengths, tanning the skin, making a hazel noose, if he didn't want the world to marvel his work. Or hers hypothetically – but most killers are men, aren't they? Anyway, you don't accidentally murder someone and bury the body like that – it must have been planned out." He drew deeply on the black mouthpiece, before exhaling the vapour out the side of his mouth – the barman did not notice the illicit manouevre. "But why would they want to make it look like a bog body? They must have realised even twenty years ago that forensics would be able to date the body once an initial investigation took place? And the bones, trying to remove them?"

In this setting he had calmed right down, the colour in his face returning to the brown suntan without the red inflamed capillaries. The past twenty years hadn't been kind to him, January thought, as she remembered the young archaeologist with ice-tipped highlights and blue-check shortsleeved shirts. He had done well at adopting the posture of a professor – with the bilious voice, nostril hair, and most likely a drink problem not far removed from hers.

"*That* is the million-dollar question, isn't it, Ms Quail? Sorry about the vape. I picked the wrong one this morning. It's been a hectic twenty-four hours."

"I am a fan of the saccharine, Setanta, don't worry. Maybe the killer was hoping the body would be reported by the media, giving them an early warning, time to make an exit." She had drunk a little quicker than she meant to and was down to the final third of the pint.

"Or maybe they were mad, who knows?" He matched her with one glug.

"Tell me, did you go up to the scene last night? I bet the gardaí are scrambling around trying to preserve the field."

"I saw that farmer's tweet in the morning and went straight up. It was the local gardaí at that point. Eventually they allowed me to take a look once the anthropologist arrived."

"It wasn't Traynor who made the initial call that it was ancient remains. She was blaming them again now."

"Traynor still managed not to notice before the CT scan. Anyway, that eejit farmer was there holding court at the entrance to the field. By the time I left, the local media were starting to arrive and he had a big poster stationed at the nearest crossroads with an arrow advertising 'Bog Body Discovery' as if it were a bingo fundraiser."

"I'm going up to talk to him this evening," January said.

"Good luck to you. I suspect the police aren't happy about him blabbing away on Twitter."

"This whole thing is a total mess," said January.

"*Hmm*," he said thoughtfully. "The Clonycavan Man and Old Croghan Man were exciting, weren't they?" His demeanour had softened from the overwrought megalomaniac he had appeared as earlier. He was quite the chameleon. His legs were now crossed like hers, one hand supporting his chin, mirroring her shape against the table.

"I got some of my first international by-lines from

those stories. I was filing stories for all the newswires. I wasn't the only one but I was prolific. Two-thousand-year-old mummies captured the imagination of the world's media," she said. "Do you ever hear from old Monty these days?"

"God, he was cracked, wasn't he? He went doddery the last few years." He leant in closer to January so that she could smell the vetiver in his aftershave and the sickly sweet scent from his breath.

"Between us and strictly off the record, the museum had some trouble getting rid of him. In fact, the Minister had to get involved."

"Fitzpatrick?" said January, the images of him in the apartment complex with two hookers jumping into her mind. "He's a pal of yours, isn't he?"

"It's complicated – although that reminds me – he asked for me to let him know how the bog investigation goes." Setanta drained the final drop of his pint glass with a sense of finality, the heavy glass bottom hitting the mahogany pub table in conclusion.

"He's in New York?" January wondered if he shared the same carnal hobbies as Fitzpatrick. Her mind wandered, imagining what sort of woman would marry him.

"The life of Rily he has, off on junkets like that. Listen, take my number and stay in touch, okay? I had better head off."

She realised that she wasn't quite finished, and

wasn't sure whether she was enjoying his company or the drink, suspecting a little of both.

"I'll see what I can do," she said. "I'm sure I'll see you again soon."

"Here's hoping," he said.

The office of the *Irish Sunday Chronicle* was quiet that afternoon. January wanted to show her face before leaving for Ardee. A little bit of work was the best thing to sober her up. The resident cobweb stretched without breaking as she opened the office door. It was relaxed here today, with mostly a handful of young online journalists combing the internet for news, and a couple of news hacks and a photographer floating around. Laura was licking an ice-cream cone and scrolling through American gossip sites for stories to rewrite. This is what constituted news these days – pictures from social media with little to no fact-checking or corroboration, gobbled up by the masses.

"January, hi, I didn't think you'd be back today?" she said, her newly tattooed eyebrows arching with mild surprise.

"I'm not."

"Is there a problem?"

"Not at all, Laura." She shook her head and went off to find Alf and fill him in on the latest findings.

"What a shit show!" he greeted her. Rings of underarm sweat had expanded as he sat cross-legged behind his desk, slurping an iced coffee through a straw. "Leave Traynor to me, I know how to shake a comment out of her."

"Well, the gardaí will have a statement – but Traynor is going to be in self-preservation mode," said January warily. "Already she is blaming the anthropologist." She watched as the drops of condensation from his coffee cup made the ink run on his notepad.

"How did they make such a big mistake? So that means the killer is still out there. You would want to be extremely careful, January, if you are going down there."

"The murder happened twenty or thirty years ago, Alf. And I'm a big girl." She massaged her fingers as that fact sank in.

"I mean it – if you had seen what I have seen, anyway. I'll leave it there, but mind yourself."

"Any word on Fitzpatrick?" January clucked her tongue as she read the opal face of her wristwatch. "He ought to be well up and about by now."

"Well, I haven't requested a response on the pictures. I still don't know where they came from. Laura has had some luck in tracking down the girls. On the Irish escort site." He pulled his feet off the desk and lifted up the pictures. Pointing to one which showed a brunette lighting Fitzpatrick's cigarette, he said, "She calls herself Lovely Lydia, Polish originally, says she's in her thirties." He clicked on to his computer and opened an album of Lydia in a number of nude

50

and semi-nude photos. One had her splayed across a double bed with dark purple sheets. She had a limber figure but a square waist, and certainly looked to January a few years north of thirty.

"Her rates are at the upper end of the scale," she said, scanning the web page. She had recently written an article about high-class prostitution in Ireland.

Alf nodded, still sucking on the straw. "Three hundred an hour. But no sign of her friend here." He tapped the blown-up pictures of a blonde woman closing the curtains, with a suspender belt visible on both thighs. "Laura has convinced Lovely Lydia to meet her this evening," he said, "so let's see in the morning which looks more like the front-page story."

January was impressed at Laura's work, surprised even – when she was out of the office a large picture of Kim Kardashian in a bikini was emblazoned across her computer screen.

"Who do you think sent the pictures in?" she asked, as Alf finally put his disgusting cup in the bin.

"Someone who wants Fitzpatrick gone," he said slowly, "if not someone who wants to take the government down."

"Doesn't he have a lot invested in Irish Aviation? It could be a business rival," said January.

Alf screwed up his face. "Perhaps. Whoever it was either knew what he was up to and took the pictures, or had an investigator follow him."

"I'm surprised he wasn't more careful. I thought he was happily married? His wife is that former press secretary." January remembered their beaming broad smiles from the *Irish Sunday Chronicle*'s thirtieth anniversary party a month earlier.

"Yes," said Alf, "she is. I wonder if she had any clue what her precious hubby was up to –"

January jumped in. "You're not going to show them to her? Don't you think that's a bit unethical?"

"January, all this hanging around with archaeologists is making you soft, is it?"

"It's not her fault her husband can't keep it in his pantaloons."

"I'm not the one who made him visit that apartment block. She's going to find out eventually."

January tried not to let him get under her skin, but it was difficult. She shrugged and sighed.

"I'm going to start writing this up," she said. "Some background colour pieces anyway, until I know what the reporting restrictions are."

"Sure, babe, work away," he nodded, engrossed in the pictures again.

The over-friendly term of endearment annoyed her, but she tried her best to conceal it.

As she sat in her swivel chair, the sweat between her buttocks squelched uncomfortably. Sipping a cup of strong black instant coffee, she shook off the afternoon's tipsiness and settled into sifting through her email inbox. She disliked the taste but accepted the beverage as a vehicle to deliver caffeine.

January digested the copy that had already been submitted for that Sunday, a mixture of album reviews and beauty articles. Laura had also written three smaller articles to fill a larger double-page spread on the bog bodies, including an article discussing the other bodies found in Europe, the two most recent discoveries and an article on bog butter. She scanned them all and submitted them for review to the subeditors, the pictures of the aged dairy product lighting a pang of hunger for some fine-smelling cheeses she had in her pantry.

She decided to go home. Powdering her nose to ward off the worst of the inevitable perspiration, she made a final scan of her emails. Her eyes were drawn to one message.

Subject PLEASE CALL

Good afternoon, my gracious girl,

Had some thoughts on the recent bog body discovered – call me when you get a chance.

Monty

She wondered if the poor old guy was just lonely and wanted some company, but she still made a mental note to call him.

Chapter 7

Living in the heart of Dublin, January's car was usually ancillary. But this evening she did require it. So she paid a visit to the garage at the end of the road where her father's 1978 Bentley Corniche was housed. It was a fabulous classic car, with forest-green paintwork and a tan hood. Its 6.75 V8 engine still had the horsepower to thump along. She had recently replaced the radio, – although she had chosen not to include a Bluetooth or MP3 player facility, she did want a working radio, and she listened to classic hour on Lyric FM as she drove out of the hot streets of Dublin.

Without air conditioning, she was soon sweating and removed her driving gloves, her hands were so tacky. She kept a steady pace, checking the speedometer which was still in miles only. She was invigorated by getting out and chasing a story. Perhaps she had become a little too comfortable writing about her little pet subjects, reviewing antiques and writing features on strange historians and unusual science experiments.

It wasn't challenging her.

Thinking about the farmer Jack Flanagan, her primary objective was to assess whether or not he could be the killer. From her rudimentary understanding of criminal psychology, she believed the perpetrator often injected himself into the investigation. It wasn't likely she would get much more information from him. But she wanted to rule him out.

The epic opening of Mozart's Requiem in D Minor temporarily distracted her. She loved this dramatic piece of music, and it seemed an apt accompaniment as she left the motorway. There was a killer on the loose, after all. Given the media attention, the murderer would also know the body was found, and still think it was being treated as an authentic bog body. He or she would be watching closely. She turned the music up until the dashboard vibrated.

Chapter 8

As the choir lurched into the heavenly 'Agnes Dei' of Mozart's Requiem, she left the fast-moving traffic for the Ardee exit. Spotting the handmade sign, she approached the village and found the Gallops Pub located after a bad bend. The dry ditch was lined with all manner of parked cars and she found a spot for the Bentley under the broad limbs of an oak tree. Further up the boreen, she saw some cars and yellow tape flapping around the site, but she would speak to Jack first.

Once inside the old porch of the roadhouse, January ordered a double crème de menthe with ice. The barman's eyebrows arched in surprise, but most country pubs would hold a dusty bottle or two. It was a fitting beverage for the heatwave.

The beer garden of the pub was half full, 10cc playing on the jukebox. January recognised Jack Flanagan from his Twitter profile. She had expected a farmer's tan, but not the deep burn on his cheeks and the back of his neck. He had bright green eyes, his strawberry-blonde hair visible under his flat cap. Attired in the red of a Liverpool FC jersey, he sat astride a picnic bench, puffing his way through strong cigarettes. The mouldy parasol slanted out from its base, providing some cover from the dwindling sun.

"Well," he said as January approached him, "are you this journalist?" He looked her up and down as he exhaled the smoke. He turned to the others sitting at the table, similarly attired country men, and said, "*The Irish Chronicle*, boys."

"Yes, Mr Flanagan, can we speak alone?"

His posse sneered and guffawed at this.

"Only if you swear you'll keep your hands to yourself."

They moved to an empty table.

January sipped her drink and ground some crushed ice in irritation.

"So is this intherview for this Sunday's paper?"

"There's no guarantee, but that's the plan."

"What's that you're drinking? It's bright green."

"Thank you. It's a mint liqueur."

"It looks like mad stuff – can I thry some?" he said, resting his pint of cider down and reaching for her glass.

"A sip," she said, tight-lipped.

Smacking his lips, he lightly declared, "Not thwo bad ath all, but you couldn't drink it all night."

"I'm not planning to. Now, tell me about how you found the body yesterday morning."

"I thold all this to the gardaí and a load of other people," he sighed.

"Well, please tell me again." January twisted the glass to avoid the edge he had slurped from. Thinking of his big fat tongue in there made her think she would leave it and get a fresh one.

"Are you English?" he asked, avoiding her question completely.

"No, I'm from Kells. What were your thoughts when you found the foot first?"

"You're a West Brit with an accent like that?"

"Something like that – now please, Mr Flanagan."

He sniffed and sat up. "Sorry. Well, I was out cutthing the thurf and on the phone. I felt the blades jam and sthopped to have a look. They jam every so ofthen especially in this heat. When I pulled it out I thought it must have been a joke. Tha's when I tweeted about it."

"So you didn't call the gardaí?"

"No, Jaysus, no, I didn't. Wouldn't be keen on ringing the coppers at the best of times, or should I say the worst of times *ha-ha*. I pulled the foot out to show me uncle, and he made me call them. He made me, because of our cousin Theresa. She went missing from the bog years ago. I wasn't even born but they say she disappeared. He thinks it's her. After we put in the call, they called out to the bog and they were picking at it with their little shovels talking about it being as old as the pyramids, so we knew it wasn't Theresa."

"I'm sorry to hear about your cousin," she said, a tug of conscience pulling her to admit the latest development. "Who from the gardaí was the first on the site?"

"It was the local lads. Sure they didn't know what to make of the fuckin' yoke. I put up the tweet. They thought it was a doll or prank first – it wasn't thil they called down the sergeant that he clocked it was a bog body. Sure I'd never heard of the thing before yesterday."

"He put up all of the yellow tape and stopped people coming and going. Me phone was exploding with the notifications – *boom boom boom!*" He lit another cigarette. "After that things moved fierce quick, hey. Louth Meath FM sent someone out to me, and the *Herald* and *Leader* newspapers sent lassies down to interview me." He flicked the ash from his cigarette with a flamboyant flick of the wrist. "If you don't mind me saying so, yous journalists take yourselves far too serious. I was joking with them about paying me to talk to them and they went off in a huff."

"Sure didn't I give you a bit of my drink?" said January, lighting up one of her own cigarettes. There was only so long she could go on sitting in a beer garden on a summer's day without a trip to the Consulate.

"Aye, but you posh ones are always half cracked anyway – I've rode a few of ye before," he said, grinning from the side of his mouth.

She couldn't imagine anyone who would succumb to Jack Flanagan.

"Anyway what happened next, after they sealed the bog?"

"The plainclothes detective came down from Dublin with an anthro-pol-ol-ogist and another fine-looking older lady."

The State Pathologist *was* a fine-looking older lady, January supposed.

"And were you in on these discussions?"

"Jaysus, no!" He gulped down the end of his cider. "They ran me and me Uncle Baby as soon as the detectives landed in. But once the anthro-pol-ol-ogist had a look –" He stopped as January's smiled broadened. "What? What are you laughing at?"

"It's pronounced anthrop-OL-ogist," she said gently, not wanting to hurt his feelings.

"Whatever. After he came down they seemed happy enough there was nothing suspicious, but got antsy about moving it and not damaging the rest of her. Anyway, will you have another of, well, whatever that is?" he said on the final swill of his pint.

"It's a crème de menthe," she said.

"Jaysus, I'll never remember that – but the barman will. He got to his feet. "*De tent*," he sing-songed as he walked off.

She paused the recording and checked her phone. Another email from Monty and a text from Cooney to call him. Alf was also looking for an update. She had three notifications on Twitter. At that stage she exhaled.

This is why she hated modern technology – everyone enslaved, tapping away on their phones instead of taking in and enjoying the moment. She put the phone back in her bag as Jack returned.

"You said earlier that you were there when they were examining the body today – what did they find?" he asked.

"Ah," she said, "nothing too surprising." She considered how much detail she would give away, especially given how prolific he was on social media.

"You lured me here under false prethences – you said they found some big stuff."

"It's more than my job's worth to say, Jack."

"Go on, I won't say it to anyone." He grinned at her. His teeth were perfectly shaped but yellowed, like the ivories on a spinster's well-played piano.

"Well, the body was found with a number of trademarks of ritual sacrifice," she said slowly. She proceeded carefully, watching his face closely to see how he would react to the details.

"*Bejayney!*" he said, aghast. "Like what?"

What she was telling him was technically true.

"The nipples had been removed, symbolic that the land had not provided abundant nourishment to the people. There was also a noose from hazel, and signs that she had been pinned down in the bog."

Jack was chewing his lip intently as she continued.

"It's thought that signifies the desire to keep the

soul in a sort of purgatory after death, neither ascending to heaven nor descending to hell."

"There you go, that's all above my head anyway," he said, changing the subject. "Are you driving back to Kells tonight?"

January's gut reaction was that he was being genuine, and although interested in the spectacle on social media, did feel the details were beyond his comprehension.

"I live in Dublin now."

"Well, are you driving back to Dublin?"

She looked at the cold condensation on the glass, wiping it away from the logo with her hand.

"Doesn't look like it," she said. "Is there a B&B nearby?"

"Down the road, my uncle runs one. I'm sure he'll have space – I warned him to make sure to keep room for the journalists who come up."

He might be right about the media descending on the area once the truth about the body was released, she thought, justifying the overnight stay to herself.

January felt the conversation consisted of the pair of them sipping, inhaling, lighting and extinguishing their drinks and cigarettes at increasing speed. Her first impression of Jack was proving to be true. He wasn't involved in the murder. He was a bumpkin and she couldn't listen to him for much longer, although she was enjoying the buzz of the beer garden. But she had been in and out of pubs all day.

Summoning her self-control, she collected her overnight bag from the boot of her car and made the short journey up the country lane to his uncle's B&B on foot.

It was only eight o'clock, but the sun was beginning to set. With the humidity it reminded her more of a walk in springtime New Orleans than April in Ardee. Her bag was heavier than usual – she had packed a large ream of writing paper into the monogram calfskin brown-leather satchel. It had been expensive and it was personalised with her gold initials.

"January?" she heard a man shout as she approached the front door.

It was wide open and a single electric light bulb hung unpromisingly from a light socket over the front door.

"January?" the voice called again, now much closer. "There you are!"

A man appeared.

He was mid-fifties and had once been good-looking. He had jet-black hair with a slice of grey across the left of his widow's peak. He stood in the hallway, hips jaunted to one side, ushering her in.

"Jack told me you were headed up. Come on in, hey." He spoke softly despite the initial roars. "Welcome to *Bothar Álainn* Bed and Breakfast – we have the best room in the house kept for you. I'm Timmy Flanagan but my friends call me Baby."

January shook his thick hand. She missed country

life for these fantastic nicknames they would put on one another.

"Good evening, Mr Flanagan, thank you for accommodating me at such late notice," she said.

"Call me Baby, it's not a problem. We've been expecting a hape of journalists since Jack found the foot. Got the Wi-Fi updated and all – it's top of the range." He led her inside the hallway, where the pine floors continued into the kitchen. All of the windows were open, but the kitchen smelt musty and dusty.

"Would you like a drink or will I show you to your room? It's the presidential suite, if you like," he said, delighted with himself.

Past the end of the kitchen counter she saw a narrow bar installed beside the dining room. She spotted the bright green of her favourite drink from the mirrored shelves over the plywood counter but thought better of it.

"It's been a long day …" she paused before she brought herself to say, "Baby."

"No bother, no bother, come on up this way."

She followed him up the bare stairs. There was an absence of any sort of softer touches you might expect in a family-run B&B – no pictures or ornaments.

"Is there anyone else staying here? Would your wife be in?"

He chuckled. "Oh, I'm not married, January – couldn't let anyone slow Baby down!" He opened the door labelled 3. It was a large room with a deep burgundy throw on the double bed. The suite also was sparsely furnished but it seemed cosier than downstairs. Baby had gone to the trouble to turn on the bedside lights.

He picked up the visitor information booklet and pointed to a mobile number on the front. "That's my number if you need anything." Sensing her uneasiness, he continued, "But you'll be doubly safe as houses as there are two detectives working on the case who are also staying here. I'll leave you to it so – and, before I go, there's a jacuzzi bath in there if you want to unwind. We put it in right before the crash – it's top of the line."

"Thanks, Baby. Eh, Jack mentioned you encouraged him to call the police?"

"Aye, he's an awful eejit, was worried about some agricultural diesel he had imported. I told him they don't care about that sort of stuff, anyway. We're delighted to have you here. And I know you probably can't say much but Miriam might well be asking you questions tomorrow."

January raised an eyebrow, already regretting her decision not to stay in the town and not be mithered by locals. But here she was. "Oh?"

"Yes, her daughter went missing a few years ago, and she half wondered if it was her that Jack found in the bog, until they clocked it was an ancient mummy and all that. She's been housekeeper here for the last few years as I'm often out in Marbella or Ibiza." Proud of himself with his chest shoved forward.

"God love her – I appreciate your letting me know, Baby." She deliberately ignored his boastings about booze-ups in the Balearics.

"I'll leave you to it. She'll be here from seven in the morning and all the other information is there on the card." He gave a small wave of his hand before closing the door.

The heels of his black crocodile boots clacked down the corridor and downstairs and January turned the lock in the door. She pulled back the thick red chenille curtains, and saw the lights on in a nearby bungalow.

Peering out, she saw a middle-aged woman hanging an array of jerseys on a clothes horse in her kitchen. As she was about to look away, a man came into the room, his back to the window. The woman stood back. He was shaking his fist and looked angry. He drew his hand back as if about to release a bow from an arrow. The woman huddled into herself as he pulled the curtains, January momentarily noting the scrunched anger in his face.

She heard the front door close and watched Baby get into his little silver car and head up the road. Should she call him back, tell him what she saw? Realising she wouldn't make it in time, she picked up her phone, anxious about the woman's welfare. Then she stopped herself, remembering the introversion that pervaded rural Ireland. The sight of a squad car in the drive, and the queries it would prompt from neighbours would most likely make things even worse for the woman.

Still perturbed, she twiddled the gold taps. She ran a hot bath for herself, making peace with her decision of inaction. The bubbly water refreshed her sticky skin. It had been a long day. The State Pathologist's office would have a lot to answer for, and January was certain that Traynor would be forced to resign for making such a mistake. She exhaled deeply, picked up the small white bottle of bath soap and emptied it into the bath, increasing the velocity of the jets beside her shoulders. When would they release the information that it wasn't a bog body? It had to have taken time to make it look like that. Whoever the perpetrator was would still think that it was being treated as an ancient find, perhaps even have had time to get out of the country.

Setanta Molloy had been more open with her than she had expected. She was quite sure he wasn't interested in her romantically but it was hard to believe that he would be interested in getting her onside. The National Museum and Setanta would have little involvement in the case, apart perhaps from an academic perspective.

She was putting off checking her phone. Alf would want an update on what she had been doing, and she had essentially nothing, apart from some detail which would make a nice colour piece.

The window frame shuddered as the front door

slammed shut. Had Baby returned? The vulnerability of her position hit her. Had she even told anyone that she was staying here? At least her bedroom door was locked, but her car was still beside the pub. The house was so thinly built.

Footsteps thudded through the pine hallway into the tiled kitchen. She listened to the beat: there must be two people. She heard a door creak and the dull murmur of conversation between what sounded like two men.

She rubbed her fingertips together, noticing the waterlogged ridges, thinking of the body as it decomposed in the bog. She sat upright in the bath, pulling back the curtain to see into the driveway. It was a burgundy Skoda Octavia – typical Garda detective car, she thought. It would be beneficial to have some more police contacts on the ground in the active investigation. She sat back in the bath, blasting a final few inches of hot water into the foam. As she lay there, she accidentally knocked a glass off the side of the bath. It bounced loudly and ominously, like a lethal tennis ball, until it came to rest beside the sanitary bin. The voices downstairs paused momentarily, before resuming their monotone conversation. She checked her phone – it was almost midnight. If she wanted to speak to the gardaí she had better dry off and go downstairs.

The steam evaporated off her flesh like a lobster pulled from a pan of boiling water. Her thin hips jutted out with the same angularity as her nose and shoulders. She wrapped her robe around her, weak from the hot bath and the day's drinking. Sitting on the bed, she surrendered to the exhaustion and slipped into a deep, alcoholic slumber, her dreams filled with the body from the bog.

Dawn came late the next day for January. She stirred, wrapped in the sheets, sweating in her white bathrobe. The morning sunbeams were already absorbed into the deep red fabrics of the room, and her thighs stuck together as she sat up, groping for her phone. The screen was full of angry red notifications from missed calls, text messages and emails. It was nearly eight o'clock. She filled the cheap white kettle with tap water from the bathroom, recalling George Orwell's advice to ensure absolutely boiling water met the tea. Waiting for the perfect moment to clutch the kettle from its plastic cradle, she noted missed calls – Alf of course, Laura, Jack.

Alf and Laura wanted an update. The call from Jack was after they met, around the time she was in the bath.

Another message popped up from a number she hadn't saved, reading:

"Dear Janie, how is the investigation going? Call when you can. Monty."

Her initial amusement at the thought of the grand old gent jabbing the keypad of an old brick of a phone with fat fingers subsided when she thought about how many languages he spoke – thirteen perhaps? Including more obscure languages like Aramaic or Danish.

The teabag was stale, spoiling her drink, but she continued to sip as she checked her emails. She maintained an orderly inbox, evading subscriptions deliberately. Living as much of her life offline as possible, the irony that this story found her through the internet was not lost on her.

Glancing at the copy for her to review for that week's feature section, she saw no Garda update. No further developments being reported by her own or any other media outlet.

There were voices chatting downstairs, doors being closed and chairs being dragged. Well-versed at hooking herself into the corset without a ladies' maid, she had the undergarment in place in a jiffy and pulled the well-plied ribbons tight. She hadn't an inch of extra flesh to encase, but enjoyed the ritual of putting one on. She quickly rolled on a black silk shift dress over it, omitting the matching suspender belt on account of the calescent weather. She quickly powdered her nose, and could smell the sizzle of a rasher.

Nearing the kitchen door, she saw two large peach plates being loaded up with a full Irish breakfast: sausages, rashers, fried eggs, a grilled tomato, and potato hash browns.

A stout lady with a tight brown perm turned around

to greet her, spooning out mushrooms from a large stainless-steel frying pan. It was the woman who lived across the road. January was relieved to see no blemishes or bruises, but still felt concern at what she had seen.

The woman wore a white V-neck T-shirt, pink striped canvas trousers with Crocs and had a simple thin gold locket around her neck.

She smiled widely at January. "Good gersha, Jane!" she said in a broad country accent. "I'm Miriam the housekeeper. Are you ready for breakfast? I made plenty." She pointed to the various pots and pans accumulated on the kitchen counter. She wiped her hand on a tea towel and shook hands.

"I'm famished, smells delicious," January said in earnest.

"The two lads are down ahead of you," said Miriam.

Seated in the dining room were Detective Colm Cooney and another officer. They looked as surprised to see her as she was to see them.

"January," said Detective Cooney, "I, *eh*, I didn't expect to see you here?"

"That makes two of us, Colm," she said as he pulled out the seat for her to join them.

"What would you like, love?" said Miriam as she plonked an enormous breakfast either side of her.

"Could I have a bacon sandwich, with a bit of cheese if you have it, please? And another cup for tea."

Miriam poured January a glass of orange juice

71

before she left. January was still observing her for signs of mistreatment. None were evident.

"I don't believe we have been introduced before," January said to the younger garda sitting to her left.

"This is Garda Peter O'Brien, a junior detective on my team," said Cooney.

They shook hands. "Pleased to meet you, January – my mom is a big fan of yours," he said in a Dublin accent. He had a broad nose, with clear white skin and green eyes. Although young, his beer belly was prominent.

Neither of the men were in uniform, and wore short-sleeved shirts. To anyone else they looked like a pair of ne'er-do-wells filling up after a night's drinking.

"So what's the latest, chaps?" asked January.

"You were there yesterday – you saw," said Colm. His skin was grey and he looked exhausted. "The radiologist called me this morning, she had looked over the scans again and saw that the victim's skull, God ..." he paused as he stoically looked out the window, "had a number of healed fractures. Most likely sustained in childhood. It seems our victim had a childhood of abuse."

January could see the pain in his face, herself feeling detached. "How terrible, how bad."

"Poor girl never had a chance," Cooney said quietly.

"I've already agreed not to publish anything that might compromise your investigation," said January, lowering her voice as she remembered Miriam cooking in the next room. "But I have to say both of you look remarkably unhurried, considering everyone thinks the body is an ancient mummy."

"It wasn't us who made the mistake," said Cooney. "And the site has been sealed – the technical bureau are back there already."

"Yes, quite – well, how the anthropologist made that mistake is beyond me," January said. Her eyes fell on the emerald-green bottle on the bar. However fond of it she was, it would not make a good breakfast drink. She knew from experience. "But the Commissioner will be looking for a scapegoat amongst his ranks too." She softened her voice and looked into Cooney's eyes. "Watch your back is all, I've seen how these things go."

"*Hmm*, well, we'll see about that," said Cooney. "You must have arrived here late last night?"

"Yes, I was interviewing Jack Flanagan in the local pub and it made sense to stay."

Miriam returned with January's sandwich, her wedged comfort shoes squeaking.

"Will ye be staying tonight?" she asked.

The two gardaí nodded.

January, slathering tomato relish between the thick pink slices of bacon and hot buttered toast, said she wasn't sure.

"We're glad to have ye, it's always so quiet here. If ye want dinner just text me." She stood a moment too long as if she might say something, before walking to the door and closing it after her.

Now O'Brien's phone was vibrating. As he answered it, both Cooney and January could clearly hear his voice through O'Brien's too-loud speaker.

"Are you with Detective Cooney?" The voice sounded panicked. "They've found another body."

They knew that she had heard about the second body. Detective Cooney stared resignedly at his colleague. "You should turn down the volume on your phone, sergeant." He tossed his napkin to the table.

"Sorry, boss, it was loud on the line –"

"Enough!" He held his hands out to the younger officer.

January understood why Cooney was exasperated. A member of the national media had overheard a major case development. Ultimately there was nothing to stop her writing up the whole story – that this was a fresh murder investigation, now with two bodies, not a historical dig. If the victim had been abused in childhood, it would cast suspicion on her parents and family. January recognised how sensitive Cooney and his team would need to be.

"Listen, detective," she said to Cooney. She was fiddling with her teaspoon – it was a light tin bit of rubbish. "I agreed to hold off on publishing this story on the basis that it would not interfere with the criminal investigation." Looking up into his eyes she spoke with conviction. "But I have a journalistic duty to report the facts as and when they happen. Everyone thinks this is an major historical find. How would you rather they learn about the developments? Through Jack Flanagan's Twitter account or documented by a professional journalist? Take me down to the site with you." It wasn't his decision to make but that small fact didn't bother her.

Cooney didn't take long to think about it. "Fine – but don't be foostering around annoying the officers. I want you there to witness the State Pathologist's examination of this body, but be cool, okay?" He stood up quickly and jangled his car keys. "I'm sure Her Highness, the State Pathologist, will do it carefully after yesterday's fuck-up. Get on to her now, will you, O'Brien? Let's go."

Chapter 9

It was the fourth time Alf had tried calling January that morning but her phone rang out again. Her anachronistic tendencies may have been tolerated by the previous editor but she should have at least thought to check in with the office.

"Any word from the Minister?" asked Laura, leaning on the doorframe. The humid heat had flattened her dark-blonde hair and she twirled a lanky lock around her finger. She had a reputation for sleeping her way ahead, but Alf had not yet benefited.

"His press secretary is going to call me any minute, sit in on it if you like," he said, leaning forward in his seat to air the sweat from the small of his back. This weather made work more intense than normal.

"Thanks." She sat down, opened the voice recorder on her phone and put it beside the landline, ready to record. "About the Minister Fitzpatrick case – the prossie didn't have much to say for herself. A woman called her, paid her in cash that morning. She didn't have a clue who Fitzpatrick and his man were when they turned up. That's all she would say without money."

"*Hmm*, we don't have budget for that, we're not the *Sun*." He chewed on the end of his vape. "Not a bad job, getting that info."

"I've had an update on the pictures," she said. "The picture editor had a look at the metadata and there's quite –"

"Meta-what?"

"It's the information that is attached to a photo file – you can only see it when you open it on a computer usually, on special software."

Alf's phone started vibrating on the reinforced glass desk.

It was the Minister's advisor.

Alf accepted the call. "Pat, how are you – thanks for the call."

"Not fucking great, Alf, to tell you the truth. I have a few ground rules before we proceed." He was a fast-talking man, the strength of his Cork accent waxing according to his audience.

"I don't think you're in a position to be laying out rules, Pat," said Alf. "No offence but you and the Minister were snapped in a makeshift brothel and we are publishing the pictures. This is your opportunity to provide a comment but, let's get this clear, the photos will be published." He was screwing off the barrel of the vaping machine, and dropping in the nicotine syrup.

"Arrah, Alf, will you hear me out first? And have a think about holding off? The truth of the matter is quite embarrassing to the Minister, but nowhere near as bad as the pictures were made out to look. We were set up, Alf."

"Set up? Pull the other one, will you?"

Alf scrutinised the ceiling as Laura shook her head. She rested her hand under her chin and sat in closer to the phone.

"Yes. Set up, I don't know by who but," Pat hesitated, coughing, "from time to time the Minister takes an unusual form of counsel, which has benefitted his career and the interests of his constituents. But, given the nature of this counsel, we have always tried to ensure it was kept private, until now."

"Spit it out, man," Alf said, sucking on the vapour, producing two big plumes of strawberry-scented vapour.

"Well, the truth of the matter is, Alf, and I've always told the Minister of my objections, but he takes counsel from mediums and psychics."

Laura scrunched her eyes up, as Alf paused and exhaled two jets of cloudy vapour from both nostrils, like a Chinese dragon.

"God save us, Pat, keep going."

"We were at that apartment for a private audience with a world-renowned Doreen Dallevi. A medium endorsed by everyone from Ellen to Obama."

"Are you advising him to go out with this *ráiméis*

instead of taking his medicine like a good boy?"

With a thick urgency, Pat said, "It certainly is no story, Alf. As soon as we were in the apartment we knew it was a set-up."

"And how did you come to be in the apartment?" asked Alf, heartened. It was sounding a lot more interesting than a political sex scandal.

"Well, Doreen contacted the Minister's Twitter account to say that she had a message from the other side for him, and would he be willing to meet? We later discovered it came from a fake Twitter page, not from the actual Doreen Dallevi."

Alf and Laura were staring across the desk at each other. Laura wasn't going to forget any of these details.

"Jaysus," said Alf. "And who do you think it was that set you up?"

"Who knows, sure it could be Man in the Moon – or Sinn Féin. But that's the long and short of it, and we are confident that the Irish people will understand how the Minister made a simple mistake."

"Hang on a second here, Pat – are you expecting us to believe that?"

"The Minister is beyond reproach on this front, Alf. Many people declare themselves spiritual or otherwise – I'm sure they will understand the Minister's position."

"One last thing, Pat – have any of the other papers been on to you about this?" asked Alf, chewing on his biro.

"Not yet, so you'd better wonder about why the photos were sent to you and no one else. You'll have a short statement in your inbox now."

As the called ended, Alf pushed back in his chair, inhaling the vape deeply.

"Well," he said. "I knew Pat was a master of spin but this is something else! Do you believe the pictures are real?"

"It's pretty out there, isn't it? Either way someone wanted to do him damage, and went out of their way to send us those pictures." Laura started tapping her tablet again.

"What about this metadata anyway?" asked Alf.

"Well," said Laura, "the envelope also contained a USB key with a soft copy of the pictures. They were taken by a pro. The camera is extremely high-end – according to our own picture editor the photographers would love to be working with it. It's very expensive so these pictures were taken by a professional. According to the metadata, they were taken last weekend in the estate in Blackrock. They weren't tampered with."

"Get a draft written in case we have to go online before Sunday, if we get wind that anyone else has it," said Alf.

He riffled through the bottom drawer of his desk until he found some real cigarettes.

Chapter 10

Yellow crime-scene tape flickered across the ditch in the warm breeze. To their left, long bars of already cut turf lay in cables across the field, like extruded soil. She had expected sods stacked in conical piles. Flanagan's tractor reminded her that most turfcutters removed the peat on an industrial scale.

Cooney found the officer on site. "Where is the body, how was it discovered?"

"It's down there – we got the white tent up as soon as we could. I found her this morning when I was walking the perimeter. I saw some bones from where the field had been ploughed. At first I thought they were of a calf or something but when I saw the skull, God, I got an awful land – anyway I thought I'd leave it alone. I rang you and the State Pathologist Office."

"Why did you take it upon yourself to call her? The detective on site normally makes that call." Cooney shook his head as he ran his hand through his hair. "I suppose she'll be here any minute." He exhaled. He felt control of the investigation slipping away. "Get some more white tents up – there will be walkers and gawkers and God knows who else out here if they think there are more discoveries. It's not to be known that it's another body, okay?"

He was silent as they traversed Flanagan's land. January didn't want annoy him with garrulous commentary about the lack of precipitation.

At the cusp of the unfurrowed soil, three areas were boxed off with crime-scene tape, and one white tent. Alf had once referred to them as "morbid marquees".

January clocked the big thick head of Jack Flanagan bobbing above the parched hedge on the far side of the field.

"Here comes trouble," she said to Cooney, her chin pointed to the farmer as he expertly jumped over the electric fence.

This morning he had decided to highlight his sporting allegiances back across the Irish Sea to County Louth, but it was still a red-and-white jersey. January considered how much his head resembled a potato sprouting eyes at the back of the cupboard. She always managed to have some go off – that was the trouble of cooking for one. Thinking of the musty potato smell in her duck-egg-blue kitchen she remembered the parrot – oh God, the parrot – she must be starving. January had been meaning to buy seed before she came over. She would have to ask someone to feed it. She sighed at the realisation it meant dealing with the likely multitude of notifications that would be lurking on her phone.

The uniformed gardaí had started to move January and two farmers behind crime-scene tape, as she rummaged in her elephantine satchel.

"You can't jam me back here!" bellowed Flanagan. *"I want to talk to the head honcho, whoever is in charge!"*

Cooney traipsed back across the bog to dispense with him. "Mr Flanagan, as you know our investigations are ongoing," he said curtly, his lip curling.

With what was likely characteristic lack of subtlety Jack yelped out, "Mossie says yous have found another one! Another body, like. Is it Theresa?"

Cooney placed a hand on his shoulder. "Mr Flanagan, may I remind you this is an open investigation, and we are reliant on your discretion. If it is your cousin, we will let you know. Mossie who?"

"The shopkeeper, inside in the town," Flanagan drawled.

"Fucking great news!" Cooney blew out of his mouth. These local uniformed officers were a joke. He would have to get more detectives dispatched.

January's eyes glanced around the little red boxes on her phone. Twelve missed calls, eight text messages and over 60,000 emails, although how many of them were actually new, she could not tell. Could she get in to place a call without seeing who was looking for her, like a technological jammie dodger?

How long could a parrot go without food? Until when? Until she dies? She didn't want the bird to suffer any more. She'd better call Alf.

Good thing the weather was so dry or she would never be able to walk into the field. At the edge of the ditch, the grass was thicker and longer. It tickled the top of her feet as she kicked through it, walking down the lane. The grass on Dublin's canals was well-manicured; it had been an age since she felt its tickle. A lifetime even, when she last walked along a rural verge.

Often when she called Alf, she would hold the phone at arm's length for a few moments whilst he issued a tranche of expletives. Today was no different. When the voice trailed to him repeating her name, she put the speaker to her ear.

"I saw you read your message."

January detested this piece of information – she vowed to check her phone less.

"I need you to feed Leopoldina."

"Who the hell is Leopoldina? And what in the God Divine's name took you so long to ring me back? What are you doing down there? Fitzpatrick's man rang."

"Leopoldina – my parrot," she said quickly. "Send someone down, please, Alf – she hasn't eaten in days and I left no nuts out."

"Jesus, January, such a thing to ring me about."

"Will you sort it? There's a spare key in the desk."

"Fuck's sake – yes, okay, as if we don't all have enough to be at."

"Thanks, Alf. Listen, things are getting more interesting here. They've found another body. The lead detective on the case, Colm Cooney, was staying in my accommodation last night."

The officer was still in the thick of conversation with Jack Flanagan who was still shouting and pointing his thick digits down the laneway.

"Is it a new body or a bog body or a new old body or what?"

"No idea, but I think they'll let me get closer in on the investigation."

"Right – but I don't want you on some wild goose chase," he said clearly.

"My gut tells me there is something strange going on with this investigation, Alf. I need you to trust me and … give me some leeway on it, okay? What did Fitzpatrick's man say?"

"Claims he was set up, or catfished as Laura calls it. But even worse – apparently he is into going to psychics and mediums. Someone pretended to be some famous one visiting Ireland, and invited him, but it was a fake profile."

January watched as Cooney entered the sealed space of the second body. "Golly – that is interesting. Did you know Myanmar moved its capital city because the emperor got a bad horoscope?"

"You don't believe it, do you?" said Alf.

"I'm not sure. Last month at the Woods auction in the Westbury he purchased no less than three sculptures from the Fianna cycle of Irish mythology." Two more police vans were reversing behind her. "*Who set him up?*" she shouted over the sound.

"He doesn't know. Look, I appreciate you have a nose for a story but we could do with you on this? I hope you didn't agree that embargo indefinitely with the guards?"

"I'm trying to move around that particular block, but I'm not sure what I will write – I'll set aside some time this afternoon to get something done," said January, hearing the pips of another call coming through.

"Okay – update me though, Janie, I need to keep the space," he said. His use of a pet name indicated he was in better form than usual.

"Please go over and feed the bird," she pleaded. "I can't believe I left her starving like that."

She picked light footsteps through the furrowed ground, approaching the white tent housing the latest body. Detective Cooney was pulling off a paper suit as he came out, spitting a generous glob of slime. The Garda Technical Bureau were removing trays of soil, stacking each in large evidence bags outside the tent. He stopped to speak with them before heading in January's direction. She considered pushing through the tent to look at this latest body herself, but the look on Cooney's face made her reconsider.

Cooney's round forehead shone with sweat as he gazed into the dry ditch. It was another hot morning. He clocked January's fingers twiddling an ivory-and-enamel cigarette-holder.

"Don't smoke here," he said, wagging his finger but still not looking at her.

She put the holder back into its leather monogrammed case, but kept it in her hand.

"Is it another one?" she asked him.

Their eyes met before following the heatwaves rising off a shining black coupé approaching down the lane. The sports car was more suited to a summertime spin around Monaco than these bog roads.

"It's another body alright," he spat another glob of phlegm on the dry earth. "It looks old, but it's wrapped in a plastic shower curtain. God forbid we make any judgement on it before the tests are done. Speak of the divil –"

"And she will appear," January finished for him as the State Pathologist Professor Traynor clambered from the low seat of the sports car.

Traynor was wearing a cream halter-neck dress with chiffon red hearts, her shiny black hair tied on the crown of her head like a vintage housewife. Her arms were tanned to the perfect shade of golden pine, and a cherry-red lipstick popped on her lips. She slipped black working boots on, removing a white paper forensic suit and silver toolbox from the boot of the car.

"Jaysus," he said under his breath to January, "where does she think she's going in that frock?"

"It's a nice antidote to the gruesomeness of it all," said January, fingering her cigarette holder. She didn't smoke that much, but once she got it into her head that she wanted to smoke, she wanted to smoke badly.

"It's nearly ..." he was flustered, "disrespectful. If you had a look in there," he pointed to the tent, "you wouldn't be so flippant."

"*Better not take any chances on an ID!*" Professor Traynor shouted down to Cooney as she traversed the thick soil. She gave January a puzzled look of irritation.

Cooney welcomed her. "Great you could make it so quickly, Professor – obviously, given this rapid development we are keen to know as much as we can."

She pulled the cover all over the patterned frock and tightened the strings of the hood around her heart-shaped face.

"You want something to go on, you always do. I will take a look now, but I'm not going to give anything away before the post-mortem." The synthetic material of the tent scratched against itself as she lifted the flap to go in.

"What is your hypothesis, detective?" January pushed a trough of mud aside with her toe.

"She was buried fairly close to the surface. I wonder could she have even be moved here since the field was ploughed?"

"She?"

"Well, she has long black hair, though I suppose it could be a man," said Cooney. "Listen, I'm not sure how much longer you can stay around here. You saw the way she was staring at you there. The lads from the Technical Bureau are going to be combing through the grass and everything."

The Professor reappeared from the tent, coolly rolling off disposable gloves. January noticed a fresh French polish on her nails. It surprised her, given the amount of sawing and slicing and physical lifting required by a pathologist.

"Well, this victim is different from our faked mummy," Traynor said quickly and calmly. "No efforts were made to make her seem like an ancient bog body. It could have been an accidental death preceding the victim whose bones were removed." She peered into Cooney's notepad as he wrote it down. "Most notably though, she was wrapped in a shower curtain – it has the old Dunnes Stores St Bernard logo on the tag, which remarkably is intact. At only three feet from the surface of the field, she was closer to the top than our first girl. It looks like she suffered some major trauma to the head but I can't of course tell if that's what killed her. Once we get cleared from forensics I'm keen to get her to the mortuary as quickly as possible this morning. I can't reiterate how important it is to wait for the conclusive results."

"Do you think it's possible she was moved recently, like over the past few days?" asked January.

Traynor looked at Cooney for approval that she could answer her.

He nodded. "Ms Quail is here as an external observer for the moment. Go ahead."

"No, in my opinion she hasn't been moved for a long time," said Traynor.

"So you think they were killed by the same person, Professor?" asked Cooney.

Traynor clucked her red lips in disapproval. "Impossible to say at this stage, detective. Once we complete a post-mortem we can see if there might be any similarities, but on the face of it they do seem quite different. You don't need me to tell you that."

Cooney nodded as he took it in. "Can you tell us any more about the first body discovered?"

"Don't put me under pressure on this, detective – we are already preparing," she coughed, "for a media frenzy. But we have been able to harvest good DNA, skin, hair and blood cells. She also had a permanent metal retainer attached to the teeth of her lower jaw, so it should be straightforward to match against dental records. There was no other DNA available on the body though. I must say that in all my years and across any of the case files other pathologists presented, I have never seen anything like it. The amount of time it would take to research the various processes is incredible. Her skin had been leathered, for God's sake. Bones were removed. She was essentially butchered. Why would anyone go to those lengths?" She had unzipped the top of the hazmat suit and was fiddling with her pearl necklace. "And that, I'm glad to say, is your job to solve, detective. I'd better get back to it."

She lifted the white door of the tent, leaving January and Cooney alone in that part of the field.

January looked down at the bog as she spoke quietly. "Whoever killed our first victim, well, they must have been extremely well-versed in bog bodies, probably obsessed. It is possible that they would have been involved directly in or on the periphery of the investigation into the previous two bog bodies discovered. There was an international team here, from the UK and the States – all manner of pathologists and scientists. It might be worth revisiting them?" She wanted to prove to Cooney that she could add something to the investigation so he would let her stick around a bit longer.

"Can you provide a list of them?" he said, holding the yellow crime-scene tape up for her to pass under. "I'd better go and see that eejit Setanta Molloy."

"Yes, also his predecessor, Monty Passmore, could be useful to talk with. I will give him a call."

"This is a murder investigation, Ms Quail – he is not one of your sources." He was speaking formally now. "One of our officers will interview him."

As they stood on the sticky black tarmac of the road,

he took out a box of cigarettes and offered her one. It was an old-fashioned brand smoked by farmers, but nonetheless she accepted.

"What's that contraption?" he asked of her cigarette holder.

"It stops my nails from yellowing," she said as he flicked open a light for her. The filter of her cigarette rested in a gold funnel.

He stared up into the blue, cloudless morning sky. The light reflected off the shiny soft skin where he had shaved that morning.

He walked away from her, answering his phone. The call didn't last long but left Cooney punching the air in delight.

"We have an ID," he smiled, "on our alleged bog body."

"Already?"

"Yes." He was stony-faced at having to explain the procedure to her. "The officers on last night traced the dental records to that of a Sinéad O'Sullivan, reported missing sixteen years ago. She was a local woman. She is the only teenager to be reported missing with aneurysm clips that decade. I'm going to tell the family now."

"Can I –"

"No, you can't come. I can't have you at a next-of-kin notification."

"But –"

"Don't push it, January."

Chapter 11

January had been unconvinced about putting power-steering in the vintage motor. She only had herself to blame for the tremendous effort it took to reverse out of the ditch beside the pub.

Approaching the town by a river, she spotted the bronze statue of Irish warriors Cuchulainn and Ferdia. Cuchulainn struggled to hold the body of his best friend and foster-brother whom he had just killed in single combat. Heroic figures of Irish mythology, the pair had found themselves on opposite sides when Queen Maeve invaded Ulster to capture the Brown Bull of Cooley. January parked the car in a convenient spot beside the fraternal tragedy.

Her appetite was ferocious as ever from the previous day's drinking. She was called to the present by the sight of a tall plaster-cast chef merrily holding a menu blackboard. This was it – The Castle Arms. As a child she had travelled to Ardee with her mother to buy a pony – the trip was so fresh in her memory – a treasured image of her mother's caramel-blonde hair as she lifted her into the front of the Jeep. In the end the pony was lame, and her mother did not go ahead with the sale, but they had gorged on steaming bowls of vegetable soup here.

The interior of the pub had changed little in the past three decades. The same dark-emerald-velour barstools surrounded a horseshoe bar with shiny brass rails. An Irish tricolour flag hung proudly over the truncated bottle-green velvet couch. There was a lingering smell of cigarette smoke under the greasy gravy scent in the air. The geometric carpet was threadbare in parts.

A television hung over the bar, the low hum of a horse-racing commentator and the thudding hooves at Punchestown entrancing a disparate bunch of older men.

She immediately recognised the man in a well-washed football jersey from last night. She recalled the split second she saw his face when he pulled the curtain closed. What had he been arguing with his wife about?

"Ah, we may give it up!" he said with a laugh, to no one in particular. "I'll be back to you in a minute, Tossy." He tapped his box of cigarettes on the counter and moved away to the smoking area.

The commentator's voice rose as the final two horses approached the finish line.

Behind the bar, an older but better-dressed man in chinos and a golf T-shirt was rapt in the race. "*Go on, you fucker you!*" he roared, slapping the well-varnished bar. "Go 'way!" he exclaimed, the final horse crossing the line. He was now abusing the screen. *"You're only an ould nag!"*

January raised a hand.

"Now, sorry, missus." He straightened the face of his watch. "Can I help you?"

She smiled at him. "Not having much luck at Punchestown? How is Gordon Elliot doing?" Elliot was a local trainer. January remembered him from the local pony camp.

"Arrah sure, the going has been hard with this weather – it's all a cod," he said with a distinctive Northern Ireland accent, from much further north than where they were currently located. "Is it the carvery you're after?"

"Yes."

He came out from behind the counter and moved behind her. She watched his thick hand with a mat of black hair on the knuckles settle into the small of her back.

He led her round the corner to a stainless-steel station with joints of ham and beef sweating and steaming. It was manned by a small lady, wearing an extremely tall white chef's hat and pristine uniform.

The barman wandered back to watch the racing commentary.

"What can I get you, love?" the woman asked.

"Um – I will go with the beef, please, with all the trimmings."

"Grand," said the woman and started to cut the beef joint. "You're not a local, are you?"

"No, well, I am from Kells but here for work," said January, hoping the cook would bite.

"Oh? Are you a nurse in the psychiatric hospital, is it?" she said, now spooning creamy cauliflower cheese onto the already heaving plate.

It was not the first time January had been mistaken for an aid to those not of sound mind.

"No – I'm a journalist. I'm writing about this bog body they have found out the road." She held up her tray to take the hot plate.

"Tossy has been lepping around since they found her." The woman wiped the edge of the stainless-steel counter. "He's big in the local historical society." She nudged her head towards the portraits of Ireland's national heroes. "Always wants to promote his version of history. But I've never seen him so wound up as when someone put up on Facebook about that foot being found." She carefully swept a lock of hair off her forehead. "And a cousin of mine is a historian, in the National Museum – he was up looking around too."

"Not Setanta Molloy?"

"Ah, do you know him, love? Isn't that Ireland for you? Our mothers are sisters."

"Now that you say it, you do look familiar – I think I may have seen you somewhere else?"

"You're probably right, love. I used to play bass in

96

a band." She blew air out the side of her mouth. "God, it must be twenty years ago?"

"In Sin É? I remember going to that gig," said January, remembering the night he stared at her throughout the set. "You did a great cover of 'London Calling'."

"Good lord, I remember now. We went back to your place in Leeson Street after. You had it on vinyl and Setanta kept playing it." The sun faded from the cook's face. "Until he put his knee through it." Sensing January's awkwardness, she pointed at her tray. "Anyway, I'm blatherin' on – go on and eat that while it's hot."

January smiled and sat at a low table. The gig was at the end of that summer. As they had sat up drinking 'til dawn, she knew it would be her last dalliance with Setanta Molloy. He left that autumn to study in England. She hadn't spent more than a night or two with any man since. Not because she held Setanta in any particularly high regard, but the mild discomfort she had felt once their casual arrangement ended reminded her too much of the grief that comes with loss, the risks associated with having any fondness for another soul.

It was early for lunch yet and she was the only one in this part of the pub. She opened her expansive satchel to produce a large napkin from a sealed plastic pouch. She hated the cheap transparent white paper serviettes, preferring to bring her own accoutrements.

The decor declared the pub's Republican allegiance. Ardee was close to the border with Northern Ireland, so this sort of memorialising of Irish heroes was not uncommon. Sinn Féin was certainly a force to be reckoned with.

Behind the bar, Tossy was well turned out. The creases in his chinos were razor sharp, and he wore what looked like a gold Rolex watch on his left wrist, wrapped around a red-tanned arm. She wondered why he had become so excited, according to the cook, about the discovery? He was obviously keen on Celtic history but bog bodies were outside the remit of the history adopted by Republicans. January was almost attracted to him. But he was approaching sixty, and the grey-black tufts of hair from his nose and ears were distasteful.

She finished her lunch, thanked the cook and approached the brightly lit beer taps.

"Are you taking bets?" she asked.

The practice of publicans phoning in wagers to local bookmakers had almost died out with the advent of smart-phone apps. It was highly illegal, of course, but rampant in rural pubs which disregarded the law. If the strong smell of smoke was anything to go by, the proprietor could be chancy. The horses on television were walking around the parade ring, the jockeys squinting in the bright sunshine.

"You're not a revenue inspector, are you?" His teeth were white, polished and clean. Cleaner than her own.

"Ah, go on!" She softened her accent, fraudulently adopting a much more rural twang. "Elliot always does well in this race." She ran her slender white finger down the race card, looking for his horses.

"Elliot's horse, Moira's Estate?" he said, casually dialling the white landline behind the bar.

"Okay, twenty each way." She handed the cash over as he phoned it in to the bookies'.

The horses were flustering around the startline now. The field was much browner than usual. All eyes focused on the television screen.

January was fiddling with a square bar mat. "What do you think about what they found this week?" she said, glancing at Tossy who turned to look straight at her.

"Unreal so it is." His eyes were wide and his long lashes pulled back. "Unreal. What the town needs." He focused the television. "And a major historical discovery – hopefully it will bring in busloads of Yanks."

"Bound to."

"Are you having a drink?" he said, his wide eyes intimating it was a direction, not a request.

She'd had a large lunch, so figured one couldn't hurt.

"Why not? A double crème de menthe with jots of ice, please?"

"Jaysus, missus, you don't get many ordering that."

He turned to survey the shelves over the bar, "I'm not sure if we have –"

"Beside the Galliano," she pointed. As soon as she placed the order with a barman who didn't know her, she would always seek out its location to expedite matters.

"You're lucky," he said, freepouring the spirit. "We've started doing cocktails so we do have a bit of everything here."

The man who had been arguing with his wife returned to his stool at the bar as the horses tussled against their jockeys – and they were off. It was a full field with nearly twenty mares running. January's horse was dead in the middle of the pack but taking the jumps well considering how hard the ground must be.

Tossy slammed his hand beside the till when his horse fell.

"*Curse a' Jaysus on it!*" he roared, as the other men at the bar continued to howl encouragement to their chosen nags.

As they arrived to the final two furlongs, Moira's Estate outpaced all but one, finishing second to an outsider Thursday's Child. The man in the Liverpool jersey cheered and jumped off his stool, tapping his heels and toes, singing "*I'm in the money, I'm in the money!*"

"How much had you on him, Speedy?" said Tossy.

"*A monkey!*" he answered, index fingers shifting up and down to the Ginger Rogers' tune.

"Five hundred? Where did you get that to put on a horse? You've been giving out stink since I put up the price of Smithwicks," Tossy said, polishing the counter with a rag.

"Congratulations," said January warmly as she totted up her own win.

"Ah, I had a tip, a real good tip. Fuckin' ten grand – can you believe it, twenty to one. Never thought I would have it. No Smithwicks today – get us down a bottle of Laurent Perrier!" He pronounced each consonant of the name. "You'll join us for a glass, love? Sure didn't you get a place too?"

"Would love to join you," she said, with her bony ankle wrapped around the barstool. She remembered her mother chatting to the stable lads and using all of the cockney slang, but couldn't for her life remember the equivalent for twenty. "Had twenty on at ten to one, 200. So I've won forty or fifty depending on what the bookie pays. What's your name?"

"Speedy. Nice to meet you, eh …?"

"January. Pleased to meet you."

Tossy was blowing the dust off champagne flutes in a cabinet to the left of the till. "I'll go get a cold one."

"The bookie is tight – he'll only pay a fifth of the win. But that doesn't bother me." Speedy started his heel-toe-routine again. "He'll be sick to see me coming."

The men fished out cigarette boxes and lighters, moving off toward the smoking area. They left a raft of betting slips and denim jackets behind them.

January looked to see where Tossy had gone – the door behind the bar was open after him. Through the doorframe she noticed some large picture frames lying up against the breezeblock. A corner of a white poster caught her eye . The word "MISSING" was prominent. January moved along the bar until she was right across from the poster. It was tattered and yellow, the once-red of the word missing now faded to orange. It was Sinéad O'Sullivan. January was shocked by how perfectly preserved she had been. Remembering the body she had seen in the hospital, it had looked as if she was asleep. Cooney would have already broken the tragic news to her mother. Would she be comforted by the body's lifelike appearance or disturbed by it?

She had wide curly hair and, although the poster was black-and-white, it looked like she had dark hair. This picture was taken in this pub – she saw the moulding of the fireplace behind Sinéad's hand which was holding up a cigarette. Her jacket had defined shoulder pads and, although she had a rather Roman nose, her eyes were beautiful.

"Are you alright there, missus?" Tossy said directly behind her ear and she jumped in surprise. He must have come back through the smoking area. She could feel his breath on her cheek.

He started laughing and walked around her, smiling. "What are you pooching around looking at? I don't have anything much you'd call exotic in case you're looking for some quare mix." He swaddled the champagne in a tea towel as it popped loudly.

"Couldn't help but notice the poster," she said, going back up to her seat. "Of the missing girl." She finished her glass, holding it up to request a refill.

"Ah, don't say anything about that when they come back in, hey," said Tossy plainly. "That man who won, Speedy – he endured torture and still does over his missing Sinéad."

"She was his daughter?"

"Was?"

"Is – I mean, she has been missing a while?"

"Yeah, sure she most likely is dead and buried. She was a beautiful girl. But let him have his moment, okay? He ended up giving up work with depression and started coming in here during the week. It's the first bit of luck they have had since Sinéad went," he said, crushing the bottle into a cooler full of ice.

"Did you know her?"

"Ah, well, there's another sore point." He looked to the floor. "Around the time she disappeared, we were starting up together, you know." He was stacking the damp pint glasses in the fridge to keep them cool. "Himself wasn't too keen on it, because of the age difference. She was home from New York and obviously wanted something familiar – that was me." He looked out to the beer garden.

103

"When was she last seen?" said January.

"Jaysus, you sound like the Garda woman. She'd been home for a few months and things weren't working out – job-wise, you know. So she gathers everyone together – the night that picture on the poster was taken – and announces she's going back to the States. So off she goes and, sad and all as we are, no one thinks much of it. This was before Facebook and that – so sure no one heard from her for a while, and her mother starts making some enquiries – she had gone over to her the previous summer and knew some of the American friends. No one over there had seen her. When the police checked out with the airport, she'd never boarded the flight." He looked at the men returning to the bar in a cloud of smoke. Quietly he finished, "So it was weeks before we realised she was missing."

"Where's the champagne?" Sinéad's father demanded.

Tossy turned to him and beamed. "Your elixir of celebration awaits, my good man – shall I pour?"

Adopting a faux-genteel accent Speedy replied, "Yes, my man, yes, you may. Let us celebrate."

Chapter 12

With Cooney refusing to take January to meet Sinéad's mother, she would make her own enquiries. Sitting in her car, she tuned in the local radio station. She needed to learn more about this victim. The ghost of a hangover still about her, she craved sweets – the dark sort filled with peppermint cream. Recalling the old sweet shop, she started the engine.

The phone vibrated from her bag and she reluctantly answered, anxious for an update on her feathered companion.

"Hullo."

"Good thing I got to that pigeon of yours," said Alf.

He sounded to be in good form but she struggled to hear him with the phone jammed under her shoulder.

"She's a parrot," she corrected.

"Well, she's fed anyway. I saw on Twitter that they have identified your first victim. What the fuck, Jan?"

"Yes, look, I interviewed her ex-boyfriend and father."

"Right – well, get on to someone in here or write it

up. It's a joke you running around up there not producing any copy."

"I'll get something written now, please, calm yourself, Mr Timmoney."

"There's something else," Alf said, his tone softer. "When I was in yours, I saw there was a brown envelope with your post. It looked similar to the one we got the pictures of Fitzpatrick in."

"Brown envelopes tend to look alike – what's your point?"

January dropped the phone to the car floor as she saw a police checkpoint ahead. Driving such an old car combined with her lack of motoring finesse resulted in a lot of points and she risked losing the licence if she got any more.

As she approached the two uniformed officers, they checked her tax and insurance disks before waving her on.

She called Alf back.

"Sorry – was at a checkpoint – what were you saying?"

"Well, the address label on that envelope was printed in the same size and font too," he said.

She knew where this was going. "Again hardly too unusual – address printed in Size 12 Times New Roman. I hope you're not trying to tell me that you opened my post?"

"Well, good thing I did," he said. "There were more pictures in it."

"Christ, Alf, you had no right –"

"I know, but it was a instinctual thing, okay? I was right, there were pictures of Fitzpatrick. Old ones – it looks like the opening of a museum, or some such. I have a gut reaction that there is something to them. I will text copies to you now. Maybe you can figure out why someone went to the bother of sending them in."

The clicking noise told her he was vaping.

"Can the photo people not do an image search?"

"They can, but you are up there in his constituency, so keep your eyes open."

"Okay, okay, goodbye."

Lugging the hefty car to a stop at the kerb of the abandoned street beside the sweet shop, she opened the images. In the first picture, a much younger Michael Fitzpatrick was being handed a scissors by Sinéad O'Sullivan. Both were standing beside a red ribbon suspended from either side of an old stone doorway. Two men wearing bottleneck glasses, awkwardly cut suits and chains of office stood either side of Fitzpatrick. In the next picture, Fitzpatrick was whispering into Sinéad's ear, in the midst of a crowd chatting and drinking teas and coffee.

They looked intimate, she thought as she sat in the car, twirling the dial to the local radio station in time for the hourly bulletin.

"The body found earlier this week in the bog outside Ardee is believed to be that of missing woman, Sinéad O'Sullivan." The

local newsreader had a strong Louth accent. *"The discovery, which was initially believed to be an ancient mummified bog body, has been confirmed as that of the Louth woman who was last seen in 1997. James O'Shea has this report."*

"A vivacious girl with a huge curiosity about the world. A friend to those in need. These are some of the descriptions locals in the Ardee area are giving about Sinéad O'Sullivan. Always interested in history, after she graduated from Maynooth University in the mid-nineties, the curly-haired brunette travelled to New York as part of a tourism graduate programme. Working for Bord Fáilte, she promoted the historical sites of the east coast of Ireland to an international audience. When she returned to Ardee in the spring of 1997, she had been looking forward to starting work as a tour guide at the Brú na Bóinne Visitor Centre for the monument at Newgrange. It was then that something changed in the life of this beautiful young woman."

The report cut to a recording of someone, presumably Sinéad, singing:

"Come with me here to my homeland
South of the border it lies
My thoughts are still a-wandering
As time bids us all here goodbye.
My dreams will always be with you
No matter where I will be
If only I could remember
What wee County Louth means to me!"

Then a tearful woman's voice spoke.

"*It was the day of the Leinster quarter-final, she said to me, 'Mammy, I am going back to New York next week. I got a job so I'm taking it instead of Newgrange –'*" the speaker sobbed.

January recognised it as the voice of Miriam from the B&B that morning. Considering Cooney had only told her a few hours ago, January was surprised how quickly she had agreed to a radio interview. No wonder Alf was on her heels.

"*We left her up to the bus stop outside the town, the following Tuesday, and it wasn't until a good while later we thought, why haven't we heard from her? We rang up the office over there and they said she never turned up and they presumed she had decided to stay at home. So we rang up Aer Lingus and they said she never got on the flight. I will never forget waving her off in the bus. That was the last time I saw her, or heard anything from her.*"

January turned off the radio, uncomfortable with Miriam's story – something about her reaction seemed wrong.

A brass bell tinkled as she pushed open the substantial wooden door to the shop and she heard the same news report continuing from a radio in the adjoining kitchen.

The report cut back to the voice of the young journalist.

"*Gardaí conducted a number of fingerprint searches around Dublin Airport and her family home but did not turn up anything. They are therefore asking anyone who remembers seeing Sinéad on the 24th of June, either in Dublin Airport or in the Ardee area, to contact gardaí. She was last seen wearing a navy blazer, blue jeans and red pumps. Local TD Michael Fitzpatrick has condemned the State Pathologist's Office and Garda Síochána, calling the initial misclassification of her body as ancient remains a gross incompetence."*

As Fitzpatrick's voice carried over the airwaves, the shopkeeper appeared at the counter, wearing a somewhat creased cambric shirt with a wilting collar. The V-neck opening allowed January to see the deep red-brown of his throat. This must be the shopkeeper who told Jack Flanagan about the second body.

Penny sweets sat in large glass jars behind the counter, with modern chocolates and bars lying on top of the crushed velvet counter, their wrappers faded by sunlight.

"You were expecting my mother?" he said in a thick Louth accent, with long, drawn-out vowel sounds. "I'm Mossie, her son."

"Yes, I used to come here when I was little."

"I always know the ones who come in expecting to see her. She is long dead now." His hands were splayed out on the counter.

"Sorry to hear that."

"Is it the penny sweets you're after?"

"Yes, four big mixed bags, with no bull's-eyes, and a packet of peppermint creams, please."

He went to work, bagging the sweets in the thin white plastic bags.

"Aye, she was working in here up until the week she passed, went in her sleep," he said now over the noise of the apple drops shaking loose. "Peaceful, thank God."

"It's great that this shop is still open," January lightly touched the velvet under the chocolate display. The layout was perfectly preserved.

"It does be fierce quiet," he said. "But sure I like it. I work from home so don't mind tipping in from the kitchen when I hear the bell ringing. You never know who will land in." He sealed the bag with red tape.

"Do you have any eating paper or chocolate cigarettes?"

"The chocolate fags have been banned for years, and there's not enough of a footfall for me to be ordering in eating paper. It all sticks together. Twelve euro, please."

January nodded as the radio news report continued.

"Shocking about poor Sinéad, isn't it?" he tutted as he spun the white plastic bags of gummy teeth and fried eggs into a knot.

"Did you know her well?" January asked.

"Aye, we were in school together. It'll be fierce hard on the parents. I know they always held out hope she went off on the run somewhere and would turn up home eventually. Shockin' now. And apparently they've found a second body, one of the lads was in to buy Lucozade and mentioned it, but don't say I told you."

"I won't."

"Anyway, you said you used to come here to get sweets when you were small, but you don't sound local?"

"No, I'm from Kells actually – we lived out the Oldcastle Road."

"Quails, is it? Awful shame about your house. It was something special."

"How did you –"

"The Louth Meath Historical Society is active in chronicling all the old homes and artefacts in the county."

Thirsty, January grabbed a small carton of blackcurrant squash from the fridge. The mention of Avonlea had been unexpected and she needed a moment away from his direct gaze to blink away the tears that sometimes came. She opened up her phone to the pictures Alf had sent through.

"Do you know where these were taken?" She held out the screen. "It looks like the official opening of something."

He stared at her for a moment, before reaching for the phone. "Let's have a look." The glass of the antique countertop groaning with the weight of his elbows as he shifted forward. His brow moved in confusion as he viewed the picture, a momentary query that he took pains to remove from his expression as he zoomed in to Sinéad's face.

"Aye, aye," he said, leaning back with a bump on his heels. "That was the opening of the the Castle. I was there. I remember I was doing work experience with the local paper. Where did you get that?"

The atmosphere in the shop had changed and January felt like an intruder. His body language was stiff, challenging, even baiting her, with the thinnest veneer of politeness remaining.

"*Um*, it was sent to the newspaper that I work for. So I'm trying to see when it was taken," she said, picking up the assorted confections. Had she revealed the information too freely?

"Aye, well, let me tell you something, missus." He now had his arms crossed. "Let me warn you about something here. No one would want too much digging around into the family on this. So you'd better put your shovel away, okay?" His thin lips spread into a sickly sneer of a smile.

The dark cloud lifted as he sharply chuckled, walking around the counter and holding the door open, bell ringing, for her to leave.

"See you now."

When she was a trainee journalist she had often come across this reaction when reporting a death in a local community. She was doing her job, she told them. But she wouldn't take it personally. As she sank into the soft leather of the car seat, the sweat on her legs still hadn't dried. The downside to such an old car was the

113

lack of air conditioning, and she was wary of leaving the windows down in case such a valuable vehicle would be carjacked. She opened the peppermint creams and took a bite. She loved the freshness of peppermint in any form.

On the 73rd page of her heavily trafficked address book, January found the number for Monty Passmore, the Chief Curator at the National Museum of Ireland. He oversaw the investigation of both bog bodies in the early noughties.

His velvety voice answered after two rings, "Hullo?" He had two black slugs of eyebrows and January imagined how they would be creeping around his face in jollity.

"Monty, hullo, it's January Quail. Would you have a moment to speak?" Her accent warbled closer to his.

"My dear January, I was expecting your call. I can't believe they have found another one. I didn't expect it in my lifetime," he said, chuffing to himself. "It's going jolly quickly for one – it seems the chap only discovered it the day before yesterday and already there's a full investigation. The team is being headed up by the current curator Setanta Molloy, with help from the State Pathologist and Garda Technical Bureau. I called them all to offer my help." A cough hacked through his amusement.

Did he not know the body was a recent kill? "They would be lucky to have an oracle such as your fine self to ask," she said. "Did they mention anything about how old it may be or any other detail?"

"You already know more than me, my dear. It seems rather rash to be moving the body so quickly, to my mind anyway, but perhaps they have new techniques."

"Do you still have the contact details for any of the international team from the last time?"

"*Hmm*, well, there was Aart Bakker, the Dutch toxicologist, and the two American ladies – if you give me some time I will dig out their contact details. I can post them to you?"

"Fantastic, thank you, Monty. I might call you again if I need to do some background articles." She had already gathered he would enjoy the attention.

"Of course, of course. You know I always read your pieces, January. I watched your career as you've moved up the ladder as they say. You've achieved a lot for someone so young."

He was a friendly old bean all the same, she thought.

"Thank you, Monty. Are you enjoying retirement?" She hoped he wouldn't drag out the conversation any longer but knew she would be contacting him a lot in the coming days.

"Frightfully. I've taken up oil painting, and of course travel. I get away a few times a year to see the home of the Old Masters – Munch – I much prefer that darkness than to be sitting in Nice painting water lilies or sunflowers. Do let me know what is going on, if you can, January?"

"I will try. Thank you, Monty, bye now," she finished.

Pressing the red button on her phone did not have the same sense of finality as placing a heavy black earpiece into its ebony cradle did. Monty had been like a big teddy bear even as chief curator. Retirement seemed to suit that personality even better.

Checking her watch, the opaline face as bright as the day her mother got it, she panicked. She needed to get some copy written for the paper and it was nearly two in afternoon.

She had sat in the same car as a child, eating the same sweets. Flicking the gummy-teeth powder from her fingers, she searched Twitter for Sinéad's name. Who had shared the victim's identity?

It was the farmer Jack Flanagan again. This time he had shared an old school picture of a class of forty people, a mixture of boys and girls in black jumpers, the girls wearing navy-and-yellow skirts. A few of the girls wore wide-rimmed lenses, in the style of popular soap star of the time, Deirdre Barlow. She spotted Flanagan – he had two lank curtains of dark hair hanging either side of his head, a pale complexion with thick sideburns, but was not unhandsome.

In the front row, she saw a beaming Sinéad O'Sullivan, high, bright cheekbones either side of a broad smile. She wasn't looking at the camera, instead she was looking at her friend, laughing and smiling. Her thick black hair was frizzy, but still seemed shiny.

She was the prettiest girl in the class and seemed to have an aura of joy about herself. Her white knee-high socks were pristine, compared to the others in the same row. Instead of clumpy black shoes, she wore brown deck loafers. Despite the low resolution, Flanagan had obviously taken a snapshot of the picture from his phone. As January looked closer, she saw Sinéad and her blonde friend were actually not looking at each other, but looking down into Sinéad's hand. January couldn't zoom any further so she pinched out of the image and read the tweet.

Sad to say the body found in my bog this week is actually that of Sinéad O'Sullivan. Glad for all she is found but condolences to the family. Here's St Imelda's class of 1994. Sinéad messing in the front row with @SarahTweedy.

January clicked into the profile of the girl he had tagged, which appeared as a mashed-up profile of Tweedy Threads, the pink-and-grey branding of a fashion boutique. Flicking quickly down, January noticed the tweets were all of new outfits and stock to the shop. She hadn't responded to Flanagan's tweet. The shop was in Ardee, on Castle Street itself, so she decided to walk over.

Chapter 13

1979

January was the first heir of Avonlea not to be born there. Venetia delivered her in the Rotunda Hospital. The weather was cold but bright and sunny. There had been opposition from her in-laws, but she did not want to take the risk. It had taken them almost five years to conceive. Still swollen, Venetia clutched the child to her chest as they walked to the hospital's door, Thomas carrying her bag, the breeze ruffling his thick black hair and flapping his Trinity College scarf.

The baby was wrapped up well, with terry vests and an all-in-one, a yellow knitted woollen suit with a bonnet and cardigan. Her eyebrows were red and the small fuzz of hair on her head was apricot. Tired, they were overjoyed to finally have a child of their own.

A car had been sent for them, the green Bentley. Dan, the gamekeeper, could manage the beast of a vehicle on the slippery winter roads. Venetia rejoiced that they would at least be comfortable in the roomy new car.

"Congratulations, Mister Thomas and Venetia," said Dan, gently teasing back a curl of wool to see the child's face as they settled mother and child on the back seat.

"Thank you. And I told you before, stop with the Mister business, Dan," said Thomas, opening his own door.

"Sorry, Mi– sorry, Thomas. Have you a name for the child yet?"

The pair exchanged glances. They had not been able to settle on one. Her mother-in-law was anxious to announce the birth, her only grandchild, in the *Times*, but what was she to be called?

Passing by a village church on the outskirts of the capital, Venetia noticed a hearse.

"Life goes on," she sighed.

"Not for that poor old sod, it doesn't," joked Thomas.

"Ha, ha – funny."

"Elizabeth," he proffered.

"Too English. Melissa?"

"Too American. Sylvia?"

"*Hmm*. Maybe. Sylvia Quail."

On they went batting back and forth names, settling on none, before Thomas desisted, and closed his eyes for a nap. Venetia's arms ached from holding the sleeping child but she refused to place her down in the carrycot.

Father and child jolted awake as they crossed the bumpy cattle grid. Thomas loosened his scarf and stroked his daughter's cheek.

119

"Now, baby," said Thomas, smiling at the doe-eyed child, as they turned up the long drive of the estate. "This is your home. Our home for almost 250 years. There's the Gate lodge where Betty and Dan live."

"She doesn't know what you're saying," said Venetia gently.

"I know, but let me continue. Dan, slow down a bit, will you? Baby, here is the lawn you and I will ride down in the early morning when the mist still hangs low over the grass. Where we will leave for your wedding day." The house was starting to come into view in the distance. "And that," he said, wiping the condensation from the car window, "is the house your great-great – well, whatever he was, built in 1823."

He and Venetia loved the house. There was no longer a title – Thomas's grandfather cast it off during the War of Independence, in a bid to avoid getting burned out and gain the trust of the Catholic rebels. He supplied them with guns, munitions, and even allowed them to train on the tennis courts.

"Over there," Thomas pointed, although the baby was now dozing once more, "is the lake, where we will paddle in the summer and sail remote-controlled yachts."

He quieted then as the house spoke for itself, the large limestone pillars regally lined in front of the three storeys.

"Can you go round, Dan?" asked Venetia. "I don't

think I could manage those steps." She winced at the thought of displacing a stitch.

Thomas jabbed a finger at each window as they drove around. "There's the entrance hall, and the drawing room, and our library. That will be your room one day, that's where Granny sleeps." They had turned the corner and were at the back of the house. "There's our room, and your nursery. That's where I learned how to sing."

Venetia looked out and there was her mother-in-law Emily and her friend Polly, both smoking cigarettes. Emily's white hair was wrapped in an African-printed turban, with a long black cloak over an Aran jumper, and riding boots. Polly had on what looked to be red woollen long johns as outerwear. They were waving and smiling at the car, beside Betty the well-worn housekeeper and wife to Dan. There wasn't a huge staff at Avonlea, quite rare for such a large estate. Betty cooked and managed the two cleaning ladies. Dan managed the estate and labourers. Emily and Polly took joy in running everything else. Venetia suspected they were lovers, Polly stayed so often and usually in Emily's room. But she never saw any point in bringing it up.

"My beautiful child," Emily hugged Venetia.

They admired the baby before concerns for vulnerable kidneys drove them into the spacious kitchen generously warmed by the Aga. Emily had not rushed to take the child, but Venetia settled her into her grandmother's arms. Betty poured them hot tea and handed out slices of fruitcake, lathered in butter.

Emily rubbed the baby's nose, with a slender purple-painted nail, her bangles jangling over her wrist. "I wish your father could be here to meet her, Thomas. People warned us that we might never get a grandchild, with only one son. But here she is and she is perfect. He loved this time of year – none of the Christmas fuss, he loved January."

Thomas cocked his head to the side inquisitively, and caught Venetia's eye as he repeated questioningly. "January?"

"*Hmm*," considered Venetia. "How about January Quail?"

Polly and Emily cooed their delight and enchantment in the name, calling for champagne to celebrate.

Under the kitchen in the wine cellar, Betty climbed up the stepladder for the vintage bubbles. She moved slowly because the cold agitated her wrist. She repeated the name to herself. "January Quail," she said. Now imitating their posh accents: "January Quail calling!" She chuckled as she blew the dust off the bottle and began her descent. "What kind of a mad name is that?"

Chapter 14

Blooming floral hanging baskets hung from the walls of Ardee's main street, and the strong sunlight reflected into January's eyes from the ornate wrought-iron benches. She breathed in the smell of the summertime, that mixture of exhaust fumes, hot, melting tarmac, and grimy concrete. The streets of the town were in the full-flow of the lunchtime rush. Schoolgirls ate ice-cream cones on the public benches, in the updated version of the uniform Sinéad had worn. The local court must be sitting today, she thought, as she saw well-dressed men in black and pinstripe suits going into another pub for lunch. Amongst them she recognised a reporter from the *Irish Independent*. Of course she wouldn't be the only journalist up here. She had forgotten about the competition amongst titles. Whenever she ran into other antiques correspondents at a Sotheby's showing, they would usually retire to the Merrion Hotel for a bottle of Piedmont. Working on this story took a different pace, and January felt emboldened by it.

As she rounded onto the main street, she thought of her own clothes. She could do with some extra outfits. She wondered how Cooney was getting on with the latest victim – hopefully Jack Flanagan wouldn't get his smartphone camera at that. They had made a few mistakes with this investigation and Cooney's career could be over before it had even started if the senior officers looked too closely.

The grey and baby-pink shop front of Tweedy Threads looked more like a bakery than a boutique, but the doorframe and woodwork around the large glass windows was painted with a thick cream paint. The mannequins wore crushed-silk dress suits: one in lilac and gold, the other in silver and red. But the middle model wore a black-and-camel shift dress with a drop waist and gold buttons on the shoulder. January wanted it.

The shop was busy inside, with a handful of well-groomed girls in black business suits riffling through the rails. In another part of the shop was a seemingly alternate universe with rails of fluorescent green and orange gowns, encrusted with crystal, frills and slashed panels. January wondered was it even the same shop? Had an earthquake shaken loose the boundary between two separate boutiques, or even two separate realities? January enjoyed the sublime and ridiculous, especially when it came to costuming, but was taken aback at the dramatic outfits.

A thin woman in her late thirties was holding up a

dress in each hand at the changing room. She had a deep faux tan, and her hair was now a dark red colour, but January saw it was Sarah, the girl who had been standing beside Sinéad in the picture.

"The gold is popular." She was shaking a sateen bolero jacket and matching top hat for the benefit of the older traveller woman waiting outside the changing room. "At least she'd have a chance of wearing it again, a lot of times – the wedding isn't the only outing."

She caught January's eye.

"I'll leave these here for her to try," she said to the woman, clipping them onto a hook beside the changing room.

She approached January.

"Now," she said, rubbing her hands together, "are you alright there?"

"I'd like to buy that camel dress in the window, please – do you have it in a size six?"

Sarah looked January up and down, not unkindly but it unnerved her. "I'm afraid the eight is the smallest, but if you don't mind me saying, you don't look quite a six –"

"I wear corsets," she said, knocking her knuckles on the hard bone encasing her waist. "I'll take the eight. If you have it?"

"Absolutely, I absolutely do." She tacked off behind the till into a storeroom and emerged with another dress, sheeted in plastic. "It's a gorgeous dress, isn't it?

Have you something coming up?" She was wrapping it in grey tissue.

"No, but I am a glutton for anything Katherine Hepburn might have worn," January said cautiously.

"Would she have worn a corset with that? Mind you, they're more popular than you might think." Thick bangles of yellow gold clattered around her left wrist as she wrapped up the dress.

"More likely a girdle, but she was naturally thin."

Leaning in to January, Sarah said, "Those that like the gaudy gear love a corset, especially if it's see-through made with netting. I know it's a strange mix between the two parts of the shop but business is tough and I had to diversify."

January felt sorry for her other customers, being held in such contempt. Then she remembered why she had come into Tweedy's Threads.

"Terrible about the girl they found in the bog, isn't it?"

"Oh desperate, terrible stuff," she said without a beat.

The bell on the door rang and two girls in the school uniform walked in.

"No fear of them buying anything," Sarah said, smiling at January.

"Did you know her?"

"Know who?"

January made a show of sounding unsure. "Sinéad, is that her name?

"Oh, yes, Sinéad O'Sullivan. I'd say the family are happy they can bury her and move on," she said distractedly, her eyes following the schoolgirls as they picked up packets of tights. She finished tying a bow into the ribbon on the large shopping bag and placed it on the counter in a gesture of finality. "Thanks so much," she said and moved away from the till. "Stay and have a look around."

"Only I saw that Jack Flanagan had tweeted to say that the body was Sinéad – did you see it? He attached your old school picture. He tagged you in it too."

"He tagged me in it?" She started furiously prodding through apps looking for Twitter on her phone.

"I'm writing about this for the *Irish Sunday Chronicle*. I'm a journalist – my name is January Quail."

"Oh my God," said Sarah. "I read your style tips every week – is that why you're here?"

January explained she was covering the broader story. After she was promised some positive spin for the shop, Sarah agreed to an interview and suggested they go for a coffee in a nearby café.

The lunchtime rush was finishing as January decanted her thick leather-bound sketchbook from the satchel and ordered a pot of tea, not daring to specify Assam.

As she waited for Sarah, she tried calling Detective Cooney's mobile but it rang out. She spent a few minutes writing up something for the website. The ink

127

of her fountain pen still wet, she took a picture of the handwriting in her notebook. She sent it off to Alf with a note that she would have a broader colour piece to him that evening. The steady supply of unpaid interns and work-experience candidates would be transcribing it into a computer document, a practice Alf was keen for her to abandon.

The doorside bell tingled as Sarah arrived. She ordered an espresso with a double shot of foamed milk on the side. January noticed a large emerald engagement ring and rose-gold Chanel earrings as she sat down.

"So tell me about Sinéad," January said and nibbled into her biscotti.

Sarah tucked a lock of red hair behind her ear, staring out the window before looking back at January.

"Sorry if I wasn't chatty in the shop," she said, focusing on January. "Trying to look after everyone and the new girl was taking a break. But I'm all yours now." She sipped her espresso, doing nothing with the foamed milk she had ordered. "I haven't spoken to Sinéad since our Debs, we weren't that close, you know. And when she came back and started tricking around with Tossy from the Castle Arms, well, you know, I didn't like it. It was unladylike to hang out with an old lad like him. I don't know what she was doing to be honest. It's not like she would be after money, even if he did have it."

"Was the relationship public knowledge?"

"Ah, public enough – sure we were only a few years out of school when they started up. There were rumours he was in the IRA. That's the only reason I could think of, that she liked the thrill of things. She had a bleed on the brain in sixth year, and after that she didn't care anymore – she lived every day like it would happen again."

"But she had it clipped?"

"Yes … how did you …?"

"Her mother mentioned it to me," January lied. "And when did she have the baby?" She was remembering the initial post-mortem.

"Baby? She didn't have any baby," said Sarah, her face now contorted in confusion.

"The post-mortem showed that Sinéad had given birth," said January.

"Jeepers," Sarah said, sitting back in her chair. "I never saw her pregnant," she was shaking her head in disbelief, "but she was off in college, and afterwards in America so I suppose you never know." She quietly sipped her coffee. "Does Miriam know about the child? Where is it now?"

"I don't know. The police were speaking to her this morning." Sarah was hiding something, January could feel it. It had been a long time since she had had to deal with tricky interviewees. If she had been down here talking about Tweedy's Threads the conversation would be flowing, Sarah chatting sycophantically like a little lapdog. It refreshed her.

Sarah looked closely at January, her chin tilted to one side. "What exactly is it that you are doing?"

"As I said, I'm reporting on the case for the *Irish Sunday Chronicle*. Trying to build a picture of who Sinéad was and what happened to her. Considering the huge blunder that was made at the start of the investigation, someone has to keep the gardaí in check."

"But you write about vases and cloaks."

"Yes, well, I am the Features Editor of the paper, but given the local and historical nature of this I am reporting on it. In fact, I grew up nearby. But tell me, did Sinéad have any other boyfriends?" January sipped the now-stewed tea.

"Ah, she had her pick of them. She was so beautiful, like one of those people you look at in school and wonder – how could I ever look like that? Even with those mad curls her hair was always perfect, and it was natural. But she was snaky enough when it came to lads. That eejit Jack Flanagan asked her to the Debs. He mithered her until she finally agreed. She only went with him out of pity. She was so good she did that."

"Jack Flanagan – who discovered her?"

"God, yes – God, it was. He can be a bit of an arsehole at times, but I can't imagine him murdering her. His wife is in buying clothes the whole time. They're not short of a few bob."

"Who else did she go out with?" January wanted to ask about Fitzpatrick, but sensed Sarah was a gossip and couldn't risk the link being made public, not yet.

"There were rumours – now she never said anything to me – but there were rumours that she had something going on with Mr Duff, the history teacher. He was always giving her grinds and extra lessons. He was a ride, and not much older than us. But he's still up at St Imelda's now not a bother on him."

"Have you any pictures from school?"

"Aye, I'm sure I do at home. I'll have a look and text you if I find any. Actually, she was in the camera club in school – they could have something – what's his name, Mossie ran that."

January thanked her and promised to feature her boutique in 'Chronicle Life' at the end of the summer, and Sarah headed off back to the shop, the soles of her tan brogues tapping off the brown tiles.

Could Mossie have taken the pictures? She sat back in the uncomfortable metal café chair and swirled the end of her tea, mentally riffling through what Sarah had told her. Sinéad seemed to be the perfect student, the perfect girl, but for her interest in old Tossy or potentially that schoolteacher, or even Fitzpatrick. But people always wanted to sully a reputation, they wanted to find something impure about a person like Sinéad. She needed to speak to her mother and father and hear their own description of her. She wondered

131

about those fractures to her skull – she struggled to think that Speedy and Miriam could have abused their daughter, but she knew that parents were nearly always responsible. As she was thinking, the waitress came to the table mincingly. Her dark brown hair was held off her face with a black bandana, but the steam of the kitchen had made her skin red and shiny.

"Sorry, love, are you Jane Quail?"

"January Quail, yes, I am. Can I help you with something?" It was rare to be recognised. When she was, it was usually by some old art dealer or other.

"There's a call for you." She pointed to a grey plastic handset on the wall.

January rose and went to the phone.

"Hullo, January Quail speaking." She was conscious that the waitress was clearly listening as she lathered tuna and sweetcorn over a stiff panini.

"Where's your phone?" Alf was pissed off.

"Sorry – I was interviewing someone, it's in the bottom of my bag … how did you find me?"

"That Tweedy Threads one tweeted about how she was out for coffee with Ireland's leading fashion journalist. What fucking around are you doing there?"

"She was in school with the victim, okay? Did you get my copy?"

"Yeah, yeah, fine. At least you're not reliant on a carrier pigeon but I wish you'd type it up. Anyway, I'm ringing to warn you that you would want to pull some sort of exclusive out of the bag here. The Board of Management were in this morning asking for an update."

"Since when are any of them journalists? Anyway, I'm probably going to be writing events listings at the end of the month. Why do they care about someone on her way to the bottom?"

"Look, I don't want to start anything – I will leave you to it. I'm going off to chase Fitzpatrick about these new pictures, okay – so I can't do your job too. And answer your bloody phone, okay?"

He hung up before she could respond. That's all she needed, a slating by Alf in front of the Board.

Chapter 15

Hurrying to her car, she spotted an old-fashioned butcher's shop. The shopfront was recently retiled white, with a border of twisted sausages. **"Boyle's Victuallers"** was printed across the window front. In the corner, a printed sign advertised rare and unusual meats, with a price list for goose, duck, kangaroo, zebra, and buffalo.

An elderly lady in leopard-print leggings and a loose raincoat shuffled out the door, popping a bag of what appeared to be tripe into her canvas shopper.

January did not have time – but she could not continue without taking a look. She stepped in and was further surprised to see a vintage-style barber's chair across from the door. Puzzled, she looked at the butcher who smiled as he dragged a side of beef into the walk-in refrigerator. He was a tall chap, with an exceedingly black bushy beard. As he came back behind the counter January saw that he had stretched out his earlobes with thick black plugs, as if he were a member of an African tribe. A black apron was tied tightly across his bulging chest, tattooed arms stretching the tartan shirt.

"If you're going to take a picture," he said, hoisting meat trays back to his work station, "please use the hashtag." He pointed to a blackboard advertising #**MeatisMassive**. "Otherwise, what can I get you?"

"I didn't realise I needed to try zebra until I walked in here," January said.

"That's what everyone says. I'm Conor, by the way."

"Conor, tell me, is there much demand for your more unusual cuts?"

"More than you would think – we sell online across the world. People having a dinner party want to thrill or shock their guests. On the traditional end, we sell a lot of geese for New Year's Eve and Christmas."

January was partial to a festive bird. "How long are you open?" she queried.

"My family have been shopkeepers since the 1800s, but there was no one butchering since my father gave up in nineties. When the unit came up for rent last year, I got a bank loan and opened it." He rested his bloody knuckles on the chopping board.

"What were you doing before," she hesitated as she reached for the word, "butchering?"

"God, this is like a job interview. I'm a barkeep by trade. But I used to help my dad out back in the day so I spent some time with a butcher to pick up my skills again. It's going pretty well."

"Excellent, Conor, excellent. And what on earth would one do with some zebra?" she asked, lifting her question as flirtatiously as a skirt.

"Well, zebra steaks should be treated like a nice piece of venison but don't cook it more than medium rare. If you want to be bold, try it as a carpaccio."

"*Hmm*, I do love a carpaccio, but I'm not going to be home to cook anytime soon. I will place an order the moment I return to Dublin."

She agreed to take a picture for social media. Conor had to walk her through the uploading procedure, adding the hashtags and a witty caption, his dirty nails tapping on her smartphone screen. An intern had set up all of these blasted accounts, which sat lurking on the screen, but she had to admit it was rather useful.

"Someone keeps ringing you here – you have like eighteen missed calls," he said, pausing in his industry.

"I'll get them again, keep going," she said.

Their conversation was interrupted when Cooney beeped from an unmarked car on the street. She nodded a goodbye to Conor and left, wiping the screen with her monogrammed handkerchief.

"Get in," Cooney said, reaching into the backseat and pushing out the door for her.

She got in and his sidekick O'Brien drove off. Both had their suit jackets hanging from a clip in the backseat. Cooney had his sleeves rolled up, the dusty fair hair on his arms resting on top of an even golden tan. Over his collar, his neck was as red as they come. Both officers were eating ice lollies. Empty plastic bottles rattled around the backseat.

"Do you not answer that phone of yours, no? I've had one of the lads driving around looking for you," Cooney said without looking at her.

January couldn't take him seriously while his pink snaky tongue licked the melting popsicle.

"It was in my bag – those lollies look good – have you any more?"

"Where the fuck would we have more, sure it's nearly thirty degrees in here," he said as they reached the small Garda station.

"How did you get on with the mum?" she asked.

"I hate those doorstep calls. But she seemed happy there was closure and she could bury her daughter." A splodge of pink lolly landed on his tie. "LMFM were standing at the door, ready to pounce."

"I heard the report," said January. "The ID was made public quickly, lots of media attention already." When she was annoyed she tended to sound posh, her curtness rendering marbles in her mouth.

"I got them down there. I had to get the heat off from this other body. Don't worry, you have the inside line. Hey, O'Brien, get in there and start writing up your reports."

"Okay." O'Brien left.

"I saw her father in the pub earlier," January said.

"Speedy, the other chaps called him. He won a big bet at Punchestown."

"I know, we were trying to call him home. He said he knew when he saw the squad car in the driveway that we had found her."

"What's the story on the new body?" January produced the last bag of penny sweets and offered one to Cooney.

"Forensics are still there and our uniformed Gardaí are conducting a door-to-door investigation. But it seems like she was there for a while. I've invited Jack Flanagan to assist us in our investigations – I want to get the fucker on tape. His cousin lived beside that field and she also disappeared thirty years ago. He's too young to have killed her, but he's a snake – all the tweeting and hanging around. I don't have a good feeling about him." His thumb and forefinger spread across his red temple.

From her seat in the back, she could really take a good look at him. His tidy brown hair had the smallest appearance of grease. January couldn't help but smell his body. Not sweaty but masculine, with the hint of an aftershave. He was extremely good-looking in a timeless way, January could imagine his face hanging from an oil portrait on canvas or a movie poster.

"Is the second body his cousin?" she asked his reflection in the mirror.

"We are running the DNA now. In I way I hope it is – these people," he flattened his cow's lick, "deserve answers. And I want to start with Jack."

"Sinéad went to his Debs ball. She was pretty. I've been chatting to a few people myself."

"I saw the tweet – I'm sure she had no interest in the scaldy head on him."

"You saw the tweet – when you're heading up a murder investigation? Golly, what is the world coming to – my editor used it to track me down earlier."

"There's a team up in Dublin monitoring all social media and linking in with that *luthar* O'Brien." He jerked a thumb towards the station. "What else did you find out?"

"She was dating an older man for a while before she disappeared. Tossy, the owner of the Castle Arms."

"He was investigated when she went missing – they didn't find anything but we will look again. Next."

"There were rumours about her having an affair with the schoolteacher but apparently there was nothing in that," said January, picking her cuticles. "And her friend Sarah didn't remember any baby. Did her mother know what happened it?"

"The baby didn't survive, she said. Now, I want you to go in there to Peter and give him a full report of what you have been up to, and if I were you I would take a back seat. If you jeopardise this investigation, you'll be put off it, January, that's the long and short of it. You must realise that yourself."

"Fine," she said, clambering out of the back seat as he held the door open for her. She looked tired and was perspiring. A fresh dress was what she needed.

Chapter 16

1987

January's tenth birthday party had to be cancelled because of heavy snowfall. The roads around Avonlea had been impassable for days. Her own father Thomas had been stuck in Belfast all week, leaving the birthday girl to celebrate in the company of her mother Venetia and housekeeper Betty. For four days the three were cooped up together, as the snowdrifts reached shoulder-height in the ditches around the Victorian mansion. The milk quickly ran out, but the family's three hens continued to lay fresh eggs for Betty to bake scones. From Sunday to Thursday, they gorged on Tunnock's tea cakes and eating paper and chocolate and mini cola bottles, all purchased for the party. They occupied the kitchen, the family lounge and two bedrooms, while the twenty-three other rooms in the house were ignored. Betty forwent her attic radiator for a camp bed in the kitchen.

January's mother loved her shoulder pads. Having spent her own youth in a haze of loose-hanging crochet tops and bell-bottoms, as a married woman Venetia

Quail wanted structure. Structure for her daughter's schooling, structure for the Friday bridge club, structure for her exotic jars of pasta. She liked things in boxes and organised with labels. She explained various means and methods of organisation to January, who enjoyed being home from boarding school.

On the Tuesday afternoon, all three wrapped up warmly with thick woollen socks and ski jackets to put the Dewey decimal system in place in the library. Even though they had lit the fire, icicles hung from the curtain rails and the whiskey was sludgy half-frozen in the decanter on the drinks table.

"It suits you, Betty," Venetia said – their homely housekeeper was wearing a black, satin-lined jacket filled with Hungarian goosedown.

"Aye, well, it's warm enough." She pulled the zip around her neck with the panache of Greta Garbo.

The books had been collected by January's great-grandfather Jonathan, who built the large house in the 1880s. As stately homes went, Avonlea was on the cosier side of things, but ultimately was absolutely freezing. The plumbing was as reliable as horoscopes.

Jonathan Quail was an avid reader and amateur detective, gobbling up every instalment from Sir Arthur Conan Doyle's *Sherlock Holmes*. At the time, his contemporaries considered his library and literary tastes quite trashy. January was the fourth generation of his descendants to make an addition to the room, with her shelf of Roald Dahl novels.

"Right, let's take each shelf related to one particular study – we can organise further from there," said Venetia, as she unboxed a brand-new label-printer. Her hair was short and highlighted blonde, and she spoke with an accent falling between Lady Diana Spencer and an Aer Lingus air stewardess.

As they worked through the dark afternoon, January and Betty were unsure of how to classify the books. Venetia found Mrs Beeton's household guide sitting between *Old Moore's Almanac* and the *A Vindication of the Rights of Woman*.

As they worked away, Betty told of all the big snows she had lived through, including the six weeks of snow in 1947.

"My sister and I were photographed walking on the River Boyne and it completely frozen over – it's a famous picture," she said proudly as she held up a biography of Éamon de Valera and *Under Milk Wood* by Dylan Thomas for Venetia to classify with her finely manicured fingernail.

As the final vermillion left the low winter sky, Venetia released Betty and January from duty. All three retired to the long pine bench of the kitchen and the heat of the Aga.

With all the doors in the house closed and the radio playing previously recorded dramas, no one had heard the phone ring all afternoon. When Venetia and January were watching television, Betty heard the phone. It rang midway through the 'Hail Mary' she was saying during the Angelus. Fecking typical Protestants calling during the Angelus, she thought as she straightened her arthritic knee to answer the call.

It was a nurse from Burns Unit in the Royal Victoria Hospital in Belfast asking for Mrs. Quail. Betty interrogated the nurse, demanding to know what had happened to Thomas.

Chapter 17

Alf Timmoney spotted the back of the fine three-storey white Georgian house. As he parked and gathered his papers, a man watched him from a white van. The local seagulls croaked overhead as Alf hurried up the steep hill. The lane was the side entrance for a number of fine houses. His calves ached as he climbed up what must be, he surmised, an ancient street. Two old ladies pushed an old-fashioned pram up the cobbles. It was full of rolls of wool and small, delicate children's clothes. At the lip of the hill, he rounded onto Fitzpatrick's Street. He could see the blue-and-white stripes of the market stalls.

Chasing January was infuriating. Her failure to deliver on this story would take her out of the running for the editor's job completely. She was a dazzling mind with brilliant writing skills, but that wasn't enough to lead the country's largest newspaper through the most challenging time in media history, with plummeting sales and circulation. A Luddite who was completely ignorant of the changing technology and refused to even use a laptop wouldn't do.

The front of the Minister's house had been painted in a tasteful taupe grey and the white railings gleamed. It was an impressive residence. A well-dressed and groomed blonde woman in her forties opened the door. A dusting of freckles between her fine lines did nothing to detract from her beautiful bones and china-like collarbone.

"Mr Timmoney, is it? Come on in. I'm Penny Fitzpatrick. Michael is in the kitchen."

He knew this house was her family's, and she was regarded by many as the Minister's secret weapon. She had spent her twenties in the Tory press office at Westminster, and reputedly had a fiercely sharp bite underneath this refined veneer.

"It's great to see the market is so popular," he said as he followed her along the finely appointed corridor, with marble flagstones and red-and-gold plasterwork. Such ornately painted architraves only prevailed in houses passed down within a family. January had pointed out something similar in her flat. As they reached the edge of the stairs, the fine marble was replaced by worn but highly polished wooden steps with a thick carpet laid over.

Fitzpatrick sat at the head of the wide pine table in the centre of the basement kitchen. It was surprisingly light and airy with modern country-style cabinets.

The Sunday papers were spread out in front of him,

even though it was Thursday, and a heavy glass ashtray held the thin wisp of a cigarette. The Minister looked haggard, grey skin hanging from heavy eyelids. He wore a navy cashmere sweater with no shirt underneath, a pair of well-pressed chinos, no socks and monogrammed leather slippers. If his appearance was dulled, his demeanour had not and he leaped up to welcome Alf.

"Alf, welcome, it's great to see you, can we get you a drink? Penny, put on a pot of coffee." The Minister ushered him onto the pine bench.

"I'm fine." Alf smiled lightly as he unpacked his rucksack, placing a reporter's pad, Dictaphone and brown envelope in front of him on the table.

It was highly unusual for a cabinet minister to agree to an interview without a press secretary present. Fitzpatrick explained. "Pat has a family funeral today but I thought it would be fine to speak with you, seeing as this is more of a personal matter in any case. Do you mind if my wife sits in?"

"Only if you are happy to speak freely. But I must warn you these pictures raise more questions," said Alf.

Despite the warm weather, the kitchen was a comfortable temperature. Unheard of in most Georgian houses, but everything was possible with money, he thought.

"It would take a lot to faze my Pen! Anyway she will float around the kitchen." Fitzpatrick was a gregarious character. Warm and chatty, like all politicians.

He poured the coffee from a fine silver pot into a dainty china cup. Most elected representatives would offer a mug of stewed tea in a cold constituency office instead of this elaborate set-up.

"So these pictures," said Fitzpatrick, holding one knee up to his chest, "can I see them?"

"Yes, I will show them to you shortly. But first I wanted to clarify some things about the first set of pictures that were sent to the offices of the *Irish Sunday Chronicle*." Alf glanced at Penelope and proceeded to lay out the dark images of Fitzpatrick arriving at the apartment complex, being met at the front door by two prostitutes and going inside the apartment as they closed the curtains.

"Can you walk me through what happened again, on the night?"

Fitzpatrick looked over the prints. "This is a set-up, Alf – sure you have to see that."

"Walk me through what happened, okay? I want to understand."

His wife reached her slender arm to the shelf over the green polished Aga. She fingered the spine of the cookbooks until she came across a plain photo album and handed it to her husband.

"I want to show you something," said Fitzpatrick as he opened the musty pages.

Alf could smell the dust. Behind the cellophane on the first page were four black-and-white pictures of a couple standing at a cottage half-door. They were old pictures, and the couple looked middle-aged, wearing black mourning clothes.

"These were my grandparents, John and Loretta. Here they are pictured on the day of my uncle's funeral in 1934," said Fitzpatrick.

As he turned the page. Alf was horrified at what he saw on the next page. It was the image of small boy, lying as if he were asleep, in a coffin. In another picture, the couple from the previous pages sat behind the coffin, propping it up to make a tragic family portrait.

The plain voice of Penny explained, "It's a memento mori, or memento of the dead, a Victorian thing. It was quite rare in the thirties, but not unheard of."

"What age was he when he died?" asked Alf, unnerved at the child, dressed in a long white robe. This is the sort of thing January would write about.

"He was only two," said Fitzpatrick, now flicking through the other pages of the albums. No other picture was so shocking. A couple in suits on the steps of a church, a young Fitzpatrick in bell-bottoms. "He was the youngest of twenty children. Only six of them survived. For most of them that died they never got any picture taken, dead or alive. So they were proud of this one."

"Why are you showing me these?" asked Alf, uneasy at the sight of the disturbing family album.

"My grandmother Loretta, she was the seventh daughter of a seventh daughter. She had the ability to cure shingles by laying her hands on someone," he said slowly.

Even where Alf grew up in Dublin, there were quacks offering to cure the incurable, with the "cure", but the practice had nearly all died out.

"But she always felt that the energy she used for that was sapped from her own children, leaving them weak, and ready to die. Today we might know if there was a genetic disorder or leukaemia to cause so many deaths. But that's what she thought. She also could communicate with the dead. I'm being honest here with you, Alf. I know that many people today have no spirituality or religion beyond a yoga class, but I have always had messages from my grandmother, even though I never met her. She convinced me to go into politics. Even the night before the news about Anglo Irish Bank and the financial crisis broke – she warned me. Told me even to sell my shares. Fancy saying that in front of the Public Accounts Committee." He smiled, running his hands through his hair and sitting back into the kitchen chair.

"What does this have to do with these two prostitutes, Minister?"

"Jesus, Alf," he said, sitting back and spreading his arms to the back of his neck. "I'm getting there, okay? So sometimes I don't hear from her in a while, no matter what medium I visit or whatever, she's not there. It has been a few years, but anyway, this message appears on Twitter. One of the girls in the office looks after the Twitter, but Penny and I have it on our phones and keep an eye on what comes in." He pointed to the iPhone on the table. As he continued to tell the story, his accent became less and less gentrified. "So this message comes in on Twitter from Doreen Dalevi. The world's most famous psychic, friends with Oprah, and the whole shebang. She says she has a message from my grandmother for me. Says she is coming to Ireland and would like to meet me. She gives a phone number and we arrange to meet her at that address, that's it." He was now folding up the newspapers in front of him. "You might not agree with my methods, but that is the truth behind those pictures. The girls were expecting two ordinary clients, they didn't have a clue about Doreen. We left as soon as we realised we were set up. In fact, Penny was due to come with us, right up until the last minute. Weren't you, love?"

Fitzpatrick looked around at his wife, now tidying a perfectly neat windowsill.

"I had been fighting a migraine all day," she said. "It was so bad I just couldn't have gone."

"You see, why would I bring my wife to a knockin' shop?"

"There's no accounting for taste, these days. But if it is a set-up," said Alf, "and I'm not convinced of that, who do you think was behind it?"

"Well – we have been asking ourselves that," said Fitzpatrick, now holding his wife's hand.

"At the time we thought it was a nasty prank by one

of the psychics I visited before." He gestured towards the pictures. "Until those showed up, and I realised it was something bigger again." His face had lost the ashen grey tinge of when Alf first arrived. "Maybe the opposition. Who knows? All the two girls remembered was that a woman had called to book their services, and had paid in cash up front."

"It's a bit of a dirty tactic for an Irish politician, isn't it?"

"You forget you're sitting in the middle of County Louth. There are boys around here not afraid to kneecap or even murder someone in the name of the 'RA. Ringing up a few hoors would be light touch by those standards – look at the stuff I get."

He opened a plastic folder and pushed it towards Alf. It contained an assortment of sheets slandering and threatening the TD. Some of them had letters that looked like they had been cut out of the paper, others were written on an old typewriter. One even seemed to have been scrawled in blood.

"Sure we have got dog shit and everything through the letterbox. The gardaí don't care!" Fitzpatrick gestured with his arms. "They're not interested. Ever since we had to lay off those reserves. Anyway, the point I'm making is that I get a lot of this shite. I'm sure this is another one of those slimy pricks trying to get at me. Surely you can see that?"

"Well, let me know the next time it happens, okay?" said Alf.

As the buzzer of the front door rang, Penelope left the kitchen.

"I will in my hole," said Fitzpatrick, the letters rounded to the Drogheda accent. "I won't be whingeing like a lost pup. I am getting a retired detective to follow it up. He has a private forensics crowd in England going to test it all."

Fitzpatrick had been leading Alf so far in the interview, even in the choice of location. It was all setting him up. He decided to take back the momentum by producing the other large brown envelope.

"We received these yesterday, and we may be forced to show An Garda Síochána due to an ongoing murder investigation," he said as he removed the pictures and laid them on the table.

"Murder? I don't know anything about any murder?" Fitzpatrick said, staring at the pictures.

They had been taken on a camera using film, and when blown up to A4 lost some of the resolution.

"Jesus," said Fitzpatrick, still confused but not horrified, "what has that got to do with anything? That was the opening of the castle in Ardee – it must be 93 or 94?"

"1997. Do you recognise the girl?" Alf watched his eyes for a glimpse of recognition.

"We may have had a flirt," he lowered his voice so Penelope couldn't overhear, "but I don't know about any murder."

"Well, her body was discovered yesterday, in the bog outside Ardee."

Fitzpatrick seemed genuinely shocked. "Sinéad something, was it? I remember her mother had come to me when she went missing. She came to the clinic downtown and asked for support to step up the search. There was something funny about it. They didn't know she was missing for so long because she was meant to be in America or something?"

"Well, the medical records show that it's Sinéad O'Sullivan," said Alf. "The same girl we have here." He pointed to the photo of her smiling face whispering something to Fitzpatrick. "A few days after her body is discovered, we get sent these pictures. What do you have to say about that?"

"Sure isn't it obvious someone is trying to set me up? Can I take a copy of these to give the detective working from me?"

Alf allowed him take pictures of the photos on his phone but refused to give him the physical copies. He also made it clear he wasn't buying the defence that someone was setting the Minister up. Fitzpatrick offered little other insight.

"Who was it, love?" asked Fitzpatrick as his wife returned.

"Jehovah's Witnesses." She began to add salt to the dishwasher.

"That's unusual," said Fitzpatrick, considering it

little further before returning to Alf. "I thought it was a bog body, like an ancient Celtic one, that they found in Ardee?" He returned the pictures to the envelope.

"It was made to look like that. But it's her. The DNA and medical and dental records have confirmed –"

Alf was interrupted by a screech from Penny. There was a streak of blood on her long blonde hair and a gash across her thumb was pouring blood.

"I dropped a bloody glass, be careful!" she shouted as Alf and Fitzpatrick crowded around her. "One of those fragile old glasses – it was my fault – I shouldn't have –"

Fitzpatrick put his large hands on her shoulders. "Please sit down, love. There. Now, let me have a look." He examined the cut. "You'll need stitches, love."

He reached over the Aga for the first-aid box and brought it to the table.

"I'll be neat, I promise," he said, smiling at her.

Alf had forgotten that he was the only doctor sitting in the Dáil.

"I think we should probably leave it there, Mr. Timmoney. But if you need anything else, let me know, okay?"

Alf shook his hand, plonked his fine china cup on the draining board and let himself out.

The interview hadn't taken as long as he'd expected, so he decided to go for a quick stroll around the market. He browsed through small perennials and purple pansies on the gardening stand, buying a small cactus. He had heard somewhere that the spikes helped bounce bad vibes off a PC.

Amongst the offerings, he came across an old lady selling antiques. She wore a purple turban and was heavily made-up, with thick spidery eyelashes. To the left of the stand, beside where she was sitting, were two large glass cases. Each was painted white around the edge and glittered with jewellery. The sun gleamed on the edge of a green rhinestone brooch set in the shape of a rose. There were at least thirty brooches pinned into the crushed velvet-backed cabinet. One large Tara brooch caught his eye.

"There's not as much call for brooches as there was," she said in a deep baritone voice. "It's become mostly the preserve of eccentric old bats like me." She threw her head back, hocking gutturally, her printed chiffon scarf unravelling from her flabby jowls.

"How much for this one?" Alf wasn't sure what he was doing, but the brooch reminded him so much of January. It consisted of a circle of ornately carved gold with a thin pure bar.

"They were used since ancient times in Ireland. Originally to hold a Celtic cloak together. Although this is a replica, so two hundred," she said, in a whisper. "I could get a good bit more online, but I couldn't be bothered with all those trips to the post office."

"I'll leave it today," he said, making a show of patting the pocket of his short-sleeved shirt. "But I'll take a card ..." He picked up a card from an ebony, colonial-style holder. "*Polly's Antiques*" it read, with only a landline number.

He reminded himself it would be inappropriate to buy January, a colleague, jewellery ... even though she didn't have a sensor for what was inappropriate. But he pushed those thoughts aside for Fitzpatrick. The politician must have a better idea of who was trying to set him up than he claimed. Alf hadn't seen anyone use those sorts of tactics in Irish politics before – it seemed the sort of set-up you'd see in England or Washington. Maybe it was a personal thing, he thought, considering how he claimed to be catfished on Twitter. That could be a lead. He would email the Minister with a list of requests when he got back to the office. Access to the Twitter account and an interview with his private detective top of the list.

He made his way back to the car.

As he set off, he directed his phone to call January – of course it rang out. As he turned right along the river in Drogheda, a sign pointed twenty-three kilometres to Ardee.

He changed lanes. If she couldn't be bothered answering him, he would go to her.

Chapter 18

1987

Thomas Quail had been tarred and feathered by the IRA, as he was walking through Belfast. Because of the freezing conditions, he had been forced to stay in Northern Ireland much longer than planned. On a short walk outside the hotel, some young lads overheard him asking for Republic newspapers in an English accent. First they poured boiling-hot pitch from the crown of his head, over his shoulders, drenching his tall frame in steaming black. Thomas Quail was well dressed, and the pitch only made contact with the skin on his hands, shoulders and scalp. The thick tarry matter dissolved his skin instantly, before the thugs dumped a pillow of feathers over him. They tied him to a lamppost and left him to the elements.

The only saving grace was the freezing temperatures. Apart from a few bruised ribs, he was fine. The burns were deep, and got infected twice before drying out into knotted purple-red matted scar tissue, white leather. Belfast was a hub for excellence in plastic surgery at the time – an advantage from proliferation of rubber-bullet injuries and burns from bombs of petrol, semtex and even dynamite.

When well enough to leave the hospital, Venetia drove him to Avonlea. She nursed him until he could feed himself and complete basic tasks with his hands. After a third bad infection, the doctor ordered him to bed with intravenous antibiotics. It was Good Friday. The staff were off, with much of the local village of Carnaross at the Stations of the Cross.

In that Catholic silence, the Protestant family usually enjoyed some quiet time at home.

The house warmed somewhat by the April air, Thomas insisted on recuperating in the library. With a special dispensation to come home from boarding school, January sat reading *Paradise Lost*, as he lay back in his portable hospital bed.

Her red hair was shorn close to the nape of her neck in a page-boy style, and she wore a wide-shouldered black-and-white chequered blouse.

"*The mind is its own place and in itself, can make a Heaven of Hell, a Hell of Heaven,*" she read. Through her elocution lessons and private schooling, there was no trace of an Irish accent.

"Repeat the line," said her father, with slightly more of a Hiberno twang but nonetheless a far cry from his local neighbours. As an avid schoolboy rugby player, he was wearing a red Munster jersey. Betty had sliced the sleeves from the wrist to elbow and turned them up into neat cuffs. Thomas preferred not to stay in pyjamas. He was quite deformed. His ears were shrunken to stubs. Thick mottled strands of white skin-grafts pulled his scalp tightly to his shoulder. The pitch had failed to curdle the garnet red of his lips, which still contrasted against the pure white skin and now thick, curling beard he wore.

"Why should I repeat it?"

"Do."

"*The mind is its own place and in itself, can make a Heaven of Hell, a Hell of Heaven,*" she read with annoyance. "So?"

"So it's important to remember, January. Your mindset creates your reality. I have always wanted to devour these great books." He raised his hands up, still in bandages with his left arm attached to a drip. Yellow pus was oozing through the gauze, as the nurse was yet to come and change them.

"You can't even hold a book."

"I could either feel sorry for myself and sit here miserable, or I could enjoy my time listening to books on tape and enjoy our fine literary canon in this beautiful room."

January had not spoken about the attack with her father. Softly, she said "Aren't you angry with them? You should have been more careful, but they could have killed –"

"*To thine own self be true*. If it wasn't me they would have got someone else."

"But they did it because you were Protestant and rich!"

"We aren't rich, January. We are lucky to have this beautiful house, but your mother and I work hard to keep it."

"Well, you were too flamboyant …"

"Where did you learn that?"

"We studied Oscar Wilde in school."

"Well, he was flamboyant – for sure. I couldn't claim to be in his league, but why should I change myself, January? That would be a far more serious injury than this," he said, waving his hands around.

She watched her stubby toes kicking off the shiny mahogany of the chair. "But isn't it better to be like everyone else?"

"Come here, January, and give me a kiss. Let me say loud and clear, it is certainly better to be oneself, always remember that. Now, how about something a little bit more fun? Do you want to choose the next book to read for me?"

"Yes, Daddy, how about, *hmm* …" She pondered at her own bookshelf, from Roald Dahl to A.A. Milne and Beatrix Potter. She chose a book.

Spotting the cover, her father said, "Great – a favourite of mine."

"*Alice was beginning to get tired of sitting by her sister* on the bank, and of having nothing to do: once or twice she had peeped into the book her sister was reading, but it had no pictures or conversations in it, and where is the use of a book, thought Alice, without pictures or conversations?"

Chapter 19

The Garda Station in Ardee was housed in a two-storey building, its primrose-yellow pebble-dash an attempt to lift the gloom that so pervades such outposts. Neat on the inside, despite decorative efforts to the contrary, it was a collection of bleak little rooms.

The air temperature was always colder than outside and January felt goose bumps rise on her arms. She still carried the new frock from Tweedy's Threads, but would wait until after the interview to freshen up. A matchbox of sun sliced across the melamine desk in the north-facing interview room, where she sat across from Detective Cooney's deputy, O'Brien.

"Okay," he stuttered, fiddling around with the tape recorder. As the tape click into place, he sat up with his notepad open. "Sarge wants you to go through exactly what you did today, who you spoke to etcetera, and I'll write up a report to include with the investigation," he said.

"Okay, or I can send you a report written up myself

– I am a journalist, after all." She shifted on the grimy plastic chair.

"This is the way he wants it done, Ms Quail, if that's okay with you."

He was a serious enough young chap, she thought.

"So this morning, after you left the crime scene," he queried, "what did you do?"

Despite his youth and an outward appearance of self-conscious speech, he confidently guided her through describing the various interactions in the Castle Arms and with the victim's childhood friend. Over the course of the early afternoon, she rehashed the stories she had been told. She made sure to portray how she managed to gain the trust from each.

"Can I speak to Cooney before I go?" she said, as O'Brien walked her out of the station.

He agreed to have a quick look for him.

As January stood in the front reception, an ashen-faced, stick-thin guy with dark stubble and a heavy gold necklace reeled off a long number to the duty sergeant. Clearly a criminal on bail, she thought. It made a nice change to be out and about in the company of ne'er-do-wells. A welcome change from her regular beat in Dublin. To truly appreciate the beauty she was surrounded by, beautiful rooms, stunning art, she needed to see this dull and dirty side to life.

Cooney disturbed her reverie. He looked unimpressed "You wanted to see me?"

"Yes. I've spent the last few hours going through my day in detail. Could you update me on how the case is progressing?" she said calmly.

He sighed and rubbed his temples. "Yes, yes, I will go through it all with you. But not now, we have a team briefing."

January raised her eyebrow. "May I join?"

He glanced over his shoulder. "Okay – if you promise not to say anything and stay under the radar you can sit in on the team briefing. No recording, and leave your shopping with Tommy over there." He pointed at the duty sergeant.

She had never been privy to an ongoing police investigation like this. Never mind a murder investigation.

There were about twenty-five gardaí gathered in this room, which was clean and freshly painted. A blank whiteboard ran the length of one side of the room. The boardroom table was equipped with a camera and microphone. January recognised a number of other plainclothes detectives from the crime scene. They were the Garda Special Squad at Harcourt Square. But more than half of the room consisted of uniformed local officers, stripped down to their light blue shirts in the muggy room. Body odour permeated the air. January ignored the noxious miasma as best she could.

A young female officer fiddled with a laptop. She summoned up the round and tanned face of the State Pathologist, Professor Traynor. The camera was so close up January could count the oversized pores on her forehead, not covered by concealer.

Cooney stood at the top of the room. "Okay. Thanks, everyone, for gathering here. Given the numerous moving parts to this investigation, I want to lay it all out so we are up to speed. We have a big team here and many of you are working together for the first time, but we don't have time to mess around. We need to scale the learning curve as we now have two murders to solve, after another body was discovered this morning. This morning the office of the State Pathologist, who is joining us by secure video link here, confirmed the identity of the first body discovered on Tuesday as that of local woman Sinéad O'Sullivan. Sinéad went missing in the summer of 1997. We have three of the investigating officers with us to brief us on the ins and outs of the disappearance. She had told friends and family she was moving back to the States, so she wasn't reported as missing for a few weeks after she was last seen. As you all know, local farmer Jack Flanagan tweeted a picture of the foot of the corpse he severed when cutting the turf. This led to speculation that this was an ancient mummy, or bog body, like those discovered in other bogs in Leinster."

Cooney spoke fluently with authority, despite the weight directing such an investigation had placed on his shoulders.

"However, during a CT scan four metal aneurysm

clips showed up. This proved that she was walking and talking at the same time as most of us. After her death – this is really the crux of it all – the body was treated to leather the skin. She was mutilated to replicate the tribal markings and injuries that are often seen in genuine bog-body discoveries. That leads us to wonder who had the knowledge to mutilate the corpse in such a manner, and why they did so." He paused to sip water from a plastic cup.

He was confident and the officers were attentive and interested, even if the weariness of the late night had greyed them.

"Just last night, another body was discovered in the same field. We can't ignore the possibility that the murders were linked. Although it could be a coincidence … but we all know coincidence is another word for poor police work so let's rule that out. So far forensics have found nothing of interest, but I will hand over now to you, professor, for a pathology update." He crunched the empty water cup in his fist.

January found herself attracted to the gesture. He led the presentation in a sort of musky, sweaty way she imagined Wellington did approaching the Battle of Waterloo.

Professor Traynor started to speak. Her voice was tinny as she spoke over the internet connection. "Thank you, Detective Cooney. Given the profile of this case, we conducted the post-mortem this morning.

This latest victim is also remarkably well preserved. Her face resembles that of a sleeping woman but, unlike the other victim, that appearance is incidental instead of intentional. As in, the killer didn't make any attempt to stage a bog body – no removal of bones, nipples – what you'll have seen in the first post-mortem report. Taking into account the unique soil composition of the bogland, I estimate this victim died approximately twenty-five to thirty years ago, before our first victim. It could be slightly longer or shorter than that, given unusual weather events over the past few months. I've had the chance to confirm that the shower curtain she was wrapped in was sold by Dunnes Stores in the late 1980s. I don't believe she has been moved from this site. I believe she was buried here, and has stayed here, albeit in a relatively shallow grave. She was in her late twenties, had not given birth, with long black hair. She suffered a massive blow to the head, but the cause of death was asphyxiation. Most likely she was suffocated with a pillow or a plastic bag. She had no defensive wounds, which indicates that she was unconscious at the time of suffocation. She could have been knocked out by the blow to the head, or it's possible she was drugged. Another possibility is that she was inadvertently buried alive. Had the knock to the head left her unconscious? Without oxygen she would have smothered. Now, most of the victim's clothing has decomposed, apart from an unusual whalebone-and-metal corset she was wearing."

January shifted in her seat, conscious of the hefty undergarments she had in place.

"Whalebone was commonplace in corsets a century ago but it is rare to see it now. Given how tight the strings appear to have been pulled, I would say our victim trained her waist – it could even be a vintage corset. I think it could be a good thing to investigate. Our victim was likely a smoker – I noted a fairly significant amount of tar in her lungs for such a young person. Given the level of decomposition, it wasn't possible to tell if she had undergone any rape or sexual assault. Something else of interest is that she actually had quite a large brain tumour. She absolutely would have been suffering from severe migraines, forgetfulness and clumsiness. Nowadays it is rare to see a tumour so advanced, without treatment. But in the eighties and even early nineties it was more likely." Traynor smiled at the assembled team. "And that's it. I've submitted a full report and will present the full findings in person to whomever Detective Cooney sends up here to Dublin."

As she finished, Cooney walked back to the top of the room.

"Did you see any similarities at all with the first victim, professor?" he said.

"Well, as I said, this is a preliminary report on your most recent victim. We will be continuing to review this body in further detail." She hesitated. "I can't say if these women were killed by the same person. In fact, there is nothing to suggest they were, apart from the choice of burial location. The earlier victim, discovered last night, was dumped in the ground unceremoniously, and the natural soil conditions somewhat preserved parts of her body and tissue. The other victim underwent a huge range of processes including tanning and the removal of her bones. That process would have taken days, and particular skills and knowledge. She was deliberately made to resemble a bog body with props. There are no similarities. If there is a link, it is for you to establish it, detective."

Cooney considered this and nodded.

A uniformed officer in the front row sheepishly raised his left hand. January recognised him from the field.

"When will the body of Sinéad O'Sullivan be available?" he asked, in a Midlands accent. He wasn't from Ardee but he wasn't from too far away either. "The funeral directors were on to me about making the arrangements."

Cooney cut him off before the pathologist had a chance to respond. "No time soon, that's for sure. We're still waiting for Setanta Molloy and some international experts to review things. I'll get on to the mother and let her know."

Cooney then thanked the Professor for joining the briefing and ended the Skype call. He distributed jobs to the team before dismissing them, leaving January alone with him.

She hadn't thought to mention it earlier, but she now remembered the pictures of Sinéad that had been posted to her door. Given the access he had granted her, she felt compelled to reveal it and came to the top of the room.

"Detective, I have something to say," she said, swaying back on her heels.

"And?"

"Well, it seems that someone left some pictures, printed images in my apartment. I think they may be related to the case."

"Jesus, January, when did you get them?"

"Yesterday, my editor found –"

"Why are you only telling me *now*?" He slammed his fist hard on the whiteboard. "January!" He shook his head, tutting as he stared into her large green eyes.

"I didn't have the right moment. They show Sinéad O'Sullivan with Michael Fitzpatrick."

"Where are they now?" He rerolled the folds in his shirtsleeves.

"In the *Irish Sunday Chronicle* office," she said meekly.

"Okay. You listen to me. Our agreement is off. This is no longer your exclusive, and I'm damn near charging you with perverting the course of justice."

His phone rang and he answered, shoving her out the door and closing it.

"Detective, please can I –"

The door opened as he pushed by her, shouting down the corridor, "*O'Brien, if January Quail is still here in ten minutes, arrest her!*"

O'Brien looked between both of them as she protested "It's just a misunder –"

"O'Brien, make that five minutes!"

Chapter 20

As he parked up outside the B&B, hers was the only car there. She opened the heavy metal door and took out her new dress. He had been watching Fitzpatrick and that new detective too. Cooney hopped between marked Garda cars so often there was no need to track him.

It was vitally important that this tale be told from his own side. He had spent a great deal of time visiting other bog bodies. He had researched the treatment of the skin and the correct sort of blade to make an incision around her areola. It was painstaking. A piece of art. A historical manifesto. Although she had been found prematurely, it was not wholly unexpected. He had reckoned that it would take about fifty or sixty years before that part of the bog would be cut and she would be found. He would have been an old man, ready for his own grave. But with this heat, Jack Flanagan had kept cutting the bog, and so his virtuosity was found prematurely.

He had made a new ancient High Queen of Ireland,

sacrificed to protect the integrity of the nation's heritage. Now, the second act of the plan was underway. Ensuring the accurate reporting, and exit. So he needed to explain his process, his art to a storyteller. January Quail. Whilst most research was academic, he was obsessed with anything to do with the great preserved men of Ireland, these other bog bodies. He spent many, many nights reading articles bearing her name. He enjoyed her style, her eagle eye and impeccable taste. She even managed to buy the only piece of decent clothing for sale in Sarah's tired little clothes shop. He looked forward to seeing her in the camel dress.

She had influenced him. He had collected many pieces of furniture, as she had picked out in her antiques column. It was always going to be her who would tell his majestic tale of Irish regency. It is a pity that January Quail would most likely have to die, but inevitable, he thought. Summoned back to the moment, he noticed the CD had stopped playing. He reset it, and as the beat of the fast jig, the sound of the fiddle rose and fell, he closed his eyes and thought of his queen.

Chapter 21

After the grime of the police station, January relished the thought of a hot shower and a change of clothes. It had been a misstep, not showing Cooney the images of Sinéad earlier. He was under stress, she told herself, he would relent. She sensed he enjoyed her company.

When she opened the main door into the B&B, she noticed the mop was inside the front doorway. It was still full of black, lemony water, with a pair of pink rubber gloves nearby. Detective Cooney had found Miriam here at work, to break the bad news. January did her best not to remember the pain of losing someone so close. But Sinéad had been missing for nearly twenty years. It was likely her family had accepted that something terrible had happened their beautiful daughter.

January jumped as her phone began to ring in her hand. It was a Dublin number, not tallied with her address book. She decided to answer, walking down the corridor to Cooney's room.

"Good evening," she said, attempting to maintain as neutral a tone as possible..

"January, how are you? It's Setanta Molloy." For some reason he was whispering.

Nudging Cooney's bedroom door open, she saw he had already removed his belongings.

"Like I've been charmed by Hypnos," she responded. "It's been a long week."

"Cooney has been evading me lately, and I wanted to see how the investigation was going." He sounded upbeat despite his low tone. "I enjoyed catching up with you the other day."

"Why are you whispering?"

"Well, my wife is putting the kids to bed."

January tried to picture his children, and such a domestic occasion as bath time in the Setanta Molloy house. "Oh. They haven't found the killer yet, but I don't know much more."

"You might tell that policeman that I have some information what would be useful to his investigation. But I want to come and consult from a historical perspective. Once all of the information is compiled, that is."

"I believe that's called perverting the course of justice, Mr. Setanta Molloy." January promptly hung up. That was enough of listening to him. He creeped her out.

Standing still in the hallway, she heard the slow crunch of the gravel as a car drove up to the old bungalow. She felt her pulse quicken and heart beat faster. Recalling the nearby police presence at the crime scene, she breathed deeply and tugged back the fabric blinds.

"Thank Christ," she said aloud on recognising Alf's silver saloon in the drive. What was he up to, following her around like this? He was only a temporary editor, they both were equally qualified.

She met him at the front door.

"Well," he said, smiling.

He had such an unhealthy look about himself, tired like a washed-out sock. He handed her a chocolate ice cream, already melting in its wrapper.

"If Mohammed won't come to the mountain, the mountain will have to come to Mohammed," he chirped.

"What are you doing here, Alf?"

"That's a nice way to greet your editor," he said, tripping over the lip of the door. "I was interviewing Fitzpatrick in Drogheda and thought I would swing by. The lads down at the crime scene said you came back up here. That car is anything but inconspicuous."

"Yes, yes," she said, unwrapping the ice cream. "How did you get on with Fitzpatrick? Do you want a drink?"

She led him to the bar and sized up the bottles of dusty liqueurs and spirits lined up there.

"Eh, I'll have a Coke," he said, standing beside the French doors looking out towards a large deck.

The spectacular heat of the past few days had begun to wane. The sun burned to an ocherous glow on the horizon. Its warm rays shone low, bouncing off the glass sliding door. She needed to find the right moment to reveal the exclusive no longer stood, and the other media would be reporting imminently. She doubted he had the wherewithal to sack her, but not admitting it would be gross misconduct in anyone's books.

January poured him a Coke, then produced a small, thimble-like blown glass from her satchel. It was in a perfectly fitting, hand-sewn leather pouch with her family crest stamped in gold. Attached to the main body of the pouch was a thin strap, the width of two shoelaces. Alf watched her fiddle around with this glass, as he recounted his conversation with the Minister.

"So, what is your take on it?" she said, pouring the green crème de menthe liqueur into the glass. She downed it in one like a shot, before refilling the glass.

They went ourside to sit at the picnic table on the deck.

"I know it sounds mad, but I'm half-inclined to believe him. It's so ridiculous I don't know why he would lie." He leaned down to pull tufts of weedy brown grass from between the boards of the deck.

They caught up on what they had both been exploring over the past two days. He seemed impressed that she had maintained such proximity to the Garda investigation.

After the second drink he took a call from the office. January thought he was quite flirtatious with Laura but accepted it as a part of life.

She checked her own emails. Monty was still looking for her. She would try and get to see him tomorrow. There was a huge outpouring of emotional posts and pictures of Sinéad O'Sullivan across her social-media channels.

"Have you done the deed with Laura?" January asked as he lay the phone on the table.

He laughed and scratched his chin "No. God, I'm not that bad, am I?"

"You're bad enough. Mad, bad and a pain to know. Anyway, what did she have to say?"

He sat on the edge of his chair, and refilled her tiny glass with some crème de menthe. He even threw a good glug of the green liqueur into his own. He must be planning to stay, January realised. Alf did not drink and drive.

"Well, the private detective has come up trumps on the Fitzpatrick investigation. He traced the IP address of the person who pretended to be the psychic to Collon, a village outside Ardee."

"So, there are two private investigators on Fitzpatrick – why don't they talk to each other and share the information?"

"Good thinking, I will tell Fitzpatrick. But don't you realise what that means?"

"Enlighten me, please," she drawled, her voice becoming plummier as the alcohol took effect.

"This is a definite link between Sinéad and Fitzpatrick – they're shitting on their own doorstep, Jan."

"Quite," she said. "Are we going to tell Cooney? We're walking a sticky wicket if he finds out I've been withholding evidence. There is no forensic link between the two cases."

She drank a thick finger of liqueur preparatory to telling him about the exclusive. But she could not get the words out.

"Tell him on Sunday, early," he said. "I'm writing this story up for the paper so tell him, yeah? Speaking of the paper, there's something else I need to tell you."

"Yes, I know about the bloody copy, I'm writing up the main story this evening –"

He interrupted her "No, that's not what. I heard the Board of Directors has set a date to hold the interviews for the editor job. They will be held next week."

She maintained a stiff lip, but it was difficult to dampen January's competitive edge. A jolt of adrenaline set her nails tapping on the side of the glass. "Oh. Who has been invited?" She didn't remember seeing anything about it in her emails.

"Not sure – they mentioned it to me at the Board meeting yesterday as an FYI."

"So you haven't received a formal invitation for the editor job?" she asked, less perturbed.

"No, no, but I thought I would tell you, yeah, love?" His Dublin accent was coming through. "They were talking about inviting some foreigners to join in, maybe a Brit or a Yank who lived here for a few years."

"Right. So better pull up my socks on this story, if I want to keep my job, or even think about the editor job?"

"You said it, love, you said it." He checked the time and decided to head back to Dublin.

"Oh, I thought you were staying?"

"That stuff is about 2 per cent alcohol, it doesn't count."

"It's more like 25 per cent, Alf."

"Oh, I only had the one. You're hardly one to be lecturing me."

"What do you mean by that?"

"Nothing. Nothing. Look, I'm sorry. You're right, I shouldn't be drinking. It's just been a long few days. But I am sober as a judge, I swear. Sorry, January."

As he stood astride the white door of the bungalow, he suggested that she should stay in the town, where there might be more action and more possible suspects to check out.

She called and arranged to interview Monty in the morning.

Alf's news about the interviews had rallied her, but also made her a bit depressed. She was coming to the table of serious journalism far too late, and no matter how well she covered this story, her artsy career to date would likely go against her.

Alf's comments about her drinking worried her. Is

that what he really thought? She would try to avoid the drink for the duration of her trip.

Back in her sleeping quarters, a large black box waited for her on the bed. The label was an obscure but expensive lingerie manufacturer she regularly purchased from. Shaking open the lid, her mind rambled as she delicately pulled back the gold crepe paper.

"Good God!" she said aloud, holding up the cream brocade corset. She felt between the stitching to the steel frame. It was a fine piece of craftsmanship. In fact, she had a black version at home.

She dumped it on the bedspread in horror. Who had sent it to her? How had they got into her room? Could it have been Baby? One of the officers? But it was made in her exact measurements, her style …

"Sarah-bloody-Tweedy," she said, remembering her exchange with the shop owner, re-examining the garment. She often received strangely personalised freebies from shops she would write about, but the specificity of the corset was unprecedented. She must have had it delivered, and Baby or someone brought it up to her room. Still unnerved by its presence, she wrapped the box and slid it under the bed. She had work to do.

At the desk, she refilled her cartridge pen and wrote the factual account of what had happened to date, once more sending off pictures of the copy.

No matter what way she put it all together, the facts

did not point to one clear suspect. She couldn't stand not having the full story. Even without the editor interviews, she owed it to herself to produce a significant piece of journalism. She owed it to her parents and her legacy as a Quail to do something of value, of note, instead of the casual frippery that constituted her current role. The job had done little more than enable her to remain isolated; always that strange lady in the room. Up until now, January Quail had been all style and no substance, and her forty years on the planet had to count for something. She vowed to solve this case for herself. If she couldn't then it would confirm that she was a louche *dillitante*.

She could see the police investigation was floundering. After being so close to Sinéad O'Sullivan's preserved remains, she felt obliged to help find her killer. Checking her wristwatch, she saw it was only eight o'clock, so she decided to speak to Jack Flanagan again.

Enrobed in the new camel dress, with shiny black brogues of soft leather, she smiled at herself in the mass-produced full-length mirror. Pinning a blue cameo brooch to her chest, she carefully reapplied the thick, black eyeliner into her signature feline tips. Her bits of daily-life equipment had been scattered around during the day so she reorganised her bag – cleaning and replacing her cigarette holder, small glass and glasses in each of their respective, gold-monogrammed and well-worn leather pouches and cases. She cringed at the pieces of modern ephemera that had made their way in, a plastic bank debit card and her mobile phone. Usually she could do without both, but not this evening. The mint liqueur exhausted, she borrowed brandy from the unmanned bar and fit it in amongst the other pieces. It wasn't for her to drink, but just in case she needed to sweeten up Flanagan.

The portion of bogland described as the crime scene was quieter than it had been that morning, but it was brightly lit by floodlights. Looking over the tawny hedge, she saw the white forensic tents were still in place along with two orange dump trucks scooping up the sticky black bog soil. An officer was reading the paper sleepily in a car parked on the grass verge. January asked him for directions to Flanagan's house, and she followed them up the road. It was so close she could have walked.

Hazel Lodge was a picturesque white bungalow, thatched in the traditional style with the reeds plaited into intricate designs at the ridge closest to the chimney. As people often do when someone pulls into their drive in the Irish countryside, Flanagan had opened the door by the time January was out of the car.

"Well, how's she cutting?" he asked, gesturing for her to come in.

Gone was the filthy sportswear. Flanagan sported an ironed navy shirt with slacks, his hair gelled into peaks, and wore a strongly smelling oud aftershave that reminded January of something a Sheik would wear.

"Good evening, Mr Flanagan, I wondered if you might have a few minutes to chat?" She extended the bottle of brandy.

"Jaysus, nice. Well, I have to tip on soon enough. I'm going to a *seisiún* in the Castle Arms, but I've a few minutes now."

January followed him into the kitchen.

"I thought it was Mam, she's late again," said a blonde woman who was standing there, wearing tall nude stilettos and a white satin close-fitting dress.

"Babysitter troubles," joked Flanagan. "This is Yvonne."

His well-made-up consort was furiously tapping on the screen of her smartphone with extended gel nails, stopping to give January a fake smile.

January barely recognised the cook from the Castle Arms in her finery.

"This is the journalist from the *Irish Sunday Chronicle* I was telling you about, love."

"I know, we met earlier," she said plainly, any trace of amiability gone. "Sarah Tweedy told me all about what she's doing, poking around in a family tragedy."

January was right not to trust the shop owner with any extra information.

"Your wife is a skilled bassist, Jack?" She ventured to lighten the mood, to no avail as Yvonne sneered, ignoring her.

Jack inhaled deeply as he poured the Courvoisier into chipped cheap tumblers.

"Hup, be the Lord, this is nice stuff!" he said sipping, his little finger sticking out in a show of mock manners.

"Quite. Chin-chin," she said, toasting him.

"So what can I do for yeh now, missus?" he said.

"I won't keep you. I wanted to hear about how you discovered the second body." January refilled both glasses as Yvonne stormed out of the room, tutting under her breath.

"She's not a fan of journalists, don't mind her."

"Believe me, I don't plan on adding any more pain to the family. I'm only doing my job."

"Aye, so the second body. It was something else all right. How in the hell would there be two in the one field? I wish they'd just tell us if it's Theresa or not. They have mine and Baby's DNA to cross-reference with the body. If the person they find is related to us apparently the DNA will say it. It has to be her – sure she disappeared from right beside there."

"Wasn't it sealed off as a crime scene?"

"Aye, most of it was. So that whole field, well, it hasn't been dug up for years, but with this good weather we were going at it hammer and tongs." Jack attempted to shake off the burn of the cognac.

January sipped a minute amount as she reached into her pocket and started to record the conversation on the Dictaphone.

"Me uncle, it was his farm originally, well, he didn't realise it was bog either. If you can believe that – I mean, there are acres of turf fields." He swallowed the last of the drink. "*Yeehow!*" he exclaimed as he chased the penultimate droplets around the tumbler's circumference. "So anyway, when I discovers the first foot, the murder squad lands in and hooshes me out – says no cutting or anything till forensics have cleared the site." He paused for dramatic effect, realigning his hips and cocking up an eyebrow. "But sure in the hustle and bustle of it all don't I realise I've gone and lost me new watch, that my better half got me?" He leaned on the glossy red kitchen, his arms crossed, half-whispering, "And to tell the truth if she thought I lost it – it was a Breitling, very expensive – there would have been another body laid out in the funeral parlour."

"So you returned to the enclosure? Back to the scene of the crime if you will?" The line came out as a joke and reminded January to watch her alcohol intake. A hyper-giddiness began to rise as Jack refilled their glasses.

"Aye, you have it now. I tipped back up to the field, real early in the morning. The tractor and all was still there so I had half an idea where it could have dropped. So I was looking around and there it was behind the wheel of the trailer. Forensics mustn't have got to it, ha! I'm loving all the lingo, hey," he said.

January could tell he was enjoying his role in it all.

"As I was leaving the field don't I sees in front of

me, a load of muck dug up, real fresh earth, you know. So I – now I know I probably shouldn't have – but I had a bit of a root around. There was a wee bit of light rising so I came across a corner of an ould bin bag. There's been fuckers dumping in all of the ditches roundabouts so I thought I would open it up and get a phone bill to see whose it was."

A set of headlights flashed brightly along the kitchen cabinets from the front window.

"Oh dear, I'm blocking that person," said January.

"Hould on, they'll live, it's only her mother. So of course I tugs the corner and, lo and behold, the smell that comes loose, well, Jaysus Christ Almighty, it was the stench of a dead body. Not much of a smell, it was all bones, but I'd know it from around the farm. I says to myself I should hold me horses here and call the gardaí in, still thinking it was someone dumping a dead ewe or something. And that was that – they come, seal it up and send me on me way. At least I found the watch."

"A just reward."

The car beeped outside.

"So that's that," he said, clapping his hands in a show of finality. "Aye, I'd better let you head on there – there'll be war if we're late out – she's like a greyhound ready to leap out the traps when we're heading out."

He escorted January to the door.

She thought he had sound rehearsed but that made

sense – he had recounted the tale a number of times to anyone who would listen – so she took him at his word. What didn't make sense is how he would smell decomposition if the body was thirty years old. Had he added that detail for emphasis or was he telling the truth?

"Who do you think put it there?" She was standing in front of him on the doorstep.

"Aye, it's a mystery all right. But it was funny – they must have buried her by the time I found the other lassie's foot." He scratched his chin.

"But they think she's been there for years," she said, before realising that information wasn't public.

"Oh, be the Lord! It has to be her. Theresa! Jaysus. And a she? God, they don't tell me anything. "

"My apologies, Mr Flanagan, I shouldn't have –"

"Don't be silly, your secret's safe with me."

The driver of the car trying to come in, an older lady with blonde hair, beeped the horn again and gestured at January's car angrily.

"Sure you have my number if anything else comes up, hey," he said.

"You were in school with Sinéad O'Sullivan, weren't you?" asked January, not budging from the doorstep.

"Aye – poor divil. It's the family I feel for, but at least they have something to bury now for a bit of closure."

"Were you close to her?"

"I mean, there were only fifty of us in the year in school so close enough. And they are our next-door neighbours." The emphatic storytelling was now replaced with a reticent anxiety. "But we didn't go out or anything, if that's what you're getting at. Now you better go and move that big unit or my mother-in-law will burst." A small smile now returning.

"Going now – but tell me, who do you think killed her?"

This time the driver of the other car honked and held down the horn to produce a low annoying sound.

"Wait a minute, Sheila!" Jack roared at the car, as she continued to beep. "If you ask me, it was that ould perve she went out with. Tossy from the Castle Arms. Apparently he was into that kinky shite."

The older woman was now out of the car, walking towards January. She looked familiar but January couldn't place her or her icy-blonde hair.

"But don't forget about Theresa. Just cos it was thirty years ago doesn't mean she doesn't deserve the killer caught," Jack continued.

"What's all this noise?" said Yvonne, returned to the doorstep.

"I've been waiting to get in here for ten minutes!" said the fussing older woman, unzipping her padded jacket as she pushed by January.

January raised her hands defensively saying, "I'm sorry – gone, I'm gone."

As January sat into the driver's seat she couldn't take her eyes off the old lady. She really did remind her of someone ... Could she be a relative of Setanta Molloy?

As she edged the large car out the driveway, the lights were all on next door in O'Sullivan's house. There were many cars in the drive. Irish people rallied around each other during mourning, even at this hour. She lurched the Bentley to the side of the road. As a junior reporter, she had often been tasked with doorstepping families of those tragically deceased. This was not new, so she pushed away her displeasure, got out and walked up the grass lawn. The front door was open. A small collection of wary smokers watched as she approached. She recognised Miriam, bedecked in a black dress, inside the hallway of the modest house. This is where she had seen Speedy shouting at her the night before. It seemed like months ago, so much had happened that day.

Miriam nodded to January and the other mourners moved along to the buffet of buns, apple tarts and vol-au-vents.

"I'm so sorry for your loss, Mrs. O'Sullivan," January said, quietly extending her hand.

"You knew it was her that morning, didn't you?"

"Yes, I'm sorry. I couldn't say."

"It's okay. I understand. Are you here to do some write-up on her?"

190

"Well, I wanted to learn about the sort of person she was."

She was surprised at the grieving mother's welcome.

"Come on," Miriam said. "I want to show you her room. I need a break from all these biddies."

They walked past a small kitchen brimming with tightly-permed older ladies washing up, their husbands quietly leaning in corners sipping whiskey.

"I never changed it," she said, opening the door to the small box room.

January was well aware that she had grown up in a position in privilege. The private boarding school, the large country estate – these diminutive houses were alien to her, yet she could still see the details that made up Sinéad O'Sullivan's life.

The wallpaper was cream with rows of purple and taupe strips floor to ceiling. There was a single bed, with a rose-pink candlewick bedspread that complemented the thin beige curtains.

"She was always in this room, you know, as an only child. I papered it myself when I was pregnant. The cot was exactly where the bed is now. We thought there would be more but, when they didn't come, we left her here. She liked the room."

The wall beside the window was covered in posters. The Red Hot Chilli Peppers, Duran Duran, the Dubliners and The Cure, the soundtrack to January's own adolescence. She didn't choose to listen, of course, but the pop music was foisted upon her by her school roommates.

The small bedside locker displayed pictures of Sinéad. She was a toothless and gummy toddler in one, as she tried to grab a pint of Guinness from her father. In another, she was about ten and sat on the lap of Santa Claus. The beard was no disguise for the eyes of Speedy O'Sullivan.

"How old was she here, Mrs O'Sullivan?" She couldn't help wonder about what horrors she had endured to result in multiple skull fractures, but these pictures captured the light in her eyes and reassured January she had some enjoyment in her short life.

"Ten. She was a daddy's girl – she knew well about Santy but still we all went along with it. They were close."

"She was a beautiful child."

The third frame had a larger picture, a group of fifty people. Young girls wearing long sateen gowns with floral corsages on their wrists. The young men wore tuxedos.

"That's her Debs photo. She loved getting dolled up. She pretty much moved out of home after that, for college in Maynooth."

From outside the room a woman's voice called *"Miriam?"*

"I better go, love – stay and have a look around."

"Thanks, Mrs. O'Sullivan. I wanted to ask, something rather difficult, should I come back or –"

"I'll be out in a minute, Madge!" she called through the door, then turned to January. "Ask me quick, before that one comes pooching in here."

"The fractures Sinéad had – it seems they were sustained in childhood," said January quietly.

"The gardaí were interested in that too," Miriam replied. "Look, them was different times, you know? Now you'd get arrested for even holding up a wooden spoon to a child. Speedy was a good father but tough, like his father before him. He might have smacked her around a bit, Lord knows I didn't like it and told him to stop. But that was the way it was." She looked at her shoes quietly. "I have so many regrets about …" A wave of tears came over her, her shoulders rocking in torment.

January felt she ought to try and comfort the woman with a hug. She managed a short squeeze to the hand. "I'm sorry, I don't want to upset you –"

"But, before you ask, I know he didn't kill her. There was one night – she was a brat, was Sinéad – she had been into the drinks cabinet when we were out. Speedy had laid into the drink that night too and he went to hit her with the buckle …" She paused, a roar of staccato sobs pausing her confession. "He went too far, you know, he cracked her head, but it wasn't until she had the bleed … he swore he wouldn't touch a hair on her again. I know, I failed my beautiful daughter, I should have stopped him."

"Miriam! What's happening in there?" the old

busybody shouted through the door, the brass handle moving as she tried to come in.

Miriam held the handle from opening.

"I'll come back tomorrow," said January.

"I'll be out in a minute, Madge, okay? Leave us alone."

"I know this is hard, Miriam, but I want to understand who Sinéad was."

"I know, love – sure it was the same with the radio people. I understand."

"This might be difficult also, but did you know she had a baby?"

"God, you're not going to publish that, are you?"

January failed to answer, and more sobs wracked Miriam's petite frame.

"That poor baby was born dead. I was with her, you know, in America. She was in the best hospital, had the best care. All laid on by the father. She never told me who it was. But he wanted her looked after and paid for top care throughout the pregnancy, for our flat, for everything ... Sinéad had suffered a lot in her life. She didn't want a baby brought home here and the father couldn't or wouldn't marry her."

January couldn't imagine Tossy had the means to support Sinéad and her mother in New York and pay for expensive obstetric care. It must have been Fitzpatrick. It couldn't be anyone else.

"Oh Lord, January, I have to go and sit down. You can ring me if you want to talk about her more. Have a look around her room, see who she was for yourself."

Miriam was a nice lady, thought January, but she couldn't reconcile how she would let her daughter be attacked so viciously.

The room was filled with a heavy air. January imagined all the nights that Mrs O'Sullivan would have come in to be close to her daughter. When her own parents had died, January would sleep in their bed, sniffing her mother's perfume and her father's pomade. Until one day she realised she was replacing their smell with her own and stopped.

Across from the bed, the mantelpiece over the tiny fireplace was covered in the detritus of a teenage girl. A mood ring now black, half of a friendship bracelet, an empty tape cassette – the pieces of an Irish teenagehood in the 1990s. January hadn't gone in for such items even as a youth, but seeing them in front of her transported her back in time when others at school did.

Sniffing sharply, she regained the composure of an alleged journalist. She must tell Alf to send a photographer. A local freelancer. That would ingratiate her into his good books again.

January closed the door firmly but quietly, as if not to stir the sleeping spirits of the room as she left. The funeral wouldn't be for some time yet. She felt guilty about imposing on the family. Walking by the kitchen again, she saw Mrs. O'Sullivan, now laughing with a friend. A jar of jam had cracked and the sticky red contents mingled with glass on the linoleum floor. She decided to leave her in that strange moment of hilarity that can come in the otherwise consuming passion of grief. Passing the small crowd of smokers, she tried to silence the thundering gallop of her own grief as it chased her heavily towards the car. She needed a drink. And she needed to talk to Cooney.

Chapter 22

January twiddled the bar on Venetia's gold watch, imagining her mother looking at the time. How had she spent it? It was almost ten o'clock. Venentia would have been getting ready for bed, listening to *A Book at Bedtime*. Or else listening to a record with Thomas in the library. She never knew her mother as an adult, but not a day passed where she didn't imagine what her life was like.

She had been sitting in the foyer of the Ferdia Arms for a while. The lobby was that of a traditional lodging hotel in a market town, the decor maintained over its century-long existence, leaving much of its original character intact. January sat sweating in her new camel dress. The camp porter carried weight around his hips. In some studies of the human form he would be classified as "pear-shaped", with soft features and flushed pink cheeks.

When she ordered a slimline gin and tonic, he told

her how the large fireplace in the centre of the lobby had had a fire lit in its grate every day since 1911. The sole exception was when Sinn Féin had requisitioned the hotel in 1922.

"They ate and drank the place dry, hey. It was an awful way of going on," he said.

"How long did this occupation last?" she asked, mildly intrigued.

"Went on for a year – no one who works here ever votes for them to this day. It's no wonder Fitzpatrick has kept on getting in." He dusted around the brass clock on the mantelpiece in a show of utility.

It was a quiet evening. January gathered he was glad of the diversion. Given the warring role the contemporaries of her ancestors had played during the formation of the state, and her obvious Anglo-Irish accent, she was keen to move on past this topic of conversation. She reckoned he was ten years younger than the victim Sinéad O'Sullivan, but still enquired if he had known her.

"Ah God, it's shockin' isn't it, poor Neady," he said, standing with one hand on his hip and the other waving a feather duster. "She used to babysit me when I was little. My mam and her mam was the best of friends so we woulda been put together to play a lot. Miriam was never the same since, that's her mam. And how weird that she was all shrivelled up and leathery or whatever happened there." He moved closer to

January and spoke in a loud whisper. "But there's a lot of weirdos around here, if you get what I mean."

She raised one eyebrow in inquiry.

"Well, there does be lads giving me the eye and that. Sometimes I used to go off down an alleyway or something with them but, well, I value meself more now. But they were all married or had partners, would you believe it? So appearances mean nothing around here, that's for sure." He clicked his tongue in disapproval. "And poor Theresa Flanagan, no one knows what became of her."

January ordered another drink.

Cooney finally made an appearance.

"January," he said flatly, "what are you doing here?"

He smelled fresh from the shower, but was wearing the same shirt he'd had on all day.

"Any new developments? How is the case going?"

"God, woman, you sound like the Commissioner. There's a lot of pressure to get this wrapped up as soon as. Sorry if I was angry earlier, but the exclusive is off. You withheld evidence in a murder investigation."

"I know, I know, I'm terribly sorry. I'm under pressure from my editor. Please just tell me –"

"Fine!" He held up his hands in acquiescence, pointing to the bar. "But only what I told the *Irish Independent* reporter."

January allowed the indignation that he had broken the exclusive simmer under the surface. No point in making a scene now, she had better play nice. She shifted in her seat as he ordered a steak sandwich, no mean feat at almost half ten at night. That journalist would have the update online immediately. Alf would know her exclusive was off. Perhaps she could say that the police hadn't honoured it? She would figure that out later, she thought, focusing on what Cooney was saying.

"We don't have anything useful from forensics on our second woman. The theory we're working on is that she had a paying customer, if you get me, given the outfit she was wearing," Cooney cupped a pair of imaginary breasts on his chest, and January wrinkled her nose in distaste.

"So the two victims are unrelated?"

"I mean that's what it's looking like – but we can't rule anything out," he said.

His sandwich arrived, directly from the kitchen's microwave, it seemed.

"So, what line of enquiry are you following? You're not telling me much, detective." She sounded harsher than she had intended to.

"January, I'm trying to eat a fucking sandwich!" He lowered his voice. "Sorry, but will you give me a minute. I've sat down to eat something and you're laying into me like that crowd in the Phoenix Park!"

She watched him down half a pint of water. She'd noticed he hadn't ordered a pint when they moved into the bar.

The pair sat in silence for a moment.

"Well, I'll tell you what I've been up to, shall I?" she said.

He nodded. January recounted her exchange with Jack Flanagan about his discovery of their second victim, allowing Cooney to masticate the beef.

"Okay. Flanagan's an eejit social-media wannabe. I don't think he's reliable." He sat back in the padded tweed lounge seat, balling his paper napkin up in his hands.

She hoped he wouldn't go looking for treasure in his teeth.

"The first murder was well planned, premeditated," he said. "It obviously meant something to him given the meticulous details and elaborate procedures he put the body through. He would have wanted to savour and enjoy the process. So he needed time, space to undertake these activities, and the inclination to do it. It's a particular type of murder. Our second victim, we can't say for sure – either she was a sex worker or it was a lover's tiff. The blow to the back of the head was messy. No attempt at preservation or any of the other activities. So it could be the same person and he didn't mean to kill the second victim but, when he did, he decided to place her next to his first victim."

He sipped his water as January looked around for the porter to order another drink from. Cooney continued. "Maybe he felt the space was safe. Who knows? But I think Sinéad's killer wanted her to be found, for his handiwork to be admired. On the other hand – if they are unrelated – why did the second killer bury her in the bog? Maybe he didn't know it was bogland?"

"Is this your first murder investigation?" January asked, changing direction in the conversation.

"Of course not."

"Is it your first time leading one?"

"No, second. Why, is it that obvious?"

"You must have some big fans up in the Garda Head Office," she said, wondering if that was her trying to flirt with him? The booze clouded her thoughts.

"You're right – I suppose on the grand scheme of things I'm fairly new. But the Commissioner is allowing me some room here, to prove myself,"

"That's charitable of him." The journalist in her was nonplussed that this sort of experimental leadership was being employed by the top brass on the force.

"He is acting on the recommendation of my immediate superiors. They are also keeping a close eye on things. Ringing me the whole time."

"And, what are you telling them?"

"That a number of local people are helping us with our inquiries. That there are a number of potential suspects." He sounded somewhat dejected.

They both knew there was no-one out in front as the potential killer.

"What does your instinct tell you?" asked January.

"That it's the same guy – but we need to rule out the possibility of a second killer."

"So what progress have you made in that?" she asked.

"Not much. The dad was too handy with his fists, it seems – he wasn't averse to leathering her. But he was at a wedding miles away the day she went missing. That leaves the ex-boyfriend. The older guy who runs the pub – he's has been mentioned a few times. Sure he has credentials with the IRA."

"Tossy. Yes, you can see the whole pub is kitted out with Patrick Pearse mirrors, and there's even a hand-painted version of the Easter Proclamation painted on the wall of the smoking area."

"Well, according to her mother, he was involved in 'disappearing' informants at the height of the Troubles," he said. "But I've asked the retired detective sergeant to come into the station tomorrow. We interviewed Fitzpatrick. He claims to know nothing about her, says it was a friendly chat … When Sinéad went missing he was at peace talks in Belfast, so a rock-solid alibi. He's hiding something though, I feel it in my gut." He punched his own stomach.

"Aren't all politicians hiding something?" She felt the earlier tension had dissipated.

"Ah, I suppose." He relaxed back into the padded lounge seat. "So, tell me, miss. Have you sleuthed any suspects on your travels?" He smiled patronisingly at her.

"What about the Minister?"

He yawned, scratching either side of his mouth, the pink skin stretched into a yellow pink.

"What about him?" He looked confused.

She wanted to put the idea in his head without revealing Sinéad's stillborn baby.

"When I interviewed the school friend who runs the boutique now, well, she mentioned that Sinéad had a few other boyfriends. There were rumours about her and Michael Fitzpatrick."

"Why are you only telling me this now?"

"Calm down, detective. I gave a full exposition to your deputy in that horrid little police station this afternoon. He has a full report."

Cooney ignored her and demanded, "What about them?"

"Well," said January, knowing well that her deceit would have to be discovered. "There was talk, apparently, of a romantic dalliance. After she finished university, Sinéad worked for the Heritage Department next door in Ardee Castle. He was a local TD on the opposition back bench, but still was a much-revered figure. He often arranged functions and drinks receptions to be held there."

He put out his hand in front of her face. "Enough, enough, okay? I am not going to entertain stupid gossip like this. This case has been messy enough without making it more of a circus and going to the Minister about this." He adopted a pinched, nasal voice and attempted to imitate January. "*He often arranged functions.*" Shaking his head, he returned to his usual lyrical Corkonian cadence. "You're not writing an 'out-and-about-in-town' column now."

January didn't speak. She was furious that he would tease her so badly. It was not in good humour, it was mean. He meant it in a horrible, spiteful way, the same way her Latin teacher in boarding school had laughed at her.

He stuck his hand up to the porter, and she stood up, slurping the last mouthful of her drink.

"I had better go." She tried to be jovial, but the mood was recast.

"I'm sorry," he said the same time.

"Stay for another, please," he said, ordering a lager.

"I'd better go, have some writing to do – and also have to check in on who is writing the 'out-and-about-in-town' column," she said fiercely, a bright defiance burning in her emerald-green eyes.

She stormed out of the hotel bar. "The British Ambassador's Garden Party is quite the highlight of the Dublin social calendar!" she fired at him over her shoulder.

The porter stood with a hand on one hip and his pink-and-yellow duster sticking out. His mouth was tight as he made a low hoot.

January wrinkled her nose at his response as if he were in the studio audience of a controversial TV chat show.

Who did Cooney think he was? He wasn't too long off the fraud squad. Or whatever Garda Puppy zone he spent the last few years treading water in, before getting onto the elite murder squad.

She wasn't too keen on returning to the quiet of the empty bungalow B&B. Not quite yet anyway. As she walked down Bridge Street from the hotel, she saw the orange glow from the window of the Castle Arms bar.

The podgy plaster-cast chef had had his blackboard scrubbed. It now read *"Live Trad @ Castle Arms"* and she could hear the rising and falling of a quick jig from the fiddle.

Venturing through the pub doors, she was immediately hit with the humidity of a hundred bodies. It was so packed. She had to look around for the Republican artwork on the walls to make sure it was the right place. In the corner in front of the bar sat a group of musicians on low barstools. A bodhrán player beat the skin of his drum deeply, staring into an unknown distance. On the fiddle, with busy arms and dark rounds of sweat under his arms was a familiar face. Although it took her a minute to place him, she recognised the guy from the sweet shop scratching the beat furiously. Two pretty girls were playing the flute. An older man wearing a priest's collar was playing the accordion. Jack Flanagan's wife was playing the guitar.

If she was unsure of the tune, she recognised 'The Siege of Ennis' from the signature set dance. For years she had thought the misheard name of the dance was about the floating Italian city, not the large town in Clare. There were at least ten rows of couples facing each other in a long line down one side of the bar. In sets of four pairs, they moved in and out, and in and out, and then twirled diagonally. The dancers were all elderly, the women with tight grey curls. Many of the men wore thick moustaches, but nonetheless the speed at which they moved impressed January. She felt the moisture in the air cloying at her skin.

The tables each side of the bar were all fully occupied by groups of all ages. On one table, a glut of young lads with too much hair gel, short-sleeved shirts and a ruddy farmer's tan passed around a bottle of aftershave. At another table two overweight women sat with two equally hefty men and Jack Flanagan. Each sipped at a drink, watching the frentic dancing without speaking.

Behind the bar, Tossy was lashing out tumblers of whiskey. He was sweating, rubbing his hairline as he caught the eye of his next customer. There was a queue of patrons all around the horseshoe-shaped bar waiting to get served. Twenty-euro notes were ridged from the folding and unfolding of nervous hands as they waited.

Realising how long it was going to take to get served, January had almost decided to leave when she remembered the drop of brandy that was left in the bottom of her bag. The hectic, loud music was gripping, filling her with an energy that blew any thoughts of real life out of her mind. She was hyper and dribbled the last dram into her glass. She was conscious of the four fat people watching her. Jack winked at her, and she knew he was regaling his fellow roisterers with a description of their interactions.

Many more could see her pour, but no one seemed bothered or likely to move. As she surveyed the bar again, she was surprised to see Sinéad O'Sullivan's father, Speedy, back on the same barstool. He swayed in time to the music as he thumped a heavy hand on the corner of the bar in heated conversation with another crony. As he went out to the beer garden, she followed him, squeezing past the top of the bar queue. Why was he here and not at home with his wife? It was surprisingly quiet in the beer garden, considering the crowd inside. She decided on taking another approach.

"Them that does be dancing don't be keen on smoking," he said, seemingly reading her mind. "Especially them Holy Joes coming up from Carrick on trad night. Aye, it's yourself! You had a winner at Punchestown too, you were here watching it with us, weren't you?" He was drunk, but spoke in a sing-songy-bouncy kind of style.

"I did," she said, letting him light her cigarette. "But not a patch on the big win you had. Tell me, have you much left of it now?"

"Well, I had a lot of boys owed pints to. And Tossy

of course. I had to clear my slate with him. Although he didn't charge me the half of it. Be sure to order yourself a drink. I have a tab going beyond inside." He was in good form, betraying no indication that his only daughter was found murdered in a bog down the road.

"Are you well acquainted with the barman?"

"Speak English, missus – you sound like Helen Mirren," he said, smiling.

"Do you know the barman well?"

"Jaysus, Tossy isn't the barman, he owns the whole place. Aye, I do spend far too much time sitting on that barstool." He started to pull the jeans behind his knee. "There's actually a weakness in the denim," he said as he stretched out the material. "There's a weakness there from rubbing on and off the carpet of the stool. When I was settling up with Tossy, I told him to deduct the price of a new pair of jeans. He said it would have to go under wear and tear." He laughed a chesty smoker's heave.

"How long has he had the Castle Arms?" she asked.

"Arrah, going on twenty years, around the same time –" He stopped himself for a moment as he dragged out the last breath of the cigarette. "A long time – anyway, be sure to get your drink."

He walked inside.

She followed, allowing him to slip back into his position with the miscreants he was bankrolling.

"Do they teach Protestants Irish dancing?" asked the sweetshop-keeper, standing close to January as the crowd pressed towards the counter for service. He had a cheeky grin. He unfolded a large roll of fifty-euro notes. "It's 'The Walls of Limerick' up next."

"How did you know I was –"

"Sure you told me who your family was. The big house that burned down in the fire. No offence by the way, I was teasing you." He had a strong and handsome face, albeit with a large nose. His fingertips were pink and crusty with blood from playing the fiddle with such ferocity.

"I didn't think members of the musical troupe providing this evening's entertainment would be reduced to queuing with the unwashed masses."

"Sure there does be no standards kept here, that's for sure. What are you having?"

"Triple crème de menthe, thanks."

He didn't bat an eyelid, and ordered a lager for himself. They were separated by two large ladies ordering alcopops, but he found a nook to stand.

January went over and took the drink.

"It's busy this evening, considering it's midweek," she said.

"Aye, well, Speedy O'Sullivan won at Punchestown so that accounts for about a third of the hangers-on here. The two lassies in the band there are back from America. And it's the last day of April, so payday for most of the town. I'd love to think they were brought here by our fine musical talents."

They watched as the band resumed with a slow air, taking pace.

"Aren't you needed on stage?"

"Nah, one of the other fiddlers can have a spin, my fingers are fucked anyway. If I don't play for a while the skin gets all soft and bleeds."

"Do you know where I might procure myself a taxi?" His name couldn't come to her. The triple measure on top of the other day's drinking was starting to make her unsteady on her feet. The music seemed to get faster and faster.

"Where are you staying? I'll drop you out."

"Oh no, I couldn't possibly ask that. I'm out on the Tara road, after the bad bend," she said, feeling quite drunk.

"That's on my way home," he said. "This is my first pint of the night. My car is outside."

As she followed him out of the pub she felt her eyes squinting, and her ankles feeling loose. She rallied somewhat when the fresh air hit her. He was now linking her arm.

"Well, missus, I didn't think crème de menthe was that strong. Are you alright?"

"I didn't have any . . ." the word was escaping her for food.

The row of taxis parked outside the pub were blurring and fading as her vision went black.

Chapter 23

1990

Venetia Quail was in Dublin to collect her Concord tickets, and decided to take January out of boarding school for lunch. Now aged thirteen, she towered over her mother as the waiter found them a table in Bewley's on Grafton Street.

"I don't know why you won't take me," January moaned.

Venetia had been concerned about how her daughter would traverse puberty with such bright-orange hair, but she needn't have worried. Her flame locks set off ice-white porcelain skin and her lips were generous and pink.

"We can't take you out of school any more and, besides, I want to cheer your daddy up." Venetia gently tapped her daughter's elbows. "Do they not teach you how to sit at a table in that school of yours?"

"He'd be happier if I was there." She was still pouting.

"Leave it there, and let us enjoy our luncheon."

Venetia poured them both a glass of Perrier. "Tell me, how the debating is going?"

"Fine, but the other first and second years are terrible," said January. There was little of an Irish lilt to her now plummy accent. "They're unable to rebut me properly." She sliced her burger in two and picked up one half. "And the motions are all for babies too."

"Such as?"

"This house believes television is man's worst invention," or "This house believes that vegetarians should be banned from restaurants," January swung her long fingers around to reinforce the point. "Honestly, they are so lame. When I practise at home, with you and Daddy, at least you try to challenge me. I wish we had something about hanging or abortion."

A grey-haired old woman sitting beside them coughed in shock at her utterances.

"January, please, try to have some decorum, some cop-on," Venetia scolded. "I will have a word with the house mistress, okay?"

"No, don't bother, she won't listen. Sabrina Consadine's mother complained about her learning too much Debussy and she's been stuck playing Clair de Lune since. Where are you going in America again?"

"There's a wine conference in New York, and we are visiting a friend on Lake Placid. You can come the next time."

"A wine conference? Is Daddy up to that?"

213

Her father had struggled to get back into the swing of commerce after his attack. His only interaction with wine had been to drink a bottle for lunch, before moving on to brandies and cognacs until bedtime. He could just about hold a glass and open a wine bottle, but had never regained the full range of motion.

Outside the school, Venetia hugged her daughter close.

"*Te amo* – I love you, darling. I love you with all my being. Be a good girl, won't you?"

They had the same fine bone structure, and looked like two swans embracing.

Chapter 24

Hotel linen was often scratchy, January thought. She twisted her ankles around, the sheets tight and pinning her to the hard mattress. She awoke to the sounds of a home décor show on the TV.

Where were her silk pyjamas? Her temples throbbed as she noticed a sour taste in her mouth. Her hair was matted. As she found the wherewithal to sit up, she looked in the mirror behind the TV and saw her green eyes rimmed with mushed mascara.

That's odd, she thought. There was no TV in her room ... but wait. This wasn't her room.

January also realised she was wearing a Rolling Stones T-shirt. From the hotel bathroom, she could hear the shower going. What had happened? The last she remembered was leaving the Castle Arms with the shopkeeper ... what was his name? But how did she end up here ... her eyes landed on the hotel information pack. The shower had stopped running.

She sighed when she saw his Garda badge sitting

beside his wallet and some change.

He stepped into the room, drying his back in a large bath towel.

"Well, girl, how's the head? You were in a bad way last night," he grinned. Thick black curly chest hair stretched from his collarbone downward, weaving across a defined chest.

"God, not good, not good at all." Each word pained her to say. Her cheeks flushed.

"There's some painkillers there beside you. And breakfast was delivered." He pointed at two plates. One had a Full Irish congealed on it, the other was smeared red with tomato ketchup.

"How did, em ..." She couldn't bring herself to ask.

"How come you're waking up here in my bed?" His lyrical Cork accent was bounding up and down. "I found you langers drunk outside the Castle Arms last night, about to get into the car with some randomer."

"I don't ..." She tried to take it all in. "There was something in my drink."

She couldn't see his reaction as he went back into the bathroom.

"There was not," he said with a laugh. "Sure I could see when you left here you were in a state, stumbling along." He was still smiling as he teased her. "You can't be doing that if you're working with me okay? That guy would have had you off with him and you would have been wakening up in his ould sack instead of mine."

216

"I'm telling you I didn't have that much to drink last night." Of that she was certain.

"Well, look, I'm no one to judge. Take it as a chance to take stock and pull your socks up," he said as he reappeared.

"Why didn't you take me home to the B&B? Did something happen?"

Cooney sneered at the question. "If I was going to take you anywhere it would have been to Drogheda Hospital to get your stomach pumped. You were that out of it. Not the most appealing state to be in, you know? I just wanted to keep an eye on you."

She was still half-numbed as she clambered over the bed. She picked up a slice of toast and began to nibble. His explanation didn't seem quite right – if he did mean it about watching out for her, it indicated he was some way fond of her.

She decided to stop thinking. It was hurting her head too much. She started on another slice of toast. Immediately she felt the lump come back up and ran into the dated bathroom to get sick. She was unsure if the second wave of nausea came from the hangover or the peach tiles.

"Look, you're not fit to go anywhere, climb back into bed, and watch TV, whatever."

It had been a while since she had been this hungover. The daily malaise from regular drinking slowed her down, like a comma to a radiocaster, but this was a big and black full stop. She had to get through the moment and consider the consequences of her behaviour after the nap. But she couldn't stay in his hotel room.

"Can you call me a taxi to go back to the B&B?"

"I'll take you out. I want to go to the site anyway. Eat something,"

She washed her face and attempted to scrape her now greasy hair off her forehead, but she still looked terrible. Then she was sick again. Cooney took the plastic bag from the hotel's small bin in case she heaved in the car.

She changed back into her vomit-smudged dress, applied a slick of bright red lipstick and donned a pair of bug-eye sunglasses. Her tongue was chafing over teeth furry with plaque.

Her mortification was compounded as she scuttled through reception, and into the waiting squad car. She had forgotten he wasn't driving himself. The porter, still dusting beside reception, winked at her as she tacked across the wooden floor. Cooney's deputy at least had the decency to look away from her out the driver's window to smirk at the set-up.

"Where to, boss?"

"Back out to site. I want to check it has been cleared and we know for sure there aren't any other bodies buried out on Flanagan's turf." He slung his hand out the window and slapped a palm on the car roof, in a macho show of power.

January said nothing as she mentally counted the drinks she had, and concluded there was no way this was a normal hangover.

Cooney had them pull into a petrol station and got out.

The conversation between January and the driver was pained. "So were you out last night?" he sneered.

"I met Cooney for a debrief, and noticed the set dancing so went into the Castle Arms. For one."

"Aye, it was meant to be a good one last night. To be honest, that trad band can be hit or miss but when Mossie Boyle is on the fiddle it's usually a good one."

Mossie, that was his name – she couldn't remember but now that he had said it the penny dropped.

"Do you know him well?"

"Ah, sure, since he took over the sweetshop he is building a profile for himself around the town. Dropping bags of penny sweets up to the station and that. And he's a fierce fiddler, fierce. He did my sister's wedding too. He's a video man. He seems a friendly enough chap, but some of the other lads aren't too keen on him."

"I see." She struggled to maintain her train of thought as her blood-sugar levels bottomed out. Her head thumped. "Has he any friends of the female variety?"

"Dunno about that. I think he scored one of the bridesmaids at my sister's wedding, but I don't think anything else came of it."

Cooney came out with a supply of ice creams, crisps

and fizzy drinks, and fired a Twister at each of them. She was keen to quiz him on the details of the previous evening but wanted to do so alone. She hadn't been this hungover since the Meath Hunt Ball about eight years ago, when she turned up in her signature tuxedo instead of a dress. The night concluded as she roamed around the dance floor on all fours pretending to be a horse, transporting people from the bar to the smoking area. She was still disgusted she had allowed the knees of her father's vintage Lanvin suit to be so destroyed. But there had been no one to put her to bed or hand her a glass of water. She was with the crowd but not with them. Her perennial condition.

Her phone vibrated with a call and she couldn't fight answering. It was a local number she hadn't saved.

"Hello?"

"Hullo, January?" It was Monty Passmore. "I wanted to confirm our appointment for this morning?"

"Monty, hi – listen, I am tied up this morning but can call out to you this afternoon?"

"Afternoon tea? I've got gullons of delicious clotted cream and will have cook rally up some scones!"

"Perfect, I'll see you at three o'clock." The battery was down to one per cent. She didn't care as she gorged on salty snacks and sugary drinks. Cooney dropped her to the still-empty B&B. She found her room, pulled the curtains and crashed out for the morning.

Chapter 25

January had a fine, firm bottom, he thought, as she climbed out of the squad car in her tight camel dress. He twiddled with the focus dial on the telescope to get an even better view. He knew she had spent the night in the detective's hotel room. He watched her window, and when she pulled the blinds in the room he saw how bad she looked. Make-up all over her face, hair stuck to her face. She looked to be going nowhere that morning.

From Theresa's house on the hill he had the perfect view of the crime scene. Of course he knew that there were no more bodies there, but it entertained him to see the rank-and-file officers digging up the turf with hand trowels. They were almost halfway through the large, three-acre field. There was Cooney now, bouncing round the field making himself known to the lads. He pitied Cooney. This could only end badly for him, given who his opponent was.

Cooney might have charmed them up in Harcourt

Square with the special detectives, but he would never solve this case. Eventually, and possibly not too far down the road, it would be taken off him. In all of his planning he never anticipated the State Pathologist would be so stupid, and buy him all that extra time to complete the final part of the plan.

Alf would want to be careful, if his investigations into Fitzpatrick brought him too close … Well, he would meet the same fate as January. But if he had to do that, he would. As long as his story was captured, memorialised forever. He would plead guilty, of course. Sinéad was his queen. It was the least he could do to honour her family but, as soon as he had the chance, he would shank himself or arrange something to end it all and join her.

He sat back from the telescope in his van, and opened a small cigar box stored in his special toolbox. It was a special day, so he allowed himself to touch it. Usually he only allowed himself feel it on the anniversary. But he always kept the soft, dried and leathered nipple of his queen close.

Chapter 26

The Brown Thomas car park was not a normal car park. Attached to the luxury Dublin department store, the cement walls were plastered and painted white. Each floor was heated, and the entire space was thoughtfully decorated and the walls bedecked with the latest electronic billboards. Yummy Mummies unpacked their expensive prams and tried to rein in expensively named children.

But it was still a car park. That's where Alf introduced his private investigator Frank to Sam, the private investigator engaged by Minister Fitzpatrick.

Frank looked like the sort of man a dermatologist would accost in the street. His skin was a deep red-purple colour from exposure to the sun's rays. His vocal chords were similarly ravaged by cigarette smoking and he spoke with a deep gravelly Dublin accent. Kicked out of the Garda for meddling in drugs, he now also worked as a taxi driver. He was gregarious and chatty, keeping his car clean and in new air fresheners. It was a cinnamon-vanilla smell that first hit Al, as he sat in the back seat of the newly valeted cab.

"You're watching too many movies, bud. Why are we meeting here?" said Frank, his fingertips drumming against the steering wheel.

"I want plenty of eyes and cameras around, okay? But not for others to overhear. What have you for me – quick before he arrives?" Alf said, looking into Frank's eyes through the rear-view mirror, as he was facing the whitewashed wall.

"Okay," he sniffed, opening the glove compartment and handing a large brown envelope to Alf. "Don't open that here. So it seems our friend Fitzpatrick was having it off with our bog body. Back then, the Minister was part of a pilot-scheme to record the official calls of public representatives. They were all warned their calls could be recorded, but most presumed it wasn't them. Anyway, our man was recorded from the September to the Christmas of 1996."

"The winter before she disappeared."

"Exactly. And I – now don't ask me how – I managed to get my hands on those tapes. They're in the bag on microtape for your listening pleasure. Lots of calls to the wife saying the constituency clinic was running late, or whatever, a swift call to Sinéad. They used a few B&Bs around Ardee, which considering his position, was risky enough, okay? But the most interesting of all is a call from the wife Princess Penny, yeah?"

"There is Sam in the blue Renault Megan," said Alf as the other man parked.

"Let me finish. The call comes in two days before Christmas – she says she found an antique Tara brooch in his golf bag. These old antique ones are not cheap – you're talking two or three grand. Problem is, he had already given the wife one for her birthday that year, so she knows that it's not for her. She puts that with all the late nights and calls bullshit on him. Starts calling him every name, and threatens to leave him, *yadayada*. Anyway, he was having it off with our victim and the wife knew."

"Fuck," said Alf.

"Fuck is right," said Frank. "Do you know what the wife studied in university?"

"What the fuck has that got to do with anything? She worked in Westminster, so politics or something?"

"Yeah, but at university she studied archaeology," said Frank.

Alf looked over at the other private detective's car. Sam was reading the paper, playing the part of the bored husband waiting for his wife. Fitzpatrick had found a professional PI, Alf could see.

"Okay, interesting, but what has this got to do with the Twitter thing?"

"Well, wasn't the victim found all mutilated like a bog body?"

"Yes," said Alf, as what he was suggesting sank in.

"You think she had something to do with the murder?"

"She had something to do with the murder is my gut. They have a big row, she threatens to leave him, in some sick plan they carve up our body in that big old gaff of his. He's a doctor, stopped practising after his intern year but still knows how to work a scalpel."

"It's a bit far-fetched. Why would he agree to that? They don't strike me as a Myra and Ian team."

"I'm still mulling it over, but I think they did it. There were always rumours about her family. You know, that they were into devil-worshipping and sacrificing virgins in their old place."

Alf rolled his eyes. "Well, we'll hardly be printing that. Frank, those tapes are great, I'll have a listen. And see what else you can find. Let's get this guy to spill first."

The blue Renault was further away from the shop entrance, but still in a busy part of the car park. Frank sat into the front seat as Alf sat into the back and leaned forward like a little boy in between the front two seats.

Sam was bald, but that's where the similarities between the two detectives ended. He wore a sky-blue shirt. The collar was perfectly starched and he had a small amber signet ring on his little finger. Heavy notes of frangipani and musk permeated the car from his aftershave. He folded up his copy of the *Sunday Times*. He was much younger than Frank, with a chiselled jaw and a hefty upper torso.

"Finally, ladies! Was there a delay at the blow-dry bar?" He spoke with a well-polished South Dublin accent.

"Frank meet Sam, Sam meet Frank. Frank has been working with me on this case for the past few days but we have known each other in a working capacity for many years. Frank – Sam is the investigator for the Minister."

"So listen," said Sam haughtily, "this little tête-à-tête is only happening because the Minister asked me. I wouldn't agree for anyone else. And I'm not saying a thing until you," he pointed his finely manicured finger at Alf, "swear that nothing here is going to be published. Fitzy will give you the exclusive, but nothing can be printed before that, okay? So what do you have?"

Alf was surprised to hear Sam call the Minister by the pet name, in such a jocular and familiar fashion.

"We are the ones helping you out here," said Alf. "What other publication would share this kind of information? Especially considering we have agreed to hold off publishing certain details. So you'd better start talking or this conversation won't happen."

"Fine, on Fitzpatrick's head be it, although I'm not sure what other part of his anatomy you'll be after."

"Well," said Alf, "Fitzpatrick has had some trouble keeping it in his pants. Rock stars and politicians suffer in the same way – the power must be such a turn-on. So over the years he has had a few indiscretions. A couple of call girls in Vegas, a young housewife." Sam looked into their eyes, "The Buswells jazz singer."

This was veering into tabloid territory, thought Alf. He wouldn't want the Board to accuse him of taking down the tone of the paper. But still, Buswells Hotel was directly across from the Dáil and a much-favoured haunt of politicians, lobbyists and their hangers-on. Alf remembered how alluring the raven-haired jazz singer was. She had French-looking sallow skin and a cheeky smile. She played there every Thursday evening. But one for another day, and he focused back on this list of transgressions.

"From looking at the IP address of the Twitter account that catfished him – God, where do these phrases come from?"

"MTV," Frank said, each letter drawn out in his strong Dublin accent. "There's a show on MTV."

"Whatever," Sam said. "The IP address is in Dublin, in Ballsbridge. There are so many houses, offices and even embassies there, but I think it might have been this jazz singer. She happened to live in the apartment underneath Fitzpatrick's Dublin bolthole there. She's a nutter, filled his keyhole up with superglue when he wouldn't text her back. She's totally mad as a bag of cats."

Alf watched Frank as he listened, trying to gauge his reaction. He was listening to Sam but fiddling with his cuticles in a show of distraction. "I know her, she's French – Serena something?"

"She calls herself Serena Sade, because her music is

comme triste," Sam said affectedly. "She's the only one mad enough to pull some stunt like that." He took a slurp from the melted Frappuccino in his cup-holder. "She sets up the Twitter account, pretends to be the psychic . . . when Fitzy shows some interest, she arranges the two hoors and takes the photos. Case closed. There's your woman. I found the two slags and they told me it was a foreigner who booked them, but it was a woman's voice."

"And the Minister doesn't want to go to the gardaí?" asked Alf.

"No way, José. Sure he doesn't want those pictures getting out, yeah? Fuck knows what she could do next."

From what Alf knew of the jazz singer, she was a quiet and watchful sort of creature. He couldn't imagine her cooking up a hysterical scheme to wreak some sort of techno-revenge.

"Now what do you have for me?" asked Sam.

Frank held his palm up to them both. His voice was one of the deepest Alf had ever heard, making Sam sound like a pip-squeaking jock in comparison. "Well, this was a fucking waste of time. Seems like we got the same read on it. She has a new camera, yeah?"

Frank was looking Alf right in the eye, with one eyebrow raised. Sam was holding something back. Alf let Frank take over.

"Camera?" Sam looked puzzled but continued. "Yeah, whatever – look, it's her."

"Righty-ho, bud, if you say so. I couldn't find the two women." Frank deliberately avoided the derogatory slang Sam had used. "One last thing though, the website told me they didn't renew their listing last month. When were you talking to them?"

"Good. I told them to, like, vamoose for a while and take a holiday in Tallinn or whatever Soviet dump they came from. This was a few weeks ago."

Alf couldn't stand his bigotry. As he looked at his biceps bulging through his shirt, he pictured an old-fashioned weightlifter with a teeny-tiny brain.

But Laura had spoken to the prostitute this week. This didn't make sense.

"Okay, I think we've heard enough. Thanks for your time and keep us in the loop." Alf nodded to Frank and they got out of the car.

"*Adios, amigos!*" Sam called as he spun into reverse and headed for the exit.

The two walked over to Alf's car.

"I don't know whether he's as thick as shit and that's what he thinks or whether he is stupid enough to try and cod us," said Frank, dragging his large hand across his chin in contemplation. "The IP address wasn't in Dublin, for one, it was in Drogheda, so it had to be someone local there. It was a foreign woman who booked the girls, that's what they told me too. But Fitzpatrick's West-Brit wife has an English accent. I still think it's her, Alf. But that camera is pro-quality only.

Unless she's big into photography there's no reason to have a twenty-grand piece of kit."

"They are minted," said Alf.

"That crowd are tight – she's not buying gear that much, okay? It was a pro job. She rang someone and got them waiting outside that apartment block."

"And?"

"And that's what I want to find out, who the snapper was. Figure that out and it is the key to the castle."

"Okay," said Alf. "But we're getting into murky water with Fitzpatrick here. We agreed to share what we had."

"Fuck that, Alf." Frank hacked a glob of phlegm into his mouth and swallowed it. "I asked around and Sam is very pally with the wife. I think he's in with her on this – and Sambo there has just led us on a merry dance."

Chapter 27

1990

The house mistress was usually a sly, mean sort. When she opened a round tin and offered January a powdery travel sweet, January was perplexed.

"You don't have any brothers or sisters, do you, January?" she asked, her strange smile still fixed across her gob.

"No, miss. My family is small, it's just the three of us," said January.

"And any grandparents, uncles, that sort of thing?"

"I have a cousin of some sort who lives in America, but that's it. My grandmother Emily lives in India. Look, I'm sorry I wasn't able to raise much for the sponsored swim but I –"

The teacher interrupted her, placing a reptilian-cold hand on January's.

"No, no, that's not what I mean. No, no. January, I … *um* …" She stood up and walked around to the other side of the desk.

At that moment, the school principal sheepishly

knocked on the door.

"Hello," he said mincingly, looking between January's confused face and the teacher's.

Half-whispering, he said, "You haven't ..."

The house mistress shook her head. The principal was an assuming figure who huffed and puffed around the school, screeching at students to walk right or move along or generally shake themselves. Now he sat strangely on the desk, like a lady attempting to mount side-saddle.

"Alright – there's no easy way to say this, January. But I'm afraid your parents were killed yesterday morning in a car accident."

January searched their faces. Surely, this must be one of their sick little jokes? The teachers often cruelly preyed on the students' fears and weaknesses.

The room became so hot, January felt a punch of nausea take her breath away. She felt the urge to vomit across the desk, across the house mistress's cardigan.

"Now, now, we know this is a terrible shock," the headmaster said, two fingers lightly touching her shoulders as she crouched over. "Everyone here at school will be here with you. We are your family, and we will help you get through it all, alright?"

January swallowed a mouthful of vomit, not before tasting bits of sausage. Little gnarly fatty bits, they fed the students such rubbish here. She stared at her arm until the headmaster produced a small thimble-sized glass of a spirit.

"Atta girl, down the hatch," he said, stroking her head.

The spirit steeled her, but hit her thirteen-year-old frame like a ton weight.

"Now, Miss Jones will take you for a little lie-down, alright? We can discuss it all a little while later."

Chapter 28

January didn't risk driving to Passmore Hall. After a long nap and a hot shower, she felt so guilty about writing off the morning that she ordered a taxi to keep the appointment. She gorged on gourmet petrol-station duck-liver pâté and cornichons in the back of the minivan. She still felt wretched, but drank the pickle juice from the mini-gherkins and felt better. It was an old Polish trick she had learnt on a junket to Warsaw.

When she ordered the cab from the local company, she arranged for an additional tip if the driver would avoid making small talk with her. As she bumped along the bog road to Monty's house, cherishing the silence, she thought about how she had got so drunk last night.

She had been, possibly, a bit tipsy in the Castle Arms, but not enough to completely black out. Had someone slipped something into her drink? And it was a little odd how Cooney had installed her in his hotel room instead of dropping her back to the B&B.

Although, there was a small part of her that ached

for him to climb back into bed with her when he was standing in his bath towel. Had anyone else seen her get into that state? Hopefully Cooney managed to get her under cover quite quickly.

Nips of nausea hit her as the taxi left the main road for a narrow country lane with a grass verge. It was splendidly bucolic, with ochre swashes of tall grass either side of the ditch. Passmore lived in a Georgian revival mansion, and the warm light of the sun touched off the limestone columns and steps, as the driver trundled up the horseshoe drive. After that long shower and indulgent nap, she was relatively fresh-looking, with a clean purple hip-skimming magenta 1940's style frock with neat yet prominent shoulder pads. She had found energy to pin the front locks of her hair into two victory rolls to conceal the matted mass of red hair at the back. With a bright smear of red lipstick and fresh foundation, January Quail felt a renewed energy. She would drill Monty for information related to the mutilation and burial of Sinéad O'Sullivan.

In spite of herself, January was impressed by the house as she crunched across the gravel. It was an almost-perfect replication of a James Gandon-designed house. The Irish architect had been credited with creating the perfect Irish Georgian style, and this house was nothing less than a monument to him. January made a mental note to feature Monty in the property magazine.

She was greeted by his housekeeper, who wore an

oppressive black uniform with a white apron and bonnet. Monty must be the last person in the country, if not in the continent, who insisted his staff wore uniforms. She was Mrs-Danvers-dour as she led January across the lawn to Monty. He resembled the Man from Del Monte in a cream linen suit with a straw sun hat. He lay cross-legged upon a chaise-longue, behind a wicker and glass table laden with treats and a gleaming silver tea service.

"My dear, I am glad to see you!" He remained reposed on the couch but opened his arms to bestow a welcome.

As she sat across from him on a far less comfortable wicker chair, a peacock flew upon the head-rest of the chaise longue, fanning his lusciously coloured tail.

"Why are you allowed to wear summer clothes but she's still funereal in black?" she said of the housekeeper, who had left them to serve themselves tea. January struggled to lift up the pot.

"Careful, January. That's original Huguenot." He was a caricature of himself, with a bulbous red nose and shiny paunchy cheeks, reminding January of a rotund piglet. His voice had a girlish trill to it, and he spoke with clipped vowels. "And Mary prefers the uniform. What would you have her in – padded sandals and an old golf top?"

As she examined the intricate silverwork on the teapot, she remembered hearing rumours of how

Monty had pilfered the museum's collections with his magpie eye.

"So our woman in the bog, she's not old at all?" he said.

"No, it has been officially announced. It is the body of missing Ardee woman Sinéad O'Sullivan."

"Yes, yes, m'dear I have heard all that."

January filled him in on who the police had interviewed, and how Cooney was running the investigation.

"It doesn't sound like you have much," he said, tucking into a large cream éclair, licking goblets of bright strawberry jam from his white whiskers. "I tried to contact the station. I'm sure he is in over his head."

"Your antecedent Setanta Molloy has been involved from the start," said January, glad of the sweet treats laid on. She sipped her tea from a thin china cup, with an intricate band of pattern. Below the band was a boar resting on the head of a knight. January recognised the Guinness family crest.

"He is a conman," said Monty. "I can't ever fathom why he was awarded the post when such other exemplary candidates were available. Anyway, armed with the knowledge that this murder was a modern one, I think the killer undertook the whole piece as a work of art." He sat up into a youthful stance, gesticulating and refilling her cup. "The work required to leather skin like that, undertake mutilations –"

"How did you know about that?"

"I am right though, her body was mutilated, under the nipple?"

January nodded.

"There is a school of thought that there are links between kingship and bog bodies. Maybe you can tell those bloody coppers about it if they won't listen to me. The bodies buried in the bog could be a king or queen who reigned during a time of famine, drought, or other times when the land may not have been fertile or provided a bountiful harvest." He wasn't looking at January, instead he was lining up the tea service on the table, shuffling the plates of pastries so that they shared a line. "They were buried in the bog so as for their soul to be stuck, unable to move to the afterlife. The mutilation was undertaken as part of the ritual sacrifice of these famine kings, or in this case queen. There were cases where stakes were driven through the victim's knees as they lay face down in the bog, still alive. In other instances organs were removed and nipples mutilated but never removed." He was distracted as the peacock once more jumped onto the raised end of the chaise longue. "Get down now, Jippity, you blasted beast," he pushed him off, "or I'll have Mary make spicy wings of you!"

"Whoever killed her must have been well-acquainted with the history of the bog bodies, I mean why else would they go to such lengths?" January stared unwelcomingly at the haughty bird to discourage him from approaching her. The fan of his tail was magnificent.

"I'm a historian, my dear, not a psychologist. But I think that the killer viewed the whole thing, from her disappearance, murder – maybe even her discovery – as an elaborate work of art or some attempt to rewrite history. No-one is saying what other items were found with her?"

"A hazel noose, but I don't think there was anything else."

"Well, check. If they haven't found anything in the vicinity of the body I'm sure that they will. Bog bodies were always buried with tools for the afterlife, thick blocks of prized and nourishing butter, gold accessories like brooches, even animals. Not quite the same haul as Tutankhamun had in his tomb but the same princiole. There might be something, and it is critical to understanding who did this."

"After there was such a mix-up initially, I'm sure the gardaí are making an extra-special effort to keep things running well. I haven't heard a report from forensics, but I'm sure it is being worked on."

"They made rather a balls-up of it, didn't they? No wonder they want to keep you close and see how well they are all beavering away now. In case the damned thing ends up in front of a tribunal or something."

He was keen to highlight the shortcomings of the

police, thought January. She had come to research the history, but was there any possibility it could be Monty, the old perve, who did it?

The peacock was gliding gracefully across the lawn towards the cast-iron conservatory. The breeze of the afternoon was refreshing after the sticky hot days over the past few weeks. January rubbed her arms as goose bumps prickled up the fair hair on her arms.

"Are you cold? Come, let's go inside for a drink."

"No," she said a little too quickly, "no I am quite fine here," the thought of any alcohol turning her stomach.

"Well, have a hot drop though," he said, refilling her cup with stewed Assam. "And there's something else to note, it seems these bog people were often buried on the boundary between different areas, which the ancient tribal lands were divided into. Sometimes a lake edge will be involved." He unfurled a large black-and-white map that had been rolled up on the other wicker chair beside January.

It was printed on thick white card, but was obviously a copy of an ancient map with the boundaries traced in emerald-green ink. Calculating the date from the Roman numerals she traced the Eastern coastline with her index finger. From the rounded mole of Howth Head in Dublin, around by the short sea coast of Meath and into the crook of Carlingford under the head of Ulster.

"The 1670 Maps of Cromwell," she said quietly.

"The same. All available online now but I'd rather work with the real thing. Right, you see here, where the body was found …" He pointed to the map near the word *Atherde*, but his chubby fingers did little to pinpoint the location. "It sits at the boundary of five ancient clans, Shanlith, Curragh Bog, Mullinstowne, Charlestown and Clunkine. It is possible the killer is one of their descendants, or that this boundary is relevant to him in another way."

"Gosh," said January, the wicker creaking as she sat forward on her seat. She felt queasy and tired, but was unsure if it was because of her hangover or Monty's historical contextualisation of the murderer.

Mary appeared raven-like across the faded-yellow grass.

"Here comes trouble," Monty chuckled.

"Miss, there's a message for you." She spoke from thin lips and lightly jaundiced cheeks.

"For me?"

"Yes, it's a Detective Cooney, he wouldn't stay on till I got you. He said he needs to see you and to make your way into the station when you can. It's urgent, he said."

"Oh, I had better get myself in order, thank you, Mary."

"I took the liberty of calling back the taxi man who left you out here, he'll be here any minute." She nodded and left them to it.

"Thank you, Monty. Thank you for all of your help and hospitality, I'll be sure to relay it all to the investigators."

"A pleasure," he said, raising her wrist to his sweaty lips in a show of exaggerated lasciviousness. "But a word of warning, if the killer thinks he is an ancient king, remember that they all had a chief poet. If this nutjob is as fastidious as we think, he will be looking for someone to chronicle his story. And it looks like you have already done a good job of making that be you."

Chapter 29

"Did you tell Detective Cooney where you dropped me?" she said, clambering up the high step of the people-carrier taxi. It was more like a cattle truck.

"Am I not to talk to you again? Yes, there was a Garda checkpoint on the road back to Ardee and I told someone I dropped you out to your man's house. Didn't know what his name was though."

"Righto – back to Ardee so, thank you."

He had trouble motoring around the horseshoe drive but finally got the car out onto the back road.

"It's a big gaff, isn't it? Where'd he get his money from?" the driver asked.

She sighed. After seeing how Monty kept his housekeeper in Victorian robes she felt hypocritical for silencing him on the way out. But it was this inane blathering she couldn't stand.

"Yes, it's big enough. I think his family left money to him," she said, tiredly leaning her head against the smudged glass.

It was loud in the car as they bounced back along the bog road, so he had to shout at her. "I'm not surprised you're hanging today, love, after last night. I'm surprised Tossy even served you, you were so langers."

"What do you mean?"

"I was parked in the taxi rank outside the pub last night, saw you come out with Mossie and keel over. Next thing some other bloke appears from the dark and starts shooing him away, telling him to fuck off, flashing the badge an' all."

"Oh God."

"Oh God is right. When the ginger lad fucked off you puked up on the road beside the postbox, before the other felly took yeh back to the hotel." He seemed to take great joy in telling her. His eyes flashed from the road back to her. "Don't worry, it was only a few of the drivers who seen you. Are yous all here investigating that young O'Sullivan one?"

She looked more closely at him. Through the mirror she could see the same cow's lick, same hairy nostrils as Tossy in the Castle Arms.

"Are you related to Tossy?"

"Maybe I am, what about it?"

"Did you know Sinéad?"

"*Ha*, not as well as Tossy. I would have only loved to get me hole with her, she was a tasty little thing. But I would have taken her around the place to and from parties and the like. She fair got around I'll tell you. I often collected her at all hours of the day and night from every corner of the parish." His lip curled as he sneered.

She read his licence as Gary Neel. He was a disgusting specimen, and she felt genuinely concerned for any of his other female customers. They were coming into Ardee and as they approached the station he didn't slow down.

"He's giving you a feed of Chinese, says to drop yeh in the Ming Garden," he said.

She paid him and clambered back out of the car. He leered at her as she pushed the heavy ebony-and-lacquered door into the Chinese restaurant.

She became ravenous with the smell of aniseed and garlic. She walked by a pool of contented koi fish. "Dancing Queen" played on the windpipes.

She was surprised to see Cooney and Sergeant O'Brien lunging into plates of steaming food.

"Well," Cooney said, standing up to help her into a seat, "how's the head now, January?" He sat again. "Black bean beef, prawn satay and chicken chow mein – dig in."

They were alone in this part of the restaurant.

"We got some good news this morning," Cooney said. "Forensics found some samples of male hair in the mouth of Sinéad O'Sullivan. They're running a DNA search but it could well be our killer's."

January looked around the place setting for chopsticks, but only lightweight Western cutlery was available. She spooned the soy-glazed beef as high as her wavering standards of decency would allow. She had already eaten three cream eclairs in Monty's.

"Jolly good, detective. I say – these prawn crackers are delicious. Did they come across any other items, either with her or with our first victim?

"Like what?"

"Bog butter, ceremonial swords, that sort of thing."

"No, and the Garda forensics has been combing the scene with the anthropologists. Nothing. But we have news on the child though. One of the lads found a birth cert from New York. She named Tossy as the father. That old 'RA dog. But I'm still working on the theory that we have the same killer despite the fact the first kill was meticulously planned and this second one sloppy. He left some hair behind – this is the one we will get him on. The hair is not Tossy's – so it wasn't him."

"What else did I miss?"

"I don't think there was anything else. The lads here will give you a copy of the report if you like," said Cooney. "Go on, email it to her," he directed O'Brien who was pained to be halted in consuming his overloaded plate.

She was distracted from the food as she considered Sinéad. First she had delivered a baby in New York, most likely for Minister Fitzpatrick, but Cooney didn't know this. Why did she name Tossy on the birth cert if Fitzpatrick was the father? To hide his identity? Maybe she was seeing both of them and she let Fitzpatrick think he was the father to pay for her healthcare in secret. Nobody but Sinead would really know why she had done it. For a young girl, she had experienced so much in her short life. January felt intrusive for knowing all of her personal trials and tribulations without the opportunity to see her laugh at a bad joke, or dance at a friend's wedding, or all the other instances of joy in life that Sinéad had surely experienced.

Nonetheless, January's hunger drew her attention to her plate. She was impressed with the quality of the meat and fresh vegetables. It was delicious. She allowed them to keep updating her as she guzzled the food back.

She paused to tell them about Monty's theories. Cooney instructed his deputy to check with forensics to see if anything like a brooch or bog butter had turned up, and if not to conduct another search of the area.

"Are there any local historians or historical societies that would know what families or tribes reigned in each of the four baronies adjacent to the site?" she asked. "He also felt that was important."

O'Brien paused from inhaling Colonel XO sauce to speak up. "Flanagan, what's his name? Baby, that's it. He owns that B&B. He runs the Louth Meath Historical Society. He'd probably point us in the right direction."

"Right – go speak to him as soon as you finish that," said Cooney.

"Isn't he Jack Flanagan's uncle, the chap who discovered the body? And the victim's mother's employer?" asked

January, refilling her plate "And cousin of Theresa Flanagan?"

"Welcome to small-town Ireland, Missus Big Shot," said Cooney, more flirtatiously than January was comfortable with in public.

"I'm sure by now you've realised everyone knows everyone," he went on. "If a mere connection to someone would bring them into the net of suspicion in London or even Dublin, it means sweet FA in dear old Éire."

"*Hmm*, also that taxi driver you had keeping tabs on me – he is disgusting. He completely gives me the shivers."

"Ah, ould Gary is sound as a pound," said O'Brien, fishing the final prawn from the non-sizzling dish. "He often brought me sisters home from dances and that."

"Shocking, the manner he was talking about Sinéad O'Sullivan. Disgusting," said January.

O'Brien shrugged and left Cooney and January alone at the table.

Cooney sat back into the chair and wiped his mouth, looking full and contented.

"Thank you, for taking such exquisite care of me last night," she said, sipping on her third Diet Coke, having had the time to remember her manners and shake off the terrors of the night's drinking.

"Do you remember what happened?"

"Did anything *happen*?"

"No, of course not. I wouldn't go taking advantage." He drew the left-hand side of his lip slightly to the side as he tilted his head and lowered his voice. "Would you have liked me to?"

Her cheeks flushed. "It would be," she coughed quietly, "complicated."

"You don't strike me as someone bothered by complication." He moved his hand to tug gently at the hem of her skirt, his index finger whirling under the soft skin of her knee. "In fact you seem like a complicated lady, January Quail."

The touch was electrifying. She did not often receive human contact, and it made her ache for more. "I usually find the most challenging things are the most enchanting," she said.

As he looked into her wide green eyes the waitress approached. He pulled back and paid the bill.

"I thought you would be mightily annoyed with me," she said after the waitress left.

"Who says I'm not?" He was sucking on the cheap bill mints.

"You're being flirtatious, detective."

He leaned back in his chair and stretched so that she saw a small piece of skin between the buttonholes of his shirt. "Ditto. But, yes, you were drunk last night and you must not do it again or I'll kick you off the investigation once and for all. I mean that. I can't afford any fuck-ups on this. Good work on getting that information from Montgomery though. I'll check with the Commissioner how they want me to play it with the current curator but he could be good to run through things with us. We're three days in now with no prime suspect, lots of unsavoury characters but no one who looks like a serious fit. And by the way your editor was looking for you. Do you never answer your phone?"

She couldn't even remember where it was. She checked her bag. No phone. She had often lost phones on drunken escapades but she hoped it was in the B&B.

"Okay, okay, I'll call him. What else have you been up to today?"

"Well, we interviewed her father again. He was a crap dad, alright. He was too handy with his fists, but I can't see him doing this. He's a plumber, been out of work since the bust, and had never even heard about a bog body." He folded his thick cloth napkin and dumped it in the middle of his greasy plate.

January hated to see such unnecessary staining of table linen.

"Right, it's nearly four o'clock. I'm dropping you back to the B&B to have an early night –"

She wondered if there was some sort of double-entendre, and held his gaze a little longer.

"I'm checking out of the B&B," she said. "It's too difficult traipsing all the way out there and back. I'm going to stay in the hotel."

"I'm flattered."

"Don't be – honestly it's for logistical reasons." Her smile revealed that to be untrue. "But I would appreciate a lift out to collect my items."

"Why don't you stay there tonight and try to get talking to Flanagan, the landlord? Move to the hotel in the morning?"

"*Hmm* …" She thought for a moment. She was a creature of solitude but something about the B&B scared her. The appearance of that corset had her rattled. "Fine, but I have to get some things before I go back. I'll get a taxi. Thanks again for minding me last night."

The Chinese luncheon was delicious but she had eaten far too much and it sat heavily in her tummy, stretching the vintage crepe into a small paunch. She had misplaced her corset the night before. Had Cooney removed it? It must be still in his room.

And so began her quest for snuff. She had meant to ask Monty for some, as it could be difficult to track down. The evening felt cooler than the past few weeks and she missed a jacket as she visited the chain-branded convenience shops on the main street. Her father had always left half-used tins of the stuff lying around and it gave her the taste for the smokeless tobacco at an early age. There used to be many different brands, but McChrystal's was the only one available now. She was about to give up hope when she arrived at Mossie's shop. She wondered what he would have to say for himself.

January caught a glimpse of herself in the window.

She looked haggard and wrecked. How would Cooney have an interest in her? The cosmetic veneer she had managed for Monty was well and truly gone and she felt like an old seaman tramping the streets. As she waited in the shop she collected all manner of sweets and spotted the snuff behind the counter.

Mossie the shopkeeper showed no similar signs of disarray. He appeared in a hum of aftershave and hair gel. January cringed more at the short-sleeved white check shirt than her own regrets about the previous evening.

"Back to see me again?" he guffawed. "I'm about to lock up early. How are you feeling?"

"A little tired, but fine. I'm sorry if I –"

"No need to apologise, it happens to us all. The policeman caused a bit of a scene. I don't know what he thought I was trying to do."

She tucked a stiff lock of hair behind her ear and all but laid bare the charge: "Yes, I can't understand how I got so drunk."

Without flinching, he said, "Well, to tell you the truth, it mightn't have been the crème de whatever you asked me for. Tossy has a reputation for selling moonshine. God knows no one else would have ordered that drink in there. I'd say it might have been *poitín* with green food colouring."

"I had some from that bottle earlier in the day and it was fine. It wasn't *poitín*. Or anything unusual. And I consider myself a connoisseur of crème de menthe. I am well used to drinking it … and I know my limits. That's what makes it all the more unusual. Like my drink had been spiked or something."

"Oh ho, sure that's what we all say, isn't it? Or maybe 'The tenth pint I had was gone off'."

January detected nothing about his demeanour which seemed rattled. No flicker of concern across his gappy smile. "*Hmm*, anyway, I've been wandering the streets looking for some snuff. I see I'm in luck here."

"Jaysus that," he spun around "I've been meaning to dump it – God knows how long it's been there. You can have it sure."

"Thank you. Are you going out somewhere?"

"Yes, I'm playing a gig in Drogheda tonight, some do that Fitzpatrick is having, a fundraiser for his election," he said without any emotion. Then changing his accent to a baritone drawl, "I'm playing the violin though, not the fiddle."

"Okay, well, enjoy it. Thanks again."

"See you soon, remember you know where I am."

The friendly comment served to remind her that he in fact knew exactly where she was staying, alone.

She hailed a taxi back out to the B&B and cursed herself for being so compromised in Mossie's company. He seemed more attractive last night. Now she was repulsed by his chicken-like, red, freckled arms peeking from that shirt from the black hole of taste that was the Noughties.

Chapter 30

This particular silk chemise had been a new purchase, in a moment of amorous aspiration. But it was yet unseen by any third party aside from Leopoldina. January enjoyed the dry and delicate sensation as she slipped it over her freshly showered skin. Rubbing some expensive frangipani body oil into her joints, she wondered if old Tossy knew about Sinéad's pregnancy. Despite his membership to the organisation that maimed her father, she was positively disposed towards him.

Exhausted, she lay down, falling heavily into a deep nap and waking after midnight. She remembered Alf's message to call and plugged in the phone to charge as she dialled his number.

He answered on the second attempt, the background noisy and bustling as he shouted into the phone. "January, what the fuck, I've been trying to call you. Where are you?"

"Sorry I –"

"I don't want a fucking apology – you can't disappear

and refuse all calls! I've had no copy from you today."

"Okay," she spat. "I was hungover, okay? We've all done it –"

"*Hungover – what are you?*" he said, getting louder amongst the hubbub. "*Are you sixteen?* Listen, get your arse to Drogheda now. I'm at a fundraiser for Fitzpatrick and I need your eyes in the room."

It was almost one o'clock in the morning and she had fallen asleep with wet hair.

"It's too late, Alf. I'll speak with you in the morning,"

"Hang on, hang on a minute!"

She heard the background noise wane and the click of his lighter.

"Are you there?"

"Yes," she answered meekly.

"I'm trussed up like a fucking monkey in this dickey bow. I was ringing you all day to get over here."

"Why?"

"It was the wife who organised the whole thing, we think. I'm running with the story on Sunday. But here she is tonight drawing the raffle ticket and working the room like Hillary-fucking-Clinton, happy as Larry. She's a piece of work. Where are you?"

"Still in Ardee."

"Give me an hour to do a final lap of the place and I'll be with you. I can't trust you to answer the phone or an email."

He hung up before she could protest. But she was

relieved not to be spending the early hours of the night alone, as much as she dreaded any sort of row Alf could make. Or perhaps an advance. He had tried it once or twice before. Baby Flanagan would be around in the morning to organise the checking-out, and had agreed to a chat with her.

She was glad of the new corset. She tugged the cream ribbons tight, restoring her svelte figure, and slipped a plain black shift dress over it. What would Cooney think of her other corset?

She mustered the wherewithal to apply some face cream but she was far from glamorous when Alf arrived. The tuxedo suited him. It was a far cry from his usual creased clobber. It was that sickening taxi driver that dropped him off though. The light outside the B&B was a bright and harsh one, and it shone into his beady and eager eyes like a rat, as she opened the horrid PVC door.

"That lad was telling me all about you last night, you eejit," he said, leading her straight into the bar. "Hopefully the Board won't get wind of that."

"Not if you don't tell them."

"I won't, but what are you doing? Trying to sabotage yourself?" He was slurring slightly but his lip was curling in a devilishly good-looking Sean Connery sort of way.

"Someone spiked my drink."

"Ah, go way out of that. Sure I've had my fair share

of 'dodgy pints'." He crimped two fingers of each hand in an air quotation.

"No, someone did, either the bartender in the pub or –"

"Or who?"

"Blast it, I can't remember his name. He was playing the fiddle. He owns a sweet shop – Mossie Boyle."

"Jaysus get a grip – Willy Wonky gave you a golden ticket?" As she moved to stand up, he hissed at her, "*Sit down!* There could be someone watching – it's exposed here."

"You're paranoid. Political conspiracies, now this. You're quite mad, Alf, and have had more than enough of your fair share of drink for the night."

"Why don't you come back to Dublin? It's about time you got the first draft of your scoop written."

"I'm writing as I go. I've submitted four different pieces to you. And I am moving to the hotel in Ardee tomorrow."

Now that he was sitting in front of her on the hard, pine, dining-room chair, she could see that his tuxedo was rented. The small mint-green cardboard label was sticking out beside his cufflinks. They were themselves labels and she squinted to read "*Stoke City for Life*" etched into the plated silver. His collar had been perfectly starched though, and held a sharp freshness to its form, which he ruined by loosening the dickie bow and massaging his collarbones.

"I hate to be dickied up like this," he said.

"It suits you." The hardwood of the chair reminded her how much her bones ached. "What are you doing here, Alf?" The new undergarment was yet to mould to her curves and pinched as she breathed deeply.

"It was the wife who set up Fitzpatrick."

"How can you be so sure?"

"Well, that's why I wanted to go to this drinks reception, see her in real life. So the catfisher logged onto Twitter from two locations, his house in Drogheda, and his bolthole in Ballsbridge. She is the only one who would have access to both."

"But I mean – it could be anyone who visited them?"

"It could be – but why would they? Listen to this – when Fitzpatrick was first presented to Penelope's well-to-do parents, they were nervous about him and the family silver. So they made him sign an old sort of prenuptial agreement in England, outlining what the payout to him would be in case of divorce. Which is rather boring and financial, but some special account in an English bank that's made huge gains and is worth at least five million pounds. That's significantly more than the house or anything else he has access to."

"But it's not payable if he has committed adultery?"

"Bingo – so she set him up with the two hookers, got the pictures taken. She gets to keep her rainy-day fund and he is a ruined politician."

"But why would she go to such lengths? It sounds

like he was having any number of affairs. It is an elaborate scheme."

"Well, she spent her twenties working for David Donald in Westminster. He had a sharp set of claws. He was ruthless, would do anything and expected the same of his staff. So there is more than meets the eye to Penny Fitzpatrick."

"And why were you there tonight? To see if she would admit it?"

"Well, I snuck up to her room – you know, pretending to be lost and pissed, and checked her browser history."

"That's quite unethical, Alf!"

"Ah, go way out of that! Anyway let me get to the next part. So I was leaving and I see her there on the landing, all sultry with her long locks swaying ..." He crudely drew his index fingers apart like windscreen wipers to hint at the shape of her bottom. "And she snogged me. Talk about that for a result."

"Talk about that for a Press Council complaint. I've heard enough – you'd better go and sleep off your drink."

"Ah, I thought we could talk a bit longer – you're a night owl."

"Well, this evening my nest is far too comfortable."

She left the room so he revisited the bar and topped up his tumbler. He scanned the shelves for a bottle of brandy and, surprised not to find any, settled on some peaty Scotch whisky.

Chapter 31

Bacon was his favourite flavour. But Sergeant O'Brien considered himself a crisp connoisseur. It was a classic. He was impressed with the selection behind the bar in the Castle Arms. It was only breakfast-time, but bacon was a breakfast food so it might be acceptable. Perhaps not, he thought as he surveyed the wall of plastic packets. First were the tangy ones. The prawn cocktail, scampi, pickled onion and salt and vinegar flavours that hit the tongue like a kneecap under the chin. There were the thick creamy flavours, sometimes with a hint of heat flavours like cheese and onion, buffalo, paprika, and nacho cheese. Lastly, the category he had no time for and thankfully didn't feature in the pub's catalogue, came the experimental flavours, too numbered and varied to categorise further. It had begun with roast chicken, the chemically manufactured oil of thyme overpowering. Lime, tomato ketchup, Marmite, English mustard – even Prosecco. He wrinkled his nose at the thought of what Frankenstein snacks would come next.

"What can I get for you, officer?" Tossy lashed a plastic bag of ice into a plastic barrel on the bar.

O'Brien glanced nervously towards the lavatory door. Cooney was still in the loo.

"*Em*, you've a fine lot of crisps."

"What flavour are you after?"

"I'm thinking," said O'Brien, breathing a sigh of relief as the toilet flushed. He didn't know whether his boss would end up arresting this lad or get him to rustle up some scrambled eggs.

"Morning there," said Cooney.

Tossy leaned in and folded a bar towel beside the glasses. "How can I help you, officer?" His lined face bore the cocky smirk of an innocent criminal.

"What time do you serve lunch at?"

"The soup is ready from half eleven."

"Okay, well, we would like to talk to you about Sinéad O'Sullivan. Can you lock the bar door till then?"

Tossy threw down the towel and said chirpily, "Not a problem, officers!"

He went and slid the bolt lock across the pub door.

"I've always been happy to help find her. She was the love of my life, you know?" he said when he came back.

Cooney ushered them to a booth, the sun lighting up dust specks on the mahogany table.

"Do you want a packet of crisps there, officer?" Tossy smiled as O'Brien snapped his head back to the table. "Or some tea?"

"No, listen, we won't beat around the bush," said Cooney. "The examination of the body revealed that Sinéad had delivered a baby."

"Delivered a baby?" Tossy stared into the air. "Oh God. She was pregnant?"

"And she named you on the birth cert. As the child's father," Cooney said quietly. "But it was stillborn."

"The child," Tossy didn't move, now staring at a small tear in the wallpaper. "The child," he repeated. All trace of the insolent grin had retreated to tightly drawn lips.

"You didn't know?"

"Of course I didn't know. Of course I didn't." Now looking Cooney in the eye. "That child would be almost twenty-one now. Was it a boy or a girl?"

"I'm sorry to give you the news. It was a baby girl."

"What was her name?"

"Eh, let me see … It was Cara. Cara O'Sullivan was the little girl's name."

Dollops of tears gathered in each eye, one thin stream sloped down the back of his hand to the gold face of the expensive watch as he batted them away.

"*Cara* means 'friend'. Sinéad never really had any friends. She must have really wanted that baby. Why didn't she tell me?"

They consoled him as long as they could, but Tossy knew the police had no more answers for him. They

263

left the Castle Arms and its red-eyed publican, and walked into the now busy village street.

"I want him arrested this afternoon," Cooney said, digging his thumbnail into the lock of the car key.

"What? Sure he was bawling in there."

"Yes, about the child. But he didn't ask about its mother. Strange, don't you think? Given how he tells us she was the love of his life?"

"Jesus, he was fierce upset."

"I'm sure he was. But he's our man. I want him arrested, and a warrant got for that pub."

The school-gate traffic blocked up the entire street, from the Castle Arms towards Tweedy's Threads and Boyle's Victuallers. The narrow street was impassable in their unmarked police car.

"None of these biddies will let me out," Cooney slammed a hand at the window.

"Boss ..."

Cooney noticed a rash of pink crossing O'Brien's cheek. "What is it?"

"Sorry, boss, we had a few missed calls – the phone was on sil–"

"*A few missed calls?* You're not at the fuckin' cinema, O'Brien! This is a murder investigation! Who –"

"Professor Traynor."

"Fuckin' ring her back now."

The phone synced in the speakers of the car as she answered.

"Professor —"

"Detective, I've been trying to contact you."

Behind her voice they could hear the swinging beat of the latest chart-topper chorus.

"I was questioning a subject. What do you have for me?"

"Sorry, I'm at a morning rave here. I have discovered something I'm sure you'll be interested in."

Chapter 32

Baby Flanagan had laid on an impressive spread. In the dining room, the buffet included fat, dusty cinnamon rolls, custardy pastries and croissants. He poured January freshly squeezed orange juice and delicate Earl Grey tea from an industrial-sized teapot.

"This looks charming, Mr Flanagan." She had slept well and, although hungry, was relieved to be spared a cooked breakfast. The room was chilly, and she was glad to be wearing a thin red cashmere cardigan over her black-and-white bateau-striped dress. She felt refreshed for her interview with the county's leading amateur historian.

"Miriam has the day off." He was dressed in navy trousers, with a worn but clean navy knitted Aran sweater, a grandfather collar peeping out. "Of course, the poor woman. I can't imagine what she's going through. Anyway, I'm not a great cook, so thought we would go continental."

"Ah yes, of course, how is she?" said January,

lumping mortadella ham to her plate.

He paused warily before speaking. "Not great, to be honest."

In the bright spring morning light she could see a clear resemblance to his nephew Jack. The same flushed cheeks and sandy hair.

Hesitantly he ventured, "Knowing what probably happened to her daughter and knowing for sure that she was killed are two different things. And the husband is a useless fart of a lad." He remained quiet for a while, becoming calm and still. "As you know, there was another woman who went missing, before Sinéad. Theresa Flanagan, my cousin. She lived beside that field, and disappeared one night – into thin air."

"I'm so sorry to hear that, Baby. What happened?"

"She was a piano teacher, but an outsider – you know, never came to family gatherings or went into the town. Kept herself completely alone. She had no brothers or sisters, her parents long dead. We kept the search going but, you know, life moved on for the rest of us. That is, until poor wee Sinéad went too. We held hope that when they were searching for her, they could find Theresa, but they didn't." His voice was now barely audible.

January sympathised, recounting the little she did know. She set Alf's Dictaphone on the table between them. She would usually take shorthand notes when interviewing, but decided Cooney would prefer some tape to listen to.

Baby relaxed once he began to speak about the Louth Meath Historical Society.

January allowed him continue through the origins of the historical society methodically, as Cooney had told her to let him lead the interview. He was incredibly animated and enthusiastic about the minute details of the organisation. If he was the killer his drawn-out lecture had certainly diverted her.

Eventually she intervened, asking about other bog bodies.

"Well, I'm nearly finished about the governance structure –"

"Not to rush you, Baby, but I do have an appointment this morning. If we could focus on – something like – well, have any items of historical importance been found in the field before?"

"Right. Well, there was bog butter found in that field years ago." He sat back in his chair, intertwining his fingers and adopting the rounded shoulders of an ancient storyteller. "My father came across it the same way Jack found this lassie. It was 1954, and De Valera was fighting his last election as Taoiseach for Fianna Fáil. I was only a gason. But I remember it clearly. I believe it was the twentieth of April, the day Michael Manning was hanged, the last person to be executed in such a way in Ireland. I remember listening to the radio when my father brought the bog butter to the house. My father tried putting it on the kitchen table to examine it – it was a big hoor of a thing. But my mother made him take it back to the yard. It smelt like a strong cheddar – you know, it had a pungent tang you could nearly taste. We didn't know what it was, of course. But he was in the historical society and rang up Paul Boyle the butcher, who came out and said that's what it was. Left as a sacrifice to the gods or something like that. I remember Boyle scraping away the peaty soil and asking my mother for a slice of bread. He spread a little on it. Can you believe that?"

Monty had told her that there would have been sacrifices like this discovered with the body, but this was discovered over sixty years ago. It couldn't have anything to do with the murder of Sinéad O'Sullivan, could it?

"Where is the bog butter now, Mr Flanagan?"

"Well, it was kept by the Office of Public Works for a few years, but it's now part of the National Museum's exhibition on bog bodies, on Kildare Street. But it's not even on show – they have it buried away in the back somewhere, excuse the pun!" He looked delighted with his quip.

"Did they find anything else in the bog?"

"Ancient butter and a body not interesting enough?"

He was smart enough, thought January. "Like any jewellery?" she asked.

"No, nothing like that. But when Jack found the body, I was convinced, because of the butter they had found before. That's what I was telling the pathologist – that they wouldn't want to be rooting and poking at it too much in case they damaged its archaeological value. Since the foundation of our historical society we have tried to protect artefacts from vandalism. Sure Paul Boyle eating the bog butter, that was vandalism. The giant stones at Newgrange are covered in 18th century scrawls. The family who owned the land of the other passage tomb, Knowth and Dowth Hall, they held picnics up there!" He thumped his fist down on the table and their teacups clinked in a saucer.

He was passionate about the historical association. He had a methodical nature. If he was the killer, what had been his motive? When she quizzed him further, she found that he hadn't even done a first-aid course, never mind had medical training of any description. He was a small town businessman and B&B owner, with a passion for learning and heritage since youth. As well as her current accommodation, he owned a garage on the outskirts of town, and had a small stake in the hotel chain that owned the Ferdia Arms.

They were discussing her checking-out arrangements over a final stewed, tepid cup of tea. The bergamot was overpowering as Alf made his appearance. It was almost 11.00am. He must have slept in his tux, the previously smooth shirt creased like a sheet of greaseproof paper an old woman might reuse. The front portion of his hair was askew, and he reeked of metabolised alcohol. When he spoke, he croaked, revealing the heavy smoking. Mr Timmoney had his own flaws. January reminded herself the decision for the new editor was not a closed case yet. It was a terrible truism that journalists and especially Irish journalists had a taste for alcohol. Binge-drinking and blackouts were perfectly acceptable, as long as the story was submitted and the paper ended up printed.

He introduced himself genially to Flanagan, and apologised for essentially breaking into the room beside January's. "I was a bit dishonest at the honesty bar – maybe look and see what's missing because I'm not sure myself."

Flanagan agreed to send a bill to the office of the newspaper, and once assured January had everything she needed, left them to check themselves out.

After he slammed the PVC patio doors, Alf picked at the meats, and nibbled a slice of brie on his pastry.

"Not like you to drink alone," she said without an ounce of judgement.

"No, it's not, but it's the first chance I've had," he said, quiet unapologetically. "With all that's going on with Fitzpatrick, the paper, and this interview next week …"

"We all deserve to blow off steam, if not act like a total hypocrite." Checking the time, she stood up. Cooney would be expecting her at the station.

"Don't say anything, please?" said Alf.

"Who would I tell? Anyway, how are you for this interview? Who else is going for it?"

"I know I was hard on you, I'm sorry."

"Apology accepted. So who is the frontrunner?"

"Hard to know," he said, slicking his hair back. "Timmy is gung-ho."

January snorted loudly with laughter. Timmy was the lackadaisical deputy sports editor who had been kept on because it would cost the paper too much to make him redundant.

"Anyone else?"

"Well, they're interviewing a few foreign candidates."

"Foreign?" she asked, although she often felt pretty far removed from the average Irish reader herself.

"One of the former editors from Charlie Hebdo, someone from *Private Eye* in England,"

"Two satirists? But this is a national newspaper."

"I know, I know, January. To be honest, I think you still have a chance. There has never been a female editor before. Your credentials are impeccable."

"Well, thank you. But I've been the features editor for the past five years, hardly on a trailblazing journalistic mission, am I?"

"Don't be too hard on yourself. I have written you an excellent recommendation."

"Isn't that, I don't know, unethical or something, given you are also applying?"

"Nah, sure they wouldn't give it to you without it.

"Think about sales," he said with a mouth full of flaky pastry. "It's a Sunday paper. The magazine, the features, that's a crucial reason for that decision to purchase. You've won an award at the journalist awards nearly every year since you joined the paper. Don't write yourself off, but that's not to say you can go in and wing it. You'll need to prepare and get your answers ready."

"And when, my good man, do you suggest I do that?" She folded her green leather-bound reporter's pad and clipped the lid on her navy fountain pen. It signalled she was finished with the conversation. "I have work to do."

She stood up, and started to walk out of the room, her black-heeled brogues tapping off the pine floor. She didn't need this patronising advice from him of all people.

"Don't blow this shot, January!" he called, as she slammed shut the door of the breakfast room.

She started her car and reversed out the drive. If she was truthful with herself, this wasn't her first opportunity to progress up the corporate ladder. She had interviewed for various news-editor roles and managing editor jobs over the years, but never wholeheartedly wanted them. She liked what she did. She took the pulse of Ireland, and broke many unheard-of stories. The coverage given to the use of gay dating apps by trainee priests radically changed their programme. Writing about the beautiful yet damned

273

Soviet children, adopted by barren Irish families was a release for them all. There were unprecedented numbers of failed adoptions, leaving some of the small wretches institutionalised. She loved antiques, those bizarre little receptacles of modern social history. It never jaded her each time she perused the objects for auction. She recalled her favourite items. An ornately decorated chamber pot passed down through four generations of women. A never-used and hidden plaque to commemorate the birth and death of a stillborn child. The well-worn kitchen dresser, designed to house indoor chickens. It was made from such heavy oak that the sound vibrations of the birds murmuring would not disturb the carefully placed willow-pattern saucers.

The sky was grey, with the first clouds January had seen in weeks gathered like gossiping fishwives at the corner of the patchwork of hedgerows up the hillside. It was a rare geographical occurrence to find bogland so close to a mountainous region. The road into Ardee via the crime scene was closed off, with a large white van parked diagonally across the laneway. Two orange signs warning of roadworks ahead.

Hesitantly, she took the right turn at the crossroads, but her attention was distracted by the radio and she turned up the news.

"Members of the Gardaí Siochana have arrested a suspect as part of their investigation into the murder of Ardee woman Sinéad O'Sullivan ..."

A red rash of choler rose across her pale chest and into her neck, fury at Cooney for failing to alert her to this major breakthrough.

She continued to listen as the newsreader proceeded.

"In a related matter, the Office of the State Pathologist has been heavily criticised after a junior anthropologist initially classified the remains of Miss O'Sullivan as ancient remains. The Taoiseach, himself facing a motion of no confidence this week, refused to answer a question about it during Leader's Questions in the Dáil today, when questioned by Opposition spokesperson for Justice, Pat McEnnanny."

The report cut to the parliamentarian calling for the resignation of Professor Traynor. As the report finished she changed station to calm herself down. She was breathing large deep breaths as the gravelly voice of Mama Cass sang the Mamas and Papas' song "California Dreaming".

This road was far narrower than she thought, and January, struggling to steer with the steep downhill twists and turns, found herself unable to slow down. She kicked off a shoe in fear and pressed urgently. But something was wrong. The huge car bumped heavily. Instead of slowing, it picked up a terrific pace. Kicking her left foot from her shoe, she pressed on the brake with both feet. Her teeth were tightly gritted as she pushed hard, feeling the constriction of her corset. No traction. She was getting no purchase. The car was getting even faster. An icy sweat of terror overcame her as she realised the brakes just weren't working.

January pulled the handbrake. She steered feverishly to avoid plunging into the steep ditch of the treelined mountain road. Panting deeply, she focused on her breathing to get the maximum amount of oxygen to her brain, but felt the blood rush to her hands and feet. Her primordial reflexes were taking over as a hard branch thwacked heavily, cracking the passenger side window, splintering the windscreen.

As the vehicle grew unstoppable, she spotted a large uneven pothole at the base of a trough in the road. It was massive, far too large to avoid.

As Mama Cass's voice rose up in a crescendo, the front wheel of the car buckled in the pothole, twisted sharply as the car rose up to standing, before pitching over and smashing hard down on the road. As she hung suspended by her seatbelt, the struggle to breathe was replaced by an instant darkness. A line of blood the same colour as her lipstick tracked the indent of her skull, dripping to the smashed windscreen, mingling with the leaking petrol.

Chapter 33

"Detective, I fear you're out of your depth. This is a shambles," said the Deputy-Commissioner.

Cooney was sitting across from the lacquer-haired senior officer in his airy and spacious office in Garda HQ in the Phoenix Park. The Commissioner ran triathlons, and had lithe and fit arms with a fresh-faced healthy glow that belied his sixty years. His slender finger slid up and down the silky royal-blue tie. Unlike uniformed gardaí, he wore a white shirt, with his jacket slung over the back of the chair. The high-ranking officers of the Garda Síochána wore red-and-gold bordered emblems on their lapels and in the centre of their hat. Cooney thought it looked like the uniform was on sale instead of denoting an official.

"I'm not sure if you've noticed, but this is the front-page news," said the Commissioner, a fleck of spittle hitting Cooney's lip as he laid out the day's newspapers across the desk. *The Irish Times* – 'Bog Murderer Arrested'; *The Irish Examiner* – 'Body in the Bog Killer

Arrested'; *The Times* – 'Gardaí under Fire'. Listen to this
– *'An Garda Síochána is the latest State Agency to come
under fire for the botched handling of a recently discovered
body in a bog outside Ardee, Co Louth. The body was
initially believed to be that of an ancient Celtic mummy, but
is in fact missing local woman Sinéad O'Sullivan.'*

He slammed the paper in front of Cooney, sending
the papers on the desk flying.

"I disagree, Deputy Commissioner. In the past twelve
hours we have made huge progress. Sure we have a
man sitting down in a cell in the Bridewell whose hair
was found on the body, who was known to the victim."

Cooney was exhausted. They had arrested the
suspect at three o'clock in the morning and had been
questioning him ever since. Despite his protestations
to the Deputy Commissioner, he had doubts over this
guy. An anonymous caller had tipped them off.

"You think any judge in the country is going to
allow any forensic evidence to be admitted after the
crime scene was left open to any Tom, Dick or Harry?
And the body classified as ancient bloody remains!"

"I've spoken to the Director of Public Prosecution,.
He is willing to accept the risk of this evidence being
thrown out, if we can secure a confession."

"Who in the DPP office said that? What's your man
saying down in the Bridewell anyway?" It was almost
teatime and there wasn't a trace of a shadow along his
trim jawline.

"He's not saying anything, but we found tanning materials in his shed. Sharp knives which could have mutilated the corpse. There's even a drain in one of the outhouses with traces of blood present."

"But he's not fucking saying anything? Look, Cooney, I thought putting you on this would be an opportunity for you on a high-profile case. I can't listen to any more of this. I want you to bring this along wrapped up in a shiny bow, okay? We are under immense scrutiny here. Get your confession and get it closed up. Now, I must go – I have a lunch down in Collins Barracks."

He stood to put on his jacket. He dusted off the shoulders and adjusted his tie.

"There's a lot of people in government looking at this too," he warned, as Cooney held his office door open. "I had Fitzpatrick on to me this morning. Now he'll be in my bloody ear at this Army lunch, along with the Taoiseach. He's about to lose his head. Get it sorted, lad."

"Yes, sir," said Cooney, nodding as the senior officer left through the wide glass doors of reception. The Deputy Commissioner was a friend of the family, but if anything Cooney was under more scrutiny than his colleagues.

Cooney's phone vibrated – it was the *Irish Times* calling yet again. He hung up. He refused to let the press office handle any of the media queries until he got a hold of January. But if she didn't answer her phone, that wasn't his problem. He left her another voicemail as the squad car sped down to the Bridewell. If she didn't respond in the next hour, the exclusive was off.

Chapter 34

1993

The drink receptions that Emily and Polly threw were famous throughout the county. The great and good of Meath were invited for scintillating conversation and wild antics. They both still smoked forty cigarettes a day, and the drawing room of Avonlea would be thick with smoke. It is unusual for any house fire to start in two places simultaneously. But that's what doomed the blaze to be fatal for the house.

But the festivities would begin on the lawn.

Emily had decided she would open proceedings by reading a passage from Mary Shelley's *Frankenstein*, and had donned a long white muslin gown with an empire line and puff sleeves. Her hair pinned up in curls, she looked much younger than her sixty years, crow's feet aside.

Polly wore a man's linen suit, and pince-nez, *a la* Joyce. Trestle tables heaving with bottles and glasses, she sat down on a heavy wrought-iron chair painted white as Emily directed the laying out of the flowers and the final preparations.

"Come and sit down for a minute before they arrive," Polly said, pouring a pint of Guinness from a bottle instead of sipping the sugary Pimms. She licked the thick creamy head from her lip as she noticed the first car coming up the driveway.

"Will you pour some water on me?"

"What? It's not that hot, is it?"

"No, but I want to make this dress cling. It's an old trick the Georgian girls used to do to enchant the men –"

"Why don't you ask January?"

"I don't know where she is," said Emily, guiltily.

She had tried so hard with her, but January refused to see her. There was a silent agreement that she would quietly bide her time in Avonlea – neither interfering in each other's business. January was only sixteen, but was ferociously independent.

"There's Monty, the old bugger," said Polly.

"Congratulations, girls," said Monty, slurping back a Pimms cup. "It was a long time coming. No hiding anymore."

They never hid, did Emily and Polly, but now that homosexuality was legalised they wanted to mark the occasion in their signature flagrant style.

There was a decent crowd assembled, including the local accountant, Lord and Lady Athenry, as well as former landed gentry and social climbers.

January decided to make an appearance. Emily smiled as her granddaughter slung her arm around her still sopping shoulder. The smile waned slightly as she smelled the vodka off her breath.

January was distracted by Polly lighting a cigarette. *"Tell me, Buck Mulligan, did you manage to shave today? Or were you otherwise engaged?"* January roared loudly.

Emily was ultimately neglectful of the child, in Polly's opinion, which didn't count for much. "Did you tie that dickie-bow yourself?" Polly teased her back, calmly. "Or is it a clip-on?"

Adopting the stupefied outrage of an extremely drunk person, January grabbed the dickie-bow defensively. "Hand-tied, by my own fair digits, Polly. Hand-tied." Then she snorted, "Who is that?"

She was pointing to Monty who was wearing a white shirt with red suspender belts. His sunglasses hung ominously three-quarters of the way up his forehead like older people who may need to consult the lens at any time but won't commit to wearing them normally do.

"That's Montgomery Passmore," said Polly. "He was a friend of your grandfather's, although a little younger. He's the curator in the National Museum. Why don't you talk to him about a summer job – that would be right up your street?" It wouldn't be good for anyone if January stayed hanging around Avonlea for the summer.

This particular evening progressed quickly, the sun lancing a red burn on those stuck in conversation with a dullard. They went through ten bottles of Pimms, crates of beers, wines and whiskeys. Empty bottles and cigarette butts cluttered the lawn outside Avonlea, where the revellers remained even as darkness set. It was almost midnight when the alarm was raised. Afterwards, everyone had commented that with so many people there, someone should have noticed earlier. But they were all bladdered and distracted.

One of the hired barmaids raised the alarm. The flames were already licking the curtain pelmet when she shouted for help. The fire in this room was one of the last three fires to remain lit throughout the year. But, it was on the other side of the house from the party and with the fine weather no one had bothered walking through.

The fire had burned through the ceiling and into the floorboards of January's bedroom.

Emily wailed in panic. Although she had married into the Quail family, she had lived at Avonlea for over thirty years. She loved it. Steam rose from her damp dress with the heat as Polly held her back from the windows.

The local architect was almost as distraught as Emily as he mourned the loss of the plasterwork and original sash windows. "If they come soon, the limestone will save it all. It isn't the first fire Avonlea has seen and, bydad, it won't be the last," he blustered.

January, Monty trailing behind, found her grandmother, all sobered by the unfolding tragedy,

"Granny, what happened?"

"Where were you, girl?" She clung on to the child tightly, but was furious at her absence.

"In the grotto, with Monty," said January unashamedly.

At that moment panes in the tall glass windows exploded in a cloud of sparks and splinters.

Emily renewed her wailing. "*Our beautiful home is burning down!*" She was raving, turning to the crowd. "Why are you all standing here, watching? Not helping. Fuck off, you freeloaders!"

"Look!" Polly interrupted, running towards the house. "In the nursery – there's a second fire!"

The fire had engulfed the west wing and was moving quickly through the house. It had not yet reached the entrance hall. January cradled her grandmother as she wept and wailed. Hot tears rolling down her own flushed cheeks as the loud sirens of the fire brigade became audible. The bright blue lights soon appeared, winding up the drive.

The sky glowed almost as bright as day with the height of the flames. The doctor sedated Emily.

The Quail women and Polly relocated to a local pub for the remainder of the night. They watched the red sky all night, the smoke climbing high.

In the morning, the head fire officer confirmed the house was gone. Despite battling the flames all night, pumping water from the local river, the two fires eventually met. The whole house was lost. It was too early to tell, but it seemed the second fire was started by a glass paperweight, that directed a beam of sunlight into a dried-flower arrangement.

"Did you find the fireguard from the drawing room?" asked January. Her dickie bow hung open and loose around her neck as she smoked a cigarette. She was sitting on an empty keg in the courtyard of the pub.

"Miss Quail – as I said there will have to be a full investigation – our officers wouldn't recognise what belonged where." He was still sweating from the night's exertions.

"It is distinctive. It has the family coat of arms across the metal mesh." She flicked the ash into her top pocket, before cursing herself. This was now the only piece of clothing she owned. The only physical item among her parents belongings – the priceless photos, videos, antiques, clothes.

"We will have to look. I'm sorry there wasn't more we could do."

Everyone thought someone had done this on purpose. Polly and Emily were also considered suspects for financial reasons. The locals who didn't know better thought January might have done it for insurance. Or perhaps out of teenage angst or even pure delinquency.

Chapter 35

In addition to the beautiful Tiffany lamps and old ebony ashtrays, there were peculiar items that Monty Passmore had pilfered from the national collection over the years. He kept these secret items in a nondescript modern suitcase under his bed. It included a handkerchief that an Anglo-Irish lord had allegedly used to pay for local savages to kill and eat a little girl in front of him. A small notebook wrapped in the tight skin of an African slave, detailing the tea accounts of a large merchant's house in Liverpool. A cork from a bottle of brandy that Wellington opened on the way back to London after Waterloo. He had managed to retain these bits as those who donated them couldn't help prove their provenance. But he had been pretty sure of their authenticity.

A certain amount of budget was always reserved for those dealers and treasure-hunters who sold an item to the highest bidder with no regard for national historical posterity. These oil-skinned cretins would meet him in a dingy alehouse around Smithfield, pawning their wares. Of course, a lot of it was rubbish, reproductions, but there was a steady demand for more unusual items. Items, not always historical, but certainly not for the squeamish or faint-hearted that made Monty always keep them away from prying eyes. They were the most disturbing items but the most fascinating.

A set of rosary beads allegedly infused with the ashes of a famous bishop.

One peculiar item was a reputed human nipple, cut around the areola and dried out into a slightly more textured circle of leather. The man who had sold it to him spun a yarn that a tanner had killed a young girl and this was one of the trinkets he took before burying her. It was a physical specimen to accompany a snuff film of the slaying taking place. The dealer might have been a pimp, or drug dealer, and did not explain how he had come to own it. Eventually Monty agreed to lay down a deposit and take the nipple, but the man had disappeared without producing the movie. Monty had a morbid curiosity. He knew he couldn't and shouldn't look, but he couldn't help himself. The current distaste at such items was merely a fashion in the history of humanity. He felt assured that he was carrying out his role as a guardian of the social history of the Irish as he collected them.

With items like the nipple, it was obvious they could be valuable evidence in a murder case. The video in particular, but the nipple could contain DNA of the victim, or even the killer. Since he had learned how this latest bog body was mutilated, he had pondered on contributing the evidence. He even considered leaving the blasted things outside the police station.

This evening he thought about it again as the shower whirred. He sat atop the quilted bedspread in red satin pyjamas, his fingers interlocked, waiting for his partner to freshen up.

Despite his grand tastes for other areas of the house, he preferred a homely comfort for slumber. The bedframe was four-poster, but carved from an understated cherrywood without curtains or hangings. The carpet was a recent improvement, a thick cream pile, with two small Chinese nightstands either side of the bed.

It especially excited him to hoard such illicit items under his own bed. At night he sometimes felt that he could overhear the conversations from those who first held and touched each item. Little wisps of historical whispers. Quite like sleeping beside a noisy dinner party. He was certain that with modern technology they could be forensically tested and dissected, but he preferred to keep his illicit collection under the half-lore slumber. It didn't matter too much to him if they weren't wholly authentic.

It was not an evening for lovemaking. Monty felt old and as fat, swollen and gouty as Henry VIII. There was a name for this sort of encounter, where no actual union would take place. He might have a massage, but it was even enough to have another heart to palpate in the room, the air imperceptibly damper from the condensation of their breath. The boyfriend experience, that was it, remembered Monty, the terrific old pederast.

The shower stopped and he tried not to watch the door of the ensuite too avidly as the young lad dripped onto the new carpet. He towelled his downy eighteen-year-old body as the steam of the shower evaporated off his porcelain chest.

He was of age, and consented to be there at Pervany Hall, but he was like a frightened goat. "Where do you want me, mister?" He knotted the towel at his hip.

"My boy, "said Monty, clasping his fingers, "stay where you are for a moment to let me breathe in your glorious frame."

With this little lamb on a platter, Monty decided to proceed. He ignored the winces and cringes of discomfort as he rallied his own bodily experience, abandoning the sort of care or concern he feigned in everyday life. As his satin pyjama bottoms fell to the floor, Monty remembered Wilde's quote. *"Sooner or later we all have to pay for what we do."*

Chapter 36

In school, the library had been over twenty-five feet tall. One of those special library ladders was required to access the top shelf. Although it was mainly ancient Greek textbooks, the girls would time each other racing to the top and back. January was on this ladder. But instead of the library, she was in the newly budded green leaves of an oak tree. It seemed she was overlooking her upturned … what was it? Her car? It felt like she was surrounded by books, but she couldn't think straight, the pounding in her head was so severe. She smelled her mother's conditioner and deodorant. All the products that made up the scent of a person enveloped her. *Mama*, she thought – looking around for the form of Venetia Quail.

From above, January watched the bumper seesaw gently. The vintage Bentley lay upside-down against the grassy verge. This was a strange, strange experience, like a dream or the sort of confusion one gets when one faints. The road and nearby fields were perfectly still. January listened as the leaves barely rustled on the still day. The sky was overcast, and the clouds looked cross as she stared at the angry, gnarled eyes of the oak tree. An annoying ringing came across the bogland. It was a siren, the blue of the police car flashing against the grey sky. Why would the siren be ringing here, on this abandoned road where the ladybirds now paused to question their motives? She knew that her real self was in the car, she was up in the trees.

Chapter 37

He walloped himself hard on the chin twice. He was losing it, God. His T-shirt was damp with sweat but he was cold as he sat at a table in the back of the van. The workbench was welded to the floor with a small stool on castors, allowing him to work at any location of his choosing. It was perfectly neat and orderly, he had even welded a wastepaper basket to the floor. It would never become the detritus-filled rubbish bin that most van drivers allowed.

From the coin-shaped hole in the van, he watched the upside-down car through his telescope. It was a terrible shame to write off such a beautiful vehicle. In hindsight, it perhaps wasn't his most judicious decision. He hadn't meant to kill her, just to slow her down long enough until he could fix his plan. The body was discovered too early.

The heatwave was well and truly over and he pulled on a fleece hoodie. It was a disgusting piece of clothing, of course. He would prefer to wear his Scottish woollen tweed jacket with a starched white shirt. But the fleece played the part of the sloppy local lad not up to much. *Ha*, but they would be so surprised. Scowling, he fretted that the wheels had come loose – the plan was unstuck. His plan needed to be fixed. He giggled as he slapped his stubble again. He always planned that the body would be uncovered sometime, so, even if it was quite a bit earlier than expected, it was no surprise. He had underestimated the stupidity of the State Pathologist and gardaí, to actually think it was a bog body. God. He hadn't anticipated that. He sipped the glucose drink and clicked his furry orange tongue against the roof of his mouth. He couldn't have imagined Jack Flanagan would have the power to persuade the public, or his followers on Twitter.

He was not comfortable with this divergence from his plan. Ah, he breathed, beating his index fingers like a beatnik drummer. An old car like that, well, it could possibly light up on fire. There was a good chance of that. Why was that bloody road closed? He hadn't planned for January to end up down that laneway with no other traffic and no other help.

He squinted back into the telescope. Her arms were hanging limply as her torso was belted in. He was surprised she wore a seatbelt. January struck him as someone so in love with the past that she wouldn't even have them in the car. But then that's how her parents died, wasn't it? Not wearing seatbelts.

He could ring an ambulance or the Garda anonymously. They could hardly put him in the frame that quickly? Although there had already been enough disruption to his plans. *Eurgh* – there were too many thoughts in his head. He used his hands to point to imaginary options: A) Do nothing and January would probably die, if she was not already dead, B) Ring an ambulance or C) Go over there himself.

The car was sitting in the hollow of the hill. They would wonder how he was so close to see but didn't go to help. He asked Sinéad what to do.

"What do you think, my queen? I need your advice."

Waiting, he looked up to the air flecks illuminated by the sole beam of sunshine incised through his little peeping hole.

She was quiet today. He received no response.

Looking into the telescope, he surveyed the network of hillside boreen and roads. The road beside the crime scene had been reopened. Jack Flanagan bobbed along in the black seat of his new tractor, complete with sixteen-foot trailer. He would find her. He was relieved, until Flanagan petered by the laneway towards his uncle's B&B. The thick fucker didn't notice.

He reached up his jumper, passed a stomach softened from idleness, to stroke Sinéad's amber rosary beads. He was surprised to find them on her, the day he took her. She hadn't seemed like the type, after hanging around with those dirty old men. But she was pure at heart. He remembered buying a set himself. In a little nun's shop beside the Duomo on a school trip to Florence in Fifth Year. He remembered trailing around after Sinéad as they saw triptych after apocalyptic scenario, medieval and renaissance beauties. Sinéad had sneaked out of their lodging that night, with her horrible friend Tweedy. When the teachers discovered she had gone, there was an hour or two of inertia. They all sat and waited for the two girls to come back. There was no such thing as calling parents …

A loud pop pulled him from his reminiscence. *January's car*. He peered through the lens to see the chassis engulfed in a bright, white light of flame. The whiter the flame, the hotter it is. No, he didn't want her to die. He clambered across the seat into the front of the van, and drove down the hill in fifth gear. As he was to turn onto the road, Cooney, the fucker in the squad car, sirens blaring, flew past him up to January's burning car. He continued straight, exhaling and breathing slowly as he puttered behind Jack's tractor on the other road. She wouldn't be dead now, and he wouldn't have to be helping. He threw his head back in a giggle and laughed.

Chapter 38

1997

It had been four years since they had worked together on a history project about the ancient High King, Niall of the Nine Hostages. Sinéad had been dedicated in her work, drafting and redrafting the essay. Beavering together in the small and mouldy local library, he watched as she stopped writing to check a reference. She would scratch the indent over her lips when linking facts together. Even at lunchtime, the fabled leader occupied her thoughts. One day they sat together outside as her friends played hockey. She was exempt from PE after the bleed on the brain.

"Do you think he existed?" she asked.

"Isn't that what we are trying to establish?"

"Yes, I know," she said, picking a blade of grass from her ham sandwich.

He fantasised about their life together. He would introduce her to the finest cuts of beef and cured meats.

"But, aside from all of the facts, do you think that he was real? Do you feel it?" she persisted.

"Thoughts and feeling have no place in history," he said. Ardee had lost the stranglehold on his accent, but he maintained as neutral a tone as possible with her.

"Of course they do – if a historian is angry about what happened, it influences his account. Even now historians think they are being objective – but they can't escape their own social and cultural conditioning."

"He doesn't need to have existed," he said. "It's so difficult to establish if the dates recorded make sense – but it is his legend that matters. What he is remembered for."

"We should create a time capsule, something that will last for millennia to come. We could put in the paper, photos, that sort of thing." She opened her pencil case. "Even this rubber that smells and looks like a banana. But with it we should create a grand tale, we should put ourselves into the mythical canon of Ireland. Queen Sinéad. Bury it in the bog."

The idea of it had been hatching inside him as the years through college passed. She stopped replying to his letters. Then one day, as she walked down Dame Street holding an older man's hand, she ignored him completely. Later he realised it was Michael Fitzpatrick the TD. His love turned to a historical curiosity. He would make her time capsule, but in it she would go.

Four years on, he had watched her when she returned from America, waiting for the cold weather. It would be best to carry out the preservation work in the winter. When he heard that she was going back to New York, well, that changed everything. He put his kit in order as he watched her for that last week. He watched as she would graze her delicate collarbone with an unvarnished nail as she chatted to the local publican, twiddling a thin gold chain.

The music of the nineties still reminded him of sitting in a red-hot Nissan Micra, watching as she walked up and down the main street, collecting items for her travel back to America. Three news rolls of film in the Kodak shop. She soaked up the sun, and chatted to her friends. She sat with that bimbo Sarah, both licking their ice-cream cones distractedly. He was thirsty, his bottle of Lilt empty.

His wasn't the only bungalow that was built without an architect. Young couples in the 1970s were given a few acres, and the builders plonked a pre-made design with no regard to local landscape or geographic considerations. It was a long, flat, squat bungalow painted cream with faux bricks flanking the facades. The interior was dark by modern standards.

The fact that his victim would have visited similar houses of relations and school friends did make it harder to secure against escape. There were no neighbours for half a mile, but the first thing he did was to add four-inch-thick insulation blocks to the walls of the unused dining room. He glued them directly to the marigold plaster, with a double layer around the sole rear-facing window, blocking out any natural light.

He removed the green-and-yellow flock carpet that his now deceased parents had. In an effort to improve the aesthetics as well as make it easier to clean up afterwards, he chose a mock parquet roll of linoleum to cover the bare concrete floor. The preparations took nearly a week of physical graft, made difficult by the oppressive summer heat. Geri Halliwell and Will Smith provided the soundtrack to his efforts, as he sweated in an old synthetic Liverpool football jersey.

The door's elementary lock had been lightly used during his childhood, as his parents strove to protect the rosewood double-leafed dining table and mock Queen Anne chairs from the boisterous games of three young boys. He left it in place, adding an additional metal bolt and padlock at both the foot and shoulder of the door. It was the only door to the room, at the end of the dark corridor. He had sold off the furniture to an eagle-eyed and opportunistic local antiques dealer a few months after his father died last year. Their mother had drowned in the river a decade previously, leaving all goods and chattels to the boys. The hundred pounds proffered by the slimy dealer was of much more interest than the obscure furniture.

There was no interest in his parents' four-foot bed, and he relocated it to the dining room without its pink-velour-buttoned headboard. He could burn the whole mattress and base afterwards. The Irish legal system had only started to use DNA evidence, but he had closely followed the OJ Simpson trial and was conscious of obliterating any trace of it from this room afterwards.

That's not to say he didn't want to get caught. He very much wanted to be remembered for this crime, but he would unveil his authorship on his terms. If he buried her twelve feet down into the bog, he estimated she might not be found at all. There was a chance they could find Theresa, which would be a shame as he wanted to control the story. Not having firm knowledge of this final piece of the plan disconcerted him, but it was necessary to the deceit.

Along with the rest of the world he had watched OJ's unravelling trial closely, and was furious that such sloppy work would enter the canon of famous killers. Ed Geins, Myra Hindley, Jack the Ripper – these were artists deserving of their place in the hall of fame. But they were serial killers, unable to avoid repeating kills. This would be his life's masterpiece, his sole entry into the history books. Not bad for a butcher's son from a nondescript bungalow.

Once the room was stripped, he sat down during an episode of *Neighbours* and wrote out all he had left to do on the back of his wages envelope. It was unfortunate that his Queen would be reduced to defecating and releasing any other bodily fluids into buckets in the room. He had briefly considered installing a porcelain toilet but, given the tight time frame, he abandoned that notion. He still had to sharpen his tools, purchase bleach and easy-to-prepare foods. He remembered that in school she loved ham sandwiches, so he would prepare a few plates in advance. The way his mother had done for his First Holy Communion. They would last a few days. He was happy with his work so far, but the difficult part would come once he had extinguished her life flame.

Nonetheless, in the final planning stages, he knew that he loved Sinéad too much to watch her crumble in captivity. He was no fool, he knew that's what it would be. He would only keep her for three days. He couldn't bear the thought of her fading away, mentally and physically. It was the perfect solution.

After the two latest bog bodies were discovered last summer, the Smithsonian Institute had published an article detailing the chemical conditions required to preserve the bodies, primarily a low-oxygen and highly acidic environment. There could be no guarantee that the bog alone could preserve her like her historic compatriots, so he would have to start the process in the dining room. He would remove the large bones and begin the tanning process on her flesh and skin. He would cut large tracts of his own bog from behind the house to pack her in whilst he worked. It was a large undertaking, he thought, as he sipped his cup of strong tea. But failure wasn't an option. From reading about his favourite killers, he knew that this sort of work was a vocation and a compulsion. Once started, it could not be stopped. But how few were brave enough to carry it out.

He found their old history project, and he touched the pages she had toiled over. Rereading the work, he realised that Niall of the Nine Hostages had been best documented by his poet. He knew exactly who the author of this tale would be, when the time came. But that wouldn't be for many years. Now, he needed to focus on the task in hand. Memorialising his Queen.

Chapter 39

January had tried heroin once at a house party in university with some bold people. Known affectionately as Team England, the crew comprised four boys and two girls with titles from the British Crown, who were studying at Trinity College Dublin, after being declined a place at Oxford or Cambridge. They were into all sorts, and took inspiration from the elite clubs they had been members of in prep school. Séances, drug-taking and sexual exploits were wild. January fell in with them out of curiosity.

They accepted her as a sort of translator or local guide to the strange workings of Ireland, like the scarcity of barrier contraceptives or prohibition of alcohol sales on Good Friday. One such Good Friday, she reluctantly agreed to smoke some of the opioid after a particularly active Holy Thursday raving session of the sort commonplace in Dublin in the 1990s. She was partially convinced because the drug was being imbibed using an antique opium pipe, similar to the hookah used by the smoking caterpillar in *Alice in Wonderland*. She enjoyed the soothing, comforting feeling but managed to avoid repeating the venture.

She was dreaming of that muddled morning and the softness of the drug as she tipped into consciousness to the slow beeping of a heart monitor. The cellular blanket was a dirgey brown colour. As she became aware of the clinical surroundings, the throbbing in her head found its voice and roared, cracking in front of her eyes.

"It's still nipping at you, January?"

January realised the red-haired nymph in front of her was a nurse.

She managed a nod and the nurse turned up the dial.

"Do you know where you are?" the nurse asked, checking her vitals.

January knew she was in a hospital, and she was down again, after feeling so ethereal amongst the tree leaves.

The nurse shouted out the door and a doctor came in.

"Now, January, I'm sure you're feeling out of it a little. You've been in a car accident."

His voice had a tinny ring to it.

He was also redheaded, and with the nurse they resembled a brother and sister playing dress-up.

She could feel the tingling of her fingers and knew she couldn't be, but she kind of expected him to tell her she had died, or was dead. The white of the room and the softness of the morphine made her feel like she was on a cloud. If this was heaven, she was disappointed at the lack of lyre-playing.

"Try not to touch your face." The doctor leaned in and held her wrists. He was an older man with grey running through his red hair. "I spent hours removing the glass from your face, and you also sustained damage to your right eye. We are hopeful you will regain some sight there, but it's hard to tell at this moment. Modern cars have shatterproof glass, so we don't see too much of these injuries now. You're okay, though, but you have sustained some serious injuries. Try not to talk too much. You have lacerated your face and cheek, and fractured your collarbone in the impact."

January wasn't fully taking the information in. He was like a TV doctor listing off injuries.

He shone a torch in her eye and trialled her annoyingly through a course of miniature tests. "Your right foot was fractured but, most significantly, you've lacerated a few tendons in your right arm. You may need an operation to repair these but for now you need to rest. Don't try and do too much – I want you to rest and sleep, okay?"

He listened to her chest, using his stethoscope.

"That Detective Cooney has asked me to let him know when you wake up." He nodded towards the door. "He even sent two officers to keep an eye on you."

Her bruised eyes widened as she noticed the dark-blue and navy of a Garda uniform there.

She smelt the apples from the doctor's shampoo and the perspiration breaking through – he must be at the end of a shift.

"What day is it?" asked January, her voice sounding strange to herself.

"It's still Thursday, you were in and out of consciousness this afternoon, and I'd rather like you to go back to sleep."

She moved her hands to the blackness on her right-hand side.

She couldn't take in what he was saying, or why she was there.

"The, *em*, corset protected your ribs, but one was still cracked, and a number of others are bruised."

The doctor now sat at the edge of her bed.

"Your father was Thomas Quail, wasn't he?"

January nodded, remembering how close she had felt to her mother when up in the trees, watching her car on the road. Was she in heaven now? She nodded at this man mentioning her father, wondering if he might appear.

"I treated his burns," he said slowly. "I was working in the Royal Victoria Hospital in Belfast at the time as a Plastics Fellow and he was transferred to our Burns Unit there. It was the worst case of tarring and feathering anyone had seen in modern history."

It had been so long since she allowed herself to remember him, their special times together reading.

The doctor became agitated as the machine beeped viciously.

"I'm sorry, I shouldn't have mentioned him. You need to rest now."

He stood up and left as the nurse entered to attend to her arm.

The Irish language news came on a television outside her private room. Along with Greek and Latin, January had studied the language in school. Although using the two ancient tongues more, some of the vocabulary had stuck and she caught the drift of the newsreader as she spoke about Ardee and the murder investigation. Yes, that was it – the police had a suspect in custody. Who could it be?

Why hadn't the brakes on the car worked? She remembered the loose feeling as she pushed her foot down, gaining no purchase – the car instead speeding up. She hadn't the power in her mind to think hard about this. Before she could consider the development, the edges of her reality became fuzzy as the nurse increased her dosage of morphine. She found herself drifting into a dazed sleep, into some sort of past-life regression. She was an observer of a busy, busy crowd at the Banqueting House in Westminster. All thoughts of her washed-out gown and teatime biscuits faded into nothing as she dreamt of King Charles being led to his death.

Chapter 40

Alf wheeled out the aged oil-filled radiator from under a ream of newspapers, and plugged it in under the drafty sash window in his office. Hard to believe it was nearly May, after the longest heatwave in decades. But his toes were frozen. He had cleared his desk, allowing him to fully spread out the pages of the paper that were complete for that week. Even without January present, her industrious writers had worked with the sub-editors to almost completely arrange the Features section of the paper. The entire fashion and arts and culture magazines were finished. Large white gaps told of the space she had warned them to leave for her articles. She had completed three feature pieces: one about the victim Sinéad O'Sullivan, another about the history of bog bodies and their discovery in Ireland – which he found shockingly dull. The final article, which she had meant to soak up any extra space as a bullet-pointed list, was an overview of the weirdest killers. This article, entitled "The Killer's Shovel" listed ten unusual corpses. They included a mummified body that was uncovered during the filming of an episode of CSI; the stomach of a tiger shark; a freezer full of newborn babies. The list was grotesque and compelling to read, but he could already anticipate the complaints that old dears with nothing better to do might submit.

But where was her exclusive content? He didn't want to screw her over the week before her interview. He was the first to admit the whole thing was bad. The Board wanted rid of January, but she was a good writer and a serious asset to the paper.

But this wouldn't be good enough. Over the past few weeks, he had missed his usual crime beat. He had even missed having a pint with one of his underworld informers, a tangential player in a city-centre drug feud. Of course the editor role was an incredible accolade and would be the golden seal on his career, but he thought that the time could be finally right for January. Despite her old-fashioned way of working, she would be fit for the politics such a role would involve. Look at how she weaved around the various State agencies involved in the mess? Could she go from almost sacked to the editor? They would have external adjudicators on the panel, so it wasn't beyond all hope.

His head still carried the fog of the late night and hangover. But in moments like this, as he sat at his chipboard desk, sipping tea and pluming clouds of vanilla cigarette vape, he had the strongest self-awareness. He had grown up in the Five Lamps, in a red-brick terraced council house. These drug dealers were his neighbours, and that was probably why he still felt so at home with them. He'd won a scholarship to St Aloysius Preparatory School on Leeson Street, before attending University College Dublin. But he had never felt at home there amongst the middle-class sons and daughters of professionals and big farmers. Was this a hang-up since ? Did he still not feel good enough, when compared to January's self-assuredness, confidence in her work and velvety posh accent?

His phone vibrated with a text message.

Lunch and afternoon delight?

He sighed. Women. A one-night fling with the pathologist had turned into something more regular, but he had been trying to end it. He ignored the message as he dialled January's number again. The bloody thing was still off. He dragged another slow pull on his electronic cigarette. The lawyers wouldn't release his story on Fitzpatrick for publication. Concerned about the risk of defamation. His private investigator had produced reams of printouts proving the location of the IP address from where the tweets to the Minister were sent, alleging to be the famous psychic. You don't write about gangsters for twenty years without knowing the laws inside out. But legals were worried that there wasn't enough evidence to confirm that Penelope

Fitzpatrick had framed her husband. What were they expecting, a bloody confession? As soon as he had proofed the paper he would pull everything he had and see what exactly they could write for the lead story. He couldn't hold the spot for January – he needed something ready to go.

Chapter 41

Cooney was glad that the smoking ban also included Garda interrogation rooms. He was worn out from going over Conor Boyle the past fourteen hours. Inhaling outside the Bridewell Garda Station, he watched the barristers traipse between the Four Courts and the Law Library in their black gowns. Some wore their horsehair wigs, but many flounced a thick head of hair. It was a profession he found few bald men in. He breathed the final drag of the fag, steeling himself for the next two hours. The clock was up and he had to charge the suspect or let him go. He moved inside in time, as he saw RTÉ News van pull up and the crime correspondent raise a finger to question him.

He had to push thoughts of January to the back of his mind, she was being looked after in Drogheda Hospital.

Conor looked exhausted. Cooney had arrested him straight from the butcher's shop. He still wore his plaid shirt, although they had taken off his black dickie bow and even his black ear-stoppers when he was arrested. His solicitor was a thin blonde whose perfect blow-dry was now scraped back in a greasy ponytail. Her suit jacket hung limply over the plastic chair. The stench of Conor's sweat was unbearable to Cooney as he entered and started the tape.

"All fresh, boys and girls?

He was accompanied by the lead detective from the elite Harcourt Square.

The solicitor spoke, with a slight lisp that hints to poshness bordering on inbreeding. "Detectives, my client has nothing further to add. He has been in custody now for nearly three days. If you're not going to charge him, please, for all our sakes, let him go."

She looked at Conor as he ran his thick hands through his mop of hair. Although he had a sink in his cell, his fingers remained filthy, stained with the blood of his work and the ink from fingerprinting.

Conor spoke, frustration seething as he slammed his hands down on the table. "Are yous that thick that you don't want to actually get the man who did this? I'm telling you I had nothing to do with it."

Cooney seized on this. "Man? So now you know it was a man who did it?"

"Man, woman, whatever. It wasn't fucking me, okay?"

"Well, why did you say it was a man?"

"I dunno." He shifted in his chair, unpicking the top roll of the paper water cup he had been drinking from

314

all afternoon, half-flattened with toothmarks. "I don't know any female butchers. It's heavy enough lugging around stuff."

"Was she heavy, Conor?" Cooney quizzed him as if they were compatriots in a school debating contest. They'd been through a friendly interrogation, an angry argument, a harsh one – now Cooney wanted it done.

"No, I mean I don't know. She was tall though. I'd say she was heavy is all. It wasn't me, I told you, okay?"

"Well, you're telling us that you happened to be back from London to mind your mother's sweetshop when she was on holidays, when Sinéad disappeared. But you sat in every night watching telly. No one saw you. That means you've no alibi."

"I got bad sunburn at Slane, okay, and loads of people would remember me being there coming into the shop. I've already given you their names."

"That's fine. But you've no alibi for any evening that week. And, most importantly, we have found your DNA on her. A nice, juicy root to conclusively put you with her after she was dead. How do you explain that one?"

"I don't know." He blew a fluster gasp out the side of his thick lips. "Maybe ye're getting desperate and put it there."

"Now, Conor, sure you know everyone says that. Sure that's stupid. The Gardaí wouldn't do a thing like that."

"Ye made up all those fake reports for drink driving

and speeding, didn't ye? So why wouldn't ye set me up?"

"This is a murder case, Conor."

The solicitor jumped in. "It didn't start out that way, detective, it began as an archaeological dig, if I may remind you. No judge is going to admit evidence that has no chain of custody from a body that was misclassified by the State Pathologist in a crime scene that was open to any local person – including the actual killer – for over twenty-four hours."

"That's it," said Cooney, as he slapped his fingers on the table with an air of finality. "Your barrister can make that argument in court. We're charging you with the murder of Sinéad O'Sullivan."

Cooney stood up, ignoring the wary glance of his chaperone detective. The plastic chair clattered to its side on the floor as he left the interrogation room.

"You're making a big mistake, Detective Cooney!" shouted the solicitor.

Conor shouted curses out the door after him. *"You have the wrong man here!"*

The Deputy Commissioner followed him into the corridor. "Are you mad, Cooney? You don't have substantial evidence and no confession. You can't bloody well charge him."

"With all due respect, we have a number of pieces of evidence against Conor Boyle. Forensics is crawling over that shop, cooler, everything to do with him.

They'll pick up some of her DNA, I know it. It's a gut feeling here, okay? We have our man."

"Let him go until they do find something," the Deputy Commissioner said, grinning his teeth at the younger officer. "See what he does, get your result."

Chapter 42

January wondered about the smell. She found herself becoming conscious of ammonia, and she peeped her heavy eyelids open. Blinking in the white room, the light was so bright, the side of her head seared with pain. The yellow printed hospital curtains were drawn back from the frosted glass window. The darkness to her right reminded her that her eye was bandaged. The smell was not urine, after all. There was a large bunch of cream stargazer lilies on the pine bedside locker.

She looked down at her hands, and noticed thick white bandages across each palm. Her bandaged arm ached.

The smell of the lilies reminded her of something … someone. It was hard to think. Her mind felt fuzzy, in a fog. The edge of her vision was humming, nearly twinkling with iridescence. The card, there was a card beside the flowers. The writing, it looked familiar, as if she remembered it from a Christmas card. But she couldn't read it. That was beyond her stretched consciousness. She closed her eyes, and fell back to sleep, dreaming of a dark and cold December day when she opened her post. Fitfully, she imagined Monty sitting there by the fire, in another life. It seemed the card was from him.

Chapter 43

The bright red dot indicated the phone was recording. It had been days since he had spoken to anyone and his voice sounded strange to himself. He was aware of the importance of multimedia. This could accompany the images online once January had written the story.

"I had taken these portrait shots specially. When you see the pictures of famous killers, they are nearly always technically terrible. It definitely couldn't be a mugshot, like the wild-looking Charles Manson with thick curling eyebrows or Myra Hindley, features cast in shadow. Instead, it is more like a feature-style photo you might see in the magazine of the Sunday papers, of a master whiskey blender with his casks. Rich in atmosphere, a golden glow highlighting the edges of the barrels in a maturation warehouse. Or like a cheesemaker in a Roquefort cave, wheeling out one mouldy piquant turn amongst rows and rows.

"I definitely don't want any sort of holiday snaps to turn up. You know the type the tabloids love. A lary sunburnt skinhead, arm draped around the shoulder of a floral-dressed ex-wife, heavy tar cigarette perched between pursed lips. Plenty exist of me in a professional capacity already but they will use these shots as I have asked. It has taken months to stage them properly. Alongside January's article, it will be the perfect package to memorialise me as the Preserver.

"For the pictures, I set up the camera to take the timed shots, gathering my props to tell the story of immortalising my Sinéad. The room had changed in the years since I used it to gut her. I returned it to a family dining room, to avoid detection. The only blemish was the discovery of that old tramp Theresa. I didn't mean to strangle her. The opportunity presented itself but, when it had happened, well, I panicked, worried about forensics and all that has come along since. I should have moved her before burying Sinéad.

"Back to the pictures, I tried to give the room the earthy feel of a cellar. I took them in the dark black light of a long December night, and a good thing too, seeing as they were discovered in April. Three large pillar candles flickering in the windowsill, tea lights giving a gentle pool of light in each corner. Laid atop the dining table, a well-worn mahogany table bought online, were the tools. Mossie Boyle Senior's old butchering knives and cleavers. Conor didn't believe they were lost, and plagued me for weeks before opening his little hipster victualler's in the town.

"As I laid them out, the hairs on the back of my neck raised bumpily as I remembered each slice through flesh, the satisfaction when tendon and muscle were cleaved cleanly from bone. Although it was intricate work, the cooling of her body reminded me of the tight time frame. In the end, I couldn't take them all out. Another small blemish I am unhappy with. For the fine detailed jobs, I had procured some scalpels and lancets. When I got to work, well, I managed to remove the bone in her arm, but it was impossible to take the bones without completely damaging the flesh.

"Behind the knives, I had three large vats, antique style. The ceramic vats you sometimes see in pubs whose decor has not been updated since the 1990s, labelled Brandy, Sherry and Whiskey. I had repainted them and stencilled in the correct lettering, the chemicals used to preserve the skin. Formaldehyde, a Victorian conservation tool, most-used for infant piglets, human livers and perfect-looking foetuses. Lime and caustic soda, used to swell the skin and dry it out. That was an unpleasant part of the process. For anyone who has ever visited a tannery, the smell of fats and water being siphoned from a decomposing body is eye-watering. Chromium sulphate to restore her supple and soft skin.

"It had of course taken many more than three chemicals, but only a chemist would want to read about them. The purpose of the picture was to illustrate. Beside the table, I stood. Holding the ponytail of her thick curly hair I had cut from the band. I needed something of hers here to make an impact on readers. I toyed with the idea of wearing a hide or animal skin myself, and whilst it was most likely an ancient High King of Ireland would wear a bearskin or the fur of a wolf, I felt it could look comic."

The phone beeped, letting him know there was no memory for more recordings. He looked hard at the final image: a dark green woollen smock hanging from his own broad frame, with a cream fur collar wrapped around his shoulders and a crown of ash wrapped around his hair.

It started to rain, little specks of soft water on the double-glazed bungalow window. The recent precipitation had begun to restore the greenness of the countryside, the purple hedges crisscrossing the hill. Some of them were drawn on ancient boundaries, others recent divisions by smallholder farmers.

Before he got up from the desk, he logged into his fan club online. These people, whatever they were, or wherever they came from, knew everything. In this forum on the dark web, they shared and traded videos of artwork, or victims in common parlance. They too were excited that the plans were coming to fruition. They wanted daily updates, knowing, like the others gone before, that when he stopped replying, things had moved to the next stage. They would watch online for media coverage.

The new replies since were congratulations and encouragement, all but one.

That one said:

Ireland must be pretty lame if two kills counts you as a serial killer. It's at least three according to all the criminal psychologists I've read.

This guy was always a pain, he thought. He had no kills to his name, so why did it even bother him?

"Because it is true," he said out loud to himself.

He decided to visit January. Once she had the story written, she would be his third kill.

Chapter 44

"I've come to break you out," said Alf.

January looked like a ghost, lying in the mechanical bed of the modern hospital room. Only the one emerald eye gave a sense of the woman who lay there.

"Oh, yes, please," she said, signalling for him to hand over the grapes he had brought along. "I want out. It smells terrible here, and I can't handle the amateur antiques of people on those daytime television shows. Their valuations are totally pie-in-the-sky." She sucked on a grape and paused for a moment – she did still feel tired. "They set an original Walter Keane print at forty quid." She pointed at the television, her hand still bandaged. "How did you find me, anyway?"

"You have the newspaper as your next-of-kin, January. As incredulous as that may sound, they called me."

"Yes, well, I'm more likely to get injured in work than any other way," she said, crankily, gobbling up more grapes.

"So they are releasing you today, I thought I would

take you back to Dublin." Alf was regretting the decision if she was going to stay this moody.

"They are, but I will do no such thing." She smoothed down the satin sleeves of her nightdress, the pocket embroidered with JEQ. "Monty is taking me to recuperate at his house. It is he who sent this lovely robe to me, and those lilies. Would have been stuck in one of those horrible little gowns if he had not."

She spoke with clipped words, a haughty and conceited tone he had only seen come out once or twice when she had out-drunk herself.

"But, you're not well enough – you'd want to get yourself home, January. Take some chill time. The board has postponed your interview for tomorrow so you needn't worry about that."

"Yes, I know all about that, thank you much, Mr Timmoney. But I am completely well, although admittedly I will need help feeding and bathing. Monty is lending me his nursemaid."

Alf was exasperated. "Would you cop on and live in the real world, January? You can't shut yourself up with that creep and play backgammon by candlelight. You need intensive physio if you're going to regain the full use of your right hand."

"He is not a creep, he is a good friend of mine," she said curtly.

"He is a letch. I think you should come back to Dublin with me, and stay in my house and I can take care –"

"The semi-detached in sprawling suburbia that is still quite dodgy but you're banking on the area becoming gentrified to get you out of negative equity – that house?"

"Yes," he said, hurt.

"Look, Alf, I appreciate the offer. But I need to stay here. I know who the killer is. I need to prove it."

"Fine," he said, standing up. "Here's your post by the way," and he dumped the envelopes at the end of the bed.

Chapter 45

What had got into her? Alf wondered. The traffic on the motorway to Dublin was heavy. Busloads of barely dressed young girls travelling to the capital for a concert by the latest elected songstress. He would be late for this editorial meeting. He slammed the base of his hand against the wheel. It had been years since he smoked in the car, but the cigarette lighter still worked. He shoved it in to heat up and called the office, warning them to tread lightly.

He dodged through the cars as he jerked the gear stick. It was dangerous – the rain was lashing his windscreen and the wipers slashed the water off. He knew January better than most people. In the almost two decades they had worked together, he had never heard her mention her family, or any friends for that matter. She was independent, her own woman, that much was for sure. But she had isolated herself. Of course she went drinking with him and the other journalists, always taking charge of the wine list at the

Christmas party. She would go drinking with almost anyone. But she was such good fun, an enchanting person. Despite her airs and graces, she had always treated him and everyone she met, including the lowly interns, with respect and good humour.

When she asked him to feed the parrot, he had taken it as a positive step in her opening up to him. But he was a proud man, and refused to try to make it happen, hoping she would come to him first. That had not happened.

The woman in the hospital bed was not the January he knew. She was the worst sort of snob, barely acknowledging any of the work he had done to try and help her. He almost sabotaged his own interview with the Board for the editorship to give her a better chance.

He hadn't even been able to tell her that the police had Conor Boyle in custody, the story now passed to staff reporters. Her gentleman's agreement was void, and the story was being publicly reported on.

In the years he had run the crime pages of the paper, the IRA men had always terrified him. But he enjoyed the cheap beer and women they laid on when he visited their drinking establishments. As he left the motorway and drove through Summerhill, he mentally noted the homes of the various criminal drug lords he once knew. In the early years he would hover on the doorstep, hoping to get a slice of coconut cake and a chat with Dum Dum Doyle's mother. Dum Dum was the underworld assassin of choice, and his sister was a fit young woman. They knocked heels a few times, like the other cheap and disposable women he went for. None could come close to January.

Both lanes choking with the red lights of traffic and cars, he massaged his chin, feeling the bristles on his unshaven skin. He had worked hard to buy that house, and January had commended him regularly on managing to maintain it and the large mortgage throughout the recession. He didn't even think that she actually knew this Monty guy well. Alf had never seen her with a boyfriend, but when she chose to copulate – her own term, not his – it tended to be with a red-faced, gout-ridden older gent. Much like Monty.

Perhaps it was the head injury. When the hospital called, he immediately called his contact in the traffic division who took a picture of the report and sent it to him. Someone had cut her brakes. When the car sped down the steep hillside road, its weight pushed such momentum that when the front wheel bumped into the pothole, the hefty vintage car spun upwards. It then twisted before thudding to a stop, the size of the engine and chassis crumpling the glass and side of the vehicle down around January. She was severely concussed, the doctor told him, with lacerations so deep in her arm that the tendons were cut. She would probably lose the sight in her right eye. She would struggle to hold one of her much-loved goose quills. But she could have been killed. January's tardiness in refilling the car's tank had saved her – only a few drops of diesel took light from the overheated engine. The flame had gone as easily as it arrived.

Already late, he resigned himself to missing the meeting. He drove straight across the Liffey. Someone had to feed that bloody parrot.

Chapter 46

"Do you have everything you need, my dear?" Monty wore a padded silk dressing gown. It was only four o'clock in the afternoon. The grand bedroom he had installed January in was dark, as the rain lashed tinnily on the single-glazed sash windows.

"Quite," said January without turning around from the writing desk. "I'd better get cracking, if you don't mind."

"Oh, oh yes, of course. Well, pull the bell if you need me or your lady. I'd best leave you to it." He shuffled out in his velvet slippers, closing the heavy door gently.

January was absolutely exhausted. She had underestimated how tiring it would be to check out of the hospital, source all the items she needed, and get set up here, although Monty had been extremely helpful.

The room was larger than her entire apartment, with high ceilings, and forest-green wallpaper. There were edgings of a mouldy darkness under the plasterwork. Original of course, they depicted Diana, the goddess of hunting, with her bow drawn back over her shoulder, ready to incise her quarry. The bed was four-poster, with heavy gold curtains. One side of the room had three tall windows, casting only a dismal light across to her desk. The crackling of fire logs in the large marble fireplace distracted her. The sparks spat angrily out onto the carpet. Where was the fireguard? She would have it put out – she wouldn't be able to sleep with the risk of fire. The only problem with Monty's house was that it reminded her so much of Avonlea. This room was like her parents'.

Mary had visited her apartment with a list of clothes that might fit her when she was not wearing her corset, and her back ached without the support.

She focused on the task at hand, sipping a coffee through a straw. She still had Alf's Dictaphone. It was difficult to do anything with her hands in bandages. She managed to use her fingernail to sift through the notes. At the minute, it was just a theory. She had to work on a timeline and find the evidence to prove who the killer was. He was obviously a danger to others, but there was a man already charged with the crime. She'd heard the story from the local radio station in the car home, and checked on Monty's iPad to read what had happened. Cooney was fooling himself. When she called him that morning he was on his way into court and refused to talk to her.

What she didn't know was why the killer wanted to create a bog body.

Another gentle knock at the door. She would regret accepting his invitation, if Monty was going to be constantly pestering her to have a drink.

"I'm still busy, I will come down in a few hours!" she called.

It was the maid, still ridiculously attired in a heavy black uniform, mud caught at the end.

"Excuse me, miss?"

The formality hung ridiculously between them.

She turned too quickly and her head hurt. "Yes, Mary, sorry, I thought it was Monty."

"You have a visitor."

Chapter 47

After feeding the bird and getting updated on that morning's meeting, Alf decided to get a confession from Penelope. The lawyers would have to let him run the story and it would be the big bang he needed to get the job.

He rang his investigator, Frank.

"Are you sure it's her?" he shouted into the phone mounted on his dashboard.

"Alf, we have the IP address the same – both in Drogheda and in Dublin. The pics were taken by a professional snapper. Only four of those cameras have been sold in the country, all to professional photographers, who are of course denying they took the pics. She paid them to do it. Okay, our hacker got into her laptop and read multiple logins to the fake psychic's profile – and even found the profile picture downloaded on her desktop. It was the wife alright."

"But why? I mean, I thought this was a blackmail job."

"Could be a revenge job. Who fuckin' knows with women. There could be a story there, wouldn't be hard to find some CCTV with different young ones on his lap. A few of the club owners keep a hold of that sort of thing – you know, rainy-day stuff. Available for the right price."

"That would be a great story," said Alf, knowing the paper didn't have the sort of slush fund to bribe greedy nightclub owners. "But there's something that doesn't make sense, Frank. "Why send us the pictures of the Minister with that girl in them, the girl who was buried in the bog, Sinéad O'Sullivan? They were taken a few weeks before she went missing. And they stayed hidden all that time."

"Easy – they were press shots taken at a launch – on film, remember it was the nineties. They had been sitting at home and she dug them out when the news broke. If he was having an affair with her, the wife would remember."

Alf wasn't convinced. "But those pictures were sent to January before the name was made public. Whoever sent those was showing off that it was Sinéad."

"You think the Minister did in the girl?"

"I don't know. He is a GP, and fanatical about mysticism. He has the room and medical skills. If the wife was involved why would she want to draw attention to him?"

"Revenge – I told you. A woman scorned. *Hell hath no fury.*"

Alf was hoping the call with Frank would give him some clarity. Instead he was confused.

Was this linked to January's story? She seemed convinced that she knew who did it. Knowing January, he decided to text her instead of endlessly calling. The message zoomed off.

"WHO IS KILLER?"

Chapter 48

Cooney was trying his best not to look wholly bowled over as they waited in Monty's library. The same could not be said for Sergeant O'Brien, whose Bic-shaven jaw hung open.

"Is that a real bear, do you think?" he said, his knees knocking together. "Those ceilings must be twenty feet tall?"

"Of course it's a real bear," said Cooney, clinking his coffee cup in its saucer. The spoon seemed to have no obvious home of its own in the arrangement. "He's wearing a fez, to answer your next question."

"How would anyone have so many books? It's unreal, isn't it?" O'Brien dropped wet tea leaves from the sieve as he attempted to pour his tea.

"Alright, Noddy, this is a murder investigation not a school tour – pull yourself together."

"Sure you're clattering around with the coffee –"

They both hushed as the large door opened and the lady in question walked in.

"Detective Cooney, Sergeant O'Brien," she said, a little brusquer than usual. She was wearing a mustard cardigan and simple black trousers, with a slash of red lipstick.

Cooney thought she looked well considering her injuries. A row of steri-strip faux-stitches tracked a semicircle on her forehead, barely visible under the bright red fringe. Cooney knew she had injured her eye, and the presence of the large white bandage around her head reminded him of what she had been through.

She sat down on the opposite couch.

He realised how badly injured her hands were when January allowed Mary to hold her teacup to her mouth.

"January, how are you?" Cooney set down his cup but still felt awkward on the old couch.

"Fine, officers. To what do I owe the visit?"

"Well, we wanted to see how you were doing. You look well."

"Apart from these claws," she raised up her hands with a bored look. "I've ordered an eye patch from Sotheby's but I have to wear this big bandage for another week or two."

"Oh, I'm sure your hands look worse than they are," said Cooney.

"Not likely. The tendons in my arm were severed by the shattered glass and pieces of metal."

"Well, you never know with physio, what can be restored. My grandad had a stroke and —"

"Excuse my curtness but I'm working to a deadline." She sucked back her tea. "If you have something to say, say it."

"I do, Ms Quail." His formality accompanied an official tone. It was hard to believe she had let him rub her thigh only a few days ago. "Someone cut the brakes on your car, which is attempted murder. We wanted to pay you a courtesy visit but we will require you to provide formal statements. After the crash, it was decided that your involvement in the case should be terminated – for your own safety." His tone softened. "So please, we need to talk." He signalled to O'Brien to sit down also.

Mary hovered by the door.

January shuffled her feet. "Detective, I told you, you have the wrong man." She tried to scratch her ear but the bandages prevented her gaining any traction.

"If you'll listen to me for a minute, please. It is my fault you were nearly killed. I should never have allowed a civilian to take such an active part in the case." He spoke louder as she tried to interrupt him. "The Garda Technical Bureau has found that the same pair of pliers were used to cut the brakes on your car as were found in our suspect's butcher's shop. There were even traces of animal blood on the wheel. Conor Boyle wanted you dead."

"Someone must have stolen them, cut the brakes and planted them back in his shop. Because he isn't the man who buried Sinéad O'Sullivan in the bog. Look, I'm sorry I was a bit abrupt. I am still trying to get my head around what happened. I need to check a few things, but I am convinced you have the wrong man. Whoever has the wherewithal to go to the lengths of making a recent murder look like a bog body is perfectly capable of framing someone obvious like Conor. A butcher is the perfect suspect, but perpetrator he is not. I need to check a few things and I will have a name for you."

"Who is it then?"

"I told you I need to check – that's why I must return to my work now."

"What, can I ask, are you checking that a team of five detectives, ten officers, the Garda forensic squad and the State Pathologist won't have already turned over?"

"Well, you'll hardly count Traynor as infallible after the start of the case. The one that allowed our killer to plan, hide, disrupt, flee, do whatever he wanted to?"

"Touché – but, January, please, for your own sake, rest, and forget about the case for a while. Conor is going to be charged with two murders and attempted murder, and will go away for a significant amount of time."

"I need to check a few historical facts and I will have a name for you today."

"Historical facts? What are you on about?"

"History is obviously important to this man, if you look at what he did to Sinéad."

341

"A team of archaeologists and historians have been providing guidance to –"

"They are looking for something to fit that won't fit with their theories. I must insist on returning to my work. Thank you for the visit, and I look forward to enjoying a nice bottle of Margaux with you when we have the right man." She rose to her feet. "Mary, will you show Sergeant O'Brien to the loo, please? I fear he's held on as far as he can."

And she walked out of the room.

O'Brien raised his hands in defence. "How did she know? Is she is psychic now too?"

"Off you go, I don't know how she knows. I don't know how she knows what she knows. But I don't think she's pulling tarot cards."

Mary hustled the young man out of the room.

The library now empty, Cooney poured himself another coffee from the silver pot. He picked up the cup and quickly perused the bookshelf as he put an order on his thoughts. The evidence all pointed clearly to Conor as the killer. But what January had said, her conviction, well, it had rattled him. What had he missed?

Chapter 49

The window frame dug into Monty's belly as he peered out from his bedroom window. The cheap little police car was petering away down the drive. He had not been summoned, so they were obviously here to talk with January. Their presence unnerved him. His special items, well, they had been acquired quite illegally. But it was his small tablet computer that he was most concerned about.

He was a voyeur, that was all. A curious sort. That's why he collected unusual items and experiences. He logged on to the forum, ensuring all of the signal-scrambling that the computer chap told him about was in place. The dark web sounded much more interesting than its actual appearance. Even the forum was a crisply designed cream and light blue, like somewhere you would go to update your antivirus software. As an additional level of security, Monty pretended to be a marijuana-smoking Californian.

There was a message for him.

RINAMARBH

You're right. Two kills does not a serial killer make. But cranking up another this evening. If you are nice I will post a video.

He replied:

Sorry, dude, no offence meant – would love to see your happy ending. Namaste.

Monty felt a twinge of guilt. RINAMARBH – Rí na Marbh – was the Irish for the "King of the Dead". It had to be the bog-body killer. And he was planning to kill someone now this evening. He couldn't go to the police, could he?

"*No*," he said out loud to himself, shaking his jowls against the lapels. There was too much of a risk. The killer would probably find some poor wretch to lay his crime against. If he had only done two, and decided to do a third in the space of twenty-four hours, he couldn't have done too much planning.

He reattached the iPad to the Velcro patches under his desk drawer on the other side of the room. Opening the large wardrobe, he slid back a thin brass cover. Its lens looked directly into January's room. She had reams and reams of paper laid out on the floor, recent printouts between old leather books. What was she up to? She was speaking into the Dictaphone slung around her neck. He could see in, but wasn't able to hear a word.

He had instructed Mary to light a coal fire in the room and the heat was getting to January. She had stripped down to a pair of black tights and a thin camisole top. She hadn't changed much, in the twenty years since their first encounter. Her long, thin spine and nubile limbs. She was no innocent sixteen-year-old as she had drunkenly led him to the grotto. She had led that particular endeavour. That sweetness of youth evaporated like the vodka on her breath. He looked forward to having her again.

Chapter 50

The heat in the kitchen of Fitzpatrick's Drogheda townhouse was overpowering. Despite the wind outside, the Aga was up full blast. Alf pulled forward his collar to air a line of perspiration. As Penelope filled a pot of tea, he read the front page of the newspaper. The headline called for the resignation of Professor Traynor for inadequately handling this bog case.

Penelope didn't seem to feel the warmth of the hearth. She wore a smart black cashmere jumper with a shiny gold Tara brooch, white jeans and red wedges.

"Now, Mr. Timmoney, what can I do for you?" she placed a plate of biscuits on the table.

"The Minister is away at the moment?"

"Up in Leinster House – he's busy with this privacy bill." She smiled, a bright white mouthful of veneers, her voice a luxurious deep accent. "He's being hammered in the Dáil over it."

"Ah, of course. So I have something difficult to ask you."

"Why else would you be here, Alf? Pat would kill me for letting you in, but Pat's my husband's spindoctor, not mine."

"Can we speak on the record here?" Alf placed his phone with the red button of the recording app clearly visible beside his Wedgwood mug.

"Tell me what it's about first and I'll decide."

"Why did you send those pictures to the paper?"

"The same reason you're sitting here and not outside on your arse on Shop Street." She was still smiling, like a friendly adder.

"Why is that?"

"My husband is a serial –" She paused as her mobile rang and shut it off. "Sorry. My husband is a serial philanderer. I am surprised it took you so long to figure it out. He has no fear about dipping his John Thomas into the honey pot. I even caught him with his tongue down the throat of one of my bridesmaids the night of our wedding. I've turfed more sluts and whores out of hotel rooms over the years. I've played the part of Jackie Kennedy long enough, but I'm calling time on it now. But, of course, this is my family house – all of our money comes from my family. I have been a faultless wife, loved and honoured him. And I've received nothing but deceit from him."

Alf couldn't believe what he was hearing. Never before in the history of the Irish State had the wife of a sitting Minister revealed extra-marital affairs. This interview was a landmark exclusive for the paper.

"Twice I've contracted infections." She tucked a lock of her long hair behind her ear. Speaking with incredible composure, she was the perfect victim, her only sign of distress a slight blush about the apple of her cheek. "Before I called time on our relations. He will be receiving separation papers from our solicitor this week. So you're in good time with the story."

Alf was so shocked at what she was telling him that he struggled to think of his questions. He paused for a moment as he thought he heard a door creak in the house, but Penelope didn't seem to hear anything so he proceeded. "And how did you come up with the idea of pretending to be a psychic?"

"Oh, that wasn't me." She shook her head.

Alf looked surprised. "But he thought he was meeting a psychic in that apartment?"

"I smelt the Hermes aftershave he usually wears and suspected he was going to a woman, so I called a photographer to follow him. The migraine story we concocted afterwards."

"Who was the photographer?" Alf was stuck to his seat, figuratively and literally with the sweat on his thighs in the polyester trousers.

"Oh, I have the name somewhere. But I didn't send him any tweets – I thought Pat had cooked up that ridiculous scheme. I just wanted to get the shots of him with his pants down."

"But he consulted with psychics over the years?"

"Aye," she said adopting a mock country accent. "Mammy Fitzpatrick was fierce superstitious – she had the cure of something or other." She laughed at her own joke, taking a bottle of Evian from the fridge. "Michael couldn't pass a tarot reader without crossing her palm."

"Okay, Penelope – is that how you pronounce it?"

She nodded.

"This is a pretty big story, you know that?"

"Of course I do, Alfred – I worked in Westminster before I met that horn dog." She nodded to a wedding picture - she with her permed hair swept to one side, him with aviator sunglasses, and both with broad smiles.

"Do you have the names of any other women he slept with?" Alf asked. "Any other occasions?"

"Yes, I have it all documented in a Word document."

"We will need to check it all out. Aren't you worried about your own reputation?"

"I don't care, Alfred –"

"Alf please."

"Alf – I am the innocent party here. I didn't want to rock the boat. I enjoyed the other parts of our life together, but no longer. For all of the other wives and girlfriends turning a blind eye to this, I want to stand up, and be heard." Her skin glowed with a sheen of sweat in the warmth of the kitchen and the excitement of telling her tale.

"And what about the woman in the other pictures –"

"Other pictures? What other pictures?" The muscles of her forehead crinkled with confusion.

"The paper received two sets of pictures, in the same type of envelope, with the same labels."

"I never sent any other pictures. What was in these other pictures?"

"They are much older pictures, from the 1990s. They depict the Minister opening the castle in Ardee."

"Yes, June 10th 1995. I remember because that was the day I gave birth to our son. Michael was nowhere to be found that night. He didn't even find out until the next morning. Now, please go on."

"Well, they show him with a local girl, a Sinéad O'Sullivan.

"The name sounds familiar, but there were so many of them."

"You might recognise the name because her body was discovered in the bog last week, outside Ardee."

At that moment they both froze.

Pat Dennehy, the Minister's advisor, walked into the kitchen, clapping slowly. A tall thin man with a brown combover, teeth yellow from smoking, and deep circles under his tired-looking eyes.

"Excellent performance, Penelope."

Startled, she asked, "What are you doing here?"

"Mr. Timmoney, it's always a pleasure."

He turned to Penelope. "The Conservative Party lost out the day you moved back to Ireland, missy."

Alf flicked his reporter's notepad over to hide the phone which was still recording their conversation.

"Looks like I arrived at the right time to set you both straight," said Pat.

He pulled a chair out from the table and sat down, as Alf moved the phone deftly to his satchel.

"It is unprofessional, Mr Timmoney," said Pat, his presence a malevolent force in the kitchen.

"Pat – get out of my house now, or I'll call the –" Penelope stood up and moved towards the landline the other side of the kitchen.

"You'll do no such thing, gersha. You'll sit down and shut your little mouth, is what you will do. If you think I've given the last twenty years of my life protecting the Minister to let you throw it all away with this two-bit chancer who shouldn't even call himself a journalist, you have another think coming!"

Alf flinched at the slight. "Pat, you've heard her now, she wants you to go – we're not living in the last days of Rome here – can you head on out?" he said unwaveringly.

"*Ha*, you're one to talk!" Pat said, the dark circles under his eyes shifting into a smile. "Now sit down until I tell you both all about Sinéad O'Sullivan."

Chapter 51

Penelope was standing at the Belfast sink in her kitchen. Her lips were drawn together in anger, but Alf detected some fear in the look she gave him. Pat started to loosen the belt of his pinstripe-suit trousers.

"That Sinéad O'Sullivan was a little tramp. A prick-tease. She met Mick at a do in Collins Barracks a few months before those picture in Ardee were taken. She was a cast of many, you know that, Penny," Pat said evenly, shooing one leg out of his trousers.

He was moving slowly, but Alf was concerned that Pat had stripped down to his jocks. In his time as a crime reporter he had been in a lot of tricky situations, downright dangerous, and his internal alarm was screaming. Pat was a big man. If he tried to force himself on the Minister's wife, he would of course do everything to stop him, but was he strong enough?

"Yes, she was one of many little tarts," continued Pat. "But, for some reason, Mick was unusually fond of her."

The tails of his blue shirt hung down over fine-thread boxer shorts. He made no attempt to move. "I tried it on once and this is what she did," he said, lifting back the material to reveal the inner skin of his leg. "She fuckin' bit me, the little bitch."

There was gnarled white skin in a semicircle.

"Anyway, they were mad about each other. Mick was going to give up his seat and they would move to New York. That was the plan. Although I didn't find out until after. Turns out she goes missing. Vanishes on the road when she's waiting for the bus to the airport. Can you believe it?"

Penelope garnered some inner strength, "Will you please put on your trousers, Pat!" she spat at him "*You clown!*"

The tension had dissipated but Alf's heart still pumped hard, as Pat put his trousers back on whilst still ignoring her, continuing with his story.

"Which was convenient." He pulled the leather tightly through the buckle, still standing. "Mick was a Junior Minister for Finance, and spent the summer trying to wrangle over money for more gardaí, bigger searches, anything, but she never turned up."

Alf's phone started to vibrate in his pocket, but thanks to a serendipitous cough from Pat, he managed to hide the fact.

It started buzzing again. This time it had shifted against the keys in his pocket and the sound was unmistakable. Alf started talking loudly. "So if she didn't send the pictures," he nodded towards Penelope, "who did?"

"You're the investigative journalist – I don't know who sent them, if it wasn't her." Pat spoke without looking at her.

"It wasn't," she said.

Pat cracked his knuckles. The sense of dread returned to Alf. Pat wasn't finished with them yet.

"But anyway. No one outside this kitchen is going to ever find out about Mick. Sure he is all set to be elected party leader and Taoiseach at the *Ard Fheis* next week, the leader of the country. And you pair of twerps sitting here gossiping."

Penelope now found her voice and walked over to the table, slamming her fists down in front of him. She looked like a woman possessed, spittle flying from her mouth.

"If you think I am enduring one more week in this marriage, you have another think coming!"

"Calm down, love," said Pat. "God, women, wha'? Is yours like this, Timmoney?"

"I don't have one." Alf now fought his own corner. "In fairness, this is a conversation between me and Mrs Fitzpatrick here. You've no remit to interfere in this."

"Mr Timmoney, I would tread fucking careful if I were you. I heard your interview went well, for the editor job. My sister-in-law was on that panel by the way. But they are a bit worried you haven't moved on past your crime days, running round drinking snakebite with scumbags, that sort of thing. Worried you might interfere with the running of the country. And they want to know what the new Taoiseach thinks."

"I'm sure they care as much about the freedom of the press and keeping the state in check," said Alf, indignant.

"*Aah!*" Pat sighed. "Not as much as you'd think. But, listen here, I have a deal for you, Timmoney. Write whatever you want about Sinéad. You'll have the first interview with the new Taoiseach when he becomes elected, and access to all of the investigating officers and files relating to Sinéad's disappearance. Just keep this madwoman's story out of the paper, okay?"

Penelope flinched at the slight.

"Sure most people wouldn't think too badly of an affair, they'd all understand it. But the truth is stranger than fiction. Sorry, honey," he turned to Penelope, "I've got something up my sleeve for you too. Mick will go back to counselling with you, promise to dedicate one evening a week to whatever you want."

"I don't believe that. Even if he wanted to, he will be too busy *if* he gets elected ..." She trailed off. "Well maybe, Mr Timmoney, I mean Alf," she whispered. "Maybe we could hold off. I mean if you think he has a chance of being Taoiseach, Pat ... I suppose it would be a shame ..."

"Neither of you are worried about who sent those pictures of the Minister to the office? Did they send them anywhere else? Who sent them? Who set up that Twitter account?" Alf asked, blowing a sharp exhale from the side of his mouth in incredulity.

"What was the name of that bloke, the photographer?" asked Pat, looking at Penelope "You sent him to follow us to those flats in Blackrock."

"Something Boyle," she said quietly, in half a daydream. Thinking of her new position as Taoiseach's wife.

"Mossie Boyle," said Pat. "The freelance snapper. He took those pictures in 1995. I remember cos he kept asking me how the Minister knew Sinéad. He was a pest."

"Mossie Boyle," Alf repeated. "Yes, he still sends stuff in to us." Things were all falling into place in his mind. "I have to go," he said.

He rushed up from the basement kitchen, jogging out to the car. He would still use her interview of course, he had recorded everything. But he needed to get to Ardee now.

Chapter 52

Her injuries rendered it almost impossible to read through the original manuscripts alone. For the past few hours, Mary had been a great help, photocopying and laying out the documents so she could read them. She suspected Mary thought she had lost the plot somewhat. Though someone working for Monty all this while would no doubt have had the edges knocked off her. Monty had not bothered them for hours, and she was relieved.

Alongside parish records and historical notes, Mary had printed a large map of the area where the body was found, from the 1650s. This was part of the Down Survey, the first ever detailed survey map of an entire country commissioned by Oliver Cromwell. The A4 printouts covered the whole bedspread. Although Monty's house was only ten miles from the bog-body site, they were on different parts of the map. Ten miles would have taken a fast rider almost an hour on horseback on a dry day.

"That's Ardee there, I'd say," said Mary, once they had assembled the map. "It was originally called Atherde," she smiled. "From the Irish *Áth Fhirdia* – the Ford of Ferdia. You know, before I came to work for Monty, I managed the archives in the local library?"

"No, I didn't know that." January regretted her previous dismissal of the kindly woman as a dithering cleaner.

She opened the large modern map to compare, flapping the large book down across the pillows.

"Flanagan's field is right here, in the modern map – which must be in 'The Great Bog of Atherde' in the Cromwellian map. That is – oh, these are different modern names, so it's smack-bang on the boundary of Curraghbeg, Grange and Gawstown. It must be the same place. That's it, we have it!"

January was invigorated. Overjoyed, she needed to check one more thing.

"Righty-o – that means the most likely spot for any other odd business is *here*. Jolly good. Move that sheet there, Mary. *Sorleybones Bog*. There's a fairy fort on this map, I think? That's where we need to go."

"You know who would be a great help to you?" said Mary. "The Louth Meath Historical Society. They are active. There was one young lad in particular, obsessed with these maps. Would always be bringing them into the library before it went digital to compare with the ordnance survey ones. He was obsessed with the lineage of the land, convinced he was descended from the ancient high kings, before the Protestants were shipped in. No offence."

"None taken, but that's exactly what I am thinking. The killer didn't pick this spot at random, he had a specific reason. Perhaps he mistakenly thought –"

Mary's face slackened, her eyes staring into space.

"What is it, Mary? Are you okay?"

Her eyes snapped to January's, her voice falling to a whisper. "He used to always talk about the bog bodies." She drummed her fingertips off her scalp. "He was only a young lad, but came with printouts from the paper, everything. Said it was for a school history project."

"Who was it?"

"Jayney, I can't remember the name ... But the historical society meeting is on tonight. If he's not there, one of the others will certainly know the name."

"Can you drive me there?"

Mary blew her fringe off her sweaty red face. She still had all the fireplaces to top up, and the dinner table to lay. But at least she could take off this bloody outfit.

Monty met them in the corridor accidentally-on-purpose. "Off somewhere, girls?"

"I hope you don't mind, Mary is going to drive me to the shop. I need to pick up some feminine items," she said, trying to put him off. She didn't have time to listen to his asinine pleas.

"Oh," he blustered, a dried line of sticky port

around his lips. "No problem, but you will join me for dinner tonight?"

"Yes, dying for some venison after all that hospital mac and cheese," January lied as she flew down the large marble staircase..

January knew she ought to call Cooney, but she didn't want to. It had gone too far already. This was the man who had tried to kill her, she could feel it. But she wanted to be sure.

Chapter 53

He knew she wouldn't stay long indoors. The crunch of the housekeeper's car down the drive gave him enough warning to turn unassumingly, now comfortably trailing January and the housekeeper along the Castletown road. He would do everything in the van. He had already sealed off the back from the seats, including soundproofing. Conor hadn't got around to branding the refrigerated truck, so in their search for his premises and vehicles the gardaí had missed it. Another fuck-up that would come back to bite them. Still, they weren't a particularly deft organisation to deceive.

They cut a strange pair, a beret sitting on January's flame-red hair and the old woman with dull grey hair in a bun. The road from Monty's house had been busier than he expected. A farmer pulled out between them, trailing a clunking horsebox. By the time they passed the local national school, there were six cars of country mammies collecting schoolboys from Gaelic football training.

He gripped the wheel as the adrenalin coursed

through his veins, his hands growing slippery on the wheel. He turned up the music, the Red Hot Chilli Peppers were Sinéad's favourite band, and he thumped the heel of his hand on the dashboard to the beat of "Suck My Kiss". The road was empty now, the daylight dwindling into the horizon. No houses overlooked this stretch of the long, straight road and the forest was thick right up to it.

Approaching a T-junction, Mary slowed the car, peering in both directions.

He accelerated and hit the back of the car. January's head jerked.

With the second hard shunt, January looked hard at him, confused. He was wearing a wig. With a third bang they were all out of their cars, January yelling at him.

He grabbed Mary's wiry frame and issued a skull-cracking head-butt. He stumbled and pulled her backwards before throwing her to the ground and managing a kick to the face. Mercifully, she was out cold.

"*Leave her alone!*" January shouted, before he muffled her screams with his glove.

He dragged her, kicking, into the van. He held her tight, crushing her bruised ribs. January bit hard onto his fingers. She was stuck to him like a limpet, pulling and looking for traction. He twisted her injured arm and she screamed with the agonising pain as she passed out.

He cut her loose, long enough to slam the door. She was trapped. The old woman was still unconscious as he drove past her motionless body on the road. He felt alive, empowered by the struggle.

He joined Anthony Kiedis in the last chorus of the song, screaming, as he took his cargo bumping down the road.

Chapter 54

The tall grandfather clock chimed nine o'clock. Monty sat in his tuxedo, angrily twirling a warm Martini glass. They had been gone for hours. He was shocked that January would refuse to be dressed and ready for dinner. She was raised better than that. Cook was anxious about timing the *Iles Flottant*. Once more checking out the window to see no sign of Mary's car, he decided to treat himself. He paired a heavy hand of Gordon's gin with a breath of vermouth and three olives and toddled upstairs to check the iPad. Still in good vantage for the drive, he sat down and logged onto the forum.

RINAMARBH has posted a photo.

Despite the dark light, he could see a woman hunched over in the dark back of a van.

The caption read: **Step 1: Capture your victim. Stay tuned, everyone**.

The movement of wheels across the drive jolted him back to reality. At last, he blustered, standing up –

before freezing. It was a Garda car, not Mary's hatchback.

Twice in one day. It was worrying. He considered taking the emergency wipe measures on the tablet but hesitated.

With the black tails of his tuxedo flapping behind his rotund silhouette, his patent dress shoes tapped down the marble steps. In a flagrant disregard for position, he opened the front door himself. Cook was redundantly standing there, taken aback with this development.

"Officers!" he exclaimed, to Cooney and O'Brien. "Back again? The neighbours will think we're washing diesel." He chuckled jauntily.

"Mr Passmore, may we come in, please? We need to talk to you," Cooney said grimly.

"Is it January? Has something happened?"

"I think it's best that we speak inside, if you don't mind. Is there anyone else here apart from you both?"

"*Em*, yes – Cook, can you see who else is here, and bring some refreshments into the library?"

He ushered the officers inside.

"No refreshments for us, Mr Passmore, but if you could assemble whoever is here, thank you. There has been a very serious development."

Chapter 55

January's hands throbbed. The deep lacerations on them meant she could barely move her fingers as she grappled for the door of the van. With her right eye bandaged, it took longer than usual to adjust to the light. They had been moving at a steady speed for a while now, and the sound of rain was pelting against the metal sheeting of the van. It was a big vehicle, she knew that. But it had been divided into at least two sections by a large sheet of plywood. The space inside the doors that January was now imprisoned in was only slightly larger than the sleeping bag he had lined the floor with.

How did he realise she knew? She had been certain he was the killer, but had not suspected he would be so vicious, so angry. The way he had head-butted poor Mary was just horrid.

She was scared, and wondered if anyone had found Mary yet. Her car was right at the T- junction. No one knew where she herself was now. Monty would realise, but it could be too late by then.

A small curved space between the straight edge of the wood and the rounded side of the van allowed the light in. Clambering to her knees, she tried to maintain her balance in the moving vehicle as she peered through the gap. The blow to her ribs made it difficult to breathe. It was dark in there too, her eye drawn to the light from the windscreen. He was singing along to a Red Hot Chilli Peppers CD. She squinted, the muscles of her damaged eye contracting out of habit. The pain raged red-hot through her whole body, thumping in her eye, her ribs, her arm and her hands. It was impossible to make out the road, but it was narrow and the tree branches were hitting the windscreen wipers as they lashed back the water. Behind the driver's seat was a black metal grid.

As the light revealed the second compartment in the van, January's stomach lurched. She felt hot with nausea as she made out what looked like an operating table, soldered to the van floor, leather manacles on each corner. More details revealed themselves, including the red dot on ... it couldn't be ... It was a camera, on a tripod, also soldered to the side of the van.

It was cold, much colder than outside. She sat down and wiggled her legs into the sleeping bag. Her heart was thumping, leaving her hands and feet cold as the blood rushed to supply the hypothalamus, her heart and brain. If she couldn't overpower him, she would have to appeal to his ego and talk him down. She closed her eye, strained from acting alone. The van slowed down along what felt like a road that was full of potholes.

Chapter 56

"We will speak with Mr Passmore first." O'Brien addressed the assembled staff at the library door. "We will call you all in, if you wouldn't mind waiting here."

"What happened?" asked the cook, a thin, small little woman with a tight ponytail. "Does he still want the dinner?" She sound harried.

"We'll go through it all," said O'Brien. "Don't worry about the grub, but if you want to take off anything that might burn or boil over, do."

She flew off down the corridor, throwing her hands in the air. *"Me custard, me meringues!"*

O'Brien closed the door and rejoined Cooney and Monty, standing beside the large window.

Cooney's black overcoat was drenched with rain and smelt of damp wool "Mary has been taken by ambulance to Beaumont Hospital. She has a gash on her head and is in a critical condition. January was with her?" He sounded exhausted.

"Yes," nodded Monty. "Was she not there with Mary?"

"No, it looks like there was a struggle. We found some of her items on the road, a Dictaphone, her emerald necklace, and a small bottle of crème de menthe." He said it without smiling.

The image of the woman in the van posted on the forum flashed into Monty's mind. Was it her? An icy thread shot up his spine, as he stared momentarily into space.

"What is it, Mr Passmore? Where were they going?"

With a deceptively believable anger, he said, "To get the real killer, the man you should have caught!"

"Where were they going?"

"To Ardee, to the Louth Meath Historical Society meeting."

Turning to his colleague, Cooney commanded, "Send a car to the meeting and tell them not to let anyone leave. I want all of the roads in and out of the town blocked, and the eyes in the sky out looking. Get cars on all of the roads and byroads between here and Ardee. *Fucking move it, now!*"

Dialling the number, O'Brien moved to the other side of the room. He rested a hand on a large globe that spun under it, leading him to nearly fall over. Cooney shot him a filthy look, before returning his intense gaze to Monty.

"What did Ms Quail do since we left here earlier today?"

"She was working away in her room. I'm not sure what she was doing."

370

"Show me. *Now*," Cooney made for the door, signalling Monty to lead the way and they started up the steps.

"Mary had been helping her," said Monty breathlessly, his legs made for lingering and loitering, not taking tall steps two at a time. "She was convinced you have the wrong man," he said, reaching the top of the staircase and opening the door of her room.

Inside, Cooney bent down to read the dozens of printouts. "What are these?" he said to himself. "Church records?"

"Detective, these are all historical documents, it seems, related to the location where the bodies were found," said Monty, wondering if he could get to the iPad and wipe it. The strings of guilt were tugging him to show Cooney. He hadn't killed anyone, just watched ... but it would be the ruin of him. But he couldn't stand the thought of his little January coming to a brutal end.

"This is a map." Cooney pulled back the bed curtain further and held a sheet of paper to the light. "How would this tell her anything? Did she speak to you about it?"

It was starting to make sense to Monty. "I think, and I was the curator when the last bog bodies were discovered – I think the person who did this is concerned with history. He wanted to rewrite it. It was common for bodies to be buried on boundaries, and that site, if I'm right, is right on the border of these five townlands. This must be significant. And this here," he held up a land register, a photocopy of an elaborately-penned document, "details the landowners."

"Hang on," said Cooney. "If January's hands were injured, she couldn't write anything so let's try this ... " He fished around in his pocket for the evidence bag holding the Dictaphone. His fingers were damp with sweat as he fumbled, sliding the buttons and clicking the start button to no avail.

"*Fuck*, it's dead."

Chapter 57

Alf drove through two red lights along the steep hill out of Drogheda. He tried to think where he might find January, as he dialled her phone and it continued to ring out. That old degenerate Monty would be ex-directory, but he texted Laura to get his number.

Then he rang Frank.

"What's up, boss?"

"January," he said, reaching a narrow side road. "When we were in the hospital she was convinced she knew who the killer was – she mentioned a name – something Boyle. I think it's the same guy who sent us the pictures from the Castle reopening in 1995, after he took those pictures for the Minister's wife. That's why they had the same envelope and printing on them."

"Why would he do that? And what about the Twitter account?" said Frank.

"Why would he make her look like a bog body? He's a psychopath is why. Maybe he was trying to send us down a wrong trail, or to take down the Minister?

The Twitter account was Pat, some stupid scheme he cooked up."

"But it came from their house in Drogheda, their flat in Dublin, where Pat seems to make himself much at home, if what I saw was anything to go by."

Alf shuddered. "He is a real scary guy – he gave me the heebie-jeebies in there. He looks half-dead or something the way his eyes are so sunk into his head. Anyway, the photographer is our man, I think. He must be related to the man they have in custody. Same last name. Hang on …" Monty's phone number was arriving by text. "I want to check the name with her first. I'll call you back, Frank."

The sky was almost black. Alf slowed slightly as he worked through the motions on his phone to disconnect Frank and call the old curator.

The call rang, and rang, eventually answered on the other end by the tired cook. "Hello, Pervany House?" she said.

"Hello," said Alf. "Could I speak to January Quail, please? I believe she's a guest –"

"She's disappeared," said the cook. "The polis are here now taking statements – they think someone hauled her into a van and they done in –"

"What? When was this?"

"This evening. Mary was attacked too, she's almost dead. They were going hunting this killer –"

"I know, I know – okay, would you mind putting me

through to the police? Whoever is there?" How could January be so careless? Hadn't he warned her off going on a wild goose chase for a reason? She dismissed him as a killjoy but she often acted profligately with her health and safety. Did she think she was Nancy Drew or something?

"A minute, who is this?"

"Alf Timmoney."

"One minute, Ralph," she said, transferring the call through to the library. She bet they would let the line flippin' well ring out and she'd have to run up there to tell them and run back to the kitchen. As the line tricked through, she thought about how she was getting too old for this *Upstairs Downstairs* rubbish.

In the library, O'Brien looked at the phone as it rang. He thought it was an antique, not a real phone. It was an old one, the sort where the earpiece hung vertically at the side of a wooden box, instead of sitting across the phone in a cradle.

Cooney roared at him from the end of the room. *"Will you answer that fucking phone, O'Brien!"*

He picked up the handle tentatively, expecting to receive a telegram or a message in Morse code. "He-llo?"

"Ralph Timmoney calling there, wants to speak to someone about the kidnapping," the cook said before clicking the call through.

"Hi, Ralph, Sergeant O'Brien here – do you have any information for us?"

"Alf, it's Alf Timmoney, the editor of the *Irish Sunday Chronicle*."

"Sorry, Alf."

"Whatever, that woman on the phone told me January was kidnapped? Where was she? Do you know where she was taken?"

"*Em*, I'm not sure we can release any information to the media –"

"I'm not writing a story, you tool. I'm looking for one of my staff members. Who is in charge there? Put me on now, or my next call will be to the Deputy Commissioner."

O'Brien didn't know what to do with the mouthpiece so waved Cooney over.

Cooney accepted the hand piece with an evil stare for his junior colleague.

"Cooney," he said coolly.

"Cooney, it's Alf Timmoney the editor of the *Irish Sunday Chronicle* here. Can you please tell me what happened to January Quail – as well as being her employer I am also listed as her next of kin."

"Okay, Mr Timmoney – she was kidnapped on the road this evening on the crossroads in Castletown. The housekeeper here was driving her to the local historical society meeting."

"Jamie Boyle, I think that's who took her," said Alf. "When I saw her in hospital yesterday she told me she knew who did it, that you had the wrong man."

"Mossie Boyle," said Cooney slowly, thinking, "Conor's brother."

"That's it. What are you doing to find her?"

"The line isn't great, Alf – this is an antique phone – let me see –"

"I'm coming there now."

The line went dead, leaving Cooney unsure if the phone or Alf had ended the call.

Cooney sent two cars to Mossie's house and sweetshop, with instructions to call him immediately before they entered. He needed to get back to Ardee as soon as they had interviewed the others. He decided to take another look around January's room, although forensics had arrived and were already checking the temperature of her coffee and taping off the area.

O'Brien had ushered the staff to the other end of the library and begun questioning them. Monty stayed, one leg anxiously bobbing on top of the other. Before his time in the museum he had briefly practised as a barrister. He offered his rudimentary and unofficial counsel to the staff as they recounted the last time they had seen Mary.

January had followed her nose, thought Cooney as he climbed the stairs, and proved the entire investigation wrong. He hoped that they would find her in time but, knowing how these things often go, he doubted it. He fingered the bust of Cicero set into an alcove at the top of the landing. The door to the room next door had been left ajar. He cautioned himself against going in. They had no sort of warrant to be investigating here, but he couldn't help feel Monty wasn't entirely blameless. He pushed in the door anyway, and decided to take a look around.

Chapter 58

The van was slowing now. Trundling up and down, it felt like they were on grass, or some unsteady ground, not paved road. January was terrified. She had passed out again from the pain and, although aware the van was slowing down, she was neither awake nor unconscious.

She thought of her parents, replaying special memories of them. She often did this at home when wallowing in a drunken stupor. If she didn't do it, they would be forgotten, their existence evaporated into the ether.

The drinking had kept her from feeling too much, missing her parents, her grandmother, Avonlea and the life that she should have been living. Sometimes she wondered if the Quails were cursed.

She imagined what this evening could have looked like in another life. She imagined her four children, Tabitha, Trixie (for Beatrix), Thomas and Theodore. The older ones had organised a concert in the library at Avonlea. Their little hands tugging and dragging at her and her parents all afternoon as they unearthed ancient sheet music and dragged the heavy harp across the newly varnished hall floor. Her husband, she was picturing Cooney, but with an open-necked shirt and slightly darker hair, carried four wineglasses upside down as they took their seats. Her father looked disapprovingly at Cooney as he blew mould off the vintage bottle, grey-green flecks falling onto the satin couch. The bulbs of the glasses chimed off one another as Cooney turned them upright. Her father was scrutinising the endeavour, but accepted the drink warmheartedly. January saw herself, in a clinging hound's-tooth wrap dress. But her hair was not bobbed, and instead it flowed softly over her shoulders, her left hand hefty with diamonds and rings, tokens of love presented at the birth of each child.

She was carrying a dozing infant on her shoulder, arguing with her mother about the safety of allowing the children eat venison that had been buried as they took their seats.

In the van, tears were rolling down January's face, and she wasn't sure if it was from the fear or the wretched sadness or both.

"I miss you, Mummy, Daddy," she whispered to herself. "Please help me," she sobbed, the saltiness of her tears stinging the open wounds on her hands and cheek. As she tucked her knees up into the crook of her arm, the van slowed to a stop.

Chapter 59

The café and shops remained open for late-night shoppers. Pockets of curious onlookers stood along the street gossiping, wherever they could take shelter from the rain. As Alf walked into the Castle Arms, he noticed Conor Boyle's victualler's shop was ominously unlit amongst the bright window displays.

There were three officers essentially facilitating a lock-in. With no one allowed to leave, they had granted permission for two rounds of drink to be served once they were all interviewed. Alf recognised one of the officers, a former detective who had been demoted to uniform when a drugs bust went wrong.

"Alf," he smiled, "my man, how's it going?" he said, slapping the sodden shoulders of his suit jacket. "What are you doing here?"

"Not so good – one of our staffers was taken. The fucker cut her brakes a few days ago too. Anything out of this lot?"

"Well, between you, me and the four walls, fuck all.

They're a boring bunch, these historical society people. There's three of them missing – Mrs Dunne is at her daughter's wedding in Cork, but two regulars are unaccounted for. Mossie –"

"Boyle – it's him who took her – have ye been out to his house?"

"There were cars sent there and also to the sweetshop,"

"Sweetshop? Did they find her?"

"I haven't heard," said the officer, now looking uneasy as the pub door slammed. "You'll have to ask the gaffer." He nodded at the approaching Cooney.

"Alf, let me get up to speed here, and I'll come back to you." Cooney ushered him to take a seat on the pub couch.

As he waited, Alf checked to see if anyone had been reporting it on social media. He cursed as he saw the entire homepage of the competitor newspaper the *Irish Journal*, plastered in red and black with the headline "Killer on the Loose in Ardee". They had pictures of Mary's car and the crossroads, the locals standing around, Mossie's sweetshop – even a fucking headshot of Mossie.

He quickly checked their own homepage and saw nothing about the story online.

He called Laura in the office. "The *Irish Journal* is plastered in this story – get something up about it, *now*. Get on to the press office!" He was furious. That was the problem with having an unpaid intern in charge of the website. They hadn't even heard January was missing.

Cooney returned and placed an empty glass and January's Dictaphone on the table between them, then shed his overcoat.

"So, any update?" Alf scratched his head nervously.

"There's no sign of them at the house or in the sweetshop. We have a helicopter doing the rounds looking for the van and the roads are closed –"

"But you've lost them." Alf helped himself to some peanuts from the table.

"I know. Do you have a charger for the Dictaphone? She was using it to make notes before they left for here." Cooney handed the device to Alf for inspection.

"That's my Dictaphone, but I don't have the charger. It's in Dublin. But I'm sure you can get another charger fairly easily." He exhaled sharply. "He's going to kill her, isn't he?"

"That's very strong, Alf – let's hope it doesn't come to that. We're doing everything we can – we even have the army scouring the fields near the crossroads."

He called O'Brien over and told him to have the Dictaphone taken to forensics to find a charger as a matter of urgency.

O'Brien nodded and rushed off.

"You didn't listen to her when she told you the killer was still out there," said Alf. "She knew that you had the wrong guy." He was furious, but remained calm. He wanted to keep Cooney onside and keep a window into the investigation.

"Look, Alf, off the record here, I presume ..." he paused until Alf nodded, "this entire investigation has been a shambles. If that body hadn't been misclassified to begin with ... Look, all the evidence pointed to it being the brother, whatever, but I am not letting him get to January, okay?"

O'Brien arrived back with two lemonades and three packets of crisps which he unloaded onto the table. He was red-faced and sweating, with large circles of perspiration around each armpit.

"Here, boss, listen, the crowd over there is getting antsy." He pointed to the members of the historical society who were sitting with folded arms and pouts with a table full of empty soft-drink glasses and crisp wrappers. "They have been here since five o'clock this evening. It's nearly ten now. They've all been interviewed and given statements. Can we let them go?"

"Fine, but tell that pub owner he's not opening this evening. We need a base." Cooney tore open the crisps. "Tell me, Alf, what do you know about this Montgomery guy? Why was she staying with him?"

"*Phew!*" Alf glugged back the drink. "He's a weasel of the highest order. I thought they knew each other from the previous bog-body discovery when he was in the National Museum. But I actually think they know each other much longer than that. I'm not sure if you know, but January grew up in a big mansion like his.

They were the two big Protestant families around many years ago but, anyway, her parents were killed in an accident and she was half-reared by her granny and her lesbian lover, before the place burned down."

"Yes, I knew there was something like that. I can tell from her accent, of course, but also from the way she doesn't use a phone and drinks this weird little liqueur all the time. I could've guessed she'd been raised by an eccentric member of the gentry."

"That's why I think she likes Monty so much. Sure you saw he has actual staff – a cook, gardener, and the housemaid that was mown down by Boyle. Wearing a tuxedo for dinner! Anyway her grandmother died not long after the fire and she has been essentially alone since … I've never seen her with any friends." Alf picked the salty remnants from the silver packet, as he watched the angry mob pass out the door.

O'Brien ushered them out and bolted the door after the last man carrying a large scroll left.

"Monty Passmore must be the last link to that whole world, and she's never come to terms with being alone," said Cooney. "Anyway, I agree there is something sort of not right about him. I'm applying for a warrant to search the house, and left two men there with instructions to watch him closely. I'm even wondering if he was working with … never mind. Sorry, it's been a long day." Cooney exhaled and stretched his broad shoulders back.

"A long day," Alf commiserated. "Do you mind if I stay around? I guess I'm the closest thing she has to a family and if she's found ..."

"*When* she's found. Of course. But everything is off the record, okay?"

Alf nodded, but his fingers were crossed under the table. Cooney would be glad he had stayed. Depending on the outcome, and he was trying his hardest to remain detached, he could be recounting this conversation and the operations taking place around him to a tribunal in Dublin Castle. One more fuck-up by the Garda and it was January who would be taking the hit.

O'Brien rushed over to the table, stumbling as his shoe caught on a stray short barstool. "They have him, boss!" he said, pulling himself upright and handing a mobile phone to Cooney.

"You have Boyle?" Cooney spoke into the mouthpiece, now standing.

Alf watched anxiously as Cooney took the call, nodding and listening to the low vibrations of the officer at the end of the line.

"*I can't fucking believe this!*" Cooney cursed. The phone hanging by his side, he kicked a barstool over. It bounced on the stained carpet. "They have Boyle! He's at home, and has been all day. Mossie Boyle didn't take January. It's someone else."

Chapter 60

After the commotion of the day, Monty had taken supper on a tray in his room. A beef sandwich with plenty of horseradish. He licked the last glob of the fiery sauce from his top lip and settled back in the armchair. He was unsure of the extent of the powers of police monitoring, and had held off on checking into the forum. Over some late-night brandies a few months ago, one of his young men had assured him that they could register the device and his activity completely under the radar. That it would look like he was logging on from Africa.

He could not hold back any longer, and sought the tablet, entering his credentials and signing in.

RINAMARBH had received plenty of cheering on from the other forum subscribers over the afternoon. Their bloodlust was strangely sanitised when written down. He was now streaming live. Monty could access it by paying fifty euro. Surely a clear link to him would be an online payment? He considered momentarily before seeking out his bank card from the wallet in the mahogany valet stand. He entered the card details. After a momentary delay, the black square came alive with a live feed. It was damned dark. He recognised the outline of this chap sitting on the edge of a table, talking to a wooden wall.

It was difficult to make anything out, then the screen split.

It now showed January kneeling in what appeared to be some sort of chamber. His heart raced as the sight of her. At least she was still alive. Once more he considered calling one of the policemen, but was unable to move from the chair, the satin cushion growing damp with adrenalin-driven perspiration.

Chapter 61

It was still heavily raining. January smelt the wet dew on the bog rows as he opened the door. She only caught a momentary glimpse of the surroundings and recognised the outline of an oak tree with a tall hedge on one side.

"No need to be too worried now," he said, his eyes squinting as they grew used to the dark.

If she could only make it to the other side of the plywood. She had been kicking it on the drive. There was some give on the left-hand corner. January had no clue why Setanta Molloy had taken her. He was wearing a navy beanie hat, and a green waxy rainjacket. He looked more like a local hurling player than a serial killer. This disguise was as affected as his cream linen suit had been.

Whilst they were in the car together, Mary had told January about her days as the school librarian in St Imelda's. After leaving Ardee for the highly prestigious Patrician College in Dublin, Setanta rarely returned to his adopted family. Due to an incident of some sort, Mary didn't know for sure, he was stripped of his scholarship before the Leaving Cert. Without funds to pay for his fees at the Patrician College, he was forced to return to school in Ardee. Mary spoke of how he struggled to adjust, occupying the library instead of trying to associate with the others in his class. Until he met Sinéad. As Mary described the teenage Setanta, January knew that he was the killer, not Mossie Boyle.

A few locks of wet auburn hair sat snugly on his freckled forehead as he unscrewed a bottle of water and stuck in a straw. "Look, I'm opening it here in front of you." He walked over to stick the plastic straw through the small gap in the plywood. It was a tall van but he still needed to crouch.

"What are you going to do to me?"

"Here," he said, ignoring the question. "I brought you some peppermint creams."

January could smell a strong odour but wasn't sure which one of them was producing it. She recalled reading about the scent of terror animals release in moments of immense fear.

"Are you not wearing the gift I sent you?" His tongue peeped out of the corner of his mouth as he licked his bottom lip. "I suppose that's to be expected. Although I know you like that make. I've been watching you for some time, January. The discovery of my Queen has come earlier than I expected, but nonetheless I'm glad to know you. And how much you like peppermint!"

The corset. He had sent it to her or had placed it in her room. Her stomach flipped at his intimate knowledge of her. He had been watching her this whole time. It made her feel queasy. She wasn't hungry, but knew it would be useful to build her sugar reserves so reluctantly accepted the chocolate.

"I gather they have found the other one now too. Funny, she also liked wearing corsets." He gazed off to the side of the room.

"I said," January pushed down the acid heartburn and spoke loudly, "what are you going to do to me?"

He was avoiding looking at her. "You should eat. You haven't had anything since that Mulligatawny soup Mary gave you for lunch. Ould Mary, she'd always have a spare copy of *Peig* for you. Not that you could call the porta cabin in St Imelda's school a library, not like the fine tall shelves of the Patrician College, lined with first editions and worn copies of the *Aeneid*."

"You must have hated going back to St Imelda's," she baited him. She was terrified but refused to be intimated yet. "I went to Patrician."

"These things happen, January. I was struggling with my identity at the time. Aren't we all? Who is January Quail? A pisshead journo? Wannabe editor, revivalist of gracious living, also known as indentured servitude. I'm lucky but I found my calling many years ago."

He laughed and handed her some more peppermint

creams. He then began fixing the camera on the wall of the car.

"What's that for?" she asked.

Without looking at her, he answered jovially. "Oh, you have such a curious mind, don't you? Always beavering away with questions. It's for a live stream, to share this little show with some of my fans." He sat down slowly on the table with his hands crossed. "What else would you like to know? I did plan to have a notepad for you to take notes, but that wouldn't be much use to you now. Go on, we have a little time."

"What are you going to do to me?"

"Oh, don't think about that for the moment. I thought you would be delighted with the chance to interview the elusive bog-body killer."

"So it was you," said January quietly.

"Of course it was, but you knew that, didn't you, January Quail?"

"Why did you make her a bog body? What about the other girl?"

"Oh, that second one was an earlier mistake, inelegant. When I got sent home to Ardee, I needed to vent my frustration. She lived in the middle of the bog, so noise was no problem. I would go to her every Thursday. I bashed out Rachmaninoff and Wagner, whatever I wanted to vent. We didn't have a piano at home, you see. She let me have her, did Theresa, my piano teacher. I was a schoolboy of eighteen, and she was in her thirties. One night I lost my temper and before I knew it I was rolling her in her own shower curtain. Don't you hate when things slide under the fridge, and you have to pull the whole thing –"

"You disgust me," she interrupted his diatribe. "You buried her alive, did you know that?"

He paused for a moment, looking away from her. "I didn't know that, but it doesn't change anything. Anyway, you had better shut it, if you know what's good for you. I have no problem hurting you badly. But that would probably impair your writing style so I don't want to do it. Let me continue … Anyway, I panicked with Theresa, wrapped her head in a towel and a shower curtain. It was black dark that night, so I carried her out to the field behind her house and started to dig. They were finished cutting the bog, and I knew that they wouldn't find her until the next year. There's no way anyone around here would cut turf twice in one year. But they didn't find her – they didn't cut the bog the next year, or the year after that. The Flanagans were incapable of properly maintaining that land. Anyway, I went to university, and worked on the Clonycavan Man. And you and I met. I got nosey and wondered how Theresa was doing. When I dug her up I was shocked to see how perfect she had remained. That gave me the inspiration to do a recreation."

"Tell me about Sinéad," ventured January.

Her vision had adjusted to the darkness and she

wanted to make him comfortable whilst she reviewed her options for escape. There was give in the plywood, but the door from the van was on the right-hand side. And she didn't know where they were. She knew she didn't have the physical strength to fight him with her bare hands, but noted some large jugs on the floor. But they hadn't been rattling when they were driving so they must be stuck to the floor.

"Sinéad was my queen. I gave her all of my love, my heart, my soul." His smile hardened to a curling sneer. "You distracted me that summer. I haven't been able to eat a minty sweet without remembering how your stiff little mouth felt."

His sickly reminder of how she had let him kiss her, combined with the pain in her arm made her skin prickle with sweat. She could feel her consciousness slipping away. She allowed her head to hang between her knees to get the blood flowing. The tape of the bandage around her eye pinched as she listened.

"But, Sinéad, yes, she was my one true love. It was unrequited, as often the best ones are. But," he spat, "she preferred to trick about with ex-Republicans and politicians. I wanted to get her, to keep her. You remember – there are a few theories about bog bodies. One was that burial was used as a punishment, to trap the soul in a sort of purgatory. In school Sinéad used to talk about heaven, and how much she wanted to go there. But I wanted to keep her, here, close to me."

He stood up and shuffled to a metal chest of drawers behind the driver's seat.

"Here," he took out a small rosewood box, about the size of one of January's winter brooches. "I want to show you something." He held it up to the gap and flashed on the torch on his phone. As she reached for the box, he pulled it back "No, you can look, but I don't want this contaminated with your bloody fingers."

January peered at the circular object, trying to make sense of its leathery appearance. "A nipple," she whispered. The body had been found without hers.

"A souvenir. I kept both of them of course. Along with her ponytail, a fine mane of thick curly black hair." He snapped shut the box and returned it to its hiding place. "I had to sell the other one, to one of my fans, when things got a little tough. There's not much money in the public sector, you know. That's who the camera is for, pay-per-view subscription on the dark web. The internet is great, you can buy or sell almost anything." He pointed to the corner.

January noticed the red light was on.

Trying to buy more time she continued, "How did you do it?"

"With Sinéad? Oh, I'm so glad you asked. Here." He pushed the now grimy straw through the gap. "Hydrate."

January sucked back some of the water. The van was now much warmer than before and she loosened her legs from the sleeping bag. She would listen to him, and conserve her strength until the moment of action came. She thought of the car – it was the last thing of her father's that she owned, and now she was left with nothing. Its absence pained her as much as the torn flesh and broken bones.

"I had been watching her for a while. She was back in Ardee from New York and, well, I asked her out a few times. But cosmopolitan woman that she was, she didn't want anything to do with me." Setanta had now removed his coat and was wearing a Trinity rugby jersey. He sat on the workbench swinging his legs as he spoke.

January had removed two hair slides and was secretly trying to bend them into a C-shape to try and open the van door. Her fingers were slow and heavy. The progress was tortuously slow. She had just about opened one.

"I got the house ready. Like you, my own parents died and left me and my brothers the house and the butcher's shop –"

"No, they didn't. I met your aunt yesterday at Flanagan's house."

"That old crone, she's not my aunt. She's my mother. You know small-town Ireland, a pregnancy out of wedlock. Well, her sister adopted me. Then her own two sprogs arrived and I wasn't good enough. They sent me away to boarding school. I was of superior intellect anyway and won a scholarship. I lost it before the Leaving Cert and was forced to attend that appalling school with –"

"Conor and Mossie." January recalled the pleasant discussion around zebra meat. She wondered if Cooney had realised he was the wrong man yet. It was difficult for her to tell how much time had passed. She guessed that someone must have found Mary by now and realised she had been taken.

"Yes, well, we don't get on. Anyway, I stripped out the dining room, prepared the house for all of the mess. Let me tell you, murdering someone is a dirty business, never mind converting their flesh to leather. The smell. Anyway. She was waiting for the bus to the airport. Imagine, Speedy O'Sullivan wouldn't even give his only child a lift to the airport. Anyway, I pulled up and offered her a lift. Said I was collecting my cousin. Sure of course she jumped at the chance. She knew how to be nice when it suited her, when there was something in it for her. Laced her lemonade with ketamine, and she soon passed out. That was the easy part."

Chapter 62

"The Garda Station is only at the end of the road," blustered Tossy as he unloaded the dishwasher in the Castle Arms. "I don't know why they won't fuck off there and let me open," he complained to Alf, who was waiting for a rock shandy.

It was almost midnight and the search teams had had no luck in tracing the van or January. Alf was trying not to think about what could be happening to her.

"She was in here a few times." Tossy shovelled ice into Alf's glass. "Your one who is missing."

"January?" Alf was not surprised to learn she had soon found a watering hole when on the job.

"Aye, the redheaded West Brit one. She was asking about Sinéad, and that. She came in the next night. Had to be carried out. She was langers, and she'd only had a few drinks."

He remembered the morning she was wiped from a hangover. Rarely did January get so drunk that she would collapse.

Their conversation was interrupted as Cooney shouted *"Timmoney!"* at him across the bar.

"What's the latest? Did the chopper spot anything?"

"Unfortunately not, but we have the Dictaphone charged," said Cooney.

O'Brien was sitting beside him with a notepad and a set of headphones on.

"What's on it?" asked Alf.

"Which lord owned what land, in the 1600s – I mean, I don't know what we're meant to take –"

"Boss, you better hear this." O'Brien pulled off the headset. He rewound and pressed play.

January's voice mid-sentence came over the small playback speakers.

The assembled officers quietened to listen, Alf's heart pumping as her sharp voice hung hauntingly over them.

"Righty-o – that means the most likely spot for any other odd business is here. Jolly good. Move that sheet there, Mary." The sound of papers rustling and movement against the microphone scrubbed over her voice before it came back clearly: *"Sorleybones Bog, there's a fairy fort on this map, I think? That's where we need to go."*

Cooney's voice jumped loud into action, as he stood up and directed the team, pulling on his overcoat, "Right, boys – let's go! O'Brien, get those cars over there. I want a local driver." He marched to the door. "Timmoney, come on the fuck, are you coming or not?"

Chapter 63

The van was moving again, to January's relief. Setanta had stopped telling his story about Sinéad after his phone rang. After reversing for a distance, it now felt like they were on a main road. They were moving at speed. He had given no explanation for where they were going. He was obviously spooked. No wonder he had fought so hard to remain privy to the investigation. Would Cooney have suspected Setanta Molloy?

He turned on the radio. It was a bawdy chat show. January could just about hear the noise of raspberries, before something caught her attention.

"We are here with the mysterious Lady Anon," the male presented jeered. *"And I can confirm to the listeners that she is indeed a lady, in every sense of the word. You're very welcome, my lady!"*

"Thanks, Panda," Lady Anon said in a broad Dublin-city accent. *"I'm bemused and amused to be on a mainstream setting such as this."*

Her voice was low, in fact so deep January was not

sure it was a woman's. Hearing her prime interview candidate prostitute herself on such a show compounded January's sense of desperation. It didn't seem real.

"I just want to describe your appearance to our listeners."

"A face for radio."

"Well, that's just it, we can't see your face. Tonight you're wearing a Venetian mask, so we have no idea who you are. What's that all about?"

"I'm sure some of your listeners will be familiar with these masks. They're very popular at sex parties."

"Oh hoo!" The presenter sounded nervous. *"Why don't you want to tell people who you are? Isn't it cowardly?"*

"Isn't it cowardly that society hides behind appearances?"

Without painkillers for over twelve hours, January's hands and fingers throbbed in agony. She had tried kicking and banging when they had slowed down, she presumed at traffic lights. No one had heard her. Peeking through the gap in the plywood, she looked past the grate and the dashboard to see a winding road of cat's eyes. By now the alarm had to have been raised. Would they not close the roads?

She tried to listen to the interview. Snippets came back and forth. The pain was too much.

"The truth is, Panda, which is not your fuckin' name –"

"Woah now, we'd better apologise to the listeners for that –"

"We are standing on the precipice of extinction, the end of the world, man. And still, you and any other media out

there just want to propagate nonsense stories about some sort of pretty pictures that get sprayed up outside a pub."

"You painted an image of the president on a crucifix outside the George. Of course people will comment on that."

"Yeah, you're all looking for something to talk about – it's sad, to see the Irish people, reputedly saints and scholars, stick their heads up their arses –"

The presenter coughed. *"Okay, I eh —"*

"And ignore the end of the world. We've had our heads up our back passage that long that the window to actually stop the climate extinction has passed. We should now be rolling out army training in schools. Teachin' kids to grow their own veggies and build a defensive base, find clean drinking water. Then there's swimming, less than half of our teenagers can swim. And probably only a tenth of them that can swim in the sea or in any sort of inclement conditions. And the country is going to be flooded like – is anyone actually thinking about this?"

"Right, that's Lady Anon, a sharp reminder of the action we need to take –"

"Take that body found up in the bog the other day. That was found in a second cutting of the bog. In other words, it was a total fluke. Those lads only did another cut of the bog cos the weather was so hot. Last year most of the turf was lost cos it pissed rain –"

The radio cut out.

What did it mean, thought January, about the weather? She hadn't been prepared for the end of the world. She wasn't sure if the interview was real, or if she was dreaming it up somewhere where the pain wasn't as bad. She desperately needed to go to the toilet, but holding on was keeping her tied to reality, the concentration distracting her from what was to come.

Chapter 64

The chiming clock on his mantelpiece sounded twice. Monty yawned, swirling a cognac in one hand with the iPad in the other. A moment such as this, what he was viewing, well, it called for a special drink. He had opened a Louis XIII Rémy Martin, alleged to have been hidden from the Nazis in an Aquitaine grainstore.

But nothing much had happened in the live video. It was not a chamber, he realised, but apparently a moving vehicle as the camera shunted and moved back and forth. January remained in a ball, her head hung between her arms as they wrapped around her knees.

He almost fell asleep, when goodness, a flash of light!

The vehicle had now stopped. January stood up to watch as the driver got out. Figuring he'd be gone for a few moments, she attempted some kicks to a weak spot of the chamber wall. It moved a few inches, but caught on the roof elsewhere. Peering through the new gap, she kicked more strongly and dislodged the wood by almost a foot.

Monty's heart was racing once more. Other viewers were commenting that she was trying to escape, trying to alert RINAMARBH to come back.

The door of the van slid open, into the makeshift middle compartment of the van. Monty recognised Setanta Molloy as he lugged a heavy body over his shoulder. It looked like a man's frame. The van vibrated, the hefty weight slung down to the floor.

Gosh, thought Monty, wiping the sweat from his brow. Things were livening up, finally. Setanta Molloy had hidden his predilections well, although he couldn't help but feel flattered that he might have impacted the chap as they had worked together.

January was watching through the hole. Setanta pulled back the door and exited.

The body lay lifeless on the van floor as the vibrations of the engine shook the camera in its holder.

A twinge of guilt about January's fate tugged on Monty's cholesterol-choked heart. He removed the stopper and refilled his glass, settling down to watch what would happen next.

Chapter 65

After an initial recce of the scene, the officers found nothing. Cooney ordered a roving van with floodlights to illuminate the bogland of Sorleybones. The white light bounced off the beady little eyes of the bog wildlife, and a panicked fox ran across Alf's path. At least it had stopped raining, the land still soaking up the much-needed moisture. They had lost almost an hour here, time that January desperately needed.

O'Brien was marching down the muddy laneway. "Nothing here, boss, but they have the tracks of the van. He came down here that's for sure, but it looks like he got out and drove straight back up."

Cooney kicked the wet black rubber of the squad car. "Where the fuck are they? *Jesus Christ!*" He raised his hands over his ears. "*Fuck it!*" He kicked the car door again as the officers stood still, waiting for more instructions.

The energy that had driven the search all evening was lagging. Cooney was drinking from an old bottle of water that had been lying in the footwell of a squad car for months. Damp and cold, he watched a yawn pass along the stationary policemen.

Alf ploughed through the thick and wet sludgy leaves over to him.

"I think I have something, Cooney. Michael Fitzpatrick has been taken from a garage outside Termonfeckin. The wife was a few minutes behind him, and found his car there. Door wide open. It has to be connected. There's something else, too."

Chapter 66

The van moved slowly. They were off a main road and onto a side road. The man lying on the floor of the van was moaning. A small shred of moonlight showed a dark slick of blood on his forehead. January could not see his face though. He was gagged with a thick black band. January had tried talking to him, encouraging him to tap back in Morse code. He did not respond. Another great tragedy in the advance of technology was the loss of this sort of knowledge, January opined. She felt hot and cold, her hair now curling from a sweat of fever and fear.

The vehicle shuddered to a final stop. The adrenalin had been hitting January in waves, each time weaker. This time, she felt her heart rate rise as Setanta opened the door. The man on the floor whimpered louder as Setanta kicked him, clearly for sport, before stepping over him to fix the camera.

"Don't want them to miss out on the action," he said to the prone body, sickening January to her stomach.

"There are over 200 people watching us here at fifty euro a pop. Already sitting in my bank account, perfect running-away money. And what are the chances of finding you like that? I meant to pick you up tonight but, God, you really made it easy for me. Going to a petrol station alone like that. You didn't even see me coming."

He flicked on a light and January recognised the man lying on the floor. It was Minister Fitzpatrick.

Setanta handcuffed him to the table soldered on the floor of the van. January could see Fitzpatrick was struggling to breathe.

"I never finished telling you the story, January," Setanta then said haughtily. "I'm sure you'll appreciate it too, Mick."

"Will you take his gag off! He's choking! Please, he can barely breathe!" January called out.

"Okay, okay, Scooby Doo," he smiled, loosening the gag.

The Minister coughed and gagged, inhaling deeply.

"Don't try anything, okay?" said Setanta who was now sitting on the table in the middle of the van. "So where was I? Yes, so I got Sinéad home. She hadn't been in the car long but her back and legs were covered in red circles, marks from the beaded seat cover. We all had them in the nineties. I remember that as I carried her in. That was the first night. I still remember the taste of her. She was salty with fear, and I wasn't the first. But we enjoyed our time together. After the third day, the ketamine ran out. She was lying in her own filth, commingled with mine." He paused and looked at her. "Hmm, I'm not sure how you're going to write it up, the state you are in. That's a misstep on my part now. The story of the bog killer. *Hmm*, you'll remember all of this, January, won't you?"

"You're disgusting," she said bravely. Her agency in his plan gave her some hope.

"So are you, January Emily."

Fitzpatrick was whimpering, pulling pathetically at his handcuffed arm, but not talking.

"You're quiet there, Minister? Cat got your tongue?" he laughed disgustingly, before taking something out of his coat pocket. He held it up to the light. It was a human tongue, and the realisation that it was the Minister's had January's stomach leap with nausea and disgust. She had to sit down and get some blood to her head. She felt hot with panic, barely able to catch her breath.

"Have you ever seen a Halal slaughtering? Bloodletting? Well, that's what I did with Sinéad."

"Oh my god," said January, "can't you give him something for the pain?"

The Minister was crying, a horrible wheezing low howl coming from his throat. She had met him a few times over the years. She didn't know him, but she badly wanted to reach out and comfort him.

"This isn't a hospital, January," Setanta said, as he hung his jacket on a hook. He started to pull a pair of surgical gloves on. "I can wash out the floor of the van, but you never know where you'll get a fingerprint," he said in a high-pitched sing-song voice.

The little light there was in the van went black. Even a crack of pain from her broken rib couldn't halt her descent into oblivion.

Chapter 67

A fine channel of drool had pooled down his chin onto the riotous grey hair on his chest. Both sides of his dressing gown had fallen asunder to reveal his silken grey boxers. The iPad was on the floor, and for a while Monty had been aware of the murmurings and sedate sobs as the action unfolded. But then he slept.

He slept through the car arriving over the gravel, but spilt the last few drops of the precious Rémy Martin with the loud door-knocking. Given the distress in the house that night, he had sent all of the staff home, so he was forced to arise to open the door himself.

In the sleepy-drunk haze he went to look out the window, and spotted a familiar car that he couldn't quite place.

At the door, he found Cooney and O'Brien, stony-faced.

"Oh gentlemen, once again we meet at this doorway! I fear it is the worst –"

"Montgomery Buxbaum St John Passmore," Cooney

leaned in to handcuff him, "I am arresting you on suspicion of perverting the course –"

"What? You can't do this, what do you –"

O'Brien buried a sneer as Cooney cuffed him. The red dragons of Monty's silk gown flapped in the cold April night air.

"And on suspicious of incitement to murder, membership of an illegal organisation and –"

"I can't believe this. You jolly well can't! Can you let me get dressed at least," squealed Monty. He was now fully awake and remembered that the iPad, and his other special items, were lying about the room. If only he could get up to kick them under the bed.

"You are not obliged to say anything unless you wish to do so but anything you say will be taken down in writing and may be given in evidence. O'Brien, go up to his room and bring down a pair of trousers and a shirt."

Cooney let him sit down in the hallway, with his hands behind his back.

"Um, if you wouldn't mind much I have a clean white Henry Jermyn shirt in the laundry room, and red chinos," Monty ventured, trying to keep them away from the bedroom. But what would he do about shoes, he thought in a panic. There weren't any downstairs apart from boots and wellies.

O'Brien looked to Cooney. He nodded and O'Brien left to trail through the empty black corridor of the house to get the clothes.

Cooney enjoyed seeing the fat old fucker like this.

"Officer, please tell me what this is about –"

"Don't give me that, you fat little prick!" Without O'Brien there Coonety didn't need to be so polite. "Do you know where January is?"

"I don't know – how would I know where she is?"

"Do you fucking have anything that could help us find her?"

Monty sat still, staring at the shiny parquet floor.

"A soft chap like you will go down well in prison. You'll be popular in there – a posho like you. Even drug dealers get blowjobs – it's the order of things."

"Okay," said Monty quietly, looking into thin air.

"If you help us now, it will be positively looked upon later."

"Okay, I said I would. Let me show you something."

Outside Monty's house, Alf fingered the condensation on the window in the back-up squad car. The officer in the front passenger seat was dozy, his forehead slipping on the wet glass. Frank had found a link to the forum. When he showed it to Cooney, the team was now so well resourced that the technical team could pinpoint exactly who was accessing the feed, and knew Passmore had been watching. They still hadn't been able to find the location where the camera was being broadcast from, and the tech guys were working on dismantling the blocks.

"Well, what now?" asked Alf, using the last few minutes of his mobile-phone battery.

"I thought you were working with the coppers?" said Frank. "Looks like your bird is fine – she's curled up in the back of the van. Can't say the same about the other bloke. Looks like he's tied down to the table. Fuck, I think it is Fitzpatrick after all!"

Then the sound of January screaming came through the iPad and through the phone to Alf.

"What's happening now? Is she okay?"

"Yeah – she's fine, Fitzpatrick is not. Are the Garda technical boys on this? Looks like she's going to be next, he's hauled the body off the table ..."

"They are tracking the signal and looking at it but the detective is arresting your man, Toad of Toad Hall. I won't ask how you came across this."

"It's best not to. Go get your detective. He needs to see this."

Chapter 68

The rosy pink of the early summer dawn shone through the front window of the van. January awoke from her horrified slumber, the sleep of terror. The metallic smell of blood sat thick in the mucous membranes of her nostrils. She had never seen that much blood before. It was dense and sticky as it soaked under the plywood wall onto the sleeping bag. They were on the move again and, as Setanta turned a sharp corner, she heard the Minister's body slide across the van floor. She hadn't watched when Setanta was at work. She tried to distract herself by imagining the tabloid headlines once it all came out. **The Killer Curator, the Museum Murderer**. What would they call him?

She curled back into her ball and tried to block it all out. But the smell, this smell. It was so strong it would stay with her forever. She no longer cared whether Setanta would kill her or not. She wanted this to end. To be over.

They had been driving for hours. He would need to

stop soon. For petrol if nothing else, and she needed to be ready. Summoning the last bit of strength in her legs she kicked the corner of the plywood. It gave way another foot, but Setanta looked into the rear-view mirror.

"Don't be tiring yourself out, love, you've got a story to write!" he shouted back.

She groaned, with relief that he wasn't going to kill her yet, but horror that he was not yet done.

She had heard sirens nearby a few hours ago, and thought they had found her. It was an ambulance overtaking them. She had hoped Cooney and Alf would have found them, but they had been driving and driving for so long. Where were they?

She closed her eyes, and imagined she was at her children's concert in Avonlea. Tabitha was strumming the golden threads of the harp to the gentle air of "Greensleeves". She found herself humming, *"Ba ba ba ba ba, ba ba ba ba ba, ba ba ba ba ba ba ba ba ba,"* as she hit the back of her skull harshly off the van wall in time to the gentle beat.

Chapter 69

Two slices of toast, five packets of crisps, half a chicken-fillet roll, two chocolate bars. O'Brien tallied the food he had consumed in the past twenty-four hours as his stomach rumbled. He was looking forward to the full Irish breakfast once they found her. He glanced down at the iPad on his lap. She was sleeping. They were close. That was something. They were less than ten minutes from them now. They were almost in Dunmore East, Waterford, and had been driving for hours. They had followed him through the night, tracking through the van's live feed. Once they got him arrested and got your one to the hospital, Cooney would surely let him go for a kip and some grub? Cooney had stationed a team of officers in each petrol station, each leap-frogging the other as Setanta passed by. The online crime investigators didn't want it made public knowledge till they caught as many of the voyeurs as possible. That's where he came in. He couldn't help but be chuffed with himself. They would say that he had solved the case. No one would want to give credit to a private investigator.

That's what everyone would say. O'Brien's stomach rumbled as he refreshed the tracker. It was so simple. They were tracking her phone. They nearly had her.

Chapter 70

January had now kicked a gap of two feet in the plywood chamber. She remained alert, ready to crawl through when they stopped. The ribs on her left-hand side ached, and she tried to keep all weight to the other side of her body. They had to stop soon. He would need petrol, or the toilet, or something. She obviously couldn't rely on anyone else to help her. She shouldn't have ever thought that they would.

"You want to see this view!" he shouted at her, half-looking around as he drove, the bright daylight illuminating the large vault in the rear of the van.

January tried to look over the Minister's body, but snapped her head back to her hands. Black with blood and dirt, she saw the dust flecks in the bright morning sunshine.

"I'm hungry. Can you get me something to eat?"

"More peppermint creams?" He had a large jar from the sweetshop belted into the front of the van.

She couldn't bear to eat another one. She had vomited a few times during the torture of the Minister, and the menthol clung to the back of her throat.

"No, please, I need something else to eat. I need to build up my strength to write your story. I need protein to repair my hands," she pleaded.

He swung the van dramatically around. He was really unhinged. Maybe all the sleep deprivation had left his judgement impaired.

January was relieved as the red-and-white logo of a garage came into view. Before he had fully stopped, she kicked her way through and crawled through the blood and over the Minister's body. He noticed, slammed on the brakes. Jumping out of the van he slammed the cargo door shut.

"*Oi*, what do you think you're doing?"

Now screaming, she summoned every piece of her strength to open the door. She was met with a hard thrust as he slammed her back into the table. She couldn't breathe. Agonisingly, it was like the air was sucked out of her lung, as it collapsed. She heard the thud of the metal against her skull, a hard thwack. But she didn't feel anything as she slid to the ground, now lying face to face with the Minister. As close as lovers.

She thought heard a familiar voice. It sounded like a CD or the radio playing. What was Alf doing on the radio? Was he on the news?

"*I'm coming, January, we have you now!*" Alf shouted, her world now dark.

She closed her eyes.

Chapter 71

"Setanta Boyle, I'm arresting you for the murder of Michael Fitzpatrick, Sinéad O'Sullivan, and Mary Baxter." Cooney was one of five officers holding Setanta down on the floor of the otherwise empty petrol garage.

Alf was kneeling on the tarmac, holding January's head in his lap. Her left eye opened momentarily. "You're okay, January, stay with me? Do you hear me, you're safe now, okay? I have you. We have him. He won't hurt you again."

"Alf ..." He was a shadow in the bright morning sun but she smelled him, his aftershave and shower gel. He smelt like safety to her. "It's Setanta. He killed Fitz—"

"Rest, January," said Alf, running his index finger over the small area of her face not covered in lacerations. Her eye only opened wider, searching his face for answers. "We have him, okay? I'm so sorry I didn't come to get you sooner. I shouldn't have let you do this all on your own. I should have listened to you."

His body ached with her, she was so delicate a creature. The gauze around her eye was filthy and soaked in dried blood, her her bandages likewise. The camel dress was torn past her thigh, the alabaster skin bared. She was like a little injured bird.

"I–"

He hushed her, pulling her closer in his arms as the ambulance appeared along the bright coastal road. She lay there quietly as Cooney continued the arrest and dragged Molloy to the back seat of the waiting squad car.

"Leopoldina," she wheezed.

"Is fed and watered, January," said Alf, as the paramedics came to move her. "Gently, lads, she's bashed up. Her name is January."

"January," said one of the paramedics urgently, "we need to put you on the trolley, okay. Where are you sore?"

She pointed to her side and used her last piece of strength to hold her arm up to them.

"My wings," she said slowly. "Are clipped." She managed a small smile, that broadened at the sight of a syringe of painkillers.

"It's okay, January," said Alf, now stroking her hair. He leaned in to her face as they hoisted her into the ambulance. "You might look a state," he chuckled, "but your breath is fresh."

She squeezed his hand in response before fading unconscious with the power of the drugs.

423

Chapter 72

The carriage clock ticked happily over the embers of the fire. January stretched her ankles, her heels relishing the soft and slippery satin of her couch. In the past week, she had slept on such a variety of surfaces, she enjoyed the comfort of that evening's accommodation. The fire was a requirement now that the Irish summer had set in, with frost appearing across the capital on May Day.

"More wine?" asked Colm Cooney, reaching for the bottle over the mantelpiece.

"You finish it, I have four different opioids in my system, so you need it more than I do," said January. Indulgently she held her hand out for a refill of soda water.

He poured from the heavy tumbler, pulling a stray pluck of mint from the jug. She drank gladly. She folded her knees up to make room for him on the sofa as he refilled the glass.

"I'm sure you're glad to have today over," he said quietly, reaching for her baby toes. She allowed him to receive her foot. In her adult life, she had never had a man caress her foot in the normal run of things. But this was not the normal run of things. She had decided to force herself into sharing more of herself with others.

"It was good to give the formal statement. It's another part of this beastly thing that's now done. Thank you for bringing me home."

"Oh, of course." His hands felt warm on her cold, small feet. "Sure you're only out of the hospital. And it's not like I've anything else to be at, now the Commissioner has me on this enforced leave."

"A chance to write your memoirs, detective. You solved a momentous case." The leather from her new eyepatch rubbed somewhat against her cheek as she spoke, but she was glad to have it instead of the mummifying bandages.

"You solved it, January. I wish you had told me who it was earlier, and he wouldn't have taken you."

"How many times do I need to tell you? I didn't realise it was Setanta until I was in the car with Mary. When he was forced to go to the local school, he was sure any girl he was interested in would want him, an educated man with fine manners. He even changed his name by deed poll for God's sake. After Sinéad rejected him, well, he vowed to make a success of himself. The country's leading historian. The world's leading historian. He played around with many monikers. Four years after they left school she had returned from

New York, and he was the deputy archaeologist on the bog-body digs, educated in Cambridge – and she still wanted nothing to do with him. So he decides to make history, and takes her, like Lucretia."

"Surely there would have been other ways to be remembered, to learn to accept she wouldn't want him?"

"Surely there are, Colm," speaking his first name seemed appropriate to the moment, "to any reasonable person. But Setanta is quite mad."

"Yes, his barrister has already asked that he be housed on the mental-health wing of the prison, lining up an insanity plea."

"Do his brothers have anything to say about it?"

"Ah, January, I shouldn't be talking about this with you–"

"You're off the investigation, aren't you?"

"For now but –"

"Well, go on," said January, sitting up to allow him to fix the cushion behind her back.

"Conor is a hardworking lad, putting everything into his shop. Mossie, well, Mossie has a touch of his half-brother's evil nature, the way he set up the Minister." He finished his glass and set it down on the Persian silk rug – his lips were slightly purple "Mind you, Mossie didn't know what Setanta was planning, but had been watching the Minister. Talk about an opportune moment. Fitzpatrick just never saw him coming.

Standing at the pumps, the noise of the petrol obscured the noise of the van pulling up. Setanta had his own axe to grind with him from years ago – Sinéad again. But Mossie was looking for a few bob. He was in huge debt. Penelope Fitzpatrick might have paid him to get those pictures, but when she decided not to let the pictures get published, he was blackmailing her too."

"God, I can't believe such evil walks among us, Dete– Colm. How do you deal with it?"

"Knowing we are stopping as much of it as possible helps. Not like I'll be doing any of that any time soon. Your pal Monty was no stranger to the dark, January. You're lucky nothing happened to you when you stayed with him."

"Monty barely wipes his own arse. I can't imagine he would have the wherewithal to actually do anything to someone. Can you pass me some more water, please? There's a 1967 Domaine des Vignettes over there, if you want another glass."

"You're a bad influence, January Quail."

"I do hope so, Colm. What is that you're doing?" She wiggled her toes in his hands.

"A foot rub, January – have you never had one before?"

"No, but I have read magnificent things – it seems to be living up to its reputation. It's rather a ... sexual thing though, isn't it?"

"Depending on the circumstances, perhaps."

"Well, I hate to quash your hopes but I'm fairly immobile –"

He chuckled. "Don't worry, I'm happy to be of service, milady. I have the most honourable of intentions tonight. Anything sexual – and I can't believe you're discussing this so objectively – it's not what you need right now. But I do like you, and your antiquated ways."

"Jolly good, detective – if you don't mind I'd rather call you that? I've tried Colm on for size, and it's not quite me."

"Okay. Will you share a Vignette with me?" He gently lifted her feet and stood up. "Miss January Emily Quail?"

Under her breath she said, "How did –" Bemused, she covered the initials on her bathrobe, as he poured two large glasses of red.

"Your grandmother was Emily – please don't rate me as that bad a detective. That's one thing I must ask, when I read about your family … I … did you set Avonlea on fire?"

She reached for the glass and drank the wine down in one. "Sit down." She directed him to refill the glass.

"You'll be asleep if you drink that," he cautioned, watching anger brighten her left eye.

"Sit down and I will tell you how Avonlea burned to the ground."

She whisked back the second glass and began.

Epilogue

January had procured a gramophone for the evening. She was lugging it up the tiny stairs of McDaid's pub, when Alf rushed to help her.

"Here," he said gently, "let me take that. What are you going to play anyway?" He was wearing his favourite leather jacket.

"I can't stand any more of these bloody Yuletide tunes, that's for sure." She smiled at him. For this occasion, she had elected to wear a black high-neck Victorian blouse, original mourning attire, and a thick woollen A-line skirt. To protect her toes from the Grafton street slush, her old favourite burgundy lace-up boots.

She had of course insisted they would serve crème de menthe, as well as the cheap plonk her publisher had laid on. Alf dumped the gramophone heavily on the table, already laden with her novel, *The Brothers*.

"Thank you, I shouldn't have the editor of the *Irish Sunday Chronicle* toiling like a foreign brickie," she said.

"I used to be a foreign brickie, remember, the summer I spent in London?"

"Ah yes," she said, surveying the room. It was set up theatre style, with a few high stools and a roaring fire in the corner. Her eyes lingered on the flames before looking out the window to admire the Christmas lights sparkling through the midwinter dark.

"I brought your carpet bag from the apartment," he said, nodding as the barman brought up the tray of emerald liqueur.

"Oh, I had sort of meant to leave those things there," she said. They both were distracted by the heavy thudding of footsteps on the stairs.

"Your adoring public awaits," he curtsied, ushering them to chat with the bedraggled crew, unsheathing themselves of coats, and snow-sodden hats. The *Irish Sunday Chronicle* crew had turned out in force and were the first to take over a corner of the room.

Laura had flushed cheeks as she bounced merrily over to January. "Sorry to talk about work, but I wanted to let you know – the authorities have agreed to let me visit a tomb in Egypt. I'm heading out in January, January," she said, giggling.

January hoped she hadn't been this silly as a junior reporter.

"That's exciting," she said, her eyes moving to the others climbing up the steep stairs. There were Cooney and O'Brien, sharing the season's jollity with festive jumpers, Rudolph and Frosty flashing gaily. Cooney winked at her, and she held on to his gaze a moment too long. She didn't want to give him ideas. He had been prolific with his requests to take her for dinner, but all declined as things progressed with Alf. Given Alf's return of her overnight bag, perhaps she needed to reconsider.

Laura, lips green from the menthol libations laid on, hadn't noticed January's wandering gaze. "Are you investigating anything interesting now?" she hiccupped.

"Oh, nothing much, poking around a few bits." Whether it was the season, or her new perspective on life, but she decided to hug Laura. "Thank you, for everything." Laura's breasts were squeezed tight between them. "I'd better go."

Her publisher grabbed January, and they ran through the event's proceedings. Professor Traynor sneaked in cat-like in spiked stiletto boots, nabbing a seat at the front. She was no longer the State Pathologist, but acted as a roving lecturer. She had also written a book about the proceedings.

As the publisher introduced her, a final figure appeared at the top of the steps. A tall, older woman, she wore a wide-brimmed hat, and a floor-length cloak pinned with a Tara brooch. She was wizard-like in appearance. It was Polly. Alf recognised her from the market stand in Drogheda.

"You could do with a staff," said January, in hushed tones as she approached the woman.

She gripped January tightly to her chest, the smell of orange-liqueur lingering between them. "My child. I am sorry I didn't come earlier. I heard about what happened –"

"No need for explanations, Polly, thank you for being here now."

The assembled crowd applauded, looking around for the star of the evening.

January touched the cheek of Polly, and ascended to the top of the room.

"Lords, ladies, and gentlemen . . ." she announced from the top of her voice.

The orange glow of the recess lights reflected off a gold Venetian mask, worn by Lady Anon as she squeezed into the room. January faltered for a minute at the artist's presence.

"A Merry Christmas to you all and thank you for coming here tonight," she then said. "I'm going to read a little from my book, so let's get started. *Huzzah!*"

THE END

If you enjoyed this book from
Poolbeg why not visit our website

WWW.POOLBEG.COM

---

and get another book delivered straight to
your home or to a friend's home.
All books despatched within 24 hours.

FREE POSTAGE on orders
over €10 in Rep. of Ireland*

Why not join our mailing list at www.poolbeg.com and get
some fantastic offers, competitions, author interviews,
new releases and much more?

POOLBEG ON SOCIAL MEDIA

@PoolbegBooks

poolbegbooks

www.facebook.com/poolbegpress

*Free postage in Ireland on orders over €10
and Europe on orders over €65.